THE SHARD CHRONICLES

Book One: The Naissance

LIAM M. TAYLOR

liamtaylor@theshard-chronicles.com

Printed in the United States of America

First Printing 2014
2nd Edition

ISBN 978-0-9924527-0-4

www.theshard-chronicles.com

Dedicated to Ange.
For everything.

The Endeavor

On the day the planet sealed its fate, the man fundamentally responsible stood on a large, moss-dappled shelf among some old and long forgotten ruins, completely unaware of his involvement in its extermination.

From the top of a carved-stone temple high in the thick, steaming jungles of Guatemala, he stared across a broad canopy of trees laid out below as trails of sweat ran down his flattened forehead and honey-brown cheeks, mixing with the raindrops that still dropped and dampened the shoulders of his cream-colored, muslin shirt. A delicate and drizzly mist remained after the heavy downpour, obstructing a normally modest view of the Pacific Ocean stretched to the south, its narrow band of azure, shimmering waters currently hidden behind a veil of low-lying cloud. The fading afternoon sun blazed close to the horizon, bringing with it a welcome relief from the dwindling heat and humidity, its stifling clamminess unrelenting up to now. Somewhere in the surrounding forest, troops of loudly grunting howler monkeys heralded the return of wildlife after the rain while a pair of majestically-colored macaws swooped abruptly overhead, their massive red, yellow, and blue wings flapping noisily. They squawked, a shrill, raucous din that tingled his eardrums as he flung his hand out to slap at a swarm of mosquitoes hovering nearby.

Taking a deep sniff, savoring the wet, piney scent, the man reviewed the questions in his mind, unsure of the motive behind the solitary, explicit instruction to visit a place he had not seen for a very long time. On his back, a khaki, canvas rucksack quivered, its vibrations trembling through his entire body, and he spun around, pacing forward and frowning while he scuffed the vibrant, green moss from its sturdy hold on the weathered rock. To the northeast, he sensed the damage in his barrier, and wondered if that could be the reason, because a third of its triangular shape was missing, starting on a point at San Juan, Puerto Rico, a mere 1,300 miles away. As the query came to his lips, at a location a little over 8,000 miles to the northwest, a crewman on the most important aircraft flying at that particular point in time activated its specially modified, pneumatic bay doors, and with a loud clank, they yawned open, exposing the interior to bright sunshine and a wind that roared furiously.

Far beneath, the scenery rolled along, revealing a countryside peppered with river systems, the occasional town, and a scattering of roads. Approaching their target, the broad brownness of tilled farms and emerald grassland gave way to the foundations of an extensive city, basking in the early morning light. At about 32,000 feet, the gargantuan plane gave regular, twinkling flashes from its silvery, gleaming fuselage, making it clearly visible to anyone observing the heavens at those exact moments. But they discounted it as just more aerial reconnaissance, for the blitzing received by other urban areas had passed them by, and the citizens knew an attack would never happen. Unbeknownst to their false belief lay a meticulously designed and deliberate motive, with the purpose being to study and record the expected destruction caused by a new weapon never before used in the history of mankind. Even the firing mechanism remained untested on that level, instead relying on the results of extremely small scale experiments and theoretical equations to achieve the required effect.

Consequently, an earlier air raid alarm remained cancelled and not one siren clattered as a device codenamed 'Little Boy' detached from its hook, spending the following forty-three seconds in gravity freefall while the crew of the B-29 Superfortress immediately employed a new flight path, their predetermined escape route to safety during the gadget's rapid plummet to the ground. At a height approximately 2,000 feet over the sprawling metropolis it detonated, and the world beheld a raw and devastating power that instantaneously destroyed everything and everyone within a one mile radius.

A thing, an entity, fumed at the moment of widespread annihilation, and at the same time fed voraciously on a death toll exceeding 70,000, including its new recipient, a baby, who cried in her creaky, wooden bassinet on the second floor of a dilapidated hospital, clenching her tiny fists the second before being vaporized, along with every other being.

An entity, captured, ensnared, confined within a part of itself, surrounded by conquerors who had failed to thwart it, failed in their duty... lured yet again by a deceptive slumber while it appraised various life forms through countless eons, waiting patiently, preparing and gauging when to begin its next endeavor.

An ancient entity, its true origin lost over an incomprehensible span of time.

An entity now undeniably evil.

And at those moments of unleashed energy and obliteration, its seething anger turned to euphoria once the strategy's failure became a resounding success. The humans had rewarded it by demonstrating their newfound ability, and now that warring, violent species confirmed their place as outright winners in a dual plan. Its final plan. A plan forced into action after an incredibly short duration, just over half a century later, when its conquerors found the real successor. Here, on Earth. Again.

Chapter One

The Homestead

Jeffrey and Deangela stepped from the cooler dining room and into warm, mid-May sunshine. Embracing the pleasant heat, they sauntered forward a few steps and paused to regard an enormous backyard as the realtor closed the sliding door behind them with a soft thump. A large, paved patio ended where the land sloped up to the extreme rear of a one and a half acre property scattered with a variety of trees, some tall and thick-trunked, and others with the same aspirations in years to come.

"Oh, honey," Deangela breathed. She took another stride while goosebumps prickled the silken sheen of her arms. "This is ideal." Twirling to face her husband, her light-brown eyes, a shade similar to the milk-chocolate colored pavers under her sneakers, sparkled between the long and wavy black hair that fanned out before settling upon her shoulders once more. "When we do have children, I can almost picture them riding their bikes, enjoying every sunny morning," she smiled.

With a hearty nod and wide grin, Jeffrey marveled at his wife's stunning beauty, something that pocketed his devotion from the moment he had first laid sight on her at high school. Slender, graceful, and six-foot-tall, Deangela's heritage became doubly apparent with the mild bronze of her skin conflicting resplendently against the white, cotton summer dress she wore.

"This place was made just for us, babe," he murmured. "It's a purpose-built, Cooper homestead. I absolutely adore it, and any child will feel the exact same way. This is definitely the one we should buy."

"Really?" Her eyes widened. "Are you sure? We shouldn't rush things. Maybe we should still look around a bit."

"Naaaah," he rumbled, shaking his head. "No need. We've looked for long enough and now I'm positive we've found it. It's everything we'd want, don't you think?" He laughed as she clapped and squealed.

"Yes, I do," she exclaimed. "I just wanted to see your reaction and I totally agree. It's been a long search, and I am so in love with this place. Let's get it."

"Fair enough." Jeffrey raised his head to the clear, blue sky, clamped his hands together in supplication and mouthed a silent, mischievously exaggerated 'thank you'.

*   *   *

Standing at the bottom of a long and steep driveway, they waved their farewells when the realtor tooted his car horn and accelerated down the one-way, looped road that formed Fairview Terrace.

"Nice car," Jeffrey remarked. "I like those Lincolns. There may come a day when I can get one myself." He took a firm grip of his wife's hand, squeezed it gently, and together they trekked their way up the coarsely-pebbled surface. "Well, my darling, success, after all these months. No more renting for us, no more tiny apartment, no more owner inspections. Just a lot of grass to keep under control." He looked from side to side, using his two inches of extra height to peer over the top of Deangela's head.

"Not quite," she stated.

"Yes quite, Dee." Reaching the house, they ambled along the front and paused to examine two towering, oak doors, set within a spacious and high-roofed portico. "That really is a lot of grass to mow and a lot of trees to circle. Not only will it take me all weekend, but I'll also end up crawling inside with my eyeballs rolling around. What will my boss think? He's tagged me as a future leader of the company, an executive climbing the corporate ladder, not being known as Conga-Eyes Cooper the paper manufacturing weirdo."

"You fool," Dee giggled. "Jeff, I wasn't talking about the lawn, I was talking about our apartment. We'll have about another six weeks there and the final inspection will be the worst ever. They'll go over it with a fine-toothed comb."

"Good luck to them," he huffed. "We've genuinely looked after that place the last three years. Hell, it looks better now than when we first moved in, and that's the main reason why I'm happy because we can do what we want with our own house. The grand plan has worked, babe. We set our sights on owning a little bit of Crescent Lake paradise by nineteen ninety-five, and by golly we did it."

"More on your part than mine," she muttered. "Secretarial work isn't the best paid job in the world."

"Every cent has got us here and don't you forget it. We made it past a tough economy and it's just a good thing my business is always in demand. Things are going to be fine, you'll see."

Dee ran her fingers through his straight, shoulder-length, brown hair. "I'm proud of you, Jeff. Thank you for everything. Without your support in my life I really don't think I could've made it this far. I owe it all to you."

"We've done it together, honey. After what you've been through it's your courage and spirit that's always amazed me. Perhaps mixed with a smidgen of hotheadedness at times, but completely understandable seeing as how you're the craziest Italian woman this side of Milan."

"Awww, yeah." Dee's eyebrows rose while a small smile played on her pink, perfectly-shaped lips. "I seem to recall a conversation at a restaurant a few years back where it was you who noted how we're acting more like each other every day. Careful, or I might start calling you Mr. Grumpy-Bum."

"Well if that's how you feel." He feigned a light cough and silly, pretentious look. "Then I'll keep the terms and any additional recommendations about our beautiful new palace to myself."

"Terms? This better be good. Recommendations I'll go for, but terms?" Dee squinted. "This better be very, very good."

Somewhere on the property to their left, a motor mower started up, its strident, unrelenting snarl shattering the Saturday afternoon stillness.

"Ah!" Jeff's face brightened. "Must thank our new neighbor for that marvelous timing. Hey, since the realtor didn't know, maybe they can tell us what's going on with those metal poles being stuck in the ground along the top part of the road. Two things to remember. Follow me, my love." Guiding Dee to the right-hand side of the house, they paused upon entering the backyard. "Okay, term number one. I am definitely getting a ride-on, because I'd rather spend my time with you than pushing a hand mower about all day. Term number two." He pointed to a spot close to the patio. "I think that position is just right for a swimming pool. Not any time soon, as we'll be using everything we've got to keep this place, but a swimming pool at some stage. And don't worry about the sloping land, I'm sure we'll come up with something. That's all I've got. If you want, this is where the recommendation part can start now."

The engine clamor from next door subsided as the mower travelled farther away.

"I'd love a pool, Jeffrey Cooper," Dee laughed. Pulling him closer, she gazed adoringly into his faded-blue eyes, a color not unlike the stone-washed denim jeans she suggested he wear for their fruitful, lunchtime appointment. "If you weren't so intelligent, handsome, and with the best temperament I've ever seen in anyone, I would have thought you a complete buffoon the second we got together. It's no wonder I call you a fool. But you're my fool."

"Then am I to believe my terms will be met? Not entirely sure how at the moment, however, there they are."

"Oh, absolutely." Dee nodded earnestly, trying to keep as blunt an expression as possible. "If you meet my terms. Not just any pool, but a magnificent pool. With an amazing entertainment area. Also servants. And a private jet. And anything else I think of later."

"Agreed," he chuckled. "One more thing, babe. It's taken us years of hard work to get here and I mentioned our plan, but never brought up our ultimate phase. That little something we've talked about for so long." Bending over slightly, he kissed Dee's forehead and the bridge of her nose. "Honey, let's fill the seats on those bikes you can see being ridden around every sunny morning." Jeff stumbled backward, barely able to keep his lean body upright when Dee leapt into his arms.

*   *   *

On a fine and frosty Sunday morning in early November the next year, Jeff's breath billowed out in white, bulbous clouds while he swept the patio and whistled a Guns 'n' Roses song stuck on auto replay in his head. Beneath his tee-shirt, jumper, and heavy jacket, beads of sweat rolled down his chest and stomach, moistening his already damp clothing when he straightened to the sound of Dee sliding the dining room door open. With a flushed face and glistening tears, she rushed across the paving stones to him, excitedly shrieking the news.

Chapter Two

The Boy

After fifty-two years, the frenzied ecstasy perceived that day still lingered. In the briefest moment the conquerors had tasted a ferocity so pure, so potent, that it immediately revealed the entity's objectives, and even though their captive quickly suppressed the exhilaration, they knew of its plans. This species, their planet, and all living things, were doomed. The cunning and resolve behind its brooding power was stronger than ever, and harder to contain. Eventually, it would win, ending their long continuation together. The next attempt would be its last, and to outsmart its plan, this time would be different. This time, they had no choice. They would have to use virtually everything they had to successfully overwhelm it.

And when they found the real guardian, when the entity struck again, they bestowed powers never given before, on a baby that now existed for one purpose.

"You're nearly there," the nurse stated, just as the room in the maternity ward of Crescent Lake General Hospital began shaking. A few ceiling tiles near the door dropped from their clattering, suspended frame and broke apart on impact, the large segments releasing small clouds of dust. On a bedside desk, a tall, half-full glass of water waddled over the edge and smashed on the linoleum floor, scattering a myriad of tinkling, glinting chunks in all directions. Without warning, the brightly lit room plunged into darkness, and as Dee gave a final, prolonged scream, the generators in the basement fired up. Two emergency lights mounted on opposite walls activated, directing pasty halos of radiance on the birth, right when the shuddering ceased.

With his wife's sweat heavy in his nostrils, Jeff's head jerked about. "What the hell was that?" he exclaimed. Outside the room he heard running footsteps, the odd, blaring shout, and piercing, infant wails. Jumbled with the activity around him, the noise crowded his instantaneously overloaded mind, and it took a firm compression of his hand to bring his attention back to Dee, who smiled as she received a mottled, pinky-mauve form into her opening arms.

"A boy," the nurse announced. "Congratulations." She wiped Dee's glistening brow and stepped back to watch the new parents.

During many hours of labor, the screeching of other newborns had prepared them for their own child's cries, but Jeff and Dee now stared in astonishment while their baby bucked the trend and peered calmly around the room. Apparently content with the different surroundings and situation, he rested his inspection first on his mother's face, then his father's, before giving a huge yawn, smacking his lips together three times and promptly falling asleep, a tiny, lop-sided smile creasing his miniature mouth.

The door drifted ajar and a short, roly-poly man with slightly graying hair poked his head through the gap. "Hello, Mary. I'm just on my way back from surgery and thought I'd check how things are on this floor."

"Thank you, Doctor Sullivan. Some minor damage, as you can see." She gestured toward the floor. "Which I'll clean up right away, but other than that, we're all fine and have recently welcomed a healthy, baby boy into the world."

The doctor gazed over the top of thick-rimmed spectacles perched on the tip of his nose. "Wonderful! Best wishes for you all," he whirred, and disappeared from the entry, closing the door quietly behind him.

*　　*　　*

While they watched the baby sleep soundly in his mother's arms, Jeff wiped away a single tear that slowly tracked its way down Dee's cheek. "Are you okay, my darling?" he whispered.

"Mmmm." She turned to him and nodded sluggishly. "Isn't he beautiful?"

"He sure is. He's our special little man. Well, hardly little, he's quite a size. And what a feeder, I thought he'd never stop. Hopefully he'll sleep for a couple of hours now."

"Hopefully. I could do with some decent rest myself. We both could. Did you notice the color of his eyes? What were they? I couldn't decide. One minute they looked blue, then purple the next, then like a mixture of the two. What's that called? Violet? Whatever it is, they're amazing."

"Yeah," he hummed, his low tone bursting with pride and excitement. "So vibrant and bright and full of life, just like his daddy. Who am I kidding? I'm exhausted. God knows how you feel. And our little bundle of coolness. Wasn't it incredible how composed he seemed about the whole thing? I wonder if it's..." Jeff stopped and rubbed the stubble on his chin. "Honey, before I start talking absolute gibberish, I think I better..."

"You're too late," Dee giggled.

"Nice," he grinned. "And touché, my love. If I'm not careful that honed, razor-sharp humor might challenge my status as chief slapstick comedian. I was trying to say, Deangela Quickwit, I better head down to the lobby and ring my folks."

"Good idea. They're pretty excited about becoming grandparents and I did promise Laura we'd ring. Actually, I told her you'd ring. She laughed and said Jeffrey will be doing a lot more than that, and it didn't matter when it happened, day or night, they wanted a call."

Jeff squinted. "I figured you two would conspire against me."

They looked up when a nurse entered the room and tread softly to the bed. "All cuddled up to Mom," she murmured, beaming at the sight. "Just conducting a final check before my shift ends."

"Okay, Mary," they responded.

"Have you filled out that verification document, Jeff? Right," she continued with the shaking of his head. "It's fairly important, so don't forget. If you want, you can leave it at the nursing station."

"The moment I get back. I promise." Rising from his seat, Jeff bent and gave his wife and son a gentle kiss. "See you soon, babe. And thanks again for everything, Mary. You've been fantastic. What a night, huh? Oh, that reminds me, do you know the time of birth? I did plan on checking, but with all the excitement..." He grimaced. "It kind of slipped my mind."

Mary smiled. "Twelve thirty. A first of July baby by only half an hour."

"Wow, you're first-rate, Mary. Able to note the time as well as deliver the goods." Jeff nodded his admiration.

"Thank you," she tittered. "However, I won't take any credit because I didn't look at my watch and relied on the ward clock verifying that. It runs on mains power, you see. There's no battery backup."

"I thought we didn't get any electricity until an hour ago." Dee frowned. "How did the lights come on?"

"The hospital has generators, but they only supply power to emergency lighting and certain outlets for critical equipment. So, the hands froze right on twelve thirty and couldn't be reset until the electricity came back. If it wasn't for your gorgeous, wee boy being born exactly when that quake struck, I would have covered my blunder with a random and yet very educated guess. Now you know my little secret," she smiled.

"I think it's safe with us," Jeff chuckled. Moving to the partially open door, he raised his hand in farewell and walked off down the corridor, his weary mind churning with thoughts on the mantle of fatherhood as he turned a corner and nearly collided with another man coming from a bank of lifts.

"Sorry," they mumbled in perfect accord, and laughed softly.

"Next time I'll try to keep my head watching where my body's going," the man explained. "I need some sleep."

"I'm with you on that one, buddy," Jeff nodded. "Our first child was born last night. Well, this morning to be exact."

"No kidding?" Beaming, the man looked up at his significantly taller companion. With his hazel eyes fully exposed to a harsh, fluorescent glare, the brightness illuminated specks and ripples of brown and olive in their cheery depths. "Ours was too, just after midnight. A boy. Right when that quake and power outage happened."

"The same." Jeff's brow shot up. "I didn't know what the hell was going on. For a second I thought I'd passed out."

They stifled their mirth as Jeff extended a hand. "Jeffrey Cooper. Call me Jeff. It's nice to meet you."

"Michael Carter. Mike. And it's nice to meet you, Jeff." His grip was firm, friendly, and they stood there for a while, grinning inanely at each other.

"Well." Jeff broke the silence. "I'm sorry, Mike, but I'll have to make this a quick introduction for now. I was just on my way to make a phone call and I'll be in deep trouble if I don't. This could take a while, so if I want a chance of getting any sleep ahead of the new millennium I'll have to move. Good luck to you and your wife, congratulations on the birth of your son, and maybe I'll see you around before we leave." A huge smile crinkled his face.

"Thanks," he replied, mirroring the expression. "The same goes for you."

They nodded and parted company. Only a few steps separated them when Michael turned. "By the way, Jeff," he whispered loudly. "I beat you to the phone. I was also doing the obligatory calls and you're right, it feels like hours ago." The two men lifted their arms, gesturing a brief, final goodbye. Jeff never saw him at the hospital again.

the newspaper

Jeff looked in the rearview mirror, but the reflection only showed the very top of the baby seat. "Is Austin okay back there, honey?"

Dee swiveled around. "He's fine. Still in sleepy-land."

"Excellent. I've got to stop here for a minute." Slowing the car, he took an empty parking space directly in front of a small convenience store.

"What are you doing?" Checking her watch, Dee stared through the windshield at the grimy glass holding its chaotic organization of old and new advertisements that swarmed over the panes, the posters trying their hardest to entice any casual observers with an abundant supply of products from bread and eggs to flavored milk drinks and underarm deodorant.

"I didn't buy the newspaper yesterday, babe, and I'm hoping this place has a few copies somewhere. I'm annoyed with myself for being forgetful lately," he frowned. "So I completely understand if you don't remember how I made a comment that when Austin's old enough we could show him what was happening in the world on the day of his birth."

"Okay. But be quick," she responded while he opened the door. "It's nighttime soon and you still want to walk the house with him when we get back, don't you?"

"Certainly do. I'll only be a minute."

Jeff found multiple copies of the latest edition on a shiny display stand at the front, beside a large refrigerator cabinet stocked with dozens of Coca Cola cans, and couldn't help but vocalize his disbelief when he saw the bold, capitalized headline splashed across the cover page. 'OUR EARTH TREMBLES. QUAKES AND TSUNAMIS STUN POPULATION.'

"Holy crap! The entire planet? I didn't realize it was this bad." While trudging to the counter, he quickly scanned the article, which reported tremors, tidal surges, and massive electrical failures on every continent and country around the globe.

"Anything else you need?" asked an elderly man, who glanced up from a shabby, dog-eared book he thumbed through.

"Yes, actually." Jeff set the chunky paper down and began digging in his wallet. "I forgot to buy yesterday's Gazette and really need a copy. Do you have any?"

"To be sure." Stooping out of sight for a moment, the man deposited a much thinner version on the countertop. "But there ain't nothing interesting. Can't get the news about that earthquake when the paper's already been printed. Everything you want is in here." He gave the current publication a hearty slap. "So if I was you I wouldn't even bother. Save your money."

"Normally I'd agree. However, my son was born yesterday and I'd like to give him the newspaper with that date on it. Although I will keep today's edition for him as well. I think the last time something like this occurred the dinosaurs acquired an incurable circumstance called extinction." Jeff grinned at the droopy eyelids and wrinkly, neutral expression.

"Hmmm. Sounds like your first time with a kid. That little rugrat won't let you read much, pal. Only thing you'll be getting is broken sleep, fatigue, constant demands plus a whole lot of tetchiness for a long number of years. And I ain't just talking about no baby, either."

The old man's braying laughter still buzzed in Jeff's ears as he walked out of the store, with the prophetic words ringing true from the beginning. Getting past two pages in the daily presented a huge challenge during the first week and Jeff didn't peruse any of Austin's newspaper at all. The baby's arrival definitely shortened those periods, from whenever to hardly-ever, and even the television bulletins became an infrequent habit for the best part of a month.

After five days Dee complained about the mess on the kitchen bench, and Jeff decided to store the large pile of papers inside an airtight plastic box, which he stashed away in the attic, only removing its blue lid and thick layer of dust many years later to scrutinize the contents with a much older, bigger son, family and friends, not long after the staggering events at the party.

Had he been able to get past three pages of the issue dated July 3rd, the small, grainy photo of a man at the top of a short column on page five would probably have drawn his attention to a caption that read, 'Young Father Slain During Carjacking', and in smaller type beneath that, 'Newborn will never know his dad'.

*　　*　　*

On the eastern summit of a sloping foothill, and from his vantage point on the roof of house number ten, a man had a commanding view of the area while he watched the summer sun slide away. Past the trees that dotted the backyard, dazzling oranges, yellows and a dusty-pink spanned the westward horizon as the burning star dropped behind the Rocky Mountains, leaving its final touch of the day on the soaring, snow covered peaks. The pungent aroma of freshly-cut grass carried on an almost indiscernible breeze that brought a fresh crispness from the subalpine region, its intention of settling on the pleasant neighborhood now a triumphant success.

Turning, he shuffled carefully along the tiles and wrapped himself tighter in the dark robe he wore before leaning against a tall chimney, the solid, brick surface rough and scratchy under his palm. A small flock of Western Bluebirds winged their way through the air, their gentle, intermittent tweets calling others for a nocturnal roost, and his head veered from a barely perceived study of their flight to fall upon the sizeable town, starting to thoroughly sparkle as the first streetlights flickered into existence, combining with the already twinkling brilliance that stretched across the plateau far below. He flicked his chestnut-brown eyes off Crescent Lake and crouched, his attention focused on the road when the rumble of an engine announced a car's approach, moments before its twin beams brightened the murkiness. A prolonged redness flared from the back as it braked and swung slowly onto the steep driveway.

"Here we are," Jeff stated. "Honey, can you get the remote for the garage door, please?" Creeping toward their spacious, two-story dwelling, he twisted his head around and gazed at the tiny, purpley-blue eyes blinking in the faint illumination. "Good to see you're awake, buddy," he smiled. "So we can welcome you to our own part of Colorado and your new home, Austin William Cooper." He looked at Dee, his face radiant in the dim glow cast from the dash-light. "You know, babe, I think the name mistake was meant to be. I'm really glad we kept it that way."

Neither of them noticed the soft, white spark beside the chimney, even with the long gradient that led to the door, which was now squealing and clunking on its journey up the guide rails. And neither of them saw the darker shadow appear within the gloom surrounding a huge Engelmann Spruce that dominated the right-hand side of the property, about halfway down the slope.

The shadow moved, and the robed man emerged to observe the vehicle entering the garage with a slight screech of its tires. He watched the father climb out, open the back and lean in, while the mother stepped away from his sight. Two long, neon tubes on the ceiling sputtered to life seconds later, and over the rattle of the doors that began sliding back down, he heard the father talking, his voice carrying clearly on the cool, twilight air.

"The hallway's locked, Dee. Okay, our little bambino, it's time for the tour. We'll start on the ground floor, obviously. Yes, Daddy looks funny, doesn't he? Maybe the kitchen or the study. No, how about the living room first? Then we'll go upstairs, because that's where your room is and I know you're going to love it. You've got some pretty cool stuff in there and Mommy and Daddy are not far away from you at all. Okay? Honey, look at him just staring at me."

Muted laughter reached the man before the door connected with a loud thud on the concrete floor, the panels quivering to a stop. In the swiftly descended night, he pulled a large, flowing hood over his short-cropped, black hair and tread backward, vanishing into the impregnable darkness underneath the giant tree.

Chapter Three

The Babysitter

"Pssst!" Dee peered around the corner of the door and ducked back when he glanced over his shoulder. "Peek-a-boo." Slowly, she returned her angled head and got a single, jolly chuckle the moment her black locks started to show. "Peeeek-aaa-boooo."

Austin gurgled around his pacifier as his mother's forehead came into view, and bounced madly up and down when she stopped with only her eyes revealed over the top of the dark timber trim.

"Peek-a-boo!" Dee laughed, and dashed forward when he began lurching himself to and fro with such vigor that the high chair he sat in trundled across the kitchen floor with a scraping, grating clatter each time the wooden legs struck the tiles. "You strong little monkey," she gasped, grabbing hold of the armrests. "Be careful, cheeky boy."

In the late-afternoon sunlight spilling through the windows, she gazed for a second at the vividness of his eyes, a flaring, incandescent blue and identical in color to the background lagoon in a recent snapshot sent from Fiji by Dee's older sister, Michelle, who travelled the world extensively in her job as a nature photographer.

"I think you're getting a bit too big for that game. Maybe Mommy should just do this." She swooped in to snuggle and blow on the exposed, velvety flesh of his neck while her son shrieked and squirmed delightedly. "Okay, honey," Dee purred as Austin picked up the pacifier that had fallen in his lap during the giggling fit. "Just a quick cleanup of all your mess before Daddy gets here." She wiped some dribble from his chin and smilingly shook her head when he commenced the game invented three days ago, which involved his dummy, his mouth, and a slow squeeze of his jaw while pulling it out at the same time. The resulting soft pop amused him greatly. Staring at it in amazement, he gave a wide, gummy grin and recommenced his fantastic new trick.

*   *   *

The journey home from the company headquarters in Denver went surprisingly fast for Jeff, mainly due to the accolades that still reverberated through his mind, and upon arrival, he breathed in deeply, gathering his thoughts before entering the living room. "Hi, babe," he greeted Dee merrily. "Hi, my handsome boy." Placing his briefcase beside the sofa, he lifted Austin off the floor, kissed his son's cheek and ruffled the delicate, fluffy covering of light-brown hair. "Too interested in Sesame Street, huh? Okay, buddy, there you go." He put him on the carpet at his feet and chuckled as the infant crawled forward and dumped his cushioned bottom down, quietly and completely immersed in his favorite show. Sighing, Jeff settled himself next to his wife and turned sideways to her, wriggling into the spongy, cushioned padding. "Dee, before we have dinner, I've got some news. Something happened at work today. Alan called me in for a bit of a talk with David Bishop. You remember Dave? The head honcho. Numero uno. Our esteemed el presidente."

She searched his face, fighting the terrifying notion that immediately entered her mind.

"Everything's okay, my love," he chortled when he saw her pursed lips. "It's nothing bad about my employment situation. In fact, it's more than okay. Now, nothing's official until the announcement at our annual general meeting next week, but it's no secret around the office. Babe." He paused and watched his wife's blank look for a second. "I've been promoted. You are seated alongside the new, and soon-to-be, chief product officer." Two hasty blinks met his wide grin.

"Promoted? That's... that's wonderful!" A quiver ran through her voice, right before her eyes widened and she squealed in delight, causing Austin to tear his interest away from the television and peer over his shoulder at the sight of his parents embracing joyfully.

*   *   *

"There is one particular thing worrying me about this progress," Jeff admitted. Spearing a lump of potato, he examined the wispy steam that spiraled above the food. "And if truth be told, it goes beyond one thing." Taking a bite, he twisted the fork slowly, watching the silvery handle twinkle under the bright, dining room light.

Dee scooped some mashed banana into Austin's eagerly awaiting mouth and swiveled her head to the right. "What things?"

"Dave informed me the position will most likely involve certain periods of travel. Not only around the state, but around the country, and I've also had ideas that could take the company overseas one day. I'm concerned with the amount of time I might be away from you and Austin. He's already ten months old and I don't want to miss stuff like his first adventures with walking, his first, proper words. The important, growing-up things. Don't get me wrong." Jeff raised his hand, palm up, when Dee parted her lips to speak. "I know this is fantastic for all of us and just about every new dad must go through the same thing, and I also know this is exactly what I've wanted with work, but I don't want it to affect our relationship. Sometimes it's bad enough driving to Denver and back every day, but now there'll be times when I'm away for who knows how long."

"Don't you worry about us, we'll be fine." Dee scraped together another dollop as Austin clapped his hands and dribbled down his chin. "This is why you've worked so hard and your efforts have been noticed. Your skill, your talent, the fantastic way you treat people. All of it. Dave and Alan told you those are some of the many reasons for your success and promotions. You are very, very good at your job and you deserve this. Without your loyalty and natural flair that company wouldn't be half as big as it is now, and one day you will be CEO."

Jeff beamed. "Thanks, honey. How much do you want for such a blush-worthy testimonial? Seriously though, that's really nice. But a lot of amazing people work there and any one of them could run the place."

"That's so typical of you," Dee laughed. "Modest till the end. Jeff, you're the best they've got and they know it." She waggled the empty spoon at her husband. "Don't forget. Being the boss-man means you can do what you want."

"I'm glad you pointed it out, my darling, because as the boss-man I'm going to highlight an additional worry, but also eliminate it with one word. Babysitter."

"I never said you were boss-man here, mister." Dee shook her head, making her long ponytail, a now regular child-rearing and chores hairstyle, whip around both sides of her neck. "Why do you think I need a babysitter?"

"I don't think you need one, I think it'd be good to have one. Just for a bit of support if I'm not around. You'll be able to relax and do something for yourself now and then."

"It does sound nice," Dee agreed. Setting the bowl on the table, she used Austin's bib to wipe his moist, rosy lips. "Actually, it's a great suggestion, honey, and we could both take advantage of that. We could go out for movies and dinner again. That kind of slipped away without us really noticing."

"Yep," Jeff nodded. "But for that task we'll need someone special. Someone who already knows Austin. Someone we can trust. Someone who loves him and is utterly, completely, totally reliable."

"And I think we know who that is," Dee finished for him.

the restaurant

Jeff stabbed a finger on the illuminated, flashing button, his touch turning its color from red to green and silencing the sharp tone that interrupted his focused attention. "Your wife is on line two, Jeff," a pleasant voice drifted from the speaker.

"Thanks, Nat." He poked the corresponding number on another button and lifted the phone off its cradle. "Hey, babe."

"Hi, honey. How's your day going?"

"Magnificent. Do you remember me gabbing about the material reclamation project? The reuse of old paper? Well, I charted the model behind a better production process and Alan's really excited with the outlook. We'll float the idea by Dave tomorrow. I think I can make us one of the leading manufacturers and recyclers in the country. Dee, this could be huge."

"I knew they'd love it, my clever man. You're wonderful," she enthused.

"Thanks, babe. You sound cheerful. Had a good day? How's my boy?"

"He's fine. Exhausted, like Mommy, and having his nap now. He was so funny when we went grocery shopping at the mall this morning. He kept putting things into the cart when I wasn't looking. Just like Daddy."

"If he's just like his daddy, then he'll grow up to be a fine, young idiot. Honey, I'm sorry to do this, but if it's nothing important and you still want to go out for dinner, then I have to get on with this paperwork. It's bigger than the Rockies and if I'm not careful I might set off an avalanche. I'm fairly certain the mountain rescue teams will politely decline the opportunity to search this office for me."

"You fool," Dee laughed. "Okay, a couple of things first. Geena's bringing Susan around earlier, so you don't have to pick her up, and I've also got a surprise for later. I'm thinking it can wait until we're at the restaurant."

"A surprise? I like surprises. Have you dug a hole for the pool?"

"How did you know? If not for Austin, it would've taken me all day. He did the dirt and I did the snow, so it only took a half hour." Her end of the line fizzled as Jeff shuffled through some documents and sniggered at the same time. "One more thing before you get back to your mountain, babe. See if you can guess the identity of the sexiest person in the world who's always cutting off phone conversa..."

Smiling, Jeff listened to the monotonous humming in his ear. "Damn, she's getting good."

*   *   *

Bouts of frenzied giggling shattered the stillness while Jeff strode to the fireplace and squatted momentarily to inspect several birch logs crackling behind two wrought-iron, glass doors. An orange glow and cozy warmth bathed his face as he breathed in the blazing wood's strong, spicy scent before turning to the comical action of Austin scrambling along the floor, nimbly evading more kisses from his babysitter.

"He's my beautiful boy, yes he is, he's my beautiful boy." The young girl laughed through her sing-song words when the infant rolled away from her outstretched hand and sprawled on his back, panting and sniggering.

Jeff smiled at their antics. "Okay, Suze, the fire's stacked and there's plenty in the basket, but just watch the little monster with that." He pointed to a metal grille sitting near the edge of the hearth. Three, large, hinged panels surrounded the fireplace and its collection of implements, each suspended from their own hook on the beige and rust-colored brick chimney. "He's fascinated with the whole deal."

"Sure, Mr. Cooper. I'll keep him away, you can both trust me."

"We know, darling," Dee hummed. She looked at the teenager sitting on the floor by her feet. "Has Jeff given you the money yet?"

"Not yet. But that's okay, Mrs. Cooper, it doesn't matter when."

"Susan Callahan, you are one crazy senorita," Jeff chided playfully. "You've always enjoyed coming here to see this monkey and now that you're getting paid for something you love doing you don't say one word when we forget to pass on the moolah." Raising a finger, he circled it round his ear. "Si. You loooooooco."

Susan laughed, her delicate cheekbones lifting a wide smile from which exuberance and happiness overflowed.

"Sorry, honey, forgive me. That's been my fault. I completely forgot again. I've done that quite a few times over the past nine months, haven't I?"

"You don't have to apologize, Mrs. Cooper. Really, it's okay."

"You are a darling, just like your mother. The absolutely gorgeous, carbon copy of her. It's no wonder you're the envy of everyone at high school. And sweetheart, please, please, please call me Dee." She bobbed her head toward Jeff. "Mr. and Mrs. Cooper are his parents."

"True story. I saw it on their mail once," he grinned. "Suze, I thought we'd covered the Mr. and Mrs. topic last time."

"We did," Susan nodded. "And I'll keep it in mind for later, Mr... um... whoops." She grimaced. "Jeff."

"Mr. um whoops Jeff." He shrugged. "Well, I guess it's a start. Just don't ask Dee for any suggestions or there'll be names that a fifteen-year-old shouldn't hear."

*   *   *

When Jeff and Dee went to a delightfully cozy, Chinese restaurant three days prior to their wedding, the conversation covered a variety of subjects, everything from their imminent marriage to a light-hearted dig at how they were frequently taking on each other's traits. But at the same establishment almost five and a half years later, they discussed only one important topic after the waiter took their order and poured wine into their bowl-shaped goblets.

Dee swirled the maroon-colored liquid and took a slow sniff, treasuring the release of its sweet, fruity fragrance. "Mmmm... delicious," she murmured. "But just this." Delicately, she clinked the side of her glass with a manicured, pink-painted nail. "And that's all I'll be having. Merlot shall pass these lips no more."

Jeff watched a light snowfall shining on its leisurely, downward exodus through the brightness cast outside. "Not good enough, huh?" he remarked, taking his sight off the illuminated street. "You know, I don't think we should blow my pay rise on top shelf spirits. They can be just as expensive."

"You fool! There won't be any alcohol for at least two years, probably three. Well, not me, anyway. And that, my darling, is one part of the surprise."

"Really? No giggle-water? Ludicrous! If that's one part of your crazy revelation, then what's the..." Jeff stopped, grasping the significance of her words the instant a radiant smile ignited her already ecstatic face.

In a softly lit area several tables to the rear, a lone man sat hunched over a large saucer, outwardly preoccupied with the immediate task of devouring his steaming soup. When the couple adjacent the front window enthusiastically vocalized their delight and sprang from their chairs to kiss and hug one another, he paid more attention to their dialogue, increasing the number of furtive peeks while slowing down the spooning of his broth.

"No way, Jeffrey Cooper. Everything will be okay and this won't change what we've already discussed. As I've said, you'll end up becoming CEO in the future, which is exactly where you wanted to be. We've come so far, sweetheart, let's not take any backward steps, or it's all for nothing."

Jeff rubbed his forehead. "I know, babe. It's just... well... it has worked out fine with Austin, but maybe you will need me more now, and I..."

"Honey." Dee patted his free hand. "This is old news and the reason why we've got Susan's help. She was fantastic when Austin was a baby. I think she could even change a diaper blindfolded she's that good, and I don't think we could keep her away if we tried. I can cope with this just like all the mothers out there with two or more children. Besides, you're missing the most important issue here. My terms. Remember? Servants. Private jet. Pool."

Jeff chuckled. "You're forgetting something."

"What?"

"An entertainment area, if my memory serves me well."

The man deposited some money under the now empty saucer, stood, and straightened his navy blue jacket before picking up a tan satchel sitting on the chair seat to his left. Taking a final glance at the laughing duo, he strolled toward a red door marked with an intricate, gold-painted symbol and the word 'Men' written below, pushed it open and walked through. As the door closed softly behind him, he moved ahead a few paces, his chestnut-brown eyes glowing a brief, muted white, and paused outside Austin's room, listening to the last of Susan's bedtime story. Looking carefully around the interior, he studied the high ceilings while she bade the child goodnight, and stepped forward to brush a fine coating of snow from the thick top-rail on a metal fence that ran along the elevated half of Fairview Terrace. Smiling, the dim, white spark fading in his eyes, he leaned against the freezing barrier and shivered for a moment before gazing up the long driveway at the house. "Good kid. Nice girl. Terrific parents," he murmured. "Pity your choice isn't somewhere warmer. The Canary Islands, Hawaii, Barbados, Australia. I could list it for hours. But I guess I should be grateful it's still this planet." He puffed out a great, cloudy breath and disappeared, a fleeting, swirling disturbance in the bitterly cold air the lone testament to his being there.

*   *   *

Around seven and a half months later, and after a much shorter labor, Stephanie Rachel Cooper was born, coming into the world at one-thirty, an early morning baby, matching her older sibling. Unlike him, she arrived screaming louder than a banshee, and her amused parents wondered at the difference. It was as if she realized something was amiss that night.

The night of the very first attempt to get her two-year-old brother.

Chapter Four

The Man

Jeff hoisted an enormous bag off the floor and threw its long, thick strap over his shoulder while he raced from the bedroom and along the hall. As the tall man plunged recklessly down the stairs, the suspended bag bounced and swung across his hips and the back of his legs, threatening a serious tumble with each strike. Reaching the bottom unharmed, he stumbled into the front living room. "Okay, okay. Ooookaaayyy, I think that's it," he gasped, and began stalking the area, his frantic eyes searching the corners when mild panic convinced him that necessary and crucial objects were missing from his mental inventory.

"Jeff, will you please calm down," Dee implored. "That's about the fiftieth time in ten minutes. You're going to end up hurting yourself and then what the hell are we going to do?"

"Sorry, honey." He looked sheepishly at his deeply breathing wife, and against his better judgment, started babbling. "It's just, you know, this is so sudden. I mean, not sudden as such, it's not like we weren't expecting this, but, you know, we had everything ready to be collected and then I had to get it all together and pack it in the bag. You've got to be able to utilize the available space in there, you realize. Then there's the checking and double checking. You can't be too careful. I would really hate to get all the way to the hospital and find out we've forgotten something, it wouldn't..." His voice trailed off at Dee's scathing expression, which indisputably stated, 'I am a pregnant woman about to give birth, you are merely a man, so do not mess with my plans or, heaven help you, with me.' He opened his mouth to speak, snapped it shut again just as quick, and took a couple of moments to contemplate her glare before composing himself, better judgment finally controlling his next, and extremely wise, move. "You're right, Dee, of course. I should just calm down." He nodded placidly. "We're all ready to go. Are you okay? How are the contractions?"

"They're still there, still regular, but I'm fine, thanks." Her demeanor mellowed. "Although, this baby is coming soon, I do know that for sure. So I think we'd better get moving."

Jeff smiled eagerly. "No problem, babe. Let's go."

Throughout their exchange, like spectators at a tennis match, two heads moved back and forth from one to the other, silently observing the interaction. And when Jeff had a challenging time levering his wife from a single, wooden chair while trying to control the large bag still slung across his back, Austin giggled at the funny face directed his way.

"Come on, darling," Dee said to the toddler. She took his hand when he slid off the sofa, and together they followed Jeff and Susan out of the living room and along the hall. Pausing near the door to the garage, she peered at the babysitter, who stood quietly by the wall, rubbing one hand atop the other. Shorter than her by about three inches, with layered, golden-blonde hair cascading like a flaxen waterfall midway down her chest, the shapely and strikingly attractive teenager was the essence of youthful beauty. "Are you okay, sweetheart?" Dee asked. "You look a bit stunned."

"Yeah, I'm fine," Susan laughed. Her eyes, pale-green, sharp and radiant, the inner color of a freshly sliced, garden-grown lime, twinkled in the ambient light. "I'm just beginning to understand that the older I get, the more I find adult relationships very difficult to grasp sometimes."

Dee nodded. "Particularly when they're of the marital kind with children involved. But don't be put off, honey, because if you ever find that someone who is so special you just know everything will be okay through life's tough times, then hold on to him with all you've got. Especially if he does have a bit of sense in that usually silly male head."

She smiled sweetly at her husband. "You'll know when he comes along," she finished as Jeff knelt in front of Austin.

"Hey, buddy. Do you remember our talk about you being well-behaved for Susan? About helping out and how you're the man around here until I get home?"

"Yes, Daddy. I memba."

"That's my boy. Protect what you love. Do I get a hug?" Jeff's heart melted when Austin gazed affectionately at him a second before smiling and jumping into an enormous cuddle. He rocked him from side to side, stroking the fine, brown hair on his small head, and chuckled when his son pulled back to perform an action that had been a highlight for him over the past three weeks, a click of his tongue and a rapid, double wink. On the first night it happened, both parents had congratulated Austin for eating his entire dinner using just his cutlery, not his fingers, and Jeff simultaneously clacked his tongue while giving a huge, exaggerated wink. Austin looked curiously at the deed before attempting the same thing, but only succeeded in blinking both eyes along with a slight 'tsk' sound, which made his father roar with laughter. Now, he had gotten better, and achieved a very passable click, yet still didn't have the eye action quite right. He blinked either one first followed instantly by the next. Jeff absolutely adored it, and he tousled Austin's hair once more as the boy moved to his mother, who embraced him when he wrapped his arms tenderly around her extended belly.

"I love you, my sweetheart," she cooed. "Very soon you'll have a brother or sister coming home. You're really looking forward to that, aren't you?"

Austin waggled his head excitedly. "Yes, Mommy."

"Me too." She stooped to kiss and hug him one last time. "You be a good boy."

Jeff checked his watch. "Honey, it's after four and we better go if we want to beat any traffic buildup. Suze, good luck, darling. Remember…"

"It's all under control, Jeff." Susan nodded reassuringly. "Mom and Dad are only five minutes away if I need them. You two get going."

Austin sat on her lap at the front sitting room window, and together they watched the car's brake lights glow as it rolled down the driveway. It slowed even more for an extra cautious right-hand turn, the suspension bouncing the vehicle gently while it eased onto the tarmac and accelerated out of sight, pumping white plumes of smoke through the cool late-afternoon air.

"C'mon, little dude, let's get something to eat. You're hungry, right?"

"Yes, peas."

Heading for the kitchen, Susan smiled when she felt his small hand slip into hers, and gave it a soft, comforting squeeze.

*   *   *

Just after seven o'clock the sun finally relinquished its hold on the day, taking the lingering reddened hues in the heavens below a dusky, western horizon, and within an hour of evening's tightening grip, syrupy, iron-gray fog spooled down from the topmost reaches of the colossal Rocky Mountains. Creeping slowly toward Crescent Lake, it wrapped a chilly blanket of haze and concealment around every town, suburb, house, car, tree and streetlight, forcing the abandonment of many late, nocturnal exercises, the walkers scurrying back to their homes when the visibility reduced to a mere two-foot limit.

Inside Jeff and Dee's sprawling abode, Susan busied herself getting Austin ready for bed. With his teeth brushed and nighttime diaper on, she dressed him in his newly bought attire, a set of warm, fleecy Sesame Street pajamas and already his favorite, for they had a hundred Bert and Ernie's printed all over them. He would sit there on his bed with Mom and Dad, pointing out each and every picture, saying, "Ert Ernie, Ert Ernie, Ert Ernie," over and over, compelling either parent to interject with a mildly stern, "Okay, Austin, that's enough now, it's time for sleepies." And tonight was no different. After reading a bedtime story about how many cookies the Cookie Monster devoured, he began contentedly and thoroughly showing Susan the two characters, until she abruptly brought it to a halt, utilizing Jeff's advice on how to curb the event that would undoubtedly occur.

"Okay, little dude, Bert and Ernie are tired and want to sleep, so it's time for everyone to get some shuteye." He dove feet first under the sheets, writhing and giggling while Susan tucked him in. She bent over, kissed him on the forehead and smoothed back his hair. "Big day tomorrow, huh? You'll be meeting your new brother or sister. You must be really excited. I know I am."

"Yeah. Big egg-site-ed," he replied, grinning broadly.

"And I'm sure they'll be just as gorgeous as you. Sleep tight, sweetheart. Nightie, night." She stepped into the hallway and wiggled her fingers at him while closing the door, diminishing a rectangular slab of illumination cast within the room. Just as it latched softly, his voice rang out.

"Sooz-in!"

Opening it quickly, she peered in. "What's up, buddy?"

"Don't coze door, peas." His little eyes blinked at her over the top of his sheets.

"Oh! Of course. Sorry, I forgot. Sheesh, silly me, I must be too excited. There you go, I'll leave it open a bit." She pulled it three quarters shut, blew a kiss to his contented, sleepy face and padded lightly down the hall, ready to relax a bit now, maybe read for a while, or watch some television. She had a computer studies essay due next week and brought the paper to work on, but that could wait for it was practically complete, so she would finish it tomorrow, leaving an almost entire Sunday free to go out and have some much-needed and well-deserved fun with her friends.

the invader

As time crept past midnight, with the moon recently set and blackness now at its peak, the fog besieged Crescent Lake, eventually obscuring Fairview Terrace. In the dwelling, the smaller of two blissfully sleeping people stirred, his disrupted slumber laced with tiny, incoherent mumbles, while outside, at the extreme rear of the property, an enormous portion of mist began thickening amid the trees, bending and flexing their creaking branches when it lowered to the ground and pressed ahead.

Reaching the clear and open land sloping down toward the house, the impenetrable smog coagulated further, becoming a solid and yet squelchy-looking, pitch-black cylinder that rolled along, flattening the blades of grass on the neatly kept lawn. As it moved, large pieces fell away from the main body until at least a hundred refrigerator-sized blobs remained. All together, they quivered, and rose into the air on long, thick tendrils that sprouted from their new tar-like form, rocking them from side to side while thousands of narrow, red stripes emerged, glowing, swirling, and darting rapidly across the surface. Every few seconds the stripes stopped their wild flight and converged in one spot, creating a crude eye that rotated left and right, up and down, expanding and contracting as it surveyed the house's wood and brick façade. In unison, the blobs inched their way forward, their luminous red eyes dispersing to resume the threadlike, erratic race.

The soupy fog seemingly abandoned its vigil, withdrawing completely when the massive, black blobs picked up speed and sprinted around the perimeter, galloping on their solid props and surrounding the house within moments. Acting as one, and in total silence, they advanced, latched onto the walls and flowed instantaneously across the exterior, merging and expanding like a giant black and red wave of oil while seeking the entrance they had observed. It engulfed the roof, spreading briskly along the tiles, and surged up the last bastion to be overrun – the chimney, standing tall and proud in the darkness. At the top, a large lump broke off, slipped under the stainless steel cap and oozed down the cold, gloomy flue while the remaining bulk compressed tighter on the house, making the structure shudder, as if trying to reject this new and undesirably vile coating.

Located at the bottom of the flue, a metal damper gave one momentary, protesting squeal when the lump pushed the dusty flap open. The iron and glass doors came next, thrust aside with a dull clunk, allowing the mass to spill upon the plum-colored, slate hearth in a puff of ash. Finger-like gelatinous strands stretched out and probed the hinged, metal grille, then reached through the gaps to examine the edge of the fawn-colored carpet. With a muted, rattling thump, it pushed the grille over, and the black lump rolled, bubbled and reared up, just as the bright stripes appeared, beginning their frantic chase around the wet-looking thing before forming the glittering eye. It swung about, inspecting the murky surroundings, and stopped to scrutinize a set of three, framed photos, hanging on the wall to the right of the fireplace, one above the other. Each of the pictures showed a widely smiling couple with an infant at different ages, a baby, one, and two years of age. Instantly, the lump changed, shifting and fashioning itself into the rough approximation of a human being, the large, red eyeball centered exactly where a face would normally exist. The eye dissolved again, and the strands hurtled around and around the body. Slowly, the invader moved, the legs jerky and uncertain at first, but by the time it reached the door, its strides were fluid and confident, and it walked purposefully down the hall, the glistening, pulsating eye reforming swiftly and pivoting everywhere.

Pausing at the bottom of the stairway, it scanned the individual treads, then headed for the two sleeping residents above.

Susan woke with a start, and raised her head to peer confusedly around the darkness. The first thing she noticed caused further disorientation to her drowsy, sleep-induced mind. On the other side of the room, to her left, a set of green numbers glowed dimly, and yet she couldn't remember why she had moved her digital alarm clock over there. Wakefulness returned with a sharp jolt while she stared at the time. It read 1:34 a.m.

"You dumbass," she quietly scolded herself after realizing she was in the guest room of the Cooper household.

The fading remnants of a bad dream, more a nightmare, left her with a troubled, edgy feeling. Sighing heavily, she fumbled for the switch on a small, bedside table lamp, clicked it on and squinted in the lackluster light flooding the small corner of the room. Blinking away the adjustment of going from complete dark to dull brightness, she pulled the comforter back, slid tiredly from the mattress and altered the nightie that had twisted around her hips and legs during the course of her movement-filled visions. Gathering her hair, flicking it over her shoulders, she picked up a fluffy, pink bathrobe from the floor and slipped her arms through the sleeves, yawning as she pulled it tight and fastened it around her trim waist. At the exact moment her hands dropped the cord she heard a sound in the hallway and paused, listening hard above the blood that began pumping loudly in her ears. There it was again. A creak. The unmistakable groan of a floorboard pushed down by something. Something heavy. Something like a foot. And the weight of the body attached to it.

With short, tortured gasps and trembling hands, she sidled gingerly to the door, keeping as close as possible to the wall in a successful attempt to not make any noise of her own. The progress seemed to take forever, and by the time she got there a harsh pain arced across her chest, gripping her in a bear-like embrace and she made a monumental effort to regain some composure, certain that her breathing alone would alert whoever walked through the house.

Don't be stupid, she thought. It's probably just Austin getting a drink or, or, wanting some food, maybe. Although the notion popped happily into her mind, the familiarity with the little boy she loved successfully contested it with, no, you are so wrong, he doesn't do that. He might lie in his bed, calling out, but he won't get up. And he might be big for his age, but he's not that big. That was something with a lot of weight, something really big.

Susan lingered at the door, her hand shaking while it hung suspended above the handle, and placed her ear to the solid, grainy surface. She listened for a few seconds more, but heard nothing else, and with a sweat-laden palm, tentatively grasped the lever, eased it all the way down, and brought it gradually open, mutely praying that no squeaky hinge would give her away now as she peeked into the hallway. She had intended on staying up late to watch an old, romantic movie from the 1930s, however, after twenty minutes, severe, wavy lines suddenly affected every television channel, and she dragged her annoyed, weary self to bed, purposefully leaving a bulb burning above the stairway landing in case of a sleep-disrupted bathroom call. And in its glow, extremely close to Austin's slightly open door, she saw some sort of creature, stocky, massive, perhaps seven-foot-tall, prowling stealthily toward his bedroom, a vision that would stick with her forever. Though the shape did seem vaguely humanoid, it most definitely wasn't human, and the sheer inability to accept that fact and the circumstances now beyond her rationality and understanding instigated a ruthlessly staggering mental blow.

The whole figure was incredibly dark, a depthless, raven ebony that seemed to suck in light like a galaxy's greedy black hole. Yet at the same time, it used the brightness to emphasize its wet-looking, ever-changing skin, which appeared to undulate across its frame, visible even at the distance of around thirty-five feet. Energetic, flickering red stripes zipped around the body, both beautiful and repulsive to observe. They churned, spun and gave the awful impression that it was a race in being the first dominant one to traverse the hideous figure. For a few moments the stripes would disappear from sight, briefly, away to the front, before coming into view again on their mad and endless journey.

Susan trembled, rooted to the spot, while moisture dripped through her white-knuckled clutch on the cool, metal handle. Losing her tenuous hold of control, she let forth with a bloodcurdling scream, and both hands flew to her mouth, unconsciously trying to stifle an already too late reaction as the door opened fully.

the shard

The molten mass rippled, propelling an enormous surge across the entire house. They felt them close by. The human, and the object he possessed. The Shard, The All, The First. Though many cycles had passed, their master's great yearning for the object never waned, it only intensified. Even here, his influence knew no bounds. Hurriedly, frantically, the mass peeled from the roof, and like giant flaps on a box, hoisted high in the air. The red strands dashing across its surface formed gargantuan eyes on all four sides, and that was when they observed them, a darkness opposing the darkness, halfway down the rough-surfaced driveway, standing calmly and staring at them. The fury of their master raged, but before they had a chance to react, the human advanced swiftly. A pair of intense, scarlet sparks, the movement of his arm, and a flash of the object terminated their failed trap as bright, colorful lights made them see no more.

The figure immediately stopped its forward motion and straightened from a slightly hunched posture. In the space of Susan's heart making the transition from one beat to the next, two occurrences happened near simultaneously. First, the primitive shape of an eye coalesced on the back of what must have been its intended head, created by the twirling bands that had sped around its form only a moment ago. The next took her completely by surprise, because now it stood in front of her, right there, no more than ten inches away. Barely able to track its progress, nothing more than intuition told her the maneuver had occurred with lightning speed.

Up close, the figure was utterly appalling, and released a nauseating smell reminiscent of sizzled hair. It mixed with the scent of her sweat and fear and lodged deep inside her airways. On the malformed, egg-shaped head, no features identified a face, no ears adorned the sides, no nose protruded out, no lips, no chin, just that one ghastly abomination of an eye, whizzing up, down, and over the heaving skin with an evil, studying intent.

Susan panted hard. Blinded momentarily by warm, salty tears spilling down her cheeks, she wheezed through a mouth that opened and closed quickly. All the horror movies she had watched with her boyfriend, Hank, as she squirmed under his arm and covered her eyes with his hand, refusing to look until the terrifying scene passed, none of it prepared her for this. They were only fiction, films, a made-up story, so how could they? Those kinds of moments just didn't happen in real life.

In a flash, the thing's arm shot out, and a misshapen, stubby-fingered hand clamped tightly to her neck, cutting off the lung's treasured flow of sweet, sweet air. As her damp eyes bulged, all she could do was gaze at the bubbling, stirring skin on its forearm, and wonder why the touch felt icy cold and not burning hot. With that single and silent contemplation the thing moved, taking two backward, partially-turning steps, dragging her along and intensifying its pressurized clench.

I've failed, her desolate thought rang out. I've been left to... to care for... and... and to... to protect the precious, beautiful child in this house... and... I've... I've failed. Austin... he's next... no... it's killing me... Mommy, help... Daddy... help me!

Fresh, fat droplets splashed on the hand around her throat. She felt her bladder weaken and her mind begin a darkening slip over the edge, its fragile continuance with stability nearly over, the last strands of saneness declaring their farewells with the information she was on the verge of two things, unconsciousness and severe, irreversible psychological damage. The event that helped her, that saved her from a dive into the abyss, came in the form of a hushed reprimand, beckoning from farther along the hallway, right by Austin's room.

"Uhhh, uhhh, uhhh," a deep voice murmured, the tone rising with each scold.

Susan stared past the thing's clumpy body, vaguely noticing the red eye swing quickly out of sight to the back of its head, and saw another figure, a man she decided due to the resonant baritone, leaning comfortably against the wall with his arms folded across his chest, lackadaisical as could be. Dressed in a dark-brown, hooded robe over black clothing, she thought his garments identical to something a priest or monk would wear if they wandered the mountains on some quest in ages past. Especially the hood, which covered his head and shrouded his face from view. Deep inside its shadow, she detected the glint of his eyes, a rich, dusky red. Not like the stripe's color on the foul creature currently squeezing her life away, but a vivid, scarlet-blood, gorgeous and radiant. Peaceful, comforting waves washed through her, cleansing her soul and instilling the certainty that this robed person meant no harm to either of the two real humans in the house.

"Whatever the hell you are," the hooded man snarled softly. "You're being extremely naughty. Now put her down, or this will end very badly for one of us. And that won't be me."

Susan felt a tremor roll through the thing's frame while it regarded the man, and blinked when the eye suddenly swung back to hold her gaze a mere millisecond before it lifted her effortlessly off the floor, high over its head.

With a deft flick of its arm, her neck broke. The echo of vertebrae snapping and grinding carried briefly in the stillness before the thing released its grip, dropping her ragdoll body in a crumpled heap where it twitched once and was still. Lashing out with its poorly constructed foot, the thing sent her lifeless corpse flying up against the bedroom doorframe, smashing it into the wood with a solid, sickening thud. Bones split and cracked with the impact, and she plunged, bent and twisted, to the floor. The crude eye rolled around, dispassionately appraising the newcomer some more.

"Through all my years, all my travels, she's been one of the nicest, most decent, genuine individuals I have ever encountered, and I'm rather fond of her. Now, when I said put her down, I meant let her go. But I think you know that." Pushing himself off the wall, the man advanced, shaking his hooded head, the swaying cloth rustling across his shoulder while he sauntered purposefully toward his foe. "I also warned about things ending very badly for you, turd-man."

The being's eye broke apart, raced around its form and reshaped a split second before it made its move, not for the man, but away from him. With stunning velocity, it reached the stairway, and abruptly froze in flight when the man threw his arm up.

"No, you don't," he grunted, his baggy sleeve swinging with the snappy gesture. "You're not going any..." He stopped, and continued facing forward, deliberately hiding his shrouded features, and the frown he wore, from view. "Boy," he snapped. "Go back to bed. You don't need to see this."

Austin was positive he made no sound during his cautious entrance to the hallway, and yet somehow this man knew he stood there, without turning around. Of average height, the stranger was neither short nor tall, and Austin felt no menace, only goodness, it radiated like heat from the fireplace, even with the stern words. He knew with a certainty that the hooded man wasn't here to hurt him, not like the horrible, black being near the stairs. That... creature... had already done something to Susan. As he studied her inert, tangled form, his small body shivered, and the small hands at the end of his pajama sleeves clenched.

"Go back to bed," the man repeated. "I don't know how you managed to sneak up on me, boy, but I'll tell you right now, you're far too young for this. Go."

Austin didn't move, didn't take his gaze off Susan. Instead, he directed it to the black creature again, slowly, while a strange, white spark flickered deep within his purpley-blue eyes. "Bad fing," he growled. "Potec love."

"NO," the man hollered. "Austin, stop!" Keeping his outstretched arm pointed at the immobile figure, he swiveled to the wall and looked directly at the toddler, who tilted his head to one side when he saw the red glow inside the hood. "Go to your bed... please," he finished gently. "You'll sleep well, and everything will be okay. I'll make sure of that. So off you go and close your door. Just this one time."

Staring at the hooded man, the white spark in his eyes retreating as quickly as it existed, Austin sensed a significance about him that his fledgling mind couldn't grasp. He didn't understand what it was and simply accepted the fact right then. "Like you," he stated. "Good."

"That's right," the man chuckled, nodding once. "I like you, too." A layer of sweat covering his brow gathered together and trickled down the bridge of his nose. "You're quite amazing, boy, but still too young. Go on, off to bed." Immediately, he spun to his captive on the stairway landing. "And don't forget your door," he added.

Austin stepped rearward to his room, seizing a final glance at Susan and the two perplexing characters. As he started closing the door he paused when movement caught his attention, and watched while something shifted along the high span of wall at the stairway. It was like a wiggling of yellowness, close to the ceiling, and brought to mind an afternoon only days ago when his mom made some Jell-O. She had taken the dessert from the fridge, called him over and shook the bowl gently, making the pineapple-flavored treat wobble to and fro and giggling when he stared wide-eyed and open-mouthed at the amusing sight, so much like the phenomenon he examined now. The peculiar spectacle hung there like a transparent curtain, until a heavy sigh from the funnily dressed person made him depart.

The sound of Austin's door finally latching spurred the hooded man into action. He strode to the figure, scrutinizing it, his scarlet eyes firing dangerously within the folds of his cowl. From one leg half raised in flight, to the skin and bright red streaks, everything appeared to be completely motionless.

"Okay, turd-man, it's just you and me. First things first, let's keep you where you are," he whirred, and forced the index finger of his raised arm inside the inky-black chest, driving it deeper, twisting and turning to the middle knuckle while filaments of energy burst into life, dazzling blue and green threads similar to lightning bolts that streamed up, down, and around his hand. They curled at the entry point, bursting like miniature fireworks, before snaking across the entire figure. Giving a rumble of approval, he reversed the motion, pulled his finger free with a small, slurping pop, and held it up, inspecting the skin and nail as the filaments faded away.

"Disgusting," he buzzed. "And really, there was no need for me to do that, but hey, pain and payback's a bitch, huh? Well, for you it is." Separating his robe, he kicked the frozen leg straight with a keen snap. "I don't recall having the displeasure of your company in the past. I don't know where you came from, and frankly, I don't care. You're here for someone. A young, defenseless boy, not even old enough to fully protect himself." Pointing at Susan's shattered body, he began a leisurely stroll around his prisoner, like a shark circling its prey. "Then, you just kill anything you can put your grubby turd-hands on. You really thought this would work? You really thought you could get away with this and roam about my planet doing whatever you want?" A cutting smile worked his lips. "Because there's no going back, not without a ship, which you don't have, and not through anything else. The Triangle's secure and there's no way you're leaving." He stopped, tapped the figure's head, and looked it up and down before resuming his ambling circuit. "You know who I am," he hissed. "You know who the boy is and yet you still thought you'd defeat me. Me? Hasn't gone too favorably, has it?" He dropped his voice to a barely-heard whisper. "Listen, I've gotta tell you something. You don't cut it as a human. Not even close. Look at you, you're just laughable. I won't have pathetic things like you thinking it's okay to jump over here any time you want. And by the way, what the hell is that stench? You smell like a hair salon on fire." Grinning, he slapped its cheek thrice, Mafiosi style. "One more thing before the fun part. Your friends are gone. All of them. But I've got a feeling you're already aware of that fact. Now it's your turn. Are you telepathic? Got someone commanding you? If so, and if there's still a link, then pass my message on to whatever spawned you. Let's see if this little trick makes them think twice. Enjoy the ride, turd-man."

His eyes blazed, like two tiny infernos firing up, the vivid, blood-red dancing on the confines of his hood. Flicking its shoulder fiercely, he moved farther away, raised both arms and rotated them in an intricate, circular pattern while the being rose into the air. Levitating about four foot off the wooden floor, it stopped, jerked suddenly, and melted into its large, globular mass again when a glittering, mesh-like ball appeared, completely encasing the now bubbling entity. An astonishing collection of colors flashed around the exterior of the sphere, masking the trapped invader as the ball shrunk rapidly, growing brighter and brighter until all the shades had blended into a brilliant white. The sphere shriveled to the size of a marble, and with a sharp crack, ceased to be, the only indication of its prior existence being the injection of a fresh, minty scent, which the hooded man fanned vigorously around the area. "That's better," he murmured. "Smells just like a Norwegian summer."

Calmly, he made his way to Susan and gazed sorrowfully upon her broken figure. "Such a beautiful girl," he sighed, sliding the huge hood onto his back, the softly whispering material blending with his exhalation. "Such a shame." The redness in his eyes, already dim and distant during his contemplation, changed instantly to a glowing gold. "I don't know how they found him," he rumbled. "I don't even know who they are. They've achieved the impossible by getting through." He fell silent for half a minute. "I agree. We can't allow him to remember. And the answer to your question is, nothing's happened to him. You know that, so why ask? Bloody hell, you haven't been this vocal since his birth." Turning quickly, he tread softly to Austin's room, and smiled at the sight of the gently snoring child snuggled under his covers. "See? The boy is fine," he hummed. Reaching inside his voluminous robe, he brought forth a multifaceted, exotic looking object and held it out toward the bed. "Apparently and mind-bogglingly unaffected by this event." The object, twice the length of his hand, quivered as bursts of gold and silver flared within its transparent interior, and a frown creased the man's honey-brown skin when a powerful tremor shot violently through his arm. "What the hell is wrong with you? I understand he's important, but what's with all the twitchy stuff? Isn't this just a simple memory alter..."

All at once, the object filled with a mass of weaving, countless colors, more than he had ever seen, more than he had ever thought imaginable. The boy's eyelids flew open, exposing the vibrant blue-purple of his irides, which transformed immediately and joined the assorted, sparkling illumination that ignited the entire area. The light show was over within seconds, and as Austin's eyes shut he sighed through a relaxed, contented smile before nuzzling his head deeper into his pillow's soft and spongy padding.

"Hmmm," the man whirred. He scrutinized the object carefully while its colors subsided to the sporadic, fleeting glint of gold and silver, punctuated now and then by a sticklike, branching eruption of coal-black. Slipping the object back inside his robe, he flicked his vision over various crayon-scrawled drawings pinned to the walls, a Colorado Rockies baseball poster, and pictures of puppet characters placed above an open, camouflage-painted toy box sitting near the window. "You won't remember me," he announced quietly to the sleeping figure. "In fact, you won't remember any of this. But one day you will, and that day will come all too soon. I'll be around and I'll be watching, so keep your wits about you, boy."

Noiselessly, he closed the door and approached Susan, the goldenness returning to his eyes when he crouched beside her destroyed remains. "Yes," he said. "Of course it's the only option. An extremely valid one and something I'd already decided on, thank you." He hunched his shoulders and lifted her from the floor with a quiet grunt. Her head sagged backward, swinging grotesquely to and fro while he carried her corpse into the bedroom and laid it delicately upon the sheets. Brushing some wayward strands of blonde hair from her face and blank, staring eyes, he removed the object from his cloak and proceeded to trace an outline close around the prone body. Starting at the crown of her head, taking particular, skillful care in not making contact, he completed the full circuit and smiled when a flashing, coppery-colored light enveloped her skin. It swirled rapidly across the surface before creating three, small radiant orbs that plunged into her forehead, chest, and lower abdomen. The second they vanished a muted cracking breached the stillness, and her body jerked as the shattered bones of her skeletal structure reassembled. Susan gave a sudden, tremendous jolt and sat bolt upright, gulping huge lungful's of air. Blinking sluggishly, she looked at the man, yawned, and flopped back down, asleep in an instant. While the man covered her with the comforter, she flicked her tongue softly over dry lips and muttered a few, muffled words.

"You're welcome," he whispered, storing the object in his robe. "I'm lucky they screwed up tonight, and I give immeasurable thanks for your intervention, Susan Callahan. Without you, things would have been... tricky." In response to his low voice she tucked the sheets under her chin and rolled to one side. "Sleep well, young lady. The life you've saved is undoubtedly the universe's most important, and he'll be a very handy person to have in your corner."

Grinning, he left the room, latched the door silently behind him, and reopened Austin's to its original position. Slowly and surely, he made his way through the house, restoring any disorder before the hazy, white shimmering of his eyes had him outside. After inspecting the foggy property, he stood on the driveway again and took a final, frowning look toward the unsullied and darkened dwelling while pulling the hood over his head. The whiteness twinkled within its depths, and he disappeared, leaving a brief agitation of the mist as it whirled in on the suddenly unoccupied spot.

the euphoria

Austin came to full wakefulness with a wild-eyed stare around his faintly lit room. The final, nightmarish image of his abnormally distorted babysitter lying crumpled at her doorway descended to an unfathomable compartment in his mind, stored quickly, and permanently. But the emotional taste stayed, causing a painful, despairing sensation.

"Sooz-in!" He threw back his sheets, raced for the door and flung it wide open. "Sooz-in, Sooz-in," he yelled again when he saw the empty hall.

"I'm here, little dude," she called, hurrying up the stairs. "What's going on?" Susan caught his look of dread that, like his dream, melted swiftly when he spotted her smiling face. "Hey, are you okay?"

"I haff bad fing. See bad fing."

Lifting him onto her hip, she stroked his pale, soft-skinned cheek. "A bad thing? Do you mean a dream, darling? Did you have a bad dream?"

"I fink," he nodded. "I see man an big back fing an you haff hurt." His bottom lip fluttered.

"Awwww," she purred, smoothing his rumpled hair. He wrapped his arms around her neck and pulled himself in for a tight cuddle. "It's okay, sweetheart, everything's okay. That's all it was, Austin, a nasty, horrible dream. Naughty, naughty dream." She pouted, and giggled with him when he pulled back and saw her expression.

"Naw-ey deam," he grinned. The relief of Susan being safe and sound had changed his whole demeanor, and his purple-blue eyes shone vibrantly in the early morning light.

"You've had a good sleep, little dude. It's almost seven thirty. I checked in on you earlier, but you were snug as a bug in a rug, all nice and warm." She nuzzled his neck, which brought on another fit of laughter.

"Ear Mommy and Daddy?"

"They're not back yet. Remember Mommy won't be home today, only Daddy. Then we can find out if you've got a new brother or sister. Isn't that exciting?"

"Yeah," he buzzed, nodding vigorously.

"And are you hungry?" Susan tickled him under his arm, holding on tight as he chuckled and squirmed.

"YEAH!"

"Wow, you sure sound like it. Come on, let's get some breakfast. What would you like to eat? Oooooo! I know." Her mouth and eyes opened incredibly wide. "How about some scrambled eggs and French toast? They're yummy, yummy, yummy for your hungry, hungry tummy," she sang.

"Yummy, yummy," he burbled, and burrowed closer, resting his head upon her shoulder.

"Okay, let's go. I'll have to put you down though, because you're far too big and heavy for me to carry all the way to the kitchen."

"I big boy," he stated when Susan lowered him.

"You sure are. I'll have to call you big dude soon."

"Yeah." He took Susan's hand, and together they descended the stairs. "What smell?" Austin asked, sniffing loudly.

"I don't know, buddy. It's weird, isn't it? Maybe Mommy and Daddy have got some strange smelling flowers somewhere."

"Yeah. Fowers."

*　　*　　*

Jeff set a new record up the 200-foot-long driveway when he got home a half hour later, completely exhausted, ready for the next whatever number of hours he would still be awake, and barely able to hold back his excitement. On entering the downstairs hallway from the garage, he stopped when a peculiar odor assailed his nostrils, still strong enough to overwhelm the obvious and completely delicious scent of early-morning cooking that wafted through the air.

"Mint," he pondered, inhaling deeply. "Aaaannnnd..." Furrowing his brow, he sniffed again, three speedy snorts in an attempt to distinguish the aroma. "Is that burnt hair? Suze, are you blow-drying with some sort of mint-enhanced, hair styling explosive?" With a chuckle and a shrug, he decided his euphoria couldn't wait any longer. "Austin! Susan! It's a girl!"

Chapter Five

The Kindergarten

The cordless phone beeped loudly as Jeff set it back upon the base. Lifting his briefcase off the floor, he took a sheet of paper from Dee's outstretched hand. "Well, that's sorted. We see her on Monday morning, my love, so I'll have to start work later." He waved the paper at an array of products strewn across the kitchen bench and studied his wife's harassed expression. "You still haven't told me what happened here."

"Austin happened here." Through taut lips, she blew away a lock of hair that strayed across her left eye. "He pulled down all the shelves in the refrigerator trying to get something at the top."

Jeff's brow rose. "I see it wasn't a successful climb."

"No. Not at all." Dee folded her arms. "Not even with the chair he dragged in from the dining room. There was food all over the place. Broken glass, the whole lot. And then Stephie races in, slips on some Tabasco sauce, and... don't you dare giggle, Jeffrey Cooper. I've only just finished clearing up the mess."

"I'm not." Jeff shook his head, a small smile playing on his mouth. "Well, not at this, anyway. I was just thinking about Stephie's version. I couldn't understand what she was going on about. Her attention to the TV overrode everything else, even Daddy being home early. Dora's a lot more important than that. But she seemed okay." He frowned. "Is she okay?"

Dee nodded. "Yeah, she's fine. Although I don't know how. The way those legs shot out from under her, she could have hurt herself badly. It was really weird, honey, and it happened so quickly, a few hundredths of a second type of thing. For a moment I swear she paused in mid-air, like she was floating, or hovering or something with her tiny arms flapping at her side." She shrugged. "I guess shock plays with the imagination, but jeez, it was weird. It was like those slow motion parts you see on nature documentaries. You know, of animals doing fantastic jumps and things."

Jeff laughed. "Where was Austin during our little monkey's circus trick?"

"Standing right beside me, watching her semi-graceful drop and subsequent whack of her tailbone."

"Owww." Jeff grimaced. "I bet that brought on a bit of screaming."

"Uh-huh." Dee grabbed a mop leaning against the bench and stuck its head of twisted fibers into a metal bucket full of foamy water by her feet. "I very nearly yelled at him for causing it, but he also got a hell of a fright. You should have seen the look on his face. So I didn't get too cranky, especially when he took her to the lounge and made up a story from these pictures in a book. It was so cute. The whole time he kissed and cuddled her and did these funny little actions. She loved it."

"What happened would have hurt him just as much. He's so protective of her."

"And that's where the problem is." Dee pointed to the paper still clasped in Jeff's hand. "What time does his teacher want to see us on Monday?"

"Nine o'clock, and she said we might as well keep both of them off for the day. Actually, I've got some leave owing." Jeff smiled broadly. "I think I'll skip school and we'll all go somewhere after the meeting. How does that sound?"

"It sounds like you're not taking this seriously."

"Honey," he sighed. "Come on, you know that's not true. He's just finding his feet. Defending his sister. It's all normal stuff."

They looked at the open window when a rattling interrupted their conversation, and saw Austin zoom onto the patio from the smoothly rising slope that cambered up and away to the right.

"Austin, come inside please," Dee called. "Your father's home and we'd like to ask you something."

With the brakes squealing on his bike, the youngster came to a halt, studying the large, glassy expanse of the dining room door. The only distinguishable objects were reflected trees, a fertile, leafy backyard, and a blazing sun dipping toward the western horizon behind him. He swung his head to the kitchen window and peered at each pane. No, he couldn't see his mother's face pressed flat to its surface, waving her arms around madly, beckoning to hurry before the ground collapsed under him, and decided she wouldn't mind if he kept riding his bike around the yard. Just for a little while.

"Austin!"

Even at the age of five, there was enough familiarity with the sounding of his name in such a way, its tone needed nothing more, and the remainder of any unspoken statement was fairly easy to fill in, bringing his current, favorite game to an end. He leapt off the seat, leaving the bike to clatter noisily on the paving stones, and raced inside, wondering how she knew what was going through his mind.

"Hey, buddy." Jeff rubbed his son's back, the paper crumpling in his hand while Austin clamped himself to one long leg. "I see you've been busy destroying the kitchen. Next time, just ask your mom for some help."

Austin looked up, wiped away the brown fringe stuck on his forehead, and nodded at the smiling face.

"Something happened at the kindergarten on Wednesday, didn't it? Can you tell us what it was?"

Swallowing a sudden lump in his throat, the boy flicked his sight over Dee's ominously raised eyebrows, trying to gauge whether or not he was in trouble. Or, to be more precise, was the trouble big or small. Uh-oh, he thought. Big. "Where's…"

"Stephie's in the lounge watching TV," Dee stated. "And yes, she's okay."

Sniffing the lingering, pleasant scent of lavender wafting through the air, Austin dropped his gaze, amazed yet again at her capabilities.

"Come here." Dee squatted and held her arms out, drawing the uneasy child closer. "Usually, I would have read the mail by now." She deliberately lightened her voice. "But because of a certain hungry boy, I didn't. It was your father who opened the letter. That letter."

Jeff knelt at her side, holding up the paper. "I've just been on the phone with your teacher," he said. "She wants us all to go and talk about what happened. Why didn't you tell us? And why didn't Stephie? What did happen, Austin? This is important, son." They stared deeply into the bright, blue-purple pools of light that were his eyes, and sighed as he held his head high with the description of events.

*   *   *

Ernie Stone was forty, overweight, fatigued, and teetering on the verge of ruinous unemployment. His life had taken off on an entirely new, grim direction when his wife of twenty years became seriously ill, and in addition to the care needed for Esther, the primary charge of their three children fell unequivocally into his hands. This had a massive impact on his ability to work, and the job that provided well enough for the family became a near impossibility to achieve. If ever he was able to drive for the company, he nearly always turned up late for either pickup or delivery, not to mention all the times he answered a call only to tell the supervisor that Esther wasn't feeling too good and he had to be there for the kids when they got home from school. And up until now, the owners understood his situation.

Hell, they should anyway, he thought bitterly, dropping the phone. I've worked there most of my married life and given a lot. But they don't see that when I'm not making money for them. "Damn you," Ernie hissed at the machine, his jaw muscles clenching as the voice still rang in his head.

"Are ya interested in keeping ya job?" the supervisor had growled.

"Yes, of course." Ernie looked at the stack of bills on the kitchen counter, rising ever higher. Only yesterday, an insistent bank manager requested an appointment to discuss the dire affair of their account, after the balance rapidly dwindled away and the demand for payments relentlessly kept coming.

"Good, 'cos I gots plenty of guys who want the work and I ain't holding it out to ya no longer. Last chance, Ernie."

Ernie turned, stared at the children silently picking over the scraps served for lunch, and flinched at the sound emanating down the hallway, something that broke his heart even more and something that seemed to be increasing every day. The sound of Esther, leaning over the side of the bed she had lain in for five weeks and vomiting into a bucket.

Later that night, Ernie perched himself on the edge of the mattress, held her frail hand and spoke of his travel plans for Monday. "I've worked out the route already, baby," he assured his wife. "I'll be in and out before you know I'm gone. Straight into Colorado Springs and back again. I'll even be home in time for the kids. I promise you I won't be long." He hoped his grin would be brimming with confidence and resolve, but it only brought about a weak nod of understanding, her fingers twitching in his as she tried her hardest to squeeze.

Ernie fought with everything he had to keep the smile on his face, and the tears from rolling down his cheeks.

the policeman

"Honey, I still think you and the kindergarten teacher are overreacting somewhat. Like I've been saying, this is all normal stuff." Jeff adjusted his sun visor when they crested a slight rise and blindingly bright rays fell directly across his line of sight.

"This has to stop," Dee whispered hoarsely. "It's Monday morning and you should be on your way to work, not doing this." Her eyes narrowed as she swiveled in the seat to look directly at her husband. "And it isn't an overreaction," she glared. "Why else would Miss Corbin want to see us?" She took a quick glimpse at the back seat to make sure Austin didn't hear them, but he was completely oblivious to the conversation, and instead played 'car colors' with Stephanie, a game Jeff used to keep them occupied on journeys. It involved guessing the color of the next vehicle they saw, and the children expanded on the entertainment by including multiple cars in advance, even anything with wheels, like the trains they passed while on a long trip to North Dakota a couple of months ago to spend a week's summer vacation with their Aunt Michelle.

"Fair enough. You're not overreacting then." Jeff glanced briefly at his beautiful wife. "Look, Dee, I absolutely one-hundred-percent agree with you that this has to stop, or at least be brought under control. But let's just see what takes place at the meeting, so this discussion can be resolved. Agreed?" Slowing the car, he scanned ahead to the four way intersection they approached.

"Agreed," she nodded.

*   *   *

A gigantic Peterbilt 379 eighteen-wheeler semi-trailer started its slow descent down the westward side of a sizeable hill on Interstate 70, and as Ernie gently decelerated the huge truck, methodically grinding his way through the gears, he stared at the sight that made his heart and spirit plummet. Columns of thick, black smoke swirled and billowed toward the now blurry sky above a crash site. He saw fires burning amid the vehicles strewn everywhere and people milling around all over the place. It was one hell of a pileup.

"Damn it all!" Slapping his palm down hard on the steering wheel, he gripped it tightly, hauled himself upright and leaned forward to peer through the windshield. With his face squashed against the glass, he looked like a kid pressed up to the window of a candy store, mesmerized by the pleasurable display while trying to get as close as possible to the tasty treats.

Getting nearer, he evaluated the scene of carnage. It had taken place about three or four hundred feet after the off-ramp that led to State Highway 71, just past the flyover on the start of the next hilly incline, and in all his many years of trucking, at only one mile away,

Ernie knew with absolute certainty that it was not only impassable, but probably one of the worst highway accidents he had ever seen.

"No," he mumbled, assessing the devastation once more. "This is the worst."

Wrecked vehicles covered the entire width of the road, at least forty or fifty of them, flung about like toys after a child's vicious temper tantrum. He even observed one car sitting perfectly atop another, both violently ablaze, their final driving experience ending in a crushing, metallic embrace. There were people and infernos far and wide, any attempt to get through would be fruitless. The day had dawned fine and sunny, and visibility for this stretch of the highway was excellent. Perfect conditions for a five hour wait.

"Damn it, damn it, DAMN IT," he screamed. His skin turned an unsettling, blotchy red, and the tendons in his neck stood out starkly above the stiff, denim collar of his shirt. Just under the surface, running across his temple from the left ear to the beginning of his forehead, a blue-green vein as thick as a pencil popped up and began pulsating rapidly with the elevated beat of his heart.

No, no, NO, he thought. I don't believe this. Please, not now, not today. Of all days, not today. How can this happen? Look at the weather! What sort of idiot crashes on a straight highway that has everything in clear view?

He gazed upward through the glass, scanning the blue sky. The radio station chattering away in the background hadn't even mentioned anything about the accident. No helicopter hovered overhead to inform everyone about the size of this crash, and nobody had called it through on CB. The destruction and sheer scale of the disaster was unknown by any except those here, looking directly at the scene.

"That's it, I'm finished." Ernie slammed the steering wheel twice with the side of a closed fist, then slumped back into the seat, his shoulders sagging. "Oh shit, what are we gonna do," he sobbed. His eyes darted wildly around the cabin before aiming back through the windshield, hoping upon hope that miraculously everything would be clear and empty.

It wasn't. But what he saw was so simple, so life-saving, it left him stunned.

About one hundred yards away was a large sign, suspended from a thick, shiny post, the green background and white lettering standing out like a lighthouse beacon, informing each and every motorist that State Highway 71 lay within reach, heading east toward Ordway, Fowler, Crescent Lake, Akron, Fort Morgan and other towns.

Crescent Lake, he thought. Of course! I've been there with Jim and Ralph many times. A long way to go fishing. But that huge trout. What was it again? Yeah, that's right, the Legend Fish. No one's ever caught it, not even old brag-mouth Ralph. Man! That's been quite a while. I'll have to get back there sometime, and lucky for me I know that place well. I'll just cut through on Shamen Drive, then it's only a stone's throw to the twenty-four on-ramp and delivery by lunchtime. A stone's throw. Ha!

Snickering gleefully at his own pun, he chewed his bottom lip when he realized the significant glitch in his plan. Although it wasn't illegal, at least, not the last time he was there, the local law enforcement frowned upon the taking of big-rigs down that route due to the many schools sitting at various points along the road. If the police caught him, and if they were in a particularly foul mood that day, they would give him a hard time about it, maybe write up a ticket of some sort, and most likely threaten to inform his employers regarding his driving indiscretions.

They're the least of my worries, he thought. Hey, I might get lucky. It's early, there shouldn't be any cops, and after all, it is a sign.

He cackled again before scolding himself aloud. "You are a stupid fool, Ernie. How could you forget? But that's the trick right here, Esther. Do not panic. Do. Not. Panic. We can do this." He downshifted, indicated, and checked his side mirror before moving to the next lane, ready for the exit. "Off here, left on seventy-one, right toward Crescent Lake, straight through, then left on twenty-four and the Springs. Make the drop, turn around and back to the interstate, which is clear all the way. Easy." Grinning insanely, he felt giddy from the exhilarating revelation that his scheme would get the job done. He could earn a bit of money, look good with the company, and still honor the promise to his wife. "All I have to do is make up a bit of time, baby, and then I'll be home for you."

The Peterbilt roared down the off-ramp and braked heavily, bringing the tractor and trailer to a quivering stop. It turned left and accelerated away, the engine's low, throaty rumbling echoing loudly around the concrete walls beneath the overpass while Ernie raced down Highway 71.

*　　*　　*

The teacher looked from Jeff to Dee and back again. "Mr. Cooper," she breathed. "I'm not saying he is ill-disciplined. He's a very well-behaved boy and that's not what this is all about. In fact, his general behavior surpasses nearly everyone."

Rubbing the palms of both hands tightly into his eyes, Jeff dragged them slowly back over his head, leaving his brown hair sticking straight toward the ceiling.

Dee stared at him. With his stern expression and spiky fuzz, he looked just like Bert from Sesame Street, now a favorite of Stephanie's as well as Austin. Nearly bursting out in fits of laughter, she barely contained herself with a stifled, high-pitched giggle. "Sorry," she apologized. "I am definitely watching too many kids' TV shows." Flapping her right hand, she smothered another snigger.

Jeff frowned at his wife, which didn't help matters, before resting his gaze solely on the teacher's face. She kept glancing back and forth between the two, a tiny smile lifting one corner of her mouth. "Well, what are you saying then, Miss Corbin? This is all very puzzling and truthfully I'm struggling to understand. Are you punishing him for following the rules? Your rules and regulations regarding this facility, I might add."

"No, Mr. Cooper, he is not being punished. Please understand that most of the time he is like any other boy in my class. The problem we have is that he's the one actively enforcing the rules and structure

I have in place, not me." She paused to examine the other occupants in the room, sitting side by side at a table near the back wall.

Stephanie leafed quietly through a book while Austin built an airplane from a scrap piece of paper. He peered over his sister's shoulder from time to time, pointing out certain pictures before leaning into her, whispering something that made them share a warm laugh. Finishing the plane he handed it to Stephanie, who ran her fingers down the edge of the wings and looked at her brother with what was undeniably love and admiration, Miss Corbin thought. "It's nice that Austin thinks of himself as the policeman on duty here. It could be his calling," she smiled. "But it is not up to him to make sure everyone abides by the rules and then chastises them if they don't. That is up to me and this kindergarten." Her steady gaze kept an equal amount of eye contact on the parents. One aspect of teacher training had taught her about mediation skills, and she utilized that competency now by keeping both of them uniformly involved in the discussion. "As you know," she continued. "What has ultimately led to this meeting is Austin's striking of another child, which is..."

"That was self-defense," Jeff interjected.

"No." She shook her head. "It wasn't. It was the defense of someone else, not himself. He hit the boy because his sister had been hit. Simple as that." She tilted forward and fixed them with a sympathetic look. "I appreciate and admire the fact that Austin feels so protective toward Stephanie, or anyone else here for that matter. On a personal note, sibling and peer affection demonstrated in such a manner makes me feel very happy. I love it. It's a joy to watch. But when it's taken to extreme behavior, blackening a child's eye, nearly breaking his nose and drawing blood in the process, then this is something we all need to supervise and keep in check."

"Absolutely. We're both in agreement with you." Dee sighed. "So what do we do now? Is Austin still welcome here?"

"Mrs. Cooper, of course he is," she replied. "He is a fantastic boy, and we all love having him at this school. From our side we'll keep reiterating to the children the important issues of respecting their fellow students and our refusal to accept cruel behavior such as bullying. It's something that's always been a part of our curriculum and I would also suggest they be recurring themes at home."

"Bullying?" Jeff's face darkened. "My son is not the bully here, Miss Corbin. All he has done is stand up for those who are being victimized and intimidated. He is the one helping them. He is the one stopping the real tyrants. The child who harassed and attacked my daughter is the bully."

"I realize that, Mr. Cooper, and as a constant offender Kevin Wotlinski has been dealt with accordingly. I am not calling Austin a bully, nor does anyone else, because you are correct, he is the one standing up for them. But the fact remains that on top of the defense is his, uhhh… persuasion… to obey the rules. As I said, those are my rules and he has to understand that I am the person to enforce them, not him, or else it could be construed as a form of harassment, and I'm sure you don't want that." She drew herself closer to the desk, clasped her hands together and laid them on its surface. "Please, let me stress once more that Austin is a fine, young boy who always strives to do his best at whatever it is he undertakes. I wish they were all like him. He is not the nasty, bullying type. In my opinion, he is the anti-bully. He has this passionate, natural drive to see that fairness prevails, and all we have to do is lead him in the right direction while refining his methods, especially with him starting first grade next year. We don't want any unhelpful influences affecting him." She leaned back in her chair, beaming. "He certainly lives up to his middle name, doesn't he?"

"What do you mean?" Dee's brow furrowed heavily.

"His name, Mrs. Cooper." She peered from one to the other, hoping that either of the couple would say, 'Oh right, yeah, not surprising at all.' But they didn't, they just sat there, gazing blankly at her. "Do you know the meaning of his middle name?"

"No." Jeff shook his head. "We don't. Actually, there's a funny story surrounding his names." Crossing his legs, he interlocked the fingers of his hands and laid them on his knee with the thumbs twirling in orbit around each other, always a guaranteed sign that he was enjoying himself and ready to narrate some interesting facts. "Throughout the entire pregnancy," he started. "And even right up until a few hours after the birth, we had two first names, Austin and William, but couldn't decide on which we liked best. We eventually decided on William as the nicest and the one that seemed to suit him. So, there I am, only hours after the earthquake we had that year, something like five o'clock in the morning. I'm all bleary-eyed, zombie intelligence, and the hospital has me filling out these documents about there being no personal injury to any of us, and I incorrectly put Austin down as his first name. Well, the next thing we know hospital staff are coming in and out at different times during the rest of our stay, saying things like, 'How's young Austin doing?' It sounded perfect, really, it kind of stuck, and in the end we liked it. But it was only a brief nap and a cup of coffee away from being William. Right, honey?" He glanced at his wife, who didn't seem to hear him, she just stared across the desk.

"What does his name mean, Miss Corbin?" Dee asked unceremoniously.

The teacher looked directly at her, outwardly oblivious to the brusque question. "It's an old name," she replied. "It was also my grandfather's. He told me the meaning when I was younger." She paused, and straightened a text book sitting to her left. "The original form was Wilhelm, being of German origin, with William being the English version. Generally, there are two meanings, depending on where it has been translated." She smiled widely at them. "Determined Guardian and Resolute Protector."

the truck

The sun blazed in a vibrantly blue and cloudless sky when they left Crescent Lake West Kindergarten and Daycare. A superb, lengthy summer with extremely hot weather had stretched its influence right into mid-October, and coverage of the state's weather reported the season as one of the best in a long time. So it was still an extremely balmy, late-morning day that greeted them while they descended the steps leading up to the front doors and meandered down the path toward their car parked on the other side of the road.

"I'm a tad on the peckish side," Jeff remarked, looking at his watch. "How about you, my love? Hungry? Let's take the terrible twosome to Halfmoon. Sound good?"

"Sounds fine to me, babe, although the Incredible Hulk doesn't really deserve any special luxuries." Dee put an arm around her son's shoulder, towed him in closer and ran her fingers gently through his hair as they walked. "He's meant to be in that classroom behind us as we speak, not going with Mom and Dad for treats. But I think we'll take him with us this one time."

"And Steph," Austin said, smiling up at her.

Dee laughed. "Of course, sweetheart. Nothing without our Stephie."

Stephanie peeked over her shoulder, giggling with delight at the mention of her name, and threw her paper airplane high into the air, where it did a big loop before landing in the grass farther to her right. "Yaaaay!" she squealed and skipped off down the path. Pausing at the edge of the manicured, green lawn, she bunny hopped to the plane, eager for its second launch.

"Hey, Steph," Austin called. "Hold it near the front and keep it low. It'll fly better that way." He patted his mother's hand, slipped out of her embrace, and trotted forward several steps.

A little to the left of the paved pathway, located smack-bang in the middle of the sidewalk, a tattered bench-seat faced the road, the paintwork stripped long ago from the exposed and rusted wrought iron. Its wooden slats were cracked, warped, a bleached, dazzling white from countless years of severe weather, the varnish having desiccated to the point where it now flaked away, shrunken and twisted as it simply gave up any desire to remain on the wood. They sagged and bowed ominously under the weight of the person sitting upon them, looking all the world like they could snap at any given moment, sending the poor character crashing straight down for a bruising encounter with terra firma, buttocks first, arms flailing, and legs pointed skyward as needle-sharp splinters of aged timber embedded themselves ably in the back of the thighs, a consequence for ending their long lives.

The person was probably male judging by the clothes. Faded blue jeans, a red and white long-sleeved, checked shirt tucked in at the waist, and dark gray, Nike sneakers, emblazoned with an oversized, white swoosh mark. On his head sat a glaringly new, Colorado Rockies baseball cap, its peaked visor shading his face from the intense sunlight, while a pair of pristine, black, wrap around Oakley sunglasses shielded his eyes. Propped against his hip was a large, tan-colored leather satchel, and he lounged on the seat like there was no tomorrow, his legs thrust outward and his shoes crossed over at the ankles. With his face tilted to the heavens, he had his hands clasped on top of the hat, fingers entwined, his thumbs drumming out a staccato beat. If not for the incessant rhythm and stirring of his two digits, anyone would have thought him to be asleep, enjoying the clement atmosphere immensely.

As the family neared the end of the path, the man lowered his arms and turned to regard them, the wood creaking with his movement. "Those are good-looking kids you've got there," he declared, inclining his head to where Austin and Stephanie walked slightly ahead of their parents.

"Thank you." Dee reflexively shuffled sideways, giving the man a penetrating, wary stare. Jeff glanced at him and dug in his front pocket for the car keys.

"Mr. and Mrs. Cooper. Austin," a voice called.

They swiveled quickly at the sound of their names and saw Miss Corbin waving from the top step, all of them inattentive to Stephanie pulling her arm back, the underside of the paper plane held between finger and thumb, readying the next takeoff.

"I'm sorry, I forgot to mention..." Miss Corbin began, before a sudden, blaring roar drowned any further words. She looked angrily to the right, knowing full well what made the noise, and shook her head as she lifted her arms up and away from the side, her palms facing upward in a time-honored, 'What the hell?' gesture.

Only two people observed Stephanie when she gave the plane an almighty heave, and they watched it soar speedily across the road, landing in the middle of the lane on the other side. With a mock wail of alarm, the small girl raced after it.

Many things happened right then, and later on that evening, lying in bed, staring at the ceiling in the partial darkness of his room, Austin tried his hardest to think through and process the events. He remembered seeing Miss Corbin's head shaking fiercely, her arms out to the side. He remembered her pointing a trembling finger their way, and yelping, her dialogue incomprehensible. He remembered his parents spinning toward her aim, his mother's eyes and lips springing wide open. And as he also began turning, he remembered catching a glimpse of something at ground level, about halfway to the building. It was a yellowish sort of color that shimmered dimly in the light, rousing a vague and distant memory. A hall? By the stairs? But the thing he remembered most was what the person on the seat said above the bellowing of a large engine.

"Boy." The man looked unswervingly at him and slipped his sunglasses off, revealing a pair of glittering, emerald-green eyes. "Welcome to your universe. Do it. Now," he ordered, and nodded toward the loud noise.

Whirling about, Austin beheld the vision that kept him awake for hours.

Ernie Stone had already checked and rechecked the delivery address a dozen times since leaving the pileup, but knew why he consistently skimmed over it, making regular updates and estimates for the remaining journey to his destination. Stress. He had never known anything like this in his entire life, and the thought of going mad with it scared him a little. "I'll be okay, Esther, I'll sort that out later." He laid the waybill on the seat to his right, checked the watch strapped tightly around his thick wrist and grinned. "We're gonna make it to the warehouse earlier if I just speed things up a little. Not long till I'll be back home with you, baby. Not long at all."

Pushing his foot harder on the accelerator, he fixed his sight back through the windshield, and felt the blood in his veins ice when an arctic chill seized his body. No more than twenty feet away, a young girl, very young, maybe three, four years of age, stood directly in front of him, bending over and reaching for something sitting on the tarmac. His horrorstricken mind took a swift, mental snapshot of her wavy, black hair, pinned behind little ears and showing her gorgeous, pale-bronze face clearly.

And with her death an absolute certainty he wasn't sure which was loudest, the screech from his gaping mouth, or the vehicle's tires when he made a two-footed lunge upon the brakes, mashing the large, rubber-covered pedal to the floor.

Austin looked at the truck bearing down on his sister like a prehistoric, metallic monster leaping toward its prey, then to the man sitting calmly on the bench, and finally the other adults, his parents, Miss Corbin, thinking, hoping, that all of them would be at his side or even past him by now, taking control of the situation and restoring order. But nothing like that happened.

What did happen was strange. Inconceivably strange.

Everyone froze. His mom, Dad, his sister, the teacher, even a bird soaring overhead, all completely and utterly motionless. And, he squinted, they were transparent. The building, trees, every object, every person. Everything. Other than the ground, which still seemed normal, the rest he could see right through, their colors dull, barely there, the translucency reducing their former luster to muted shadows. They hadn't disappeared, they just looked washed out, used. Circling slowly, gazing at the spectacle, he didn't understand why, but the experience never frightened him, not once. Instead, he had a surprisingly enjoyable sensation, there was a sense of naturalness about it, like he expected this to take place at some stage, and his brightly glowing, bluey-purple eyes opened wide again with the astonishment of such a remarkable scene. Staring at his mother, he adjusted his theory when the awareness came that one leg was a bit higher than before. No, they haven't stopped, he decided. They are moving, just really, really slowly.

"Ahhh... Austin," a voice rumbled.

He turned to the man on the seat, not at all surprised he couldn't see through him. He was solid-looking, and his clothes glistened as if they were sopping wet. "How do you know my name?" Austin asked, peering down at himself, fascinated that his own attire and form were an exact match. Like the yellow shimmer, a deep, shadowy remembrance stirred. "Have we met? Do I know you?"

"If I've observed this correctly," the man said, ignoring his questions. "You're alert to the fact that things still move. Including the truck, boy."

A heavy panic gripped the young child at the realization he merely stood there, gawking for what must have been ages.

"Hey!" The man leaned forward, smiling warmly. "Austin, be calm. You've done amazingly well and given yourself enough time to do what you've got to do, so let's not stay on this level any longer, okay? I know things are pretty interesting right now, but someone needs you." Raising his arm, he pointed at the girl. "Go get your sister. Touch nothing else but her and get off the road as quick as you can, because the moment you make contact is the moment you reenter that phase. Keep your wits about you, boy. Remember." He paused, his lifting brow furrowing his honey-brown skin. "Get away from the truck. Understand?"

Austin nodded and spun around to Stephanie, alarmed at the closeness of the enormous machine from her tiny, delicate frame. Feeling a strong surge of energy, he sprung off, his legs powering him across the distance. As he neared the massive vehicle, he glanced at clouds of translucent, white smoke ballooning sluggishly from the locked tires, and peered up at the cabin, glimpsing the driver's pale, drained face, bulging eyes and widely-parted mouth, issuing its silent, virtually motionless cry of dismay.

Heeding the man's instructions, Austin positioned himself facing the kindergarten, spread his arms wide and crouched behind his sister, ready for what would happen next. He tilted his head to one side, took a final scan of the gargantuan, chrome bumper, the louvered grille with its Peterbilt logo placed above, then the trailer at the rear, looking straight through the whole lot. Drawing a huge breath, he grabbed Stephanie around her waist and hoisted her aloft, thrusting backward and to his right in one smooth, flowing motion, using all the strength he could muster. Instantly, she became normal again, the colors of her pink, long sleeve tee-shirt, blue jeans and purple sneakers returning with a clarity so vivid, so bright, he had to narrow his eyes.

Away from the danger, shielding her body with his, an intense cacophony overwhelmed him when the truck screeched ear-piercingly past them. It swerved, jumped, and shuddered to a stop, the momentum carrying it far along the road as an acrid pall of smoke, thick with the stench of burning rubber, enveloped the two children, followed at once by a powerful draft that thumped violently into their bodies, sending them sprawling to the ground. Jumping to his feet, coughing and spluttering, Austin hauled Stephanie upright, her screams mixing with Jeff and Dee's while they sprinted across the blacktop. On seeing their children standing by the gutter, their wails subsided, leaving Miss Corbin the one howling like a mad woman as she tore across the lawn, her skirt and blouse flapping briskly behind her.

Warm, caring hands searched his whole body the second his sobbing parents reached them, the pair darting back and forth between him and his sister. He remembered saying, "I'm okay, I'm okay, is Stephie all right?" several times while they bustled about. He remembered seeing the truck driver, staggering, quaking, and weeping uncontrollably as his father rounded on him, joined now by Miss Corbin, a bellowing, veritable force to be reckoned with. And he remembered the man in the jeans and the baseball cap levering himself unhurriedly off the old, rickety bench. He slung the strap of his satchel over one shoulder and stood for a few moments smiling the cheeriest smile Austin had ever seen. The man nodded once and winked at him, put his sunglasses back on, then sauntered up the road, whistling a merry little tune.

the witness

Halloween was a little over two weeks away, and with the exception of one child, everybody in a classroom on the second floor busied themselves, given the task of cutting out pumpkins and witches riding on broomsticks that would hang from lengths of string already suspended across the ceiling tiles. Among a flurry of activity and noisy chatter, no one, not even their teacher, Mr. Bainbridge, noticed one student move to the window, drawn there by the escalating roar of a large vehicle.

In complete disbelief, an extremely pale face watched a small girl, someone dreadfully familiar, chase the paper airplane she threw, and pause on the road, directly in front of the truck rushing toward her. The child had no desire to witness the devastating, nightmarish vision, but was powerless to turn away, to wrench rapidly blinking eyes from the frightening spectacle. Panic-stricken, incapable of speech, a little pink tongue darted fretfully between desert dry lips as the child's stare flicked over Stephanie, the machine, and the others safe from harm.

Then, suddenly, two extraordinary events happened. They stopped. Stephanie. Her parents. The truck. Even the teacher, coming into sight, running wildly across the grass, her motion frozen in place like a game of statues they played every so often during lunchtime. And something else, something particularly alarming. They were all see-through. See-through and nearly colorless. Everything. Quivering, the child rotated slowly, inspecting the room. It was exactly the same, transparent, drab, immobile. Studying the other children brought on the prompt understanding that they did move, very, very slowly, and the child watched while a young, blonde girl bit by bit dipped her hand to a plastic container full of red paint, readying her brush for the finishing strokes to a big, capital 'T' on her orange pumpkin, concentration still evident on her pretty, translucent face.

On circling to the window, the child observed how close the truck was to Stephanie, and with another huge shock, the difference between everybody else and two people down there. Austin Cooper and the man sitting on the seat. They faced each other, normal looking, solid, wet? Were they talking? Yes. The man lifted his arm toward the girl and Austin dashed to his sister's side, pulling her away from death. All at once, everything returned to its natural state, and the gigantic truck shrieked past them in a cloud of smoke, just when the other people ran, screaming in what the child now understood as the ordinary flow of time.

Classmates hurried to the windows, pressing their noses to the glass. They jostled about, babbling incessantly, until organization was restored by them being sent back to their work. With further insistence from Mr. Bainbridge, the child turned and shuffled away, bewildered, stunned, and above all else, incredibly afraid.

*   *   *

A loud, high-pitched whoop halted the man in the Rockies cap, the melody dying on his lips as he turned to view the resulting pandemonium. Two blocks back he saw a patrol car, its red and blue lights flickering crazily.

"I hope you're satisfied," the man growled. "That was risky. The boy, his sister, they could've been seriously injured, or killed, possibly beyond our help. Don't tell me to do this again, because I won't. I remember everything Khoul said about the transitions and not once did she say this happened. And she would have. It's a spontaneous technique, instinctive, and there was no need to push it upon him. Especially when it doesn't even apply to his own survival. Why did you do this? To judge his success? See how he handled the situation? It's not necessary for him to show us, we can feel how good he is. I don't understand why, but I'd like to know."

With no response offered, he carried on. "Fifty-two years of silence, then ever since his birth you start jabbering away. Except for now. This morning I've done all your demands, without refusal. What do you want to know? That he's strong? Quick? Then, yes, he's quick, extremely quick. And very strong. His level jumps were perf..."

A jolt, some kind of forced insistence, like an uncomfortable electric shock, cannonballed its way through his every fiber, jerking his head upward. Behind his sunglasses, chestnut-brown eyes flashed to a concentrated, golden glow. "Yes, you got my attention. Thank you for such delicate feedback," he muttered acerbically, and gazed about, scanning the few white, puffy clouds floating past. "What is that? I don't think it's the boy." He scrutinized the road, peering up and down its length, his sight resting briefly on the accident scene. There were a number of people milling around, but he couldn't see Austin. "Something's wrong, so why don't you know? You know about his near discovery when he was two, and you never explained that, as well. Has this happened before? Is it the boy?" Pausing, waiting for a reply, he lifted the flap on the tan satchel, stuck his hand inside and ran his fingers over the object lying within. "It could be an attempt on the portal. The barrier feels intact, but I'll check. Just realize I can't do anything about this if you won't help me," he added. Sighing heavily, with no answer given, he shook his head, frustrated, puzzled, and worried. Worried for the way he couldn't detect the wrongness, and worried for the way he now recognized it. Something was amiss, a distinct intrusion that did not belong and one he struggled to identify.

Deeply disturbed, he continued an immediately preoccupied stroll through the neighborhood, temporarily ignoring any thoughts on returning the commandeered bench-seat to its rightful position in an unpretentious and quaint little park just outside the expansive metropolis of Paris.

Chapter Six

The Crash

Austin gazed at the bright-yellow sand surrounding his feet, warm and coarse under his bare soles. As he sifted it through his squirming toes, he looked out upon an enormous body of water that spread, uninterrupted, to a very distant and blurry horizon. Directly in front of him, small, blue waves rolled toward a perpetually flat and endless shoreline, stretching left and right for miles on end. With each cresting, muted plunge, the sea dumped a sparkly, frothy foam and strong currents of salty air that Austin sniffed tentatively. Licking his lips, screwing his face up at the tangy flavor, he lifted his head to the sky and watched while its peculiar, dusky-green color changed. Hmmm, he pondered. Yep, I reckon that's gonna be purple, no, it's, ahh...

His thought fled with the gentle, scarcely perceived, yet unmistakable crunch of approaching footsteps. Whirling around, he saw a vaguely familiar figure step out from behind the only visible object on the eternally smooth and sandy landscape, a thick, glossy, and absolutely pitch-black pillar. Standing straight and true, the circular structure soared at least thirty feet into the air, and Austin, no more than ten paces away, felt his heart skip a beat when its highly-polished and apparently flawless surface showed two brightly smoldering, orange eyes in the sockets of his clear and staring reflection. Turning them on the stranger, he studied the long, brown robe and enormous hood, the interior dark and lifeless until a dazzling golden-silvery light flashed within its murky confines.

"Intriguing. We embrace this perspective," a voice said. Soft and silky, it wafted through Austin's ears, a scantily heard sigh. "You are the first, the last, among all, with nothing clear, nothing set. Let him guide before you lead. Show him."

"Who? Show what? Do you mean that?" Austin pointed at the towering column. "What is it?"

"Come no closer," the voice cautioned. "To touch is to release, to reveal. It will know. Only now are we alone, and this is not the way. Make your discovery. Grow. Mature. Begin. Trust who you are and what you are. Only then can you resist."

"What? Please, I don't underst..." Austin stirred, and peered about his bedroom while an incessant beep-beep-beep hammered at his semi-consciousness. Rubbing the sleep from his eyes, he sat up, reached across to the latest birthday present from his aunt and prodded a long, rectangular button, immediately silencing the intrusive noise. For a few moments he stared at the green, glowing digits of the nifty camping and travel clock on his bedside table. 6:10 a.m. "Great," he muttered. "A new one. At least it was a beach. Kind of." Throwing his sheets aside, he shivered against the frosty air that nipped instantly at his skin, and yawned while pulling on a pair of cozy, woolen slippers and dark-blue, fluffy robe lying in a crumpled heap on the carpet. Glad of the increasing warmth his extra clothes provided, Austin judged the day to be as chilly as yesterday. Weather reports warned of an early winter, but once the sun fully rose, every day that week had turned out pleasant, and he figured it would be the same.

Making his way to the kitchen, still tying the cord around his waist, he found the room already occupied. "Morning, Mom." He plonked heavily onto one of the stools lining a recently installed bench and storage unit. In the middle of the floor, like an island at sea, the family had taken to it quickly, creating a very handy location for meeting and eating.

"Good morning, sweetheart," Dee smiled. She leaned forward and rummaged briefly in a cupboard before depositing a stainless steel bowl upon the bench top. "Did you sleep well?"

"I guess," he mumbled, stretching his arms wide.

"You don't look happy at all. What's wrong?"

"Nothing," he said, returning her smile.

"It's not another nasty dream, is it?"

"Huh? What dream?"

"Some big, black monster thingy with a red eye. Remember? The number of times I got up to you in the middle of the night. You used to yell really loud."

"Awww, yeah." Austin grimaced. He thought of his anger, the preparation of an attack, and how, inexplicably, he knew the tar-like creature. He also knew a big part of him wanted to punish it, and had a strong sensation that something wrong happened. Something very wrong. He couldn't explain why, but he just knew that it wanted to get him, take him. Kill him? And always, right before the moment of wakefulness, he would see the bright red streaks, swirling around and around its abnormal head. "Mom," he frowned. "That was months ago."

"Ahhaaaa." Dee winked at him on her way to the fridge. "A mother never forgets these things."

"Never?"

"Uh-huh," her voice came from behind the open door. "Ever."

Puffing his cheeks out, releasing a sudden, gusty breath, Austin decided on a change in topic, worried at the astonishing way she recalled the most mundane facts. "How come you're up so early?"

"I thought I'd bake some treats and a lovely, cooked breakfast before we go. Why aren't you still in bed, honey?"

"I must've forgotten to turn my alarm off last night. I should be used to having a clock in my room. And yes, before you say it, I am a silly sausage, but I'm glad it happened, 'cos now I'd rather be up and looking forward to Susan coming over. You know, I could've looked after Stephie myself, Mom."

"It's true there are moments," Dee said, carrying back handfuls of ingredients. "When you act so grown-up I have to remind myself you're still a child, who is a bit young for their first babysitting assignment." Her brow arched high. "We'll be gone until late afternoon, so not this time, sweetheart. One day it'll happen," she nodded. "I know that because I trust you, and believe me it takes a special, special person to earn my trust at seven years of age. Let me say how very proud I am of you and how much I love you."

"Mom," he moaned. And grinned.

"I mean it, Austin. You may not be getting high grades at school, but your attitude and behavior has been fantastic for ages, and that matters more than anything, because it shows you're trying, and I'm very, very proud." Measuring items into the bowl, she glanced at him. "You also say 'Mom' like a teenager. Are we going through all those horrible years now? I love it. By the time you are a teenager you'll be acting as if you're thirty. Yippee," she cried out quietly.

"Mom!"

With an impish giggle, Dee bustled about. "By the way," she said over her shoulder. "Talking of special, I like your eye color this morning. It's nice."

"What?" Austin snapped. For a second he believed his mother had now gone from mundane fact retrieval to amazingly nonchalant psychic powers, specifically, the ability to read his mind. "I mean, pardon?" With great haste, he made amends. "Sorry, Mom... ummm... what color are they?"

"Really, really blue." Dee studied them. "A vibrant blue and very shiny. But they were so different in the den last night. A lot darker. That warm, regal purple I love. It's definitely my favorite among all the blues and purples, purpley-blues and even blurpley-pues you conjure up."

"Last night?"

"I knew it. You and your father," she chuckled. "I was the invisible person who put two cups of hot chocolate on the table and kissed you both goodnight. I think I might have got a 'mmmrrrpfff' in-between you laughing your head off. The universe stops when it comes to beating Dad at video games and nothing else exists. That, my darling son, is when I noticed them."

"Mmmm."

"See? Perfect example." Dee reached across and rubbed his messy bed-hair. "It's always amazed me how much those extra-special eyes change depending on the light. Or maybe you're using some kind of power, my not-so-little magic boy. Hey," she grinned. "How about orange? Now there's a nice color."

Austin stared at her. Power? Magic boy? Orange? Oh my God, he thought. She can read my mind. She's doing it right now!

Dee laughed at his stunned expression. "Are you all right?"

"Yeah, I'm fine. Still a bit tired, I guess," he yawned, shaking off the silly idea.

"Really? Gee, I'm sorry, honey. I'll tell your father that weekend nights are for early sleep time instead of video games."

"I'm not that tired, Mom."

*　　*　　*

Striding down the hallway, Jeff reached the front entrance on the second chime of the bell. He flung the door open dramatically, nearly sent it banging into the wall when his grasp slipped. "Suze!" he cried out. "Haven't seen you in ages."

"Hi, Mr. Cooper."

"Ahhh," he beamed. "You loco, Susan Kirk. Looooco. After all these years you're still having fun with that one, huh?"

"Yep. Wait until I bring out the um whoops Jeff part again. Anyway, it's your fault. Your wit can be extremely contagious at times."

Laughing, Jeff ushered her into the house where they embraced warmly. "And it'll be your fault if I end up going gray prematurely. You, Dee, and the kids."

She snorted at his comical scowl. "It's your work doing that and nothing to do with me. But I will agree with you about Austin and Steph. They're growing up way too fast. I'm starting to feel old at how big they're getting."

"I know what you mean," he nodded. "I think I age five years to their one. So how long has it been? Two months? Three?"

"Very nearly. It was Austin's birthday."

Jeff whistled as they strolled through the house. "Of course. Wow! Time flies when you're having fun."

"And when you're not," she sighed. "I'm really sorry we haven't seen you since then. We've been so busy."

He waved away her apology. "Don't even think about it, Suze. I, of all people, know what it's like when you've got a lot on your plate. Come on, Dee's been looking forward to this morning and the terrible twosome haven't stopped bouncing off the walls. I had to chain them up to the patio table, which is why they're not swarming over you right now."

*   *   *

"It's lovely to see you again, Susan. And thanks for coming over early."

"No problem, Dee. I've missed you all," she smiled. "But things are a bit more organized now, so I daresay you'll be seeing more of us again."

"Here you go, girls." Jeff laid a tray on the table and handed out two steaming cups before sitting opposite the women.

Susan sipped her coffee. "That's perfect, as always. Thanks, Jeff."

"Do I need a recap on anything important?"

"No, not really." Susan shook her head. "I was just telling Dee how busy this year has been. With the wedding, the honeymoon and now the business, it's no wonder we haven't seen you guys for a while."

Austin and Stephanie suddenly raced by, swooping across the rising land on their bikes, the chains and guards loudly rattling while they chased each other on endless circuits of the house. Silence descended when they disappeared, and in the cool air, a lone bird warbled its song, seemingly giving thanks for the bright, September sunshine bathing the patio.

"And I've missed those two more than anything."

"It's a good thing you're like a sister to them," Jeff said. "That way it won't be too much of a surprise when you find them knocking on your front door one day saying Mom and Dad have run away."

"You fool," Dee laughed. "But seriously, honey." She rubbed Susan's arm. "You might want to think carefully about having kids. They accelerate the aging process. Look at him, for example."

"No argument from me." Jeff shrugged at her pointed finger. "We've already covered the topic. All that time you've spent with them, Suze, you're lucky to have escaped any permanent damage. Although I can't say the same about Greg. And he should be here to defend himself."

"I know. The poor thing," Susan giggled. "It's my fault. I insisted he go to that auction. We're trying to source a particular work, and unfortunately it may show up in New York this weekend."

"Susan." Dee's eyes widened. "Have we ruined it for you? Honey, why didn't you say? I know I said the people needed us to pick it up today, but we could've organized something else."

"No, no, no," she countered, waving her hand. "Dee, it's nothing like that. I had to open the shop for a meeting with a client yesterday. He flew in from Chicago to personally examine an acquisition, so it worked out fine. And Greg will be having the time of his life. Who wouldn't? All of those rare and antique books to drool over. Anyway, they'll be having another auction at the end of December, so we might spend Christmas there and see in the New Year at Times Square. I've never done it, and it's always been on Greg's wish list. Sorry, guys, we probably won't be here for Christmas." She stuck her bottom lip out.

"That sounds like a wonderful time, honey, and fits in perfectly because we were thinking of taking the kids to see Michelle. It's been a while since we took any flowers to Mom and Dad, so we'll do that on the way. Those small, gradual trips have really helped Steph. She's fine travelling now, with absolutely no fear of vehicles anymore, and even watches NASCAR with the boys."

"Just in case they smash themselves up." Jeff rolled his eyes. "And Austin's still fantastic with her. We have never had a problem with him regarding the incident. All this time we thought he might be harboring some deep-seated issue and really, he didn't so much as bat an eyelid about the whole damn thing. Like saving his sister was just another day of the week."

Susan smiled. "I guess he's living up to his original name."

"As mentioned by his teacher, right before it happened. But she didn't know about the name mix-up until I told her. Funny you should say that. Uh. Good timing." Jeff watched as the children flew past on another lap of the patio. "You see the speed, Suze?" He pointed at Austin, who glanced rearward, laughing with Stephanie, his brown hair plastered across his forehead. "Guardian and protector indeed. He must have been going even faster than that to rescue her."

"I've always liked your Superman theory," Susan laughed. "If not for the fact that Dee did give birth to Austin and you didn't find him inside an alien capsule half-buried in a cornfield, then I think you might have something. And yes, Jeff, I know." She giggled at his hoisted finger and grin. "I'm also taking the earthquake into account. I remember reading an interesting article years ago about the human body being able to do unbelievable feats in times of immense distress, trauma, panic, danger... that sort of thing. Like this woman who lifted a car off her child after a road accident. Something that is usually impossible to do under ordinary circumstances." She shrugged. "It could be a fairly logical hypothesis for what happened."

"Either that, or how wrong were we?" Dee remarked. "I could've sworn he was right by us, but he must've been a lot closer to Stephie. As you've always stated, honey, the perception of time can change in those situations."

Susan nodded. "According to certain scientists and witness accounts, like yours." She stopped when the children cycled around and slowly cruised down the gentle incline toward the pavers, the brakes squeaking with their descent.

"We're not finished here. Give us a few more minutes, please. Off you go."

"Okay, Mommy," Stephanie beamed.

"Awwwww." Sighing heavily, Austin lifted his head to the sky.

"Shoo, shoo." Jeff grinned at his daughter. "She knows something's up," he whispered, examining the corner of the house as the bikes disappeared. "Twice this morning she's asked me why we're going out."

"She'll be so excited," Susan enthused. "A puppy for her fifth birthday. And a week early. Does Austin know about the newest addition to the family?"

"Yeah, he's just as excited. It's a good thing he knows how to keep a secret. Stephie's been asking about this for ages. I'm just happy the dog beat the pony in her animal ownership catalog."

Susan sniggered at his joking. "So, what time do you have to leave?"

"To be honest, honey, we'd better get going very soon, since the people have been kind enough to hold the puppy for us all week. The traffic won't be too bad for a Sunday, but it's still a good enough journey to Kit Carson to keep us out of the house for a few hours. And we were thinking of getting some lunch out there as well. Do you mind?"

"Of course not, Dee. You two make a day of it, okay? It'll give me a chance to catch up with them and get away from the baby."

"The baby?" Jeff made a face. "Greg again, huh?"

"Yes and no," she laughed. "A couple of months ago I told him he had dark rings under his eyes and he blamed the shop. He said it was keeping him awake at night, so we started calling it the baby."

"Ahhh, yes. Babies do that. When's he back?"

"Around lunchtime on Tuesday."

"Superb." Jeff clapped his hands. "We'll bring the kids down after school to see how the baby's developing, and while we're there we may as well have a look at the shop."

"Oh no," Susan moaned, rubbing her forehead. "Jeff and Greg together again. Two years of banter hell keeps going." She joined in on their laughter. "And bring the newest Cooper for him to meet." Looking each of them in the eye, she leaned forward, smiling. "He absolutely adores the way you've received him as part of your family, and it's just made it so much easier for him living here. I can't thank you enough."

"He's a great guy, Suze. A terrific guy. We enjoy his company and the kids love him." Jeff shrugged. "You're family, anyway. You were an honorary Cooper long before your mom and dad had the sense to retire in Florida."

"Thanks, that really means a lot to me. To both of us. If our relationship is as strong and long-lasting as yours, then that's all I could ever want."

"Suze." Jeff fanned his face. "Careful, you're gonna make me cry. Besides." He straightened in his chair. "Greg's taught me his secret Kiwi and London languages. Now we can have conversations right in front of our wives, annnd…" Grinning, he slapped the side of his thigh. "You can't understand a thing."

"Yeah." Dee's eyes narrowed. "You're bad influences, and now my son's becoming part of your speech conspiracy. Just don't forget that Susan is fluent and she'll be able to tell me what's going on."

Jeff stared at her, open-mouthed. "Bro, I don't know what the bleedin' 'eck you're gobbin' 'bout, luv. Bleedin' trouble 'n' strife. Cor blimey, mate."

"You sound like some weird pirate, you fool." She sniggered and blew him a kiss. "Come on then, No-Beard. Get those creaky, decrepit bones moving. Perhaps I should get you a walking aid this week?"

*   *   *

Susan held Stephanie's hand and Austin straddled his bike while they stood at the bottom of the driveway watching Jeff and Dee vanish over the gradient in the road. Briefly reappearing thirty seconds later, they made the tight, leftward turn on the loop and managed a final, distant wave before the sloping land blocked further sight of their car.

"Susan." Stephanie looked up. "Can we go and play with my Barbie?"

"Of course, sweetheart," she smiled. "That'll be great fun. And what do you want to do, Austin?"

"I'm gonna ride this." He patted the handlebars. "I've always wondered how fast I can go down here."

Susan scuffed her sneaker on the rough surface and peered at the driveway's length, from the garage door all the way to their location near the road. Newly developed during the mid-1980s, and purpose built to take advantage of the magnificent panorama presented from the hilly terrain overlooking Crescent Lake, Fairview Terrace divided ninety yards from its curving entrance and became a one-way road that circled back on itself. Long grass and stumpy shrubs covered the steep, middle area of its slightly squashed, oval shape and the imposing structure capping it, which Susan's sight finally fell upon.

"Uhhh... I don't think that's such a good idea, big dude." She appraised the five-foot-high, gunmetal gray fence, sitting like a faded crown on the slope's top level. An extremely sturdy looking, heavy-duty, chain-link mesh hung on a framework of thick, steel posts and rails, fastened together by immense brackets bigger than Austin's hands. "How about coming inside and I'll make us all a banana smoothie. That way we can still play with Barbie." She stroked Stephanie's head. "And I can make sure Austin the Daredevil doesn't have to be scooped into a box and taken to hospital, where they may or may not be able to glue him together. What do you think?"

"Banana smoothie!" they choentered.

"Let's go, then." She swung Stephanie's hand back and forth as they walked up the incline.

"Susan." Austin jumped off his bike and pushed it beside them. "When does Three-Gee come home?"

"On Tuesday, sweetheart. Mom and Dad are picking you two up after school and bringing the whole family to see Greg and the shop." She winked secretively at Austin, who mouthed an "OH" and nodded smilingly.

"Hey, do you think he could help me with some school stuff?"

"He'd love that. What's it about?"

"It's this reading and writing thing we have to do."

Pausing at the sound of an engine starting, they angled their heads to the left, and saw the glint of shiny metal through a thin stand of pines when a car reversed slowly in a great, gliding arc next door.

"Kaye, pull the wheel down more," they heard a male voice yell. "Why are you going so wide? To the right. No, damn it, that's left. Turn right. Your right. Do you know left from right?"

"Anyway." Austin looked back. "We have to choose a person we admire and give a speech on why we look up to them. I thought maybe Three-Gee and all the cool stuff he's done. Plus everyone has to look up to him, they don't have a choice," he grinned at her.

"Well put the window down if you can't hear me properly," the voice called. "Just go forward a bit, then come back. And don't forget to put the parking brake on."

"Austin, it's so nice of you to do that and Greg will be over the moon. But are you sure? What about Mom or Dad? Or a teacher?"

"Yeah, I'm sure. This'll be the best one, 'cos we'll be giving facts about where they grew up. I'll be able to tell them about New Zealand and him playing rugby, and all the travel he's done, the way he talks and how he's always asked where he's from. I bet no one even knows..."

High-pitched screams and sudden, loud shouts pierced the air, seconds before a white car hurtled down the driveway, an open trunk lid flapping up and down. Crunching into the tarmac first, it flew across the road, smacking head-on and dead center with one of the solid posts. Breaking glass and the screech of metal upon metal reverberated across the hillside, merging with a heavy, ringing boom as the fence shook wildly, vibrations rattling the mesh along its entire length.

"Coooool!" Austin exclaimed.

"Awesome," Stephanie breathed.

"Oh shit!" Susan cupped her mouth. "Whoops... um, I mean... sorry, guys," she muttered, and slowly dropped her hand while she stared at four people now visible on a faltering scurry toward the wreck.

"Oh my God," a man, the same voice, shrieked from the front. "You idiot. I told you to put the parking brake on. What part of put the parking brake on didn't you understand?"

Wide-eyed, Austin twirled around to Susan. "Can I go see?"

"Ahhh." She studied a hissing plume of steam billowing from the car's crumpled hood. "All right. But just wait for us down the bottom and don't get in the way. That man doesn't look too happy."

"No worries." Austin leapt on his bike and cruised down the slope, heading for a short, thickset man whose staggering trot came to an end when he clasped the top of his head and simply stood there, gawking at the damage.

"Are you okay, honey?" Susan squatted at Stephanie's side and rubbed the small girl's arm through her knitted sweater.

"Uh-huh." A mass of wavy, long black hair framed her pale-bronze skin and animated, twinkling brown eyes when she turned them upon Susan. "It's just like a crash on TV," she squealed, clapping her hands.

the visit

As several neighbors helped push the vehicle off the road, Susan looked at the crowds that had gathered in barely one minute. "Wow," she whispered, nudging Austin. "Everyone must be home today."

"Yeah." Peering over his shoulder, he scanned the clusters of excitedly chattering, pointing people, and paused when his sight landed on a single figure in the background, just on the cusp of the road before it disappeared from view. Unlike the shuffling groups stretching their necks to see better, this man stood motionless, his face masked by dark sunglasses under the shadow of a baseball cap.

"Hi, Susan. Hi, kids. Exciting stuff, isn't it?"

Austin turned to see an elderly man approaching them, a large, friendly smile beaming beneath soft, blue eyes and a heavily grayed covering of hair, neatly combed across his head.

"Hi, Mr. Evans. Is everybody okay here?"

"Yes, I think so. Thank you, Susan. Except for the car, that is." He grinned and sneaked a peek behind him.

With a hasty, rearward glance, Austin saw the crest now devoid of the man wearing faded denim jeans, a red and white, checked shirt, dark sneakers and a tan satchel hanging from one shoulder.

"And, Susan, call me Henry. Please," Mr. Evans insisted. "Jeff wasn't teasing that time. I really will be the most popular old fart in town if you do."

"You said fart," Stephanie giggled, blinking up at him.

"Oh." He put on a surprised look. "Sweetheart, I'm very naughty. No dessert for me tonight."

"If that's the case, with my colorful language earlier there'll be no dessert for me until next month." Susan grimaced. "What happened?"

Henry regarded the wreck. "A probable mishap concerning the parking brake and gear selection. Unfortunately, they only stopped by to pick up my mini air compressor and were just about to leave. I guess it wanted to go first," he chuckled. "But no one was hurt, and you couldn't ask for a better result. Barbara and Kaye, Mrs. Baxter, have gone up to phone for a tow truck, so it looks like they might be staying a tad longer."

The other man, Mr. Baxter presumably, stalked the perimeter of the car before wrenching the passenger door open. Climbing in, he began rifling through the glove compartment, scouring over folded-up pieces of paper and throwing them aside with a loud, disgusted huff.

"It's a good thing this fence is here," Susan remarked. "I remember Jeff telling me about an accident he saw on his way to work one morning."

"Yes," Henry nodded. "That was only a year after they moved in. Let me show you something." He ambled across to the steel structure with Susan and the kids in tow, and gazed down the grassy embankment before pointing to a roof, barely visible at the end of a steep driveway, farther along where the looped road travelled below them. "This fence was the result of a luxury automobile ending up in someone's front room. Christian and Maria Jasam's sedan, to be exact. They moved out not long before Jeff and Dee arrived." He smiled at Austin as the boy shifted around to his side and grabbed hold of the mesh, its gray paint drab and peeling. "I met your parents the day they inspected the house. Your father asked me about this." He patted the top post with a wrinkled hand. "I was mowing the front lawn when they were just about to leave and we all got talking after they came over to say hello, which was a very polite gesture."

"It must be strong to stop a car." Austin ran his finger over the woven, steel strands.

"Incredibly strong," Henry agreed. "And it held up nicely again. That's the third vehicle to test its design and strength, so it's a good thing those posts are deep in the ground. About two thirds their entire length. I had a chat with the contractor when they built it and he told me..."

A harsh sob made them turn, clearly audible now that the cracked radiator had emptied its sizzling contents, and they looked across to see two women trudging down the driveway, one slumped and attempting to muffle her unmistakable weeping while being led by the other, who waggled her fingers at them and smiled.

"I think my assistance is needed." Henry inclined his head toward the slumped figure, his blue eyes twinkling. "Barbara and I will pop over later. You never know, we might just have to say hello again. So you take care, kids, and I think this is another great lesson in expecting the unexpected." He laughed and moved off with a wave of his hand. "Kaye, everything will be all right," he called. "Let's get you up to the house for a nice, hot cup of coffee. Rick, come and comfort your wife inside, buddy. I know you're annoyed, but these things happen."

Smoothing out a crumpled piece of paper, Rick glanced at him, a dark scowl etched upon his face. "Sure," he grunted. "As soon as I find some insurance details. I've got a copy in here somewhere."

Susan watched Henry shrug and addressed the children. "Okay, guys, let's go. We'll have that yummy smoothie soon."

"Yay!" Stephanie sang.

"Can I stay here and watch the tow truck?" Austin asked.

"Sure. We'll go up and I'll start on the smoothie soon. I'll call you when it's ready. But stay off this road, okay? We don't need any more dramas today."

"Okay, Susan." He held her gaze with a serious expression. "Trust me. I won't go on the road and I won't get in the way. That banana smoothie sounds better every time you say it."

Susan smiled, and frowned at the same time. "Austin Cooper, sometimes you act so grown-up, sweetheart."

"Mom said that to me this morning."

"And Mom's right," she laughed. "See you soon. Be good."

For a while, Austin pedaled leisurely around the front lawn, catching several glowering stares from Mr. Baxter, and by the tenth minute, when roaming aimlessly along the roadside stretch of grass, he saw the last group of onlookers climbing their driveway. As if on cue, the man levered himself from the driver's seat and leaned against the car body. "Okay, kid," he barked. "That's enough. Everyone's gone back to their homes. You've had your look, now how about doing the same."

Bringing his bike to a stop, calmly appraising Mr. Baxter's attitude, Austin thought it best to go for his smoothie, and half-turned to check the road behind him, just in case the tow truck suddenly arrived. With nothing in sight he pushed off, heading for the rear of the house and his favorite, backyard game of zooming across the patio pavers from the ascending slope. Swerving to the right, his legs pumping on the steep terrain, he steered toward the fence line, and slammed the brake lever shut when a figure moved amid the dim shadows cast by an abundant collection of tall spruce trees. He threw his feet down, sliding the bike's frame sideways on the soft dirt, and watched a man step forward, his arms raised high, palms out, the fingers splayed in a show of goodwill and reassurance.

"Hello, Austin. I hope I didn't scare you, and apologize if I did. I judged this the better option than simply appearing inside your home. But then I have gotten things wrong before." Taking off his Rockies hat and Oakleys, he studied the boy. "You don't look scared. It's wonderful to see that's still the same." He chuckled at the silent, answering blink. "Another thing that's the same are these clothes. Do you recognize them?"

With the headwear and sunglasses removed, Austin had a clear view of the man. Short black hair, meticulously cut, topped the honey-brown skin of his face, which Austin thought could be a tan, but without sun-damaged wrinkles the school principal bore after his surfing expeditions in California every vacation and arriving back at Crescent Lake West Elementary looking like a dried, shriveled prune. The thing that took Austin by surprise were the eyes, a warm, cheerful brown, the color of lightly-roasted chestnuts or the darker cones lying scattered around the many broad tree trunks populating that side of the property. Certain they had glowed a bright green during the event at the kindergarten, now he wasn't so sure, and as he examined the man a memory emerged, bringing the faint image of a hooded, shrouded, and finely-sculpted face. Still breathing hard from the ride, Austin frowned at his momentary vision. "I remember you," he stated, nodding cautiously.

"Then you remember what happened that day. You remember doing something very strange to save your sister. Something incredible. Did you tell your folks?"

"No." Austin shook his head. "I don't think anyone would believe me."

"Mmmm," the man hummed, and dropped his haunches promptly upon the ground. "Sit here with me, boy," he rumbled, patting an abundant carpeting of dry pine needles. They rustled when he crossed his legs inward and dragged the satchel onto his lap. "I need to tell you something. Don't worry, this visit won't take long. I'm aware of Susan calling you soon."

Glancing at the house, Austin dismounted, and lowered himself and the bike by the man's side. Through the open collar of the checked shirt, he spotted a single, thick line tattooed near his neck, the muted green-blue tapering as it ran down his chest and out of sight. "How do you know Susan?"

"In a way, I know all of you very well. I've been watching since the day you were born. What's difficult about this is that you can't speak of me, and you can't be seen with me. I'd have everyone wanting to rip my head off. Your father. Probably Greg. Definitely your mother. The world has changed a lot since I was your age." Although his words were softly spoken they pulsed with a firm and constant strength. "We'll discuss those topics later. Right now, I want you to know two important things. And you'll have to accept them without questions, because the answers wouldn't make any sense. Do you understand?"

"Not really."

"It's a familiarity we both share and it's been like that for a lot of us, maybe all of us. I know it's hard to accept something you don't understand, but that's just the way it is." The man stuck the cap back on his head and slipped his sunglasses over it, resting them on top of the peaked visor. "You're a very special person, Austin…"

"Yeah. Mom told me this morning."

"She did?" The man's brow climbed, wrinkling the skin on an unusually flat and backward-slanted forehead.

"Twice. About trusting me and about my eyes. She says they change color when the light's different."

"Ahhh, I see. Your physical eye color. You had me worried for a moment."

"About what? My eyes? Why?"

"Not now, boy. We can chat about eye color another day."

Austin shrugged. "Okay."

"Has your mother made other comments? Or anyone else?" Carefully, the man gauged the child's manner as he contemplated the question.

"Only Mom. She said it might be some power and called me her magic boy."

The man chortled quietly, a rich, deep baritone in his chest. "The eyes again, right? I must admit, the colors are stunning depending on the light. They're a dark blue or even purple in this shade. But I'm sorry, you're not magic, if that's what you wanted to hear. Some people are just born with strangely colored eyes. It's a simple, natural feature they have." He gazed straight at Austin. "Do you think you're magic?"

"No."

"Good," he nodded. "You're not. That craft fled this world many, many years ago and has nothing to do with what you are. The ability you possess came from something else and there are no others like us. It's just you, me, and the day you are ready to understand everything."

Austin wriggled on his spot, a growing frown deepening, bringing his eyebrows closer together. "But I don't understand. Who are you, anyway? Why are you telling me this?"

"It's fairly obvious this isn't going to plan," the man muttered. Running a hand over his short hair, he looked at the boy's troubled appearance and gave a heavy sigh. "You're young. A hell of a lot younger than me when I was told anything, and I had to go through the same stuff without answers, so what I'm about to say is all that I can. Even I don't know everything, which is why I'm here." He held a pointed finger aloft. "Without any questions this time, boy. I came to tell you I'm going away for a while. It could be a year, a few years." He shrugged. "I don't know how long. While I'm gone, you need to do something. You need to be careful in how you act. In everything you do. Be sensible. Where there's trouble, just walk away, because your mother is correct with one idea. You do have power, and when you're old enough, there'll be more. It comes from an object that I hold. It was given to me a long time ago, to protect, to keep until its next owner, the next Keeper. You. When you're ready. And what you did at the kindergarten is a little trick that gives us a bit of an advantage in moments of danger. It helps us protect ourselves, lets us get away from any sticky situations. Kind of nifty little thing, really. But here's the interesting part. Your sister's rescue didn't feel quite right, and as far as I know it's never been this way. My predecessor, the Keeper before me, never mentioned any glitches during the handover stage. Like me, she thought it a pretty easy thing to do. So, there's the reason I have to leave. To visit old acquaintances and possibly a frenemy or two. They may have something, then again, they may have nothing. Just be careful while I'm gone. Can you do that?"

Austin's sight dropped briefly to the tan satchel. "What's a frenemy?"

"Well," the man smiled. "A few years back I provided a bit of tactical knowledge during the creation of a certain text, and told this guy that with my experiences it was best to keep your friends close and your enemies closer. He absolutely loved that, but declined using the word because it sounded too comical for serious military strategy. Although he was still very amused. It was the only time I ever saw him la..." The man paused, and chuckled softly at Austin's blank stare. "Anyway, these, uh, people I might call on aren't exactly friends, but they're not enemies, either. They're a frenemy. I've helped them with the odd problem and in return they've been useful for information. I haven't seen them in a long time and that's fine with me because they kind of stink."

Austin laughed.

"It's true," the man laughed with him. "Some smell really, really bad and others not so much. It's all very political."

"What's your name?"

"That's a reasonable question and one I will answer." He jabbed a finger toward the driveway. "But we've got company."

"Austin," Susan's voice called from the front of the house.

"Time to go." The man hauled himself off the ground, slung the satchel's strap over his shoulder and brushed the dirt off his backside.

"Will you be okay?"

"I'll be fine," the man replied. "And so will you. You're well protected here, I've spent two years ensuring that particular detail." Squinting, he tilted his head to the side. "You've just listened to a lot of stuff and don't seem bothered by it at all. You're very grown-up for one so young."

"Yeah." Austin shrugged. "Everyone's saying that today."

"Austin!"

"You better move. Susan's around the other side and she'll be entering the backyard in about five seconds. We can talk more as soon as I'm back. Look after your family, but remember... don't get into any situations. Go."

Jumping on his bike, Austin pushed off, and zigzagged his way past the trees. "Keep your wits about you, boy," he heard a soft call behind him. He stopped at a well-kept, grassy clearing, just short of the gradient that would send him racing to the patio, and peered over his shoulder, scanning the shadows. Seeing nothing, he turned and tensed his leg muscles for the thrilling ride.

"Austin." Now, a drop of panic buzzed through his name. "Where are you?"

"Sorry, Susan," he yelled. "I'm here. I was just riding around." And he shot off down the slope.

Chapter Seven

The Bully

"Quiet please, everyone." The teacher stood in the open doorway, surveying the throng of rowdy students, knowing most of them probably hadn't heard his words and the rest chose to ignore him. It was always like this during the first month of a new school year, they derived pleasure from testing the boundaries and the patience that went in maintaining them. So, for the moment, he simply stood there and scrutinized the heads stuck close to bags, hands fumbling through their belongings, the gawking through windows at the beautifully sunny day outside, and the groups that chattered incessantly with no awareness, or concern, of the events going on around them.

Only two children waited calmly, both taught by him last year, as well, and familiar with his demeanor. The tall boy with brown hair and blue-purple eyes, who sat one row back from front center, curiously observing his entrance, and the other, also brown haired, but without the same height, peering intensely through four excitedly babbling girls another three rows directly behind, watching nothing else but his classmate.

The teacher flicked his inspection to one of the closest desks when a screwed-up lump of paper flew straight past his ear, dropping suddenly and bouncing off the nose of a small boy standing several feet behind him in the brightly lit hall. Austin shook his head at the chubby, pinkish face that swung around and grinned at anyone who witnessed the deed. Under a mop of scruffy, medium-cropped, blond hair, two pig-like eyes narrowed as they held his gaze for a moment before moving on. Turning away from the rabble, the teacher regarded the tiny boy, who took three steps backward, rubbing his snout with a trembling hand.

Skinny, and very short for his age, wide, hazel eyes looked up from an otherwise handsome, pale face, made even pastier by his contrasting, jet-black hair, cut in an old 1950s style with a long side parting greased flat across the top of his skull. Twitching fingers kneaded the edge of a tatty, blue backpack, held like a shield in the tightest of grips while he moved rearward some more at the raucous laughter flaring within the classroom.

This kid is in for a rough time, the teacher thought, appraising the holes in his worn-out shoes and shabby, faded clothes. "Everything will be all right, young man," he offered. "The first day is always the hardest, so what I'll do is put you beside someone I can really trust. He'll look after you, okay?"

The protruding Adam's apple in the boy's scrawny neck bobbed up and down as he gave a huge swallow.

"Let me restore order, then I'll come and get you. Just remain here." He pointed to a spot near the wall, where thirty pairs of judgmental, prying eyes couldn't prematurely assess the newcomer. There would be plenty of time for that when he first walked in. With an encouraging smile, the teacher strode through the doorway and to the blackboard. Beneath it, a narrow ledge held various quantities of multicolored chalk and a long, thick wooden ruler, which he picked up and whacked three times on his desk, releasing small clouds of dust that billowed into the air with each loud crack. "QUIET," he hollered. "PLACES, NOW!"

A mad scrambling of bodies, a screeching of chair legs on the timber floor, and the thump of swaying desks superseded the former racket when the children scurried about, aware now of the disgruntled person in their presence.

"Your attention on me," the teacher barked. Not an exceptionally tall man, reaching around five-foot-ten, he was stockily built, with broad shoulders and thick forearms covered in a mat of dense, dark hair. On his head, the same trend waned with the mousey-brownness showing visible signs of male pattern baldness, starting at the temples, where two, curving arches crept back across the top of his scalp. Beneath his receding hairline, gunmetal-gray eyes waited for them to comply with his order, the tolerance and joviality usually present within the steely-blue color wilting drastically while he glowered at the sea of staring faces. "We are merely two weeks into our first semester, and other than a few individuals, nearly all of you have broken at least one rule during that time. This is unacceptable behavior, which I will not tolerate. If you would like to stay behind after lessons finish, then you are certainly going the right way about it. Any repeat of this morning's event and communication with your parents shall inform them of your subsequent detention the next day. Or the following week, if you consider yourself smart enough to act like this on a Friday. Do I make myself clear?"

Everybody nodded, except one child, who scowled as he turned his head away.

The teacher returned the ruler to its shelf. "Tess Anderson," he declared, rubbing the dust from his fingers. "Stand up, please." A beautiful, blonde girl seated two rows behind Austin jolted out of her chair, rocking it back and forth with her quick movement. "In case we have one or two students confused with the consequences of their actions, explain the significant speech just given. In your own words, please."

She fidgeted with her dress, her amber eyes blinking rapidly. "Um. If we behave badly and disrespect the rules of our classroom again, then you'll tell our parents and we'll have detention the next day, or the week after."

"Impeccable. Wonderfully said. You may sit down, Tess. Now then, I trust everyone understands. Do you, Kevin Wotlinski?" He singled out the paper thrower, a tall, overweight boy near the doorway. His head swiveled slowly at the resonance of his name.

"Yup," he droned, rolling his eyes.

"I hope so, because most of the time you don't listen, whether it be your obstinate refusal, your frequent problems with comprehension, or your persistent disruptiveness. I just don't know." The children laughed boisterously, many not actually grasping the meaning of their teacher's scathing dialogue, only knowing he had put the nasty individual in his place quite magnificently. Kevin twisted round in his seat to glare at them, ending their amusement as quickly as it started. "Once we're finished here, you will do a couple of things for me. One of which is picking up the paper that is, at present, lying in the hallway." The teacher paused, and strolled to the boy's desk. "And if I ever catch you throwing anything at me again it will be detention every day for two whole weeks. Do you understand that, Kevin Wotlinski?"

"Yup," he growled. In his pink and flabby face, inky-brown eyes, almost black, darker than a moonless night, deepened even more when he fixed them on his teacher.

"Splendid. Okay." Clapping his hands, ignoring the daunting stare, the teacher moved to the open door. "Let's all start again, shall we? Good morning, class."

"Good morning, Mr. Foley," they chanted harmoniously.

"Today, we gladly receive a new student not only in our school, but specifically in this room." He leaned out and gestured to the boy, who remained glued to the wall before somewhat reluctantly shuffling forward, the bag still clasped against his chest. Dragging his leaden feet, the teacher guiding him with one hand between protruding shoulder blades, he looked out at an endless ocean of what seemed like baleful, defiant scowls. "This is Paul Benton," he heard a distant voice announce while his stomach commenced a series of violent, unsettling somersaults. "Let's give him a good old, West Elementary greeting."

"Good morning, Paul," they chorused, and watched the small boy lower his head, lifting it every so often with a momentary glance.

"Paul has recently arrived from his birthplace, a specific location in Texas, so to find out where, here's a quick quiz. Can anyone name the state capital?" He surveyed the blank expressions, and addressed the first, well-mannered person noted upon his arrival. "You can answer this," he smiled. "And I'll give you a big clue. Even though it's been around a lot longer, your name is identical."

"Austin!" The boy beamed.

"Correct. It's Austin, Austin." Mr. Foley laughed along with the children. "Welcome to Crescent Lake, Paul, and we hope you enjoy your new school. As for seating arrangements, I think it's only fitting you sit beside your prior capital's namesake. So, in order to achieve that, we'll need an extra desk, a chair, and some shuffling around before we belatedly sing our national anthem and get into the first subject of the day." He cupped a hand to his ear. "Which is?"

"Algebra," they mumbled drearily.

"Your enthusiasm is overwhelming," he chortled. "Okay. Wade and Kevin, both of you go to Miss King and politely ask if we can have the spare desk and chair that is currently in her classroom. When you get back, Wade, you'll be where Kevin is, Paul, you will sit beside Austin, and you, Mr. Wotlinski, can now have the constant pleasure of my inimitable company." He pointed to the end of his own, larger desk. "You're moving to a fresh and probably permanent workplace."

Kevin glowered at the teacher and mumbled something under his breath as he levered himself up, while the boy sitting next to Austin packed books into his bag and dumped it by his new spot on their way to the door. A sharp reminder made the bigger one pause.

"Wotlinski," Mr. Foley snapped. "Don't forget that paper."

As Paul slumped into his chair he took a quick peek of the departing students, and caught the full, piercing brunt of Kevin's stare before he left the room. The hatred rising in those glittering eyes left a disconcerting, bad taste in his mouth, but nothing like the chill shiver that crept along his spine.

*   *   *

A shrill clanging broke the classroom into a frenzied hive of activity. Everyone jumped up, their instantaneous babble mixing with the long, intense screeches of twenty-nine chairs pushed backward. Austin remained seated, and tapped his new classmate on the shoulder when he knelt beside him. "Hey, Paul, what are you doing for lunch?" He smiled at the small boy, who was searching through his threadbare backpack for the food lovingly made that morning.

Something happened to Paul the night before school. Extreme nervousness had set in causing severe loss of appetite, and after a fitful sleep he woke feeling the same way. Usually, he loved his food, with breakfast the best meal of the day, although a delicious dinner finished off with Mom's steaming apple and cinnamon pie regularly challenged that opinion. His father often shook his head, asking how he could eat so much and still have the physique of a toothpick. Now, he was simply ravenous, and couldn't wait to chow down.

"You can hang out with me and Wade if you want," Austin suggested. "It must be pretty hard not knowing anyone."

Paul studied the inquisitive, yet kindhearted face, evaluating what may be either a genuine request for company, or a possible setup of some sort, aware he had already angered one boy within moments of walking in. The biggest and ghastliest nine-year-old he had ever seen. All morning he fretted about the impending mealtime, scared by the vision of being the outsider, left alone in a grimy and long forgotten corner somewhere. But, hopefully, here was a guy friendly enough to come forward and offer their company. "Okay," he blurted, his enormous grin showing the scale of his gratitude.

As several girls rushed past, one thumped the side of his head with her bag. Tess, Paul remembered the name. She peered back over her shoulder, her long, blonde ponytail swinging. "Sorry," she called, and smiled at Austin before disappearing from the room.

"Come on, Paul." With slightly flushed cheeks, Austin jumped up and grabbed his snazzy, Adidas backpack. "You'll get trampled down there. Bring your bag, we're gonna eat outside today."

Paul stood and gaped as he scanned the boy's height. "Whoa," he boomed. "Jeez, you're big!"

"Yeah, whatever." Austin glanced around the near empty room. "Let's go."

the gang

"My name's Pauly." The straightforward statement came while he followed them out through the open front doors. Glaring sunlight dazzled his vision when he looked up and swiveled his head either side to view his taller companions. "I mean, my real name is Paul," he continued. "But my parents call me Pauly. Mom says Dad started calling me that as soon as I was born, and now everyone does."

"Cool. Pauly it is, then. It's nice to meet you. I'm Austin Cooper, that's Wade Fitch, and you should tell Mr. Foley, or you might always be known as Paul." Austin half turned and stuck his hand out.

Wide-eyed, the small boy blinked at him before taking it in his own. Having only seen grown-ups perform this type of ritual, he had never experienced anything like this from his peers, and reciprocated the warm, firm grip.

"Hey, do you like fishing?" Wade's handshake was just as friendly.

Pauly shrugged. "Dunno. I've never done it."

"Me and Austin go to Lake Crescent every summer. Usually Sunday, 'cos we play baseball on a Saturday, and loads when we're on vacation. You should come with us next time."

"Okay." Pauly examined the straight, brown hair that hung to Wade's shoulder. Unlike Austin's short and well-kept style, it covered his ears and fell across his calm, blue eyes, making him push his bottom lip out every so often to puff it away. Like the tallest of the three, he possessed a laid-back demeanor and broad, cheery smile, particularly when he wasn't removing the frequent annoyance from his lashes.

"Looks pretty jam-packed," Wade observed as they rounded a corner.

Arranged on a huge concrete slab, fifteen bench-seat tables buzzed with activity, and Pauly pointed at one located near the extreme edge, just outside the shadow of the main building, its lone occupant monitoring their arrival vigilantly. "It's just that guy there," he declared. "Or how about the cafeteria? Do you have one? My old school did."

"Yeah," Austin chuckled. "We've got one. But Wade's a sun-loving hippy and gets sulky if he's not out in the fine weather." He laughed at the gentle prod in his back and stooped to hear his friend's hushed tease when they ambled forward.

"Someone's waving at you," Wade crooned.

Austin blushed when he saw Tess gesturing grandly at him. She dropped her hand quickly at the wild giggling that erupted from her friends, a rosy hue matching the colored appearance of the tall boy. "Jeez, Wade," he mumbled, and averted his eyes, which shone a vivid blue in the balmy, glaring light.

"Only trying to help," Wade sniggered. "Just in case you missed it. Yo, Xander," he called as they approached the table. "Mind if we sit here, dude?"

They stopped, and looked at each other when their brown-haired classmate began packing up his food, shoving it haphazardly into his bag. Saying nothing, he stood and made his way across an adjacent field already teeming with rowdy children playing various ball games.

"What's wrong with him?" Austin frowned at the uneasy, rearward glances darting their way.

"No idea." Wade shrugged as he sat opposite Pauly, putting his back to the noisy, lunchtime contests. "He's always been a bit weird. Hey, maybe he likes your girlfriend."

"Wade." Austin plonked on the seat beside his friend, the wood creaking under his added weight. Stealing a furtive peek to the right, he felt another bout of burning cheeks when Tess did the same thing. "What have you got to eat, Pauly?" he asked, eager to stave off further embarrassment.

"Uhhh." The small boy shrugged the backpack off his shoulders, slapped it front of him and began rummaging around the interior. Austin noticed it looked even worse up close, ragged, old, the straps so frayed they could snap at any given moment, and probably would with the treatment they received as he dropped it at his feet and raked it unceremoniously to one side. "Yum," he exclaimed, holding out an opened package of greaseproof paper. "A peanut butter sandwich! Do you guys like peanut butter?"

"My favorite," Austin replied. "That's what I've got." He deposited a rectangular Tupperware container on the table, stripped off the lid and separated the bread.

"Hey, there's jelly on yours. That's my favorite, too."

"And it's all mine," Austin beamed. Sticking his nose close to the spread, he sniffed the delicious aroma, a sweet, salty blend of fruit and nut that had his mouth watering instantly. "What have you got, Wade?"

"Mom's leftover macaroni something," he moaned, screwing his face up.

The other boys cackled before launching into their meals, and as Pauly chewed his way through a crunchy lump he peered about the school grounds. "I always heard it was freezing in Colorado," he remarked, rolling his gaze to the blue, cloudless sky. "But this ain't so bad. Are you both from here?"

"Yep. Born and raised," Austin answered between bites. "What's it like in Austin? Is it cold? It's been really warm here lately."

"It's okay. A lot hotter than this in summer." He motioned with his hand. "And how awesome is that? I'm from Austin, and you are Austin!"

"You don't sound like a cowboy," Wade said, and joined in on the laughter. "When did you get to Crescent Lake?"

"Ummm... last weekend, on Saturday. I was meant to start school a week ago, but I've been helping my mom unpack our things." He paused before adding quietly. "And cheer her up. I don't think she's happy right now."

Austin was ready to ask why, but before he could say anything, Pauly suddenly brightened. "Say, do you like watching TV?" In his hazel eyes, flecks of caramel-brown and army-green flashed while he alternated his gaze from one to the other.

"Sure," they nodded.

"Me, too! I love cartoons. I used to watch them back at our old home. Batman's my favorite, and Spiderman. Oh, and X-Men. They're cool. Hey, maybe we could watch them together one weekend. You could stay over at my place. Saturday or Sunday, 'cos they're on both mornings."

"Little league's finished for us, so we'll do that. Wade used to like Spiderman and Batman, but now he's into Wonder Woman." Austin grinned at Pauly as Wade's elbow prodded his ribs. "Where do you live?"

"Ummm, I think it's called Fitzpatrick Drive. It's at the bottom of this big hill somewhere."

"Really? That's not far from me. I live at the top, on Fairview Terrace. Maybe a twenty minute bike ride to your place. I can probably see your roof from my house."

"Awesome!" Pauly's exuberant holler drew the attention of two groups, the girls still sitting near them, and five boys strolling across the field, led by the biggest of the lot, who pushed aside any smaller children unfortunate enough to get in their way. The joy of making friends so quickly had banished his initial fears of the new environment, but the happiness collapsed instantly when Pauly spotted a mass of unkempt, blond hair. Horror stabbed his heart when he watched the large head swing his way, knowing with an absolute certainty that the spiteful pig-eyes latched entirely on him. Sure enough, the right arm rose, pointing directly at him, and they veered off their original, meandering course to set a brisk pace precisely for the eating area. "Oh crap, he's seen me." Pauly's eyes swayed wildly from side to side.

"Who?" Austin glanced over his shoulder, chuckling as he turned and popped the last piece of sandwich in his mouth. "Yeah," he chewed, placing the lid back on his lunchbox. "I saw the dirty looks he was giving you during class. That's funny him ending up smack-bang in Mr. Foley's lap. Do you care you got moved, Wade?"

"Nah." Briefly, Wade examined the approaching boys. "It's not your fault, Pauly. Although he'll blame you for everything, and it looks like he's got the whole mob."

Pauly stared at them, positive they had gone totally mad with their incredulous display of flippancy, before peering at the gang closing in fast. "He sure looks angry." His head dropped. "This is just great. Now I'll probably get a black eye or a broken arm. Or both. Right before my birthday."

Austin's brow shot upward. "Yeah? When is it?"

"Tomorrow." He began scratching at a splinter on the seat.

"Cool! Uhhh, is it the eighth today?"

"Yes," he mumbled.

"My sister's birthday is on the nineteenth. She's turning seven. I'll have to tell her she's got a September birthday buddy."

The small boy made no response, so Austin reached out and patted his forearm. "Everything will be okay. Just relax, this can be an early present."

Pauly peeked at him, convinced the words indicated his impending and vicious beating. To his left, loud murmurs buzzed in his ears. The girls, everyone. This was exactly like one of the nightmares that kept him awake for long periods last night, and he swallowed hard when footsteps thudded upon the concrete.

"Hey, shorty," a voice sneered. "Ya got's some new friends, huh?"

Pivoting leisurely on the seat, Austin passed his gaze over the gang spreading out, all of them standing with legs wide apart and a smile on their lips. "Leave him alone and go away, Kevin." He fixed an icy stare on the largest of the five. "Please."

"No, Cooper. Ya faggot friend gonna get's it. Ya listenin' shorty? Liff ya gay head and show's ya faggot hair. Look'a ya. You's all gay buddies." Wotlinski howled with laughter and looked to his cronies, seeking mirth and adoration at such witty repartee, and his portly chest swelled when they accorded their master with hearty bouts of sniggering.

"Have you guys got nothing better to do?" Ignoring Wotlinski, Austin isolated two of them with a pointed finger. "Tyrell Jones and Joe Harris. I've known both of you since we went to kindergarten. Joe, you used to be friends with me and Wade." He hooked a thumb at Wade, who glanced backward and nodded his head in agreement. "So what's the deal here, Joe? Is this creep better company than us?"

Joe's head sagged, and he took a faltering step away.

"Shut ya face, Cooper!" Wotlinski bellowed. "What make's ya fink ya can talk ta me like that? ME!" Stabbing an index finger into his flabby torso, he directed his close-set, beady eyes on Pauly. They glinted with his snarling threat. "Ya gone in mess wiv the wrong person, shorty. Ya fink ya can come here in get's me move around like some piece'a meat by that idiot Foley?"

"Leave him alone, Kevin. You're nothing but a bully. Just go away."

Pauly stole a sideways look, Austin half turned, and everyone, including a red-faced, gob-smacked Wotlinski, gaped at the blonde, pony-tailed girl who stood there defiantly after her tremulous yell.

"What?" Wotlinski's chubby face hardened, but the ruddy flesh still quivered as his jaw muscles clenched. "WHAT? Who the hell... shut ya fuckin' face, bitch, it got's nuffin' ta do..."

Austin moved. Quickly. So fast nobody saw him, and in a flash, Wotlinski was down, thumping onto the concrete and dragged to the very edge where it merged with the neatly clipped grass. Straddling the fat chest, his big hands clamped to the dirty, red collar of Wotlinski's tee-shirt, Austin shook him fiercely, a force that wobbled the large head to and fro. "Don't talk to her like that," he hissed. "I'm sick of you getting your thrills by picking on those smaller or worse off." With minimal effort, he dragged the body upright and pushed him back. "You're the idiot, not learning your lesson last time. Remember my sister? Remember Wade? Now Pauly. Now Tess, and probably everyone in this school. You just don't know when to stop, do you? It must be that tiny, stupid brain, and because of that, Wotlinski, today it's your turn. In front of your tough pals, you've ended up on that fat ass of yours. Again."

At Austin's last word, Pauly finally looked up and viewed the immediate change of circumstances. Open-mouthed, he watched the bravado and stature wither on the second tallest boy in grade four, his superior bulk insignificant when compared to the confidence and authority of the lofty, naturally well-developed person he had obviously challenged before, and obviously lost. Again.

Wotlinski stepped farther away from his adversary, a rapid, burning flush blossoming through the existing crimson glow of his skin. Suddenly realizing a lack of presence, he sneaked a quick peek behind, and saw his gang shuffling rearward, casting worried glances among themselves at a confrontation not going to plan, reluctant to stand beside their leader any longer. "I ain't got's no beef wiv ya, Cooper. Only him." He directed a withering scowl toward Pauly, just when a massive bead of sweat trundled across the center of his forehead and curved into the left eyeball, triggering a quick jerk of his hand to rub at the stinging liquid. As everyone stared, he grasped what the action must have looked like and instantly dropped his hand.

"Yyyyeaaahhh," Austin slurred. Squinting, he rubbed his chin and nodded. "I seem to recall you crying the last time this happened. Even my little sister didn't do that much after you punched her to the ground."

The entire area exploded with thunderous, bursting hilarity, including the mesmerized gang, and Wotlinski stared wide-eyed at Austin, his face now a truly gleaming and enraged ruby-red. Pauly thought it amazing no steam blew from his ears in great, bulging clouds, just like the olden-day cartoon characters he loved to watch, and giggled hysterically at the notion.

"Laugh it up, shorty," Wotlinski rasped. "Ya can't's haff ya bodyguard round all the times. So watch ya back."

"Get it in your thick skull, Wotlinski." Austin advanced on him, his blue eyes blazing. "Leave Pauly alone, leave us all alone, and try to figure out the result if you don't. Let this be a test to see if you're as stupid as you look and sound. And next time, pay attention in a subject called English, 'cos ya ain't got's no intelligence, that's what ya ain't got's no of. Now get lost. Go eat another sack of donuts."

Wotlinski recoiled, and spat his final outburst at Austin with a gushing, radiating hatred. "Ya fuckin' freak. I'm gonna get's ya, faggot. Nobody's speak ta me like that. Ya dead, Cooper. Ya hear's me? Fuckin' dead." Spinning quickly, he stormed over to his buddies and lashed out at Joe, punching him solidly on the upper arm. The boy howled and gripped his clobbered spot while Wotlinski physically herded the group across the field, mouthing silent words as he glared twice over his shoulder, once at Pauly, and the second, longest time at Austin.

Requiring extra supplies for the period following lunch, a teacher used the stairway nearest to his classroom, and paused on the half landing between levels after glimpsing a possible disturbance through the full length windows running down that wing of the building. Peering outside, contemplating an immediate involvement, he watched a certain person applying his usual practice of intimidation, the bullying brought to a halt instantly when his opponent gave him a dressing-down he would never forget. The moment it ended, a loudly cheering crowd surrounded the tall boy, bestowing appreciative pats on the back and vigorous shaking of his arms. And during their raucous celebrations his strange-colored eyes found the window.

Austin's head swung back and forth, trying to take in the sudden throng of smiling faces, blaring calls, and jovial thumps. Everyone thanked him at the same time, Tess blushed, Wade was grinning, and he held his hand high, struggling to diminish their praise. "No, really, that was a close one. He's a lot bigger now than what he was four years ago. And I'm supposed to keep out of trouble. Look, it's nothing, really. Anybody would've done it."

"Anybody? Nothing? A close one? What are talking about?" Pauly babbled. "You were awesome. That was awesome. Holy crap, he's the one scared of you! He cried, Austin. Cried! And his friends laughed at him. Not me, him! Thanks man, you're the best. Oh my God!"

"Yeah, he had it coming," Wade said.

"He'll never try anything like that again," someone yelled.

"He still might," Austin admitted. "Because he didn't cry. It was sweat."

"What? Sweat? Get outta here," Pauly hooted.

"Yep. It went into his eye. But when he started rubbing at it." Austin shrugged. "Well... you know." Through the hysterical laughter and more good-natured blows his sight fell upon the stairway window, and saw a smiling Mr. Foley nod once before turning away.

Chapter Eight

The Ornament

Austin stumbled to the kitchen sink, grabbed a clean glass from the dish rack and quickly filled it with water, his hand trembling while he guzzled it down. "Ahhhhh," he sighed, savoring the revitalizing coolness on his aching throat. Breathing heavily, he topped it up and turned to watch two red dots flashing on the wall oven's digital display, just as one of the numbers changed. 04:57 it now glowed, and with a momentary glance through the window, Austin noted day's first tenuous light, gradually subduing and withering the gloom. He took another sip, leaned upon the bench top and closed his eyes, unwillingly reliving the latest dream, nightmare, that had started three months ago and plagued his usually peaceful slumber at least twice a week. It was identical every time.

He found himself floating far above the blue and white planet that he and over six and a half billion people called home, marveling at the beauty of the brown and dark-green continents, the indigo oceans, the swirling, flowing weather patterns and cloud cover so thick and puffy it really did seem like giant tufts of fleece had been thrown excitedly about. With an intoxicating serenity he gazed at his world and smiled.

Then it happened, and it was always the same. A vast, black shadow made its way rapidly across the surface, eclipsing the rich, vibrant features as it swallowed Earth whole. Hesitant to confront something so big it could cover the entire planet with such impenetrable darkness, Austin shivered while turning his head, momentum swinging his body to the unending depths of space, littered with undoubtedly millions of brightly shining, far-flung stars. And nothing else. Frowning, he began looking left and right, up and down, just when a rush of heat slammed against his back, rotating him again to find Earth replaced by a world that dwarfed it completely.

This thing was gigantic, more the size of Jupiter, another planet he knew after completing a school project about the Solar System. But there the similarities stopped, for this world was totally ablaze. It was not a star, a sun, not in any way, it was simply on fire, and Austin felt panic, swift, vicious, like a surging electrical current, race through him with the realization he was moving closer. Wide-eyed, his skin sizzling, he thrashed about, trying to gain some distance from the gargantuan, blistering world that dominated his vision. Every breath was a hugely laborious task, scorching his lips, tongue, mouth and searing his esophagus on the way down, and at the moment when he thought it impossible to escape his predicament, when collapse and instantaneous combustion seemed imminent, a voice would murmur something in his ear and he would wake, in his bed, his body and sheets drenched with sweat. Lying there, panting, that one word receded as quickly as the guttural cry from his parched and gaping mouth.

"Destroyer," it whispered.

*　　*　　*

Sitting near the garage door, Austin contemplated the dreary, early-morning cloud blanketing the heavens over Crescent Lake. A tinkling bell broke his broody thoughts, announcing the arrival of a large gray and white dog, which trotted around the corner of the house to his left. Upon spotting the boy, its curved, furry tail swished madly over its back while it bounded across and skipped around, lunging between flailing arms in a desperate attempt to plant as many cheek licks as possible. Nearly four years old and still imbued with the limitless, playful energy of a puppy, the Alaskan Malamute's yellowish-brown eyes twinkled mischievously.

"Okay, Duke, okay. Hello," Austin laughed. Through his cotton shorts the driveway's rough surface ground at his buttocks as he dodged another brush of the wet tongue. Grabbing Duke's collar, he held the dog and stroked its luxuriously fluffy coat, his mood brightened by the good-natured and bubbly temperament of Stephanie's pet.

"There you are. What's happening, buddy?"

Austin tore his gaze from the many roofs and tall trees sprinkling the hillside, and picked himself off the ground when Duke bounced over to his father. "Nothing much," he shrugged. "Just thinking about stuff."

Jeff nodded. "Fair enough." Stepping out of the shaded portico, he rubbed Duke's fur with his free hand, a pair of thick, leather gloves held in the other. "Do you need help with anything?"

For a brief second, Austin considered telling his father about the dreams, even the hooded man, one of only three people who could have a solution or idea about their ambiguous meanings. He's been gone four years now, so don't be stupid, he thought. No one would ever believe you. They'll think you're making it all up. They'll think there's something wrong with you.

"What's wrong, mate?" Jeff wandered over to him. "You'll give yourself a neck injury throwing your head around like that."

"Oh." Austin grimaced. "Sorry. I didn't realize I was doing it. Um. Yeah. It's, uh. It's because... um... um," he floundered.

"Austin," Jeff smiled. "Although you're turning eleven next week, I've always considered you to be emotionally and mentally well past whatever age you were. Even when you were that little boy who loved clamping himself to my leg and swinging from it when I walked down the hallway. It's just the way you are. Hell, you're the biggest eleven-year-old I've ever seen. I can't remember being that tall when I was your age, and I swear you've grown an inch overnight as it is. But remember this. Anytime you need my help, a question answered, maybe about girls, you know, stuff like that, I'm always here for you. Whatever you're going through is normal, mate, and you don't have to do it alone. You're my son, and I love you very, very, much. Hey, us guys gotta stick together, right? Just don't tell your mother I said that or she'll make me sleep in the laundry with Duke."

Laughing hard, Austin pounced, grabbed him around the waist and squeezed tightly. "Thanks, Dad. You're the best." Releasing his father, he was now certain of how much he couldn't disclose, but a strong yearning to reciprocate the heartfelt words brought about one question his perplexed mind had pondered over after quenching his insatiable thirst. "Dad, there is something you can answer for me. Two things, actually. Without a spacesuit it's impossible to breath in outer space. Is that correct?"

"Yep, according to the clever people who study that sort of thing. I've always been under the impression it's a vacuum out there. No atmosphere, no oxygen, no breathing. Why? Are you thinking of becoming an astronaut? I'm pretty sure it's an extremely important thing to memorize if you do."

"No," Austin grinned. "It was just a thought I had. It might have come from some crazy dream, I dunno."

"A dream. Hmmm. You know, I must admit, I do like the sound of you being the one and only Cooper to reach outer space. NASA, for your next shuttle pilot, here he is." Jeff tousled his son's hair. "Next question, please. Maybe something more Earth-based, because that's about the limit on my knowledge of space, buddy. The whole universe, in fact."

"Yeah, this one is." Austin rubbed his backside. "Some of the stones on this driveway are really sharp. Why is it so rough? The one at Pauly's house is smooth."

"Well, Pauly's driveway is flat and short. It's not long or steep like ours, so they probably don't need an exposed aggregate finish like this. When it's wet, or if the concrete's got mold on it, we'd be slipping and sliding all over the place, so it gives a better grip not only for the car, but your feet as well. And thanks for the reminder. It's probably time we got out here with some brooms and mold remover."

Austin studied his father's beaming smile. "That's a big job, Dad. So it's a good thing I inspected it yesterday. No mold at all," he stated, shaking his head.

Jeff laughed. "I don't know where your sense of humor comes from. It can't be me. Hey, another big job is keeping the lawn under control and that's why I was looking for you." He waved the gloves. "But I think you need a bit of cheering up, so how about this. I'll mow the lawns, and when I'm finished, what do you say to us going fishing at the lake? You get the gear ready and we'll see if Mom can make us some lunch to take there."

"That sounds awesome. Can Pauly come, too?"

"Sure. You've gotta take your best mate. Give Wade and Joe a call, and see what they're doing. We can all make an afternoon of it. This'll be the day we catch the Legend Fish."

"Awesome!" Austin whooped. "Thanks, Dad." Looking up at Jeff, his eyes gleaming, he gave another constricting hug before racing off around the side of the house, the dream, and all its after-effects, very much forgotten.

*   *   *

From his chair on the patio, Austin watched the mower rattle noisily across the incline, heading left for the fence-line that separated the Evans and Cooper properties. On the ground at his feet, two fishing rods lay side by side next to an open, bright-red, plastic tackle box, its three collapsible trays expanded up and outward on their hinges, displaying a colorful array of different sized lures, dull gray sinkers, and sharp, shiny hooks. Returning a wave to his father, he continued checking the contents of a green and brown camouflage rucksack nestled on his lap, figuring the lawns would be finished in another half hour.

On the other side of the table, Dee sipped a cup of coffee and leafed through a thick magazine, while Stephanie sat cross-legged on the pavers, brushing Duke's hair. Stretched out close to her lap, the dog sighed, his blissful enjoyment of the pampering evident with his half-closed eyelids.

A sudden, streaming brightness made Austin tilt his head skyward to see the dense cloud cover slowly breaking apart, and as he squinted at the exposed sun, feeling its immediate warmth bathe his face, a fleeting image of the gargantuan, burning planet whizzed through his mind.

"Mmmm... finally," Dee murmured. She swept her dark hair over her shoulders and smiled at Austin. "Looks like the gods of fishing bless you with some beautiful weather after all. It's always nicer when it's sunny on your vacation, isn't it?"

"Yeah. Although I read somewhere that fish actually take the bait better if it is cloudy. Something about it being harder for them to tell whether it's real or not."

"Interesting." Dee nodded. "Well, I hope it doesn't spoil the trip."

"It won't," he grinned. "I can't wait to get out there. It's all Pauly talked about before school finished."

"You boys just bring your father back uninjured this time. Remember last year when he stuck that hook in his finger and it got all infected and yucky?"

"Poor Dad," Austin laughed. "I'm pretty sure he won't do it again."

"Hmmm. I hope so. But maybe you should keep an eye on him, just in case." Dee closed her magazine, drank the last of her coffee and rose, stretching her arms out wide. "I better get inside now, honey. My hungry men will need food on their quest for glory and it won't be too long before the lawn's finished. Don't forget to keep away from the ride-on, and make sure Stephie does, as well."

"Can I come inside, Mommy?"

"Sure, darling. You can help me make lunch."

"Okay." Stephanie patted Duke. "I've got to go and help Mommy." The instant she unfolded her legs the dog jumped up and peered expectantly at his owner, his large paws spread and his tail going berserk over the rump he threw high in the air.

Dee laughed. "I think he wants a game of chase the child on the bike."

"Awww... I'm sorry, Duke, I'm going inside. But Austin's here, he'll play."

With a soft sigh, Austin evaluated the picture of hope on his eight-year-old sister's face, witnessed it shining in her light-brown, milk-chocolate colored eyes, and deposited the bag next to his equipment. "No problem, Stephie," he smiled.

"Thank you."

As Dee slid the dining room door shut, she winked at her son through the glass and turned to follow Stephanie, who skipped toward the hall, her long, wavy black hair swinging across the mild bronze skin of her shoulders and neck.

"Come on, Dukey-boy," Austin warbled. Rising from his seat, he moved away from the table, plonked himself upon the pavers and hugged the dog's neck, stopping another bout of slobbering when Duke jumped into his lap. A decline in the mower's roar made him look toward his father.

"How are you going with the gear?" Jeff called, coasting the machine closer to the patio.

"All checked, Dad. I'll pack it up and then we're driving outta here. The only thing we need is some bait."

"Yeah, I was thinking we'll get it from the store after picking up Pauly and his dad. How does that sound?"

Austin grinned. "Sounds like we're going fishing."

"Do you need to ring Pauly, or will he be ready for us?"

"He'll be ready," he laughed. "Right now he's probably hopping up and down on the road outside his house."

"Okay. Another fifteen minutes, buddy. I've just got this bit to do." Jeff turned the mower around and pointed at a rectangular portion of uncut grass. In the middle, a large cherry tree grew about twenty feet from the paver's edge, planted there by both parents as a living symbol of the love for their children, something to watch and cherish while they all developed together.

The decision for which sort of tree had turned out to be a relatively easy achievement when the family visited a nursery in Pueblo one bitterly cold weekend, and wandered the long aisles, wrapped up snugly in defiance of a biting wind blowing in from the Rockies that week. Austin sauntered quietly alongside the stroller his father pushed, and with his small, gloved hand gripping the curved handle, he leaned forward, occasionally peering within to inspect his deeply slumbering sister.

"This is nice." Dee stopped by an assorted display of saplings and examined a label hanging from the trunk of a particularly robust example, standing about five feet tall. "It says it's a new variety, self-pollinating, very resilient, loves the cold and the sun, and in the spring it blossoms with the most beautiful flowers before yielding a delicious crop of deep-red cherries. Look at the photo."

Jeff stooped to inspect the tag. "Mmmm. It can grow up to thirty-five feet. Wow! But pruning them back still gives you lots of fruit. I like it, babe."

"It'll look gorgeous in the backyard, and think of all those yummy cherries. You know, the selling point for me is the name. It matches perfectly with the whole theme we wanted. Did you see what it was?"

"I sure did." Straightening, Jeff stroked his wife's cheek and smiled. "It's called Sweetheart."

Seven years of nurturing and vigorous growth had produced a superb, twenty-five foot specimen, spreading a magnificent canopy filled with fragrant, attractive blossoms every spring and bountiful crops for three summers. On the lowest branch dangled a Christmas gift from Susan and Greg, an exotic, intricately-made hanging ornament, comprising a metal ring and twelve variously-colored, solid-glass balls, each wrapped with a thin strand of wire and suspended at assorted positions around the ring's circumference by progressively differing lengths of thread, creating an enchantingly corkscrew, helical effect.

"Oooo... it's beautiful, Susan," Dee had gushed. Huddled outside with the children, blowing great, steamy breaths through the frigid, morning air, they watched while Jeff and Greg attached the decoration. "What an amazing design."

"I know," Susan nodded. "I absolutely love it. We bought one for the shop, as well. Greg calls it Mr. Twister." She rolled her eyes. "Give it a whirl, Jeff."

"Wheeeeee," Stephanie squealed, and clapped along with everyone when the ornament spun, its quick rotation flinging the longest-held balls out wide. They lit up and gleamed brilliantly as sunlight illuminated their depths, yet not so much at the present time, due to the broad, leafy shade hindering most of the sun's penetration, that and the fact it was near its highest point in the sky, and with only the odd glimmer coming off metal and glass, Jeff pushed the mower lever to full throttle, commencing the final patch of lawn. Half-turning in his seat at the sound of loud laughter, he saw Austin by the table, rubbing Duke's side briskly, and smiled when the hind leg waggled crazily in mid-air. Always a favorite with the family, they named it The Motorbike Maneuver, and Duke had the children in hysterics every time, for it was the exact motion of someone trying to kick-start an old motorbike engine.

Shaking his head, Jeff swiveled forward, giving the hanging ornament a solid knock with his shoulder when he passed, and while it swayed recklessly from side to side, the thread snapped on the lowermost ball, sending it tumbling into the uncut grass, unseen by father or son. Reaching the end of his straight run, he swung the ride-on to his left and circled the cherry tree, leaning over at the last second to check his distance from the trunk. In that brief instant, he missed a momentary ray of light break through the canopy and shine upon the pinky-hued, glass ball and its metal binding. As the mower ran right over the top, the hefty blades scooped it up and tossed it around under the forty-two-inch diameter cutting deck. At full power, 3,600 revolutions per minute, they shattered the glass and stripped away the encircling wire, fashioning it instantly into a somewhat straight, long, and wickedly-sharp arrow. Fired out at over 100 miles per hour, the projectile headed straight toward the patio, the young boy finishing the packing of their fishing gear, and the loyal, loving dog standing close to his side, curiously observing his activity.

They both spun to the deafening clatter, and Austin's eyes widened at a vision he hadn't seen or experienced for nearly six years. He saw his father's head, his body, bit by bit turning to the right, he saw the spray of grass, gradually dispersed from the mower's angled chute, intermixed with a myriad of tiny, twinkling objects. And he saw something larger, something glittering in the sunshine as it flew a few feet above the ground. Instinctively, he peered around the property, also expecting to see a smiling, hooded figure offering calm words of guidance, and his shoulders slumped at the apparently empty land. He was in this alone, with no one to help him.

Looking back at his father, he frowned. There's something different, he thought. It's like that day at the kindergarten, but there's something different. I can't really see through anything, they're more solid, and... and... things aren't moving slowly. It's quicker. Things are moving quicker than before! And what is that? It looks like a dart, or maybe... maybe a tiny arrow. Where's it come fro... oh no. No. No!

His heart skipped a beat with the realization that Duke still stared at Jeff and the mower, directly in front of the speeding object, and its target was not just the body, but on a billion-to-one, precise, unswerving trajectory with the dog's left eyeball. His blood chilled at the vision of it piercing the spherical structure, penetrating deep into the skull before coming to rest, impaled fatally in Duke's brain. It was only a couple of inches away, another second from impact.

Launching himself, he slammed into the dog's chest and wrapped his arms tightly around the fluffy coat, the force of the collision sending them crashing to the ground, where they cartwheeled over and over, Austin releasing his grip when Duke's rear end smashed into his solar plexus. On his back, gasping, fighting to draw breath against the pain and alarm, he screwed his eyes shut and tried to relax, remembering some reassuring advice from Greg, who had inadvertently winded him during a spontaneous game of rugby played in the backyard last summer.

A peculiar, gurgling sound made Austin roll on his side, and through the clouds of red dust billowing around him, he saw a strange, horrifying creature standing ten feet away. Massive claws raked the dirt before it suddenly lurched forward.

the valley

"What the hell was that?" Jeff reached for the mowing deck handle and wrenched it up fiercely, thumping the oval-shaped tray into the steel undercarriage with a loud clunk. Reversing the machine, he flicked the key, switching off the engine's roar, and leapt from the seat, grunting softly when his boots hit the ground. Ahead of him, only a few steps away, he spotted something twinkle in the shortened lawn and stooped to pick up a lump of broken glass, its edges razor-sharp when he touched them to the spongy pad of his finger. "What the hell?" he muttered and raked his boot over the ground, dislodging another small, jagged piece, then another, and another. "They're everywhere." Glancing at the empty patio, he went down on one knee and began picking up the fragments. "Where the hell have they... aahhhhhh." Jeff turned and scrutinized the gently winding ornament, a bit lopsided with the missing ball and its metal wrapping. "Dee," he called, searching the ground on his way forward. "DEE!" Bent over, he heard the faint scrape of the dining room door.

"What's up, honey?"

"Are Austin and Duke in there with you?"

"Not with me and Stephie. They could be upstairs, I guess. Are you almost ready?"

"No." He straightened. "Well, almost. But something's happened. Can you see if Austin's in there and then come take a look at this."

He heard her voice from deep within the house, and after a minute, she reappeared. "I can't find them. They're not in here. I thought they were still outside with you."

"So did I. Maybe they're somewhere out front. That's where I found them after breakfast. Hey, have a look at this. But put some shoes on, babe."

Dee scuffed her feet on the pavers as she slipped into a pair of sandals sitting alongside a cluster of footwear they kept outside in the summertime. Approaching her husband, she examined his furrowed brow. "What's wrong?" she asked, and stared at the particles in Jeff's sweaty palm when he held it out. "What are they?"

"They're the remains of a glass ball from our cherry tree ornament. I knocked it with my shoulder when I was mowing and it must have fallen off. I think the weather's decayed the string, the way it's just broken like that, and... well, this is what's left after I ran over it."

"Oh my God," Dee breathed. "That's bad."

"I know. It's all over the lawn and I can't find the wire that was coiled around it. It could be anywhere. I don't want it getting stuck in the kids' feet or Duke's paw when they're running around out here." He suddenly brightened. "Maybe it's under the mower, you know, on the blades or something. I never thought to check."

"Okay, honey. You check it, I'm going around the front to look for Austin. Where did you see him last?"

"Over there." Jeff pointed at the table. "He was doing the..." A silvery flash had him trotting across to one of the chairs with Dee on his heels, and as they hunched down, side by side, they turned their heads to each other, wide-eyed. Embedded about a half inch in the wooden armrest was the thick, straightened wire, shining in the midday sun, light shimmering up and down its sharpened length as Jeff pulled it free. "Shit," he fizzed, rotating it in front of them. "This could have seriously injured them. This could have killed them." With a trembling voice, he looked at his wife. "And they were near. In this area, Dee. Not long before it happened. Right when it happened." Jumping up, he spun a tight circle. "AUSTIN! AUSTIN! AUUUUSTIIIIIIN!"

Stephanie burst onto the patio, drawn by the raucous bellows. "Mom? Dad?" She stared at her parents. "What's wrong?"

"Nothing."

"Who yelled?"

"Dad."

"Why?" She looked around the backyard. "Where's Duke?"

"I don't know."

"Where's Austin?"

Dee rounded on Stephanie, her light-brown eyes flashing. "I don't know. Jeez!" Heaving a sigh, she rubbed her face with both hands. "I'm sorry, sweetie. They've gone for a walk and now Dad's going to get them. Okay?"

"Okay."

"I'll be inside soon, just go and watch some TV. Immediately." The note of finality in her closing word stopped Stephanie's opening mouth. She snapped it shut and crept away, taking a single glance over her shoulder.

"Jeff." Dee turned. He saw tears racing down her cheeks, spilling down the front of her tee-shirt. "Find our son. Find our dog," she implored as he wrapped his arms around her. "Please."

"I will, babe. Austin's a good, strong, brave kid, who knows how to look after himself. I'll find him, I will. You'll see." He pulled back and gazed deeply into her eyes, his heart breaking at the anguish contained within. "Sweetheart, everything will be fine, I promise you that, and when I've found him, you can spank his naughty bottom. Just leave enough of his ass for me to whip by bringing home the Legend Fish later. He'll be sore about that for a long time." Smiling broadly, he wiped her tears away.

She couldn't help but laugh. "Okay. I'm going to ring Henry. Maybe he's next door. I'll ring Pauly, as well, he might have gone there, and also..."

"Dee." Jeff stroked her cheek tenderly. "I doubt he's next door. In fact, with all my screaming, the whole neighborhood's probably wondering what the hell is going on. Let's not create too much panic. Not yet. Give me a half hour and if I haven't found him in that time, then you can call as many people as you want. I bet him and Duke are just up the road, anyway. So look after Stephie, and we'll all be back soon. Open the garage door, and bring the car keys and my cell phone. They're on my desk in the den. I'll meet you round the front."

Her hand on his forearm halted a quick pirouette. "After you bring them home, do something about that ornament, Jeff. Replace the string, or whatever you've got to do, I don't care. Just make sure this doesn't happen again. Ever."

Nodding his accord, Jeff sprinted for the corner of the house as Dee ran inside.

*   *   *

While Austin stared, he weighed up his chances of escape. And judging by the creature's appearance, they were nil. Four short and stocky legs supported a lofty, bulky frame of hardened muscles. They bulged under a slimy-looking, pale pink skin, completely hairless and mottled with angry, dark blotches, some small, the size of a dime, others bigger than his hand. The creature dug the ground again, plowing red soil aside with three thick, ebony-colored claws, curving high from its huge paws. Stretching its jaws open, it released a fat, luminescent-green tongue that flopped out over pitch-black, needle-point teeth, and uttered a harsh, rattling groan, emanating from deep within its throat as it stepped forward.

With an icy cold pain jolting through his still-convulsing abdomen, Austin scrabbled in the dust, raising more clouds when his arms and legs pistoned him backward, but paused when it collapsed, crashing to the ground with a swift, heavy thud. He watched the body arc while a stumpy, rear leg scratched at its neck, the action growing weaker with each stroke. Halfheartedly, the creature raised its head, locking its vision on the boy, and as a shudder passed through it, Austin heard the smallest of tinkles over the blood pumping in his ears. Frowning, his breathing rapid and shallow, he peered at the beast. There was something distinctly familiar about its yellowish-brown eyes, and recognition struck him with the force of a freight train. He knew this creature. He knew it very well. Springing to his feet, Austin rushed across and threw himself down at its side.

"Duke?" A liquidy gurgle answered his crackling whisper. The animal lifted a trembling paw and laid it feebly upon his thigh. "DUKE!" he screamed. "WHAT'S WRONG?"

Apart from his gentle, friendly and fun-loving eyes, everything about the dog had changed. He was gigantic. Taller, longer than the biggest, fully grown Great Dane, more the size of a large pony, and another wheezy, labored sigh had Austin mentally kicking himself for not identifying the problem sooner.

The collar, he thought. It's strangling him. That noise I heard. It was his bell!

With the neck way out of proportion to its usual size, the band had vanished beneath two engorged folds of skin, and as he groped between the rolls, a potent stench overwhelmed him, filling his nostrils. Coughing, he gave silent thanks when his slippery, fumbling fingers found the collar's sturdy plastic buckle and side latches, and he pressed them in, feeling the strap detach. Wrenching it free, he hurled it to one side, where it wheeled away across the ground, picking up a layer of red dust over the dark-brown leather and jingling bell.

"Duke, come on," Austin pleaded. "Breathe. Please!" He shook the animal forcefully and gave it a solid thump on the shoulder. Straight away, it gulped in a great lungful of air, the eyelids flickered open, and with each inhalation, its revival strengthened. Austin sat back heavily, watching the chest rise and fall. Closing his eyes, he let out a great sigh and dropped his head, raising it at a sudden scraping and loud snort. Duke was struggling upright, his movements wobbly and fatigued.

"Take it easy, boy," Austin cautioned, hauling himself to his feet. Licking his lips, he took a few rearward steps when the animal turned its head at the sound of his voice and stumbled across to him. "Sit. Sit, Duke," he ordered, smiling at the obeyed command. "Now stay. Don't move." He waggled a finger and began circling the panting beast, which was very similar to some of the cartoon monstrosities he and Pauly saw in comic books or watched on television when they stayed the night at each other's house. "Holy crap, you're up to my neck. And where's your tail? It's gone." Austin paused at the missing appendage and leaned in to inspect the clear, mucus-like substance flowing slowly down the dog's body. Mixed with red dust, it shimmered in the dreary light and dripped off the torso in long, glutinous strands that pooled under the animal. Realizing he had already touched it, Austin sniffed his palms hesitantly. "Aw, yuck," he burbled, and wiped them vigorously on his shorts, his face a screwed-up grimace. "Jeez, you smell like rotten eggs. A load of really rotten eggs. You are one ugly, stinky critter."

Continuing his walk to the front, he studied the changed ears, which looked nothing like their usual, upright elegance. These resembled two strange, shriveled half-donuts stuck to the side of an enormous head, triangular in shape and absurdly large for the body. While he studied them Duke yawned, spreading his muzzle extremely, frighteningly wide, exposing the razor-sharp teeth yet again. Black and shiny, the bottom row curled in slightly, allowing the top set to slide past his closing mouth, and a shiver raced along Austin's spine at the sight. There was one purpose and no questioning the reason for this physique. Running, attacking, overpowering. Shredding. He was an outright killing machine.

"Dukey-boy," Austin murmured, gazing into the bright, beautiful eyes, alert and full of life once more. "That body might be freaking gross, but it's a good thing your personality's still the same, and it's a good thing I know you, 'cos if it was any different…" He whistled. "I think I'd be in big trouble."

At the shrill noise, Duke jumped up, shook his backside, sending syrupy strings of goo flying through the air, then scampered about, his giant maw open and the green tongue flapping up and down. Broad at its base, the long, fleshy organ narrowed to a quick and spiky, pointed end.

"So," Austin laughed, watching the muscles ripple under the blotchy, pinkish skin on its powerful back and shoulders. "The main question now is, where are we?"

Warily, he examined the surroundings. On one side, a dusty, flat land seemed to go forevermore, barren and dry, the vastness of it unbelievable, while far on the opposite horizon, a line of mountains soared upward, their colossal, craggy peaks looking cleaved, chiseled and sharp, even from that distance. The entire range was so immense the Rockies were like gentle hills in comparison, but without the spectacular display of white, pristine snow Austin admired when viewing it from the very rear of his home. In the middle, rising higher than any others, one summit appeared relatively level, as if the top had been sliced off with a giant knife, and everything, everywhere, was the same monotonous, reddish-bronze. Although the terrain gave the impression of a sweltering, arid desert, it wasn't overly hot, just a comfortable enough temperature.

Looking up at the cloudless sky, a dour gray like the ashes of a cold and lifeless fire, Austin saw the only break in its unceasing dreariness, a dim, orange sun, yet nothing like the star he was accustomed to, for this one burned farther out in space, a small dot progressing slowly and visibly across the heavens. With a lingering sigh, he stirred his tongue inside his parched mouth before calling out to the dog, who roamed the vicinity around them, sniffing the air and ground. "Duke, I don't think we're in Colorado anymore. And it's no use staying here, so we may as well start walking. I think we should go this way." He pointed toward the mountains. "At least there's something to look at."

*   *   *

The cell phone rang, and as Jeff snatched it up, ending a piercing chirp that split the stillness, Dee's strained voice sounded at once, overriding the unspoken greeting on his lips.

"Have you got him?"

"Not yet, honey, I'm still looking. I haven't checked the whole neighborhood and it's a big area to cover."

"Okay, I'm ringing Henry to ask if he can drive around. I think we'll find him quicker that way." A tinge of panic resonated through the speaker.

"It's only been fifteen minutes, babe. Give me five more and I'll probably find him. Please. Besides, he can't have gotten far, it's not like he's in a car."

"But he could be, Jeff. We don't know that. What if he's been abducted?"

"Dee, there is no way in hell Austin would let that happen. Are you kidding me? And the dog would probably rip their arm off if someone tried it." Exhaling noisily, he softened his tone. "He's a big, athletic guy, who's got a good head on his shoulders, and he'll be fine. Honey, Stephie needs you to be strong, and so do I. Okay?"

"But... but," she sobbed. "This is completely out of character for him. Why would he do this? He just wouldn't. Something must have happened. You always say there's a reason for everything, don't you?"

"I know, babe." He rubbed his forehead. "I know. And we'll find out what that is when he's home. Okay, look. Ring Henry. Ring Greg and Suze. I'll ring Pauly's folks, although I'm sure he's not there. If you want everyone involved now, then let's do it."

"Jeff."

"Yes, sweetheart?"

"I love you."

*   *   *

As Austin detected an extremely minor variation with the landscape he froze, kneeled in the dust and tilted his head. "Mmmm," he hummed, studying the ground ahead. "Dukey-boy, something's wrong. You stay, I'll check it out." He looked at the creature while it sauntered to his side and plonked down on its haunches with a wide-open, panting mouth and rivers of slime flowing freely over its body. "I know, buddy, I'm thirsty too. But we've only been walking about... I dunno... twenty minutes... so maybe we'll find some water soon." He moved off and turned, still strolling backward, when Duke got up to follow. "No. Stay. Sit." The dog lowered himself again at the return of the wagging finger. "Good boy. I'm just going over here." Austin hooked a thumb over his shoulder. "I'll be back in a minute."

Forty feet from where they stopped, the consistently reddish terrain gave a dangerous optical illusion of uninterrupted flatness for hundreds of miles, all the way to the base of the mountain range, and Austin slowed his pace when the land suddenly ended at a cliff edge. Breathing a sigh of relief for spotting the anomaly, he dropped to his belly and crawled forward, approaching the rim cautiously. Below him, he peered into a huge, perfectly squared trench, a thousand foot deep and at least that wide, extending left and right as far as he could see, matching the span of the mountains sitting on the opposite plateau.

"That has gotta be the weirdest valley ever," he muttered. With the miniscule sun now directly overhead, a momentary flash in the abyss caught his attention. Squinting, he focused on a multitude of scattered objects, barely distinguishable against the identically colored floor, and although the height was great, he recognized some familiar enough shapes amid the chaotic jumble occupying the imposing depth. "Look at them all," he whispered. "Planes. Boats. Ships. Holy crap, there must be hundreds. How did they get here?"

Inching closer, his shoulders just clearing the lip, he looked straight down the sheer cliff face, and deemed the climb an impossible task. Even with the possibility of hand and footholds on some of the exposed rocky layers, the notion of such a descent made him break out in a cold sweat.

And I can't leave Dukey-boy, he thought. We need to look after each other. Jeez, what if we'd been more tired? Or distracted? Or if it was dark? We'd have fallen right in!

Waves of dizziness washed over him, and shivers raced up his spine as he scuttled away from the edge. Rolling onto his back, trying to swallow a lump in his throat, he gazed at the dreary sky, wondering what they were going to do next.

A few seconds later, he heard the voice.

*   *   *

"Hi, Jeff. No, we haven't found him yet," Susan blurted to the unasked question. "Honey, I think Greg should take me to your place."

"Why?" Jeff's fingers tightened on his phone while the uneasiness inside him grew. "What's wrong, Suze?"

"Dee's really upset. I just called her and she won't stop crying. Even I started when she said she wants her baby back. I think she's determined to join the search."

"Okay. Ummm." He pulled the car over and stared through the windshield. In front of him, parked under a mass of towering trees, the bleak shadows mirrored his soul. "Is Greg okay with that?"

"Of course he is. Listen. We'll head back. Dee needs some adult company right now and someone needs to be around in case Austin turns up at home. Hang on, Greg wants to talk to you."

Jeff heard a staticy, electrical scratching as the cell changed hands.

"Gidday, mate. Where are you?"

"Close to the shop on East Lake Road," Jeff answered. "I've already asked them to keep an eye out for Austin and Duke, so I thought I'd pop in there again."

"Great idea, brother. They've got a pretty good view of what goes in and out. Hey, if it's okay with you, I think Suze should be with Dee. There's enough of us looking for him right now and if need be we can all do it in shifts. I also think it's time to bring the cops in on this. Henry's gonna call in some favors and he told me they'll want a recent photo, so I'll get it when I drop her off."

Jeff glanced at the digital clock. "Okay, mate," he sighed. "Thanks."

the tooth

At the start, Austin thought it came from the dusty landscape around him. Sitting up quickly, he stared at the surroundings, and his heart hammered violently when he realized the murmur came from inside his head. One voice spoke, the words soft, ancient, evil. They crackled like desiccated paper squeezed slowly in a closing fist, the inflection jeering and condemning.

"Human. I see you. We see you."

"Yes. Human. We see you. Yes. We feel you. We smell you. Yes."

Now, more sounded, a few at first, but others joined, rapidly growing in volume as they multiplied, until it seemed there were millions of them, all entwined, and rolling over the top of each other to form a single, sinister, unnerving speech.

For a moment, there was silence, then the single voice began again, raw, abrasive, and with a renewed vigor that shrank Austin's spirit.

"You come here. To my domain. Our domain."

"*Yes. You come to us. Yes.*"

"And where is the Keeper? Where is the Shard?"

"*Yes. Where is your guardian? Where is the All, the First? Where is it?*"

"The human is alone. He is unchanged."

"*Yes. Alone. Yes. Unchanged. Yes.*"

"No Keeper. No Shard. Be mine. Be ours."

"*Yes. Ours. Yes. But he can defeat us. The Keeper. Will destroy us. Yes. Your friend, master. Our friend. Destroyed. Yes.*"

"FOOLS," the voice roared. "Enough! I AM the defeater. I AM the destroyer."

"*Yes. You, master. You. Yes.*"

"No error. Not this time. I want the Shard. It is mine. I need it. Restore me. It can be mine, will be mine. Again. Like before."

"*Yes. Before. The All. The First. Yes. Again. Yes.*"

"The human is alone. It has started. We have him. He will come."

"*Yes. Alone. Have him. Yes. Alone. Yes. Alone. Alone. Alone. Alone. Alone.*"

The voices chanted the same thing over and over, getting faster with each turn. All of sudden, they stopped, and then that one voice spoke for the final time.

"Take him," it crooned.

"*Yes. Take him. Yes. Take him. Take him. Take him. Take him. TAKE HIM!*"

They resonated with pure triumph, and Austin sprang to his feet, a chill blade of horror stabbing at his core. He searched the flat wasteland they had travelled, but there was nothing at all except Duke, who also leapt up and prowled forward, a low, rumbling growl coming from deep within his massive throat.

An abrupt, severe boom came from behind Austin. He flinched at the intenseness and squatted instinctively, his head drawn low. It was like an enormous clap of thunder, although a thousand times more powerful and louder than anything he had ever experienced, and he spun around on hands and feet, staring at the mountains as the reverberation rolled on and on across the plain. Duke gave one loud, forceful bark, a formidable noise compared to his usual self, as if in warning for Austin to retreat from so close to the edge of the precipice. From the towering, flat peak, great, dark shapes appeared, rushing through the air toward them. It was hard to tell how many, and one raced ahead of the others, coming at a velocity that turned it to an indistinct blur.

"Duke." Austin staggered away from the cliff edge. "RUN! COME ON!"

Even with the shouted command he knew that fleeing was hopeless, they would be on them in seconds. But he pushed off with adrenaline-charged legs anyway, turning and sprinting all at once, and his heart sank after two, long strides when the thing thudded to the ground twelve feet in front. Skidding to a stop, he lost his balance and dropped backward with the monster looming over him.

In his scant, momentary sight, Austin thought it could have resembled an enormous bat, but he wasn't sure, as its huge wings were still spread and beating rapidly after alighting. They whipped up a thick cloud of dust that carried over him, cloaking the creature and making him throw an arm up defensively, his eyes shut tight against the onslaught of wind and soil. Struggling to draw clean breath, he choked and coughed, and in that instant, felt something grip his right upper arm firmly, painfully, just when the thing lifted off the plateau, dragging his body with it.

Something dry and rough wrapped itself around his head, rasping over the skin on his cheeks and forehead. He gagged uncontrollably as scorched dust penetrated his open mouth, clogging his already struggling lungs. Terror flared at the feeling of suffocation, and with his free arm, he clawed unsuccessfully at the coarse, lumpy membrane enveloping his face, his legs kicking and thrusting at thin air while it tightened even more. A multitude of bright, milky lights popped behind his closed eyelids, at the exact moment when he heard a resounding, bellowing roar, followed instantaneously by a savage sideways jerk and ear-piercing screech. Immediately, the thing released its grip, and Austin plummeted into the chasm. No more than two minutes ago he had experienced extreme giddiness at a brief and frightening vision of toppling over that cliff, and his body stiffened with the nightmare now a reality. Tumbling end over end, he caught swift, spinning glances of the rock face and the dark creature hovering above him.

As he spun, an intense whiteness flashed within his vibrant, purple-blue eyes, just before something peculiar happened. He felt warmth spark deep in his body. Like the speeding wire earlier, a thin and slender thread of concentrated heat coursed through the middle of his arms, legs, head, and torso, and in the split second it took for him to understand his fall had slowed considerably, a heavy weight slammed into his shoulders, halting the spiraling motion and pinning him face forward, staring at the valley floor and its collection of reddened, tarnished treasures, growing steadily larger while the hundreds of feet decreased.

Austin whipped his head around, furious and ready to fight the thing from taking another hold of him. It was Duke. He glimpsed a wild-eyed stare before the dog whimpered and slid off his back, a long, thick black object hanging from his clenched mouth and his legs pedaling furiously as he dropped quickly away. With a final check on the floating creature, noting the arrival of many others, Austin tucked his arms and legs in tight at the side, just like Superman did in his movies, and plunged headfirst after the animal, unsure why the things were now holding back, reluctant to seize them. Nearing Duke, he spread his arms wide, feeling the dive decelerate again, and thumped lightly into the large, slimy body. He grabbed hold of one muscular foreleg and slithered onto the animal's back, encircling his legs around the narrower stomach area. Gripping on with all his strength, Austin clutched at the broad neck and reached around to grasp the tough, leathery object still clamped between Duke's sharp teeth. About four foot long and as thick as his arm, it looked like the jointed limb from a giant spider, and he shuddered at the disgusting sensation of tiny, tingling prickles on his palm.

"DUKE, LET GO," he hollered, tugging strongly. "DROP IT!"

When the dog somewhat unwillingly opened his mouth, Austin tossed it away, and brought his arm back just in time to interlock the fingers on his other hand before they thudded softly upon a grassy embankment and slithered down, coming to rest at the bottom of a natural, moss-strewn culvert. They stayed there, taking mighty, puffing mouthfuls of air, exhausted, overwhelmed and with no thoughts of disentangling themselves.

Eventually, after a few minutes, Duke stirred and writhed his way out of Austin's hold to stretch and sniff the new surroundings. Austin raised his head and gazed at the dog, confirming a fact he had been conscious of while they caught their breath. Duke was perfectly normal again, albeit a very filthy looking and revoltingly smelling normal. The remains of the mucus substance, already drying and encrusted with dust, flattened the fur in places, while in others it stuck straight up, and his reinstated tail wagged madly behind him, the bushy appendage the only thing that appeared unsullied.

Austin heaved himself upright on shaking legs and turned to inspect a thick forest, inhaling its fresh, cool air, and incredibly grateful for the piney tang that now permeated his airways. Barely discernible through the trees, orange, pink, and golden hues heralded a low-lying sun, and somewhere overhead, a flock of noisy birds flapped past, their caws dwindling as they disappeared across the sky.

Duke padded up to him, snuffled a moist nose to his knee and followed it with a gentle lick. As Austin knelt, taking the dog's head in his hands, he noticed a sizeable trickle of crimson-red staining the jawline on the bottom, right-hand side. "Duke. You saved my life. Thank you." No sooner had he spoken, then Duke laid a paw upon his thigh once again, and when Austin clasped the soiled fur, he received another single flick of the scratchy tongue. "Good boy," he chuckled. "Let me have a look in your mouth, Dukey." Stroking the muzzle gently at first, he pried the jaws open to reveal a blood-filled hole where a long, curved, fang should have resided. "Awww, jeez," he whispered. "That looks sore. But you got it, Dukey. You ripped a piece right off that thing. You're a good, good boy!" Austin jumped up, narrowly avoiding another flurry of licks. Laughing loudly, he stared at the embankment. "Hey," he grinned, glancing back at the woods. "I think I know where we are. I think we're home."

Slipping on the damp grass, he ran up the slope, the dog loping along beside him, and reached the top to find a bitumen road that stretched either way into the darkening distance. "Yeah!" he whooped loudly, pumping a fist into the air. "Duke, this is East Lake Road. Lake Crescent isn't far from here." He pointed to the right, where the black tar crested slightly before dipping away, roughly a mile farther on. "It shouldn't take us that long to get home. An hour, maybe a bit more. But there's no way I'm running, Dukey. I'm too tired and thirsty." He looked at the dog. "And I know you are. We better move, 'cos I've got a lot of explaining to do when we're back. Come on, boy." Austin turned and began walking, with Duke plodding along at his heels, the pair oblivious to the black, spider-like limb hidden within a patch of soggy pine needles lying thirty feet back among the trees. Illumination, the last, stray beam of light to pierce the dense foliage, glistened momentarily on something lodged deep near a knuckle-like joint. Something long, curved, and white.

"That place really freaked me out, Duke. I mean, what the heck was that all about? Where were we? How did we get there? How did we get out of there? And what happened to you? Jeez, I wish that dude was here. He'd know what was..."

A faint noise behind him, a low, mechanical rumbling, made Austin stop. Peering over his shoulder, he saw the twin headlamps of an approaching car, the dimly glowing lights bobbing up and down as it trundled along the gently undulating terrain, and for a moment he considered sticking his thumb out, just like the odd hitchhiker he sometimes spotted in and around town.

His parents always drove straight past them, and he would watch as the arm sank to their side, the thumb still sticking out while the look on their face turned to one of pure misery and rejection.

"Why don't we give this guy a lift, Dad?" Austin had asked one Saturday afternoon when they journeyed home from a washed-out baseball game and passed a particularly sodden, bedraggled individual, trudging dejectedly through the pouring rain. "Son, there's a good reason for that. It's because we don't know who they are. They could be... dangerous. I know it might not seem a nice thing to do, especially in this sort of weather, but unfortunately that's how things are nowadays, and I've got to be careful if you and Stephie are in the car with me. I did do it all the time and it never used to be like this. Not when I was your age, anyway. Jeez, listen to me. I'm sounding more like your grandfather every day."

Austin examined himself. He must have looked terrible to anyone passing by. Everything about him was utterly filthy, from the disgusting goo on his hair, skin, and clothes, the remains stiffening each second, to the thick coating of dust covering him completely. With the grimy dog standing by his side, he resigned himself to the fact he was walking the whole way, thumb or no thumb, and his brow rose when the car slowed, pulled into the left lane, and stopped three feet away. Stepping back several paces, scrutinizing the darkly tinted windows, he felt relief wash over him when the door opened and a familiar figure stepped out.

"Austin! Oh boy, what happened to you?" Wide-eyed, the driver looked the disheveled boy up and down. "You look like something the cat dragged in and then beat the living hell out of." He sniffed the air. "And you reek! What is that? Burnt hair? Sulfur? Come on, son, let's get you home. Everyone's worried sick. You and Duke hop in."

"Hi, Mr. Evans. Uhhh..." Austin frowned at the immaculate, silver vehicle. "Is this your car? Is it new?"

"Yep. Just bought it yesterday," he beamed, patting the roof. "Do you like it?"

"Yeah, it's really nice." Austin glanced down at himself. "I dunno, Mr. Evans, we're pretty dirty." He shook his head. "I don't think we should get in, we'll get stuff everywhere."

"Please, Austin, you're old enough to call me Henry. And any mess in the car is the smallest problem I'd ever have if I were to leave you here. I'm quite sure your mother would take great joy in creating numerous methods in which to slowly and painfully torture me. Hop in," he chuckled. "Don't worry, I'll have it detailed on Monday. Come on, I'm under strict orders to ring if I found you and the longer we're here the more trouble we'll be in."

"Okay. But I don't think you're the one in trouble." He scanned the murky sky. "Why is it getting so dark?"

"Are you all right? Have you taken a knock to the old noodle?" Moving closer, Henry peered at the boy's head. "Austin, that's not an eclipse we're going through. It's just on nighttime. Son, you've been missing for eight hours."

*   *   *

With an unsteady hand, Austin deposited Henry's cell phone into a recessed slot below the radio. "Mom's ringing everyone now. She sounded really angry."

"It'll be okay," Henry assured him. "She's been very worried. Everyone's been worried. You've had a few search parties out and about today. Pauly and his father. Your dad. Me. I think Susan and Greg are still at the other side of the lake, as far as I know. Even my good buddies at the department have got a patrol car roaming the town."

"I'm really sorry I caused all of this." Sinking farther in his seat, Austin stared out the window at the dark scenery flashing by, silent the whole trip, and his nervousness swelled to epic proportions when they accelerated up the steep driveway to his family waiting beyond the open garage door. He saw Stephanie hopping from one foot to the other, wringing her hands together before swatting at a large moth attracted by the fluorescent strip lighting that bathed them all in its brightly dispersed glow. The moment the car stopped, Dee was there, flinging the door wide and physically pulling him to her. He felt her body quiver as she sobbed, and saw his father and Henry embracing, the two of them grinning from ear to ear.

"Ewwwww... you're soooo dirty and smelly, Duke." Stephanie's nose wrinkled while she bustled around her pet. "Dad," she yelped. "Dad, he's got blood on him."

"Steph, it's all right, we'll sort it out after." Jeff grabbed Austin, wrapped his arms around him tightly and rocked him from side to side. Releasing his grip, he stepped back and wiped some of the muck from his son's chin. "Are you hurt? Are you okay? Tell me."

"I'm okay, Dad. Really. It's Duke who's hurt. He's lost a tooth."

"A tooth?" Stephanie howled.

"Stephie, please, we'll see to Duke in a minute. He'll be fine." Jeff was still gazing at Austin, evaluating the scruffiness.

Dee stood at Henry's side with her arm around his waist and rubbed his shoulder before moving to Austin. "What happened?" she asked softly, pushing her fingers through his stiff hair. "Where have you and Duke been all this time?"

Austin swallowed. Here it was. The moment he had been dreading since his observation of the setting sun, and he dropped his sight to the driveway, ready to tell the biggest lie of his life. Everything the hooded man said rang true, they would never accept his reality, what really occurred. It was implausible, preposterous, and the foolish, immature sounding of fact, to stand there and insist that world, those voices and creatures were real would lose the trust of his family and friends, and he loved them all far too much to gamble with that prospect. Although the thought of deceiving his parents this way made him feel physically ill, he knew deep in his heart he had no other choice.

"Duke ran away, Mom," he began. "We were by the table and I think Dad hit something with the mower. It made a lot of noise and that's what scared him. The next thing I knew he just took off and I ran after him. He's really fast, you know. He went all the way down to the lake and up the hill on the other side. I called and called, but he wouldn't stop." He looked his mother right in the eye. "I couldn't leave him alone out there." The words flowed naturally, which both surprised and upset him even more.

Dee shook her head and threw a withering glance of blame at Jeff. His brow furrowed. "Dee, I didn't know it was on the..."

Another scornful glare stopped him cold, and Austin jumped in, eager to prevent any squabbles that might develop. "Mom, it's not Dad's fault. Not at all. He didn't do it on purpose, it was an accident."

"Mmmm." Her shoulders slumped. "I know. I'm sorry, babe," she apologized, looking at her husband. "It's just been one hell of a day. A day I'd rather forget."

"You're telling me. Holy cow!" Austin exclaimed, blushing and grinning when the surrounding adults burst out laughing.

"How did you get so filthy?" Jeff chuckled.

There was no going back now, and although Austin hated it, he thought he might as well make the story as convincing as possible. "Well, somewhere in the forest we both rolled down this bank. Actually, he more dragged me down there after I finally got a hold of him, and then we fell into this huge pile of garbage. And man, did it stink. There was all sorts of stuff lying around. It took us ages to get back to the road, and it wasn't too long after that when Mr. Evans found us. I mean, Henry." He smiled at his neighbor.

"Austin. Where's Duke's tooth? His collar's gone as well. He had his beautiful bell on it."

"I don't know, Stephie. They're probably with all the garbage."

"Don't worry, darling," Jeff said. "We'll take Duke to a vet first thing in the morning, and get him a brand new collar, okay?"

"Okay," she beamed. "A blue one. And he'll need another bell, too. Can we give him a bath now? He smells really bad. So do you, Austin! But thanks for looking after Duke. I knew he'd be all right with you." She grimaced at her brother. "I think I'll give you a hug when you're clean."

Henry Evans rubbed his hands together. "This is a great result. All's well that ends well. So, I'll be heading off since I've got such a long trip home."

"Thanks again, Henry. And leave the cleaning of your car to me. It's the least I can do after all your help."

"Anytime, Jeff. Come over tomorrow and have a proper look at this thing." They watched while the car reversed and waved as he pulled into his driveway next door.

"Stephie, bring Duke inside and we'll have a look at his mouth. Austin, mate, Suze and Greg should be here very soon, and you've never needed a shower more than right now, you big stinky bum. After that, Pauly wants to you to ring him. I'm sorry I screwed up your day, son. We'll go fishing next weekend. That's a promise."

"You didn't screw anything up. It's pretty obvious that weird things can happen, but I'm hoping they don't happen anymore. I really thought you and Mom would be mad at me."

"I'm sorry if I came across like that," Dee said, stroking his cheek. "I think tonight your father and I will be talking very seriously about two subjects. A cell phone for you, and something to keep that naughty Duke from running off."

"It's not his fault either, Mom. He's been a great friend. You wouldn't believe how much we've helped each other today."

"Just never disappear without warning again, buddy. You don't have to do that stuff by yourself." Jeff laid his hand on Austin's shoulder. "Let us know first. I'm sure we'd all like to be a part of your adventures."

"No, Dad." Austin shook his head and smiled. "I don't think you would."

the lightning

Huddled on a throne-like chair, a man absentmindedly stroked the bushy whiskers of his dark beard while staring at the creamy-colored object in his left hand. Usually clear, he had never seen it this way, and he watched, fascinated, as small, bright sparks of gold and silver swelled within the cloudiness, counteracting erratic flares of a sinister, ebony-black that struck like miniature lightning, sending thin, spiky branches blazing their way through the interior. And each time it occurred, a growing frown wrinkled his forehead.

Around him, a huge feast was in progress. Essentially a custom held for dignitaries, this was an extra-special banquet, for an extra-special person, as the inhabitants considered him a deity, and eons had passed since his last visit. Periods so long that not one individual remained alive, only records noting the honor, and as a result, wild celebrations followed his arrival. By his measurement of time, the festivities had been going close to five days now, and would almost certainly continue for at least another week.

Gazing out at the proceedings from a large dais preserved specifically for him, he reached down, lifted a large, tan satchel onto his lap, and placed the object between the folds of a neatly wrapped, dark robe stored inside. While smoothing the thick material flat his eyes shone a deep, sky-blue and his long, ruffled hair tumbled back when his head tilted to the sky. In a flash, he stood, gripping the bag tightly, his knuckles white through the honey-brown skin of his hands. "The boy," he rasped. "Where are you? That's... that's impossible. What is this?" His eyes widened. "I've come too far." Slinging the satchel over his shoulder, he moved forward, the bizarre garments he wore flowing with his progress, stretching and widening the russet and indigo colors while they shifted and formed to his body. "Friends," he declared, motioning to the enormous gathering. "I thank you for your hospitality. It pleases me greatly." He spoke in their native tongue, a series of chirps and clacks to the human ear, the high and low notes emphasizing certain words. The mastering of their dialect had taken many lifetimes, made possible only with their patience and respect. "This feast delights me, as does your narration. The Annals of the Ancients imparts remarkable wisdom, and I thank you once more. However, it is with the utmost regret that I inform you of my immediate departure, for I am needed elsewhere."

A resonant, collective moan soared before subsiding to a sad and delicate sigh. But no more than that, for his announcements were decree, and never questioned.

"I will return," he continued. "Soon. Your knowledge is vast and there is much to learn. Care for your young." Raising both arms to the pasty, purple sky, he inscribed a grand circle around his body. "Your young shall care for you."

The crowd acknowledged his use of their formal incantation, although sorrow clearly showed in their replicated speech and action. They watched as his eyes blazed an intense, blinding white, visible even to those a great distance away. And then he was gone.

Chapter Nine

The Surprise

"Who's that?" Stephanie asked. She nudged her brother's arm and looked up at him, her light-brown eyes sparkling when they caught the late afternoon sunshine.

"I don't know." Shaking his head, Austin watched as a large, shiny, red pickup turned from their driveway and rumbled away down the road. "Hey, Dad's already home." He pointed to the house while they stepped onto the grass and tramped diagonally across the property, heading for their father, who stood outside the open garage door, waving at them.

"My sometimes favorite offspring," Jeff called. Loosening his dark-blue, stripy tie, he smiled at their approach. "How was school?"

"Good thanks, Dad," Stephanie chirped.

"It was okay. But I'm glad there's only one week left," Austin grinned. "We've got loads of fishing to get in. Wade and Joe want to go every day."

Jeff bent and kissed his daughter's forehead. "And am I correct in presuming the same goes for Pauly?"

"Yep," he chuckled. "With the number of things he's got planned, I reckon he'll either be staying here our whole vacation, or holding us hostage at the lake."

Together, they approached the side of the house and turned the corner just as Duke loped toward them from the backyard. Completely ignoring the other two, the dog greeted Austin by bouncing around his legs and prodding him with his snout, not stopping until the tall boy lowered himself to the grass. The second

Austin's knees touched the ground, Duke laid a paw upon one thigh and gave the hand that stroked it a soggy and tender lick.

"Duke, you crazy thing, are you going to say hello to me?" Stephanie grumbled.

"Who was just leaving, Dad?" Austin rubbed the malamute's furry coat as he got to his feet.

"A man."

"What did he want?"

"Some of Mom's baking, I think." Jeff patted his son's shoulder. "Come on. We're going to play a little game." He jiggled his eyebrows at their perplexed stares.

*   *   *

"Mmmmm, yummy as always," Jeff raved, and swiped another cookie off the floral-decorated plate. "What do you think, kids? Should we go global with these? Of course, we'll have to rename them. Instead of Dee's Household Famous Brownies, we'll call them Dee's Dee-liciously Dee-lectable Worldwide Famous Brownies, and international domination will be ours. Ours, I tell you, mwahahahahaha." His crazed, manic expression brought muffled guffaws from the children.

"That's nice," Dee remarked. "And will our power over the world mean I can get a maid to help me out in there?" Seated opposite her husband, she took aim across the patio table. "My entire day has been spent cleaning up after you lot."

"Anything's possible, babe, and as king and queen we will rule fairly. In fact," his eyes widened. "We can pay her with cookies."

"You fool," she laughed.

Savoring the soft, squishy mass in his mouth, laden with chunks of warm, melting chocolate, Austin flicked his gaze sideways to his father. "So what's this game we're playing, Dad?" he asked, licking his fingers.

"It's a guessing game. We've got an out of the ordinary, exceptional, unusual and unequaled surprise coming, and you two have to figure out what it is."

Stephanie half-turned toward her mother, bouncing up and down in her chair. "Oooo! Are Susan and Three-Gee staying over?"

"No," Dee chuckled. "That's the absolute opposite of exceptional and unusual. Try again."

"Aunt Michelle's visiting us."

"No." A small smile curled the edges of her lips. "Actually, now that you mention your aunt, she's going overseas again soon. I'll tell you all about it later."

"Then I must be getting another dog," Stephanie squealed. She looked at Duke, who sat snuggled up to her brother, his head propped on Austin's lap and receiving a gentle caress of his muzzle. "Duke doesn't seem to like me anymore. Only Austin."

"Don't be silly, Steph." Austin rolled his eyes. They shone bright blue in the late, tepid sunshine. "He just wants another cookie."

"Fair enough. I know the feeling," Jeff agreed, reaching for the plate. "And you're not getting another dog, darling. Or a cat, horse, pony, elephant, dinosaur, and any other animal you can think of. But nice try, anyway. Your turn, son."

"Hmmm." Austin's brow creased. "I think Mom let a big clue slip. I think we're going on vacation with Aunt Michelle."

"No." He shook his head. "Although we did consider a holiday, right, babe?"

"Yes, I most certainly did," Dee smiled.

"But in the end," Jeff laughed. "We decided on something that will last a lot longer than any holiday. Something the whole family will be able to enjoy all year round. Well... not all year round. That'll be a couple of years away. And your mother's been waiting a very long time for this."

"Ooooohh, yes," Dee nodded. "A long time. My terms have never been met."

"Cooperville wasn't built in a day, my love." He blew her a kiss.

"Mom. Dad." Stephanie looked back and forth at her parents. "We give up. What are you talking about?"

"Hang on, Stephie, I'm not giving up," Austin countered, and began tapping his chin. "Dad, who was the guy in the pickup, 'cos you're not usually home at this time."

"I know. Being the boss does have its advantages now and then, especially with this being such an unusual, exceptional, unequaled and out of the ordinary day."

"Honey." Dee shook her head. "Look at the poor things. Let's stop teasing and just tell them what's happening."

"Spoilsport," Jeff pouted. "Okay. The surprise, the treat, the something for us all, the something that is coming, the something we are getting, is..." He paused, milking the tension as the seconds ticked by, and not making it any better when he started an intentional drum roll on the table. "A swimming pool!" he exclaimed, flinging his arms out high and wide.

Due to the children's mouths literally dropping open, they were speechless at first, and when Stephanie sprang from her chair to begin a bizarre dance of exaggerated joy, Duke jumped up, staring curiously, his head cocked to one side and the ears ramrod straight. Jeff and Dee laughed at the antics and returned her elated hugs and kisses after Austin's warmhearted, thankful embrace.

"There are a couple of things we need to discuss," Jeff stated, once Austin and Stephanie had taken their seats again. "The most important is how we'll keep it clean. I'll need some help with that, so we'll draw up some sort of roster. And of course, there will be a set of rules regarding how you and your friends use it. Okay?"

"Okay," they chorused, still grinning widely.

"What happens to it during winter?"

"Excellent question, son," Jeff smiled. "We've got some ideas for developing more of the backyard, and depending on how much those cost, we might be able to have it heated. But that may not be until next year, or even the year after. We'll see how we go."

"A heated pool. Man, that'll be so awesome."

"Yeah, man. Awesome." Jeff reached across and ruffled Austin's hair.

"When's it being done, Dad?" Stephanie gushed.

"Next week, sweetheart. That man you saw driving away is doing it. He's a good friend of my sales manager, and comes highly recommended."

"How long does it take?" Austin's eyes widened while he pushed himself upright. "Will it be ready for my birthday?"

"No, I'm sorry, it won't." Jeff glanced at Dee, his lips pressed tightly together at the sight of their son slumping back in his chair. "Ben, the guy who's building it, said it'll be at least six weeks, maybe eight, depending on the weather. So even though thirteen is a really special age to turn, I'm afraid it won't be a pool party, buddy."

"There's always next year." Dee smiled encouragingly. "And plenty of summer vacation left to have loads of fun with your friends."

"Yeah," Austin nodded, beaming at them. "It doesn't matter. This'll be so cool. It's gonna be the best time ever. Can I ring Pauly and tell him?"

*　　*　　*

"Seriously? They've finished digging the hole? Awesome. It's the best news I've heard all year, Coops," Joe Harris grinned. "Even better than finishing early today, and that takes a lot of beating."

Austin joined in on Wade and Joe's merriment while they waited near the school entrance, their mirth adding to the hustle and bustle of children running, screaming, talking and whooping, the incessant, escalating racket an indication of a hard-earned summer vacation that commenced five minutes earlier with the shrill peal of a bell.

"Who wanna beatin'? If it one's of you losers, I'll happily do's it."

The friends turned to the obnoxious intrusion, and saw four youths sauntering across the grass, preceded by their bulky leader, who halted his approach and gazed at the trio, his spiteful eyes glittering beneath disheveled, blond hair.

"Ya gonna hang wiv them's faggots all ya life, Harris? Why don'cha ya join's up wiv me a'gin, huh?" Wotlinski sniggered. "Nah. I wooden have's ya. Look'a'cha. Ya even got's long, girly hair. Ya must's be in love wiv Wade Bitch, ya gay pussy nerd. Is that it, Harris? You's in love wiv him?" Barking his laughter, he lifted his thickset arm and steered a chunky finger back and forth at the two lads standing either side of their notably taller companion. With the dark-haired styles they sported, their matching height and same, average build, the likeness seemed remarkable. Apart from the face. There, the similarity ended. Wade possessed a softer, smoother profile, whereas Joe's was quite angular, sharp toward his chin, and his blue eyes held a sterner edge, a harshness that rose quickly to the surface as he answered his former oppressor.

"Get lost, Wotlinski," he growled. "You're a douche. You're the douche of a douche, asshole."

"Tough words, faggot. Bet'cha wooden be sayin' that ta ma face if he ain't's here." Wotlinski nodded at the blue-purpley eyes calmly regarding him. "Where's ya gay pal, Cooper? Hidin' in ya pocket?" Raucous hooting bellowed from his cohorts. "Hey, here's the shrimp. Where's ya bin, Smally? Ya girlfriend's' a' waitin' for ya's."

Plodding along, glancing rearward at a throng of highly excited, shrieking youngsters rushing behind him, Pauly stopped midstride at the sight of his nemesis, only revealed now that his friends had partially separated to follow Wotlinski's sneer. "Austin," he warbled, his voice quivering.

"Austin, Austin, help me, Austin, safe me," Wotlinski falsettoed.

"Don't worry, Pauly. Come here, mate, he can't do anything to you." Austin beckoned the tiny lad forward with a sweep of his arm.

"Ya really fink that, Cooper?"

"Nope." Austin shook his head and stepped closer, his eye level well above those contained within the plump, reddish flesh he confronted. "I don't fink's that's, Wotlinski, you idiot, I know that. Now do as Joe says. Get lost. You've been a good child lately and I'm sure you don't want to end up on the ground, crying again. The entire school is here to see it this time, if that's what you want."

Wotlinski skimmed his squinty, pig-like eyes over Austin's lofty, muscular frame. "Ya fuckin' freak," he snarled and stormed off, his followers scurrying in his wake.

"Holy shit, dudes," Wade sighed. "He just doesn't give up."

"Yep." Joe nodded his agreement. "And I don't think he will. That guy is pure evil. All he ever talked about was how he was gonna get Austin and Pauly, Pauly and Austin, Austin and Pauly, over and over. I couldn't stand it any longer. Jeez, I was such an idiot. The worst thing I did was hang around with him."

"That's in the past, bro." Austin smiled at his friend. "And the best thing you did was apologize to us. Joe, you're a bigger, better person than he'll ever be."

"Thanks, man. But just watch out for him, Coops, 'cos he is gonna go for you one day."

"It's possible," he hummed, shrugging his broad shoulders. "Then again, I've always got Pauly to back me up. He'll take him down."

"Hi, Austin." A loud call interrupted their laughter, and they all turned to see an attractive, blonde-haired girl waving at them as she passed by with five giggling, pointing companions. "Have a great vacation," she sang, nearly tripping over when one girl grabbed her by the arm and pulled her closer.

"Thanks very much, Tess. I hope you have a great time, as well."

"Awww, now there's true love. Ain't it sweet," Wade chuckled, and patted a widely smiling Austin on his stocky arm.

"Coops, we should ask them if they want to come over for a swim when the pool's ready. Hey, d'ya think they'd also like to go fishing?"

"Humph," Pauly grunted. Brushing his long, black fringe across his forehead, he peered up at Joe. "Why the hell would Austin do that? He doesn't want any girls ruining our break."

the phantoms

In his sleep, dreaming, Austin's eyeballs rolled around, rippling the lids with their darting, erratic movements. With one quick, fluid motion, he ripped his top sheet off and flung it to the far side of his room where it landed in a heap, crumpling the many printed depictions of a variously-posed and fully-suited Batman. A Christmas present when he was eight, he still liked it, and just didn't have the heart to discard the item so easily. Except for now, and with the covering gone, his sweat-swathed body rasped against the remaining, fitted sheet as he writhed upon it, his clammy hands clenching and unclenching a solid grip on the damp cotton, gathering and stretching until it nearly freed its elasticized, resilient hold of the mattress.

While the internal visions continued, a collection of randomly strange images, his muscles flexed, tightening under the glistening flesh of his arms and legs when a familiar figure stepped into view, and he gritted his teeth as his foe appeared from around the corner of the house, towing something large behind him. With a hoarse, grating cackle, Kevin Wotlinski lifted one bulky arm to reveal his captive, an absolutely gorgeous girl, her limbs bound securely. Through the long, blonde hair that swung to her shoulders, exposing her pale face, Austin saw the wide, amber eyes and watched the tears flow down her cheeks, running over a strip of thick, brown tape plastered across her usually smiling and beautiful lips. Using his free hand, Wotlinski raised a finger to his pudgy neck and dragged it slowly from one side to the other.

Confused, Austin examined his surroundings, certain that a few seconds earlier he had walked in the middle of Lake Crescent, the pristine, blue waters utterly motionless, like crossing an enormous slab of smoothly polished crystal. And yet here he stood, in his own backyard, in the presence of two people. One, the most detestable creature in his life, and the other the most delightful. A girl who had started some perplexingly special emotions welling up each time he laid eyes on her, and now cruelly suspended, the life-force draining from her body. Pure rage seized him at the atrocity being committed, and as he surged forward, roaring, the pair faded rapidly away, replaced by a blackness so impenetrable, so oppressive, unnerving and absolute that it seemed to touch him, caressing him with its desire to lure him farther in.

Convinced he had gone instantaneously blind, Austin tasted an all-embracing, paralyzing fear overwhelming him for the first time in his life, and when a tiny, dazzling speckle of light flared momentarily, like a precious jewel glinting miles upon miles away in the expanse of a never-ending desert, he nearly screamed, elated that the treasured sense of sight had not abandoned him. Suddenly, something tugged him forward, like a firmly tied and forcefully pulled cord around his torso, and he raced at an unbelievable velocity to the light. In a flash, he reached it, slowing just as quickly to stare, open-mouthed, at a huge planet floating big and bright before him. It was immense, gargantuan, a veritable colossus of a world.

"Holy crap," he whispered, and stretched his neck outward, peering left and right in a futile attempt to establish an exact width.

With a geography comparable to Earth, he looked down on lush green and brown continents, the gigantic landmasses separated by oceans of vibrant blue. Every few seconds, assorted colors sprayed the magnificent scenery; gold, silver, bronze, yellow, pink, an infinite variety that shimmered across its surface, appearing and disappearing haphazardly.

As he watched the kaleidoscopic display, Austin saw small, blazing balls of whiteness popping into existence; hundreds, thousands, possibly millions. They began orbiting the planet within the upper reaches of its atmosphere, some hurtling at a tremendous speed while others tracked along rather leisurely. The slower ones reminded him of the times he sat outside with his family, sipping hot chocolate from steaming mugs and scanning the nighttime sky for any man-made satellites that seemed to meander their way through the stars. There was always a competition and ensuing bonus for the first, lucky person to spot the gleaming objects, the 'Splendiferous Optics Reward' as Jeff called it, with the prize coming in the form of an extra marshmallow or two being immersed in their drink, where it would melt with the succulently tasty goo already present.

I've won that contest hands down, Austin thought, nearly laughing at the whirlwind activity. But his delight vanished when three of the bright orbs veered toward him. Moving at an astonishing pace, they whizzed past his shoulder, and as he spun around to follow their progress, he ignored the grand and speedily swooping, downward arc they performed the moment his sight fell upon a spectacle that left him gaping. "Whoooooa," he breathed.

In all directions, the endless depths of space was filled with galaxies scattered far and wide, an amount rivaling the glowing spheres circling the planet at his back. Many were simply distant, vivid dots, but most he viewed clearly, and he was able to distinguish the differing shapes and sizes of those in close proximity. He saw vast spiral formations, tilted at all sorts of angles, their cloudy-looking, massive arms curving out from radiantly shining cores. Farther away, one particularly long, thin system hovered side-on, the disk-like structure showing a large, spheroidal bulge at its center, and beyond that, Austin spotted the oddest galaxy yet, a mammoth and irregular ring, its giant arms drawn inward from the gravitational lure of the much smaller, compact form that had plunged right through its middle, trailing streams of gas, dust and stars in the damaging aftermath.

An abrupt nudge on his arm broke Austin's mesmerized gaze, and he twirled to face a widely spread cluster of the luminescent balls. Numbering at least forty, they waited just out of reach, and as he wondered how the situation could get any worse, or better, they changed, expanding from orbs no bigger than his head into misty and translucent, full-sized copies of himself. It was like looking at his reflection in a partially frosted mirror after a long and delightfully warm shower.

One moved closer. "Is this acceptable?" it asked, passing a hand down its figure. The voice was friendly, soothing, with a sweet, melodious quality that triggered a release of treasured memories and emotions, and Austin thought of a time when he was four years old, a happy, experienced-filled time during his early childhood when everything in life was wonderful, carefree and right.

"I... I guess," Austin shrugged. "Who are you? What is this? Am I..." A startling transformation in the planet's color stole his attention, and while he gazed through the phantoms, he saw a deep, purplish-red, like venous blood, consuming its former, glorious splendor. "Is that your home? What's happening to it?" Eruptions of orange and black spurted across the entire sphere.

Without turning, the duplicate Austin smiled. "Our end. Our beginning. The naissance." The others nodded. "Your beginning. Your naissance," they murmured.

"What's that? I don't understand."

A gauzy hand stroked Austin's cheek, the touch soft and warm. "You will, young one. For now, grow, mature, discover. Trust yourself. Trust what you are, who you are. Above all, trust him. Let him guide, then you can lead. Show him the way."

In Austin's blinking eyes, fire engulfed the world, burning with a rapid and savage intensity that, thankfully, lacked the searing heat he had experienced before. "I've heard those words. In a dream, years ago. Was that you?"

"Then, as now, you call on us. We are together and everything is yours, in time. Destroy it, or all you see." The hazy arm pointed over his shoulder. "And all you do not, will be no more. Finish what we started. Finish what you started."

"What do you mean? Look, can't you just tell me what this is about?"

"No." All of them shook their heads. "Not that method. The result is perpetual failure. Be who you truly are. Find what you have, and use it. We will meet again. The last will call." One by one, they reverted back to the radiant, white balls, leaving the solitary figure, who took Austin's left hand and placed it on top of its own. "Awaken now, young one, for you are in danger."

As his eyelids sprung open, he swayed unsteadily at the rim of a massive pit, one leg raised and ready to take another stride into the unfinished steel cage forming the pool. Inhaling a sharp, hissing breath, his grip tightening on the bright-yellow plastic cap under his hand, he took two, staggering steps rearward from the edge and released his hold of the spiraled reinforcing rod that protruded four feet above ground level. With his heart hammering relentlessly in his chest, Austin stared at the galvanized coating on the structure deep below. It glittered malevolently in the full moonlight, and straightaway, he remembered a worker, earlier that afternoon, explaining the function of rebar, along with some tales of people unfortunate to have fallen upon them.

"Austin, is that you?"

Startled at the loud whisper, Austin spun to see his father stepping out from the open dining room door, dressed only in boxer shorts, as he was, the result of an early summer heat-wave that had descended on Colorado and its neighboring states yesterday.

"What the hell are you doing?" Peering at his son, Jeff reached back inside, switched on the external light and inspected the area cautiously, utilizing the narrow band of illumination now cast over the patio.

"Dad, please believe me when I say I don't know," Austin called in a low voice. "I was having these weird dreams and then I woke up standing here. I don't even know how I got over this." He aimed his finger at a waist-high, chain-link panel fence surrounding the sizeable hole, mere feet from the edge. Each section had two knotted strands of red and white striped, polyethylene tape keeping them together, with every third propped up by a thin stick wedged in the dirt.

"You don't know? Mate, come out of there." Jeff trotted across the pavers while Austin used his long legs to clear the short barrier. "And what's that all over you? Is it sweat?" Even with his back to the light and his face shadowed, Jeff's skin paled visibly as he ran a trembling hand down the sheen on Austin's arm. "You're soaking wet. Son, are you okay?"

"I feel fine, Dad." He shrugged, and glanced back at the rickety, lopsided panels. "I just don't remember coming out here. Not one bit of it."

"What do you mean?" His brow creased. "Are you saying you've been sleepwalking? Holy shit! You could have been seriously injured. Or killed." He glared at the construction site behind Austin. "Right, I'll be talking to Ben first thing tomorrow. The pathetic fence his workers put around that deathtrap of a hole wouldn't stop a small child, let alone someone like you. He's seen how tall you are. I'm paying enough money for this pool and all the groundwork, and there should be a high, proper barricade around the whole, goddamn thing. Highly recommended. I'll sue his highly recommended, goddamn ass." Jeff's chest heaved after the tumbling rush of words, and when his blazing eyes rested once again upon his offspring, they softened quickly. "It's all right, buddy. I'm just very pissed with myself, as well. Are you sure you're okay?"

"Yeah." A brief shiver raced up Austin's spine at the thought of what could have occurred without the timely, wraith-like warning. "Am I in trouble?"

"Absolutely not. This isn't your fault. It's scared the shit out of me that it's happened, but you haven't done it on purpose." He grimaced. "Have you?"

"No. I promise."

"Then you're not in trouble," Jeff smiled. "Come on, let's go inside. You can grab a shower, and get yourself back to bed. You'll feel much better after that, and in the morning we'll talk more about this."

"Dad."

Already turning to leave, Jeff stopped and looked back. "Yes, mate?"

"How did you know I was out here?"

"I didn't," he laughed softly. "It was your mom. She woke me up, said she heard the door opening down here and someone yell. There are times when she bears an uncanny resemblance to one of those antelopes in the African savanna, with her little ears rotating like radar dishes." He cupped his hands behind each ear and swiveled them around. "Of course, I'm the one who has to drag your sorry butt back to bed." He rubbed Austin's hair. "But I wouldn't have it any other way. That's part of my job description, buddy. Remember that."

Stepping forward, Austin gave Jeff a huge, surprising hug. "I will, Dad. Thanks."

"No problem. And I'd also like to give my thanks."

"For what?" Austin stepped away, his eyebrows raised.

"For your affection, your company, and..." Jeff wiped the wetness and dirt now coating his skin. "For kindly passing on your exquisite perspiration and general grubbiness. I don't know why you enjoy doing this," he chuckled. "Come on." Reaching out, he grabbed his boy around the neck and pulled him into a gentle headlock. "Remind me to tell Stephie that Duke's not sleeping in her room while it's so hot. If he was out here, I'm sure he would have barked and woken you up."

"Yeah, probably," Austin agreed. Although I think Duke might've done more than that, he thought, grinning.

*   *   *

"That sounds terrible, honey, you poor thing." Dee placed her knife and fork on an empty plate and shook her head. "It's no wonder you walked everywhere."

Sitting outside in dazzling, warming sunlight the next morning, the family finished their breakfast while watching the contractors assemble a new fence using eight-foot-high sturdy panels supported by large, bright-orange rubber blocks. After Jeff's irate phone call, the owner of the company, Ben Richards, had turned up within one hour, bringing his full crew, a truck load of materials, and a displeasure matching his clients, upset with the carelessness shown in his absence the previous afternoon. Taking complete responsibility, he arrived with comic books for Austin, continual apologies, and reparation through an entire days work on a weekend, free of charge.

Behind her dark sunglasses, Dee's eyes narrowed. "I didn't know you were still having weird dreams. How often are they?"

Impossible to gauge her reaction, it was the tone of her voice that alerted Austin, and he chose his words carefully, recalling an offhand comment two months ago about a woman's intuition. "Hardly ever, Mom." He swallowed, hating the occasional need to fib, and looked across at Ben, who stalked the perimeter of the hole, barking sporadic instructions. With her curiosity obviously kindled, it was his father who came to the rescue.

"It's nothing, babe. Just the odd nightmare probably brought on by all those cartoons he watches. Talking of which, did you miss them this morning?"

"Yeah." Austin restrained a grateful sigh. "I didn't feel like watching TV."

"Mmmm," Dee mused. "Well, I don't like the sleepwalking part. It's dangerous. Jeff, do you think Susan and Greg might be able to help us with that one?"

"How would they help, honey?"

"Ahhh… let's see now. They own a store specializing in old, rare and elusive books, as well as the mainstream editions, so there's a wealth of information available." She started ticking off her fingers, sarcasm dripping from her words. "They're very intelligent. They have extensive worldly knowledge and experience. They love these two children with a passion. There's one more thing, what was it? That's right, they'd do anything for us."

"Oooooh… that Susan and Greg," he smiled. "Why didn't you say so?"

"You fool." Laughing, she threw a balled up paper napkin at him.

"It's a good idea, buddy." Jeff rose from his chair. "You should give them a call and see what they have to say on the subject." He rubbed his hands together. "Right. I might take a wander over there and see what's happening. It looks like the cage is nearing completion and Ben said the concrete would be sprayed today if they did."

"I'm going inside, Mom," Stephanie declared. Jumping up, she stretched her arms out wide. "Do you want any help with this stuff?"

"Yes please, sweetheart. You take the utensils and I'll bring the plates. Austin, if you're staying, can you keep Duke with you? I don't want him getting hurt."

"Sure." Austin reached down and patted the dog sprawled by his side. There's only one person who can explain the subject, he thought. And he's not here. Where are you? I didn't think it would be this…

Dee removed her sunglasses and leaned forward, speaking softly. "Honey, you don't have to go through the growing up process alone. It's hard enough with all the changes that happen physically and emotionally. We are always here for you, ready and willing to listen and help if we can, and if you want us to. So, if there are girl issues on your mind, or anything else, just remember that. Okay? You never know, your father and I might have a few ideas. Or Susan and Greg, if you're embarrassed to talk to us about things. You think of them as your brother and sister, so different ears can be very useful, especially this topic about nightmares. I'd like to hear how they interpret them. That sort of thing has always interested me, but I don't know much about it."

"Thanks," he smiled. "But it's no big deal. Nothing I can't handle."

"Somehow, I thought you'd say that." She rolled her eyes. "All in your own time then, sweetheart. Whenever you're ready. However, there is a big deal about one precise matter, and a thing we've all learnt regarding this chat."

"What's that?"

"You still haven't taken out the trash this morning." She winked and set about collecting the dishes, humming a silly tune.

Watching her, Austin grinned. "Mom, sometimes you are just so like Dad."

Chapter Ten

The Birthday

Directly beneath a sign on the wall stating 'Everything Barbecue', the lettering itself just plain red on white, Jeff pulled an apron off a rack and slipped the strap over his head. Smoothing the rustling cotton flat with one hand, he passed the empty hanger to Austin, who placed it on the bracket with a small, metallic clink. "How's the size?" he whispered.

"Perfect," Austin nodded, giving him a thumbs-up.

Together, the two snickered quietly.

"Excellent. I'll have this, and we'll get the other one for Greg. It's something like an extra, extra, extra, super extra XL, so it should fit the big galoot." Peering to his right, making sure they weren't under observation, Jeff saw his wife and daughter's attention captured by a display cabinet full of various gadgets and knickknacks the novelty shop offered.

"Look, Mom, this could be a good present." Stephanie took her mother's hand, squeezed it gently, and pressed her free finger up to the glass, at a Newton's Cradle, its suspended steel balls and polished framework gleaming brightly under the stark, fluorescent lighting.

"It's nice, honey." Thrilled, Dee returned the gesture, clasping Stephanie's hand just a bit tighter. She relished physical contact like that with her eleven-year-old, and made the most of those phases she knew would end soon, as it had with Austin when he was eight. Never again would there be the cherished moments of kneeling opposite a small, sweet, innocent boy and girl, or having them sit on her lap, gazing into their adorable, shining eyes before the closeness of a cuddle, a cry, and the reassurance they yearned. Occasionally, when she was alone in the house, her mind would wander, stirring many thoughts of the differences now that her children were maturing quickly, growing older by the day. They highlighted the tragic loss of her own parents, how much she missed them, the memory of their love for her still so strong, and sometimes, overwhelmed by haunting emotions, she would find the nearest chair, collapse heavily, and weep.

But then there were the happy times, brought about by a certain, special person when he entered her life with abundant love, support, understanding, and a wicked sense of humor, the latter clearly evident on their shopping trip to Halfmoon Mall, one week before her son's fourteenth birthday pool party. And with the widest of smiles, he turned to his wife, the soul he adored above all else.

"You," Jeff called. "You woman. You look. Me like. Me buy."

Now tied around his waist, the apron had a picture of three Neanderthal cavemen, covered in furs and gathered around a large, modern barbecue laden with jumbo-sized chunks of meat. One of the males, his big, bushy eyebrows crossed low on an overhanging forehead, aimed his thick and hairy finger at a nearby rock face, directing two scruffy-looking, prehistoric females toward a dark opening. 'Me Man. Me Cook. Me Eat. You. You Woman. You Wash' was written below the image in rough, gray, stone-hewn letters.

"No way, mister," Dee retorted, shaking her head. "All it'll do is give you the stupid idea to talk like that every time the dishes need cleaning."

"It will not!" he protested, feigning an extremely offended expression, and in the next instant, he stuck out a quivering bottom lip while fluttering his eyelids. "Please, please, please." Crossing his pinky and thumb on his palm, Jeff raised his hand and gave the three-fingered salute. "You have my word I will not say it more than five times per year."

"You fool," she chuckled. "You weren't even in the Boy Scouts."

"True," he agreed. "Which is probably a good thing, or else it may have stifled my ability to find this next item so amusing. On top of it making a great welcome home gift, the resemblance to a certain fair-haired maiden we love is uncanny. Austin, my lad." Jeff beamed at his son. "Please introduce Mr. Greg Kirk's newest attire to your mother. And you won't believe where it's made, Dee."

From behind his back, Austin brought forth another apron and held it high for inspection. Much larger than Jeff's, the foremost image was of a young, blonde woman, clothed in a checked shirt tied at the waist and exceedingly short, cut-off jeans. Undeniably the caricature of an intellectually challenged Barbie, her eyeballs stared off in opposing directions while a pink tongue lolled from one side of her mouth, drooling long, shiny strings of saliva down her ample breasts. In the background, a decrepit billiard table blazed, as well as her arm, part of her hair, and the entire cue she held out to a denim-overall-clad yokel, who had a hand clapped over his eyes in exasperation. 'No, dang blammit! When I says t'set ma barbeee-cuuu on fire thass not what I means' was written in stick-constructed letters above the straw hat perched on his head.

"Jeffrey Peter Cooper," Dee managed between her laughter. "It's bad enough you've got Greg as your jesting partner, now you two are passing on your traits to the children. It's no wonder our household is like a comedy show."

"I don't get it, Mom. Why does Barbie look like that? What's she doing?" Stephanie's bemused appearance brought on fresh bouts of cackling. "Dad! Austin!" she complained, and peered up at her mother, scowling.

Dee stroked her daughter's long, dark hair. "I'll tell you later, honey. It's just typical, brainless, male behavior. Ignore them. Jeff, I think getting that apron for Greg is a fantastic idea. The moment you bring it out will be hilariously funny."

"Really? Hey." His eyes narrowed. "Wait a minute. I know that devious grin."

"Mmmm." She nodded. "You should. I bet it's the last thing you see while Susan's throttling the living daylights out of you."

the backyard

"Boys," Jeff shouted. "Let's go over those orders again. I'm ready for you this time." Standing on the soaked decking near the edge of the pool, a notepad and pen in his hand, he squinted as sunlight flashed off the crystal-clear, choppy water. Pauly laughed shrilly when Austin missed him with a tennis ball, pushed himself backward and landed with a large splash, his hand groping for the fluffy, green object floating at his side. "Come on you rowdy hooligans, if you want anything to eat we'll have to do a quick recap."

"Love of my life," Dee hummed. "I just saw Stephie waving from the dining room. Susan and Greg are here." Strolling behind her husband, she ran the tips of her fingernails gently across his back and glanced over her shoulder, smiling. "I'll go and meet them." Dressed in a sarong, the vivid pink and white-streaked material flowed with her movements, accentuating the sensuous curves of her body, and Jeff gazed at the sight, his appreciative distraction broken when someone sent a spray of water cascading against his legs.

"Hey," he chuckled. "Keep the master chef dry, you lot, or I won't be able to cook up a feast worthy of your never-ending, teenage appetites." Consulting the pad, he pointed at each one in turn. "Okay, let's see if I've got this right. Wade, you want four sausages. Joe, you want two sausages and a piece of steak. Pauly, you want three sausages and a piece of steak. Holy moly, buddy, I don't know where you're putting all that food. You must have hollow legs. But that's cool, we need to fatten you up a bit." He grinned at the small, skinny lad. "And Austin, you also want three sausages and a piece of steak. Pauly, if you can match him, then you're doing okay. Now, have I got it all correct?"

A roar of approval met his question, just as Dee came into view from around the corner of the house, arm in arm and laughing with a stunningly beautiful blonde woman. On their heels strode a giant of a man, extraordinarily tall and powerfully built, his muscles bulging with the weight of two large, black bags he carried in each hand. His deep blue eyes, sparkling like the tranquil surface on a measureless stretch of ocean, creased above the wide smile that plastered his handsome face when Stephanie rushed across the patio. "Susan! Three-Gee!" she squealed.

"There's my gorgeous girl." The man placed his bags on the ground and remained stooped, hoisting Stephanie up as she flung herself into his waiting arms.

"Guys," Austin said. "I'll be back in a minute." After a few, strong strokes, he was out, grabbing a towel and hurriedly wiping himself dry before trotting away behind Jeff to meet the new arrivals. His three friends glided to the pool edge and hauled themselves onto the warm, beige coping stones, leaving their legs dangling in the refreshingly cool water.

"Jeez." Wade stared at the joyful group hugging each other warmly. "I kinda remember Greg being big, but not that big. He is freakin' huge. Hey, man." He nudged Pauly in the ribs. "It's like comparing you and Austin."

"Shut up, shithead, you can't talk. Even Joe's taller than you now."

"Ha!" Joe whooped. He turned and pointed at Wade. "Burn, dude."

"How was the trip?" Austin heard his father say. He lobbed the towel to his left and stepped forward.

"Fantastic, Jeff. It's an absolutely beautiful country and we'll tell you all about it soon, because at the moment, I've got someone very special to greet." Susan held her hand out and drew Austin into a massive cuddle. "Happy birthday, darling."

"Thanks, Susan." As they separated, Austin looked down on her smiling eyes and beamed at her next words.

"Look at the size of you. I know it's been four months, but I reckon you've grown about another inch, maybe more. It's hard to believe you were once that tiny, gorgeous baby who needed his diaper changing." She rubbed his arm and shared a deliberate smile with her husband when he moved alongside.

"Happy birthday, mate," Greg rumbled, returning the teenager's firm embrace. "Suze is right. It looks like you've got your old man beat. And just wait until we hit those proper weights, bro, then you'll really explode." He clapped Austin on the shoulder. "But we'll have to call off our arm wrestles. There's no way I can beat you."

"Yeah, right," Austin laughed. "Hey, did you have a nice time?"

"We had a great time. But it's good to be home, even if I need a holiday after the holiday. It was pretty hectic."

"It's really nice to hear you say that, Greg."

"About having another holiday? I knew you'd have the same opinion, Dee. Although I think Jeff will have to pay for it. We better make the most of him before he's the one in diapers."

Jeff chuckled at Greg's cheesy grin. "Touché, mate," he said, high-fiving the gigantic man. "But I'm afraid Jeff's got no more money, so we ain't going nowhere 'cos of this." He swept his arm over the backyard.

"And what a way to be destitute, eh?" Greg whistled softly. "It looks freakin' awesome. What do you think, Suze?" Surveying the area, he crossed his arms, his swelling biceps tightening the sleeves of his tee-shirt.

"It's magnificent," Susan breathed, and hugged Stephanie to her when the young girl leaned in. "I'm so proud of you both. The transformation since we've been gone is simply astonishing. Dee, I love how it's worked out with the cherry tree being incorporated this way." She pointed at a massive, rectangular decking, which spread across the extensively developed property, surrounding the pool and the prized family tree before dipping on a gentle camber to the patio pavers. "It looks amazing."

"It does," Greg agreed. "Exactly like the plans. Bravo."

"Thanks," Jeff beamed. "I've got to say, Ben and the landscape artist he brought in were superb. They did a fantastic job. At what stage was it when you and Suze left? Was the pool protected?"

"Yeah, the scaffold platform was over it and they'd already started digging a hole for the spa. But nothing else. Nothing like this." Greg nodded at two enormous, oblong terraces cut into the sloping land. Along with the swimming pool and hot tub, the lower terrace included a small shed that housed pumps, filters and cleaning equipment, while the upper level held an alfresco kitchen at the back and large dining area, where a sturdy, carved oak table dominated the center. Stained dark-brown like the deck below, twelve matching, cushioned chairs encircled its sizeable bulk. All but four had occupants, and the hum of their chatter carried down on the still, warm air. "Now… well, mate, now it's the best outdoor entertainment area I've ever seen. You've certainly made the most of the terrain."

Jeff sighed. "It's been a long time plan. Holy heck!" Tilting his head to the cloudless, azure sky, he squinted. "That sun is nice, but just a tad relentless. Might have to roll the shade out before everyone ends up redder than a lobster. And while we're on the subject of burning meat." He grinned at Greg. "How about joining the maestro for a barbecue cook-off? I bought you something just for the occasion."

"Sounds good. Hey, we've also got a few gifts from NZ, and I figured since we're staying overnight we may as well do that later. For now it's the big fella's present. I'll just go and get them from the car."

"Three-Gee, if you want, we can do that after lunch. You guys must be starving. I know I am."

"You're the boss today, brother." Greg fist-bumped a beaming Austin. "Lead the way, Jeff. I've a load of snags and fresh prawns to chuck on the barbie, and I need to get my wonderful wife out of this heat so she can relax."

"What's a snag?"

Greg gazed into Stephanie's brown eyes and laughed. "You've probably not heard me use that slang before. They're sausages, sweetheart, and in this particular case, a barbie isn't a doll, it's…"

"Yeah, we've explained that one already." Jeff winked at his daughter. "Anyway, I suppose I better appease the birthday boy, and we'll make some introductions to our other guests. Greg, there's a beer waiting for you, and Suze, Dee's got a nice white wine up there."

"Not for me. I'll have an orange juice, please."

"Just OJ? Nothing else?"

"No thanks, Jeff. Honey, do you want some help with the bags?"

"You're not lifting anything." Greg bent to pick their luggage off the paving stones and kissed Susan on the cheek. "It's all under control, darling. Just be careful going up the stairs."

"Yes, Gregory dear," she droned, and slapped his arm playfully. "Take that silly grin off your face." Grasping Dee and Stephanie by the hand, she sauntered past the three teenagers still sitting at the water's edge. "Hello, boys. Having a nice time?"

"Yeah," they chorused.

"Are you feeling okay, honey?" Dee studied Susan's smile. "What's going on?"

"Nothing. I feel fantastic. It's just... you know... Greg being Greg. Oh wow! It looks even better up close," she gushed, and paused to admire some wide, curving steps leading up to the next tier. Built using the same mahogany decking they stood on, the wood's dark stain complemented a smoked glass and stainless steel railing, the highly polished surface twinkling in the bright light. It continued across the second level before swooping down an identical set of stairs on the opposite side. Anchored atop the wall behind the kitchen an additional barrier prevented any accidental falls from the slanting, grass-covered backyard above.

"Hey, guys," Austin stopped by the pool while his friends hauled themselves to their feet. "You remember Greg, right? Pauly, I didn't mean you," he grunted when the small boy scowled. "I know you were here the weekend they left."

"Sure, I remember," Wade replied.

"Dude, who could forget you?" Joe stared at the towering man.

"Gidday, lads." Greg placed a bag down and stuck his massive hand out, which completely enfolded the returning shakes. "Wade. Joe. I haven't seen you for a couple of years. You guys are growing up quick. Hey, Pauly, how's things, mate?"

"Hi, Greg. Good, thanks." Pauly cleared his long, black fringe from his eyes and peered upward, smiling, his head skewed back at an outrageous angle.

"How did you get so big?" Joe blurted.

"Eat all your veggies, bro. It's true," he laughed with them. "Get plenty of exercise, too. Weight training will give you the bulk and food is your fuel. I've been doing a light program with Austin for a little while, strengthening the tendons and getting them ready for some heavy iron in another year or so. But speaking of food, I better get going. We've got to cook it yet." He laid his hand between Austin's shoulder blades and jerked his head sideways at the pool. "Mate, that water looks awesomely inviting. Are you going for a swim soon? Before lunch?"

Austin flicked his gaze over the pool. "Definitely. It is so nice in..."

Greg gave a tremendous shove, sending the teenager flying. Barely able to vocalize his surprise, Austin splashed into the glittering depths and surfaced with a grin. "You are so gonna get it, Three-Gee," he laughed.

"Great dive, brother. Okay, see you dudes soon and we'll all go for a swim. It's gonna be fun." Greg picked his bag up and walked off with Jeff, the pair of them sniggering. "Good kids. I take it the people around the table are their parents?"

"That's them," Jeff nodded. "Finally we have a nice setting in which we can mix and mingle properly. It's always a rushed kind of affair, those brief chats you have at things like school functions, or if we're picking up Austin after he's stayed the night. Never an appropriate place to socialize."

"Everybody leads busy lives. Look how active we are. I think, I hope, people realize and understand when the situation's like that."

"You're not wrong, Greg." He moved in closer, his voice lowered. "And surprise, surprise, Pauly's folks came along. The amount of time their kid spends here and it's never been more than a mandatory sort of greeting with Sean and Jackie." Frowning, he looked up at the huge man. "Did you ever meet his father?"

"No, mate." Greg shook his head. "Just his mother. Twice. I collected Austin that one weekend a while back, and the second time was when Pauly stayed here last New Year's Eve. Remember when we dropped him off the next morning and she was on the driveway screaming at the little fella because he hadn't called her?"

"I certainly do. That date seems to be flagged for dramas," Jeff chuckled. "Well, I guess this is the perfect situation to become better acquainted with them, and the others seem nice enough. Hey, what's the delay? Use the right-hand lane, girls." At the midway point on the stairs, they caught up with their wives and Stephanie.

"... beautiful every time I see you, Stephie," Susan was crooning. "Hi! Yes, that's my fault," she laughed. "Too busy marveling at the changes here. I'm so proud of you both. You've worked really hard to achieve this and not once have I ever seen or heard you brag about your success. I can't think of anyone more deserving."

"Thanks, Suze. That means a lot. I'm pretty sure the slog has been worth it."

"Absolutely. It's just wonderful, Jeff, and the color scheme on each tier blends in perfectly. That's something only a woman can mastermind," she giggled.

Dee gazed back over her shoulder and poked her tongue out. "See?" she declared. "I told you."

Reaching the top, they stepped onto a myriad of randomly shaped and sized flagstones that checkered the entire floor area and high walls on both levels. Composed of light-gray, maroon, pale-brown and muted-blue, the stonework was an effective contrast to the long, coffee-colored, brick kitchen and its collection of stainless steel features set under a terracotta-toned granite counter.

"Excuse me, everyone," Jeff proclaimed. "My apologies for breaking in on your conversations." Silence descended on those gathered around the table as their attention focused on the group. "I'd like to introduce two very dear people, Greg and Susan Kirk. Susan was Austin and Stephanie's babysitter. No. Correction. She's still a highly treasured minder now and then, it's just we can't seem to get rid of her husband. Every time we try throwing him out, we're the ones who end up sleeping in the car." Jeff paused while the guests laughed and called out cheerful greetings. "Greg, Susan. This is Jon and Sarah Fitch." He indicated the closest couple. "Their son is Wade. Next to them, we have Tom and Rachel Harris, Joe's parents. On the opposite side, I'm not sure if you've met Henry and Barbara."

Henry chuckled at his neighbor's impish grin. "It's great to see you both," he smiled. "We can't wait to hear about your trip. I think Barbara's planning some overseas jaunt for us and I keep telling her we're too old, but wine and sun is a bad combination, so she'll be full of questions."

"I better get that canopy up, or Barb might have thoughts about dancing on the table again." Jeff winked. "And last, but certainly not least, Sean and Jackie Benton. Jackie, you probably remember seeing this big lump before. He's not the sort of guy that goes unnoticed. I was just telling Greg how nice it is to have you all here for..."

"What do you mean?" A chair screeched sharply backward, and the short, skinny woman seated there leapt to her feet. As she gaped at Jeff, a faint pinkness spread across her pallid skin, highlighting an already inflamed appearance on the many pimples dotting her face and neck. "That's a horrible thing to say."

"Ahhhhh..." Startled, Jeff looked about at the similar expressions. "Pardon?"

"Her husband," she blurted, glowering at him. "About getting rid of her..."

"For Christ's sake, Jackie, the guy's joking. Sit the hell down." Amid his rumbling interruption, a portly, unshaven man stretched his hairy arm across the woman's midriff and eased her back onto the soft padding.

Like a snake, Jackie Benton whipped her head around, sending her long, black hair flying outward momentarily. It settled on her shoulders again, hanging limp, straggly, and with an oily sheen that suggested neither washing nor brushing had occurred for some time. "Don't touch me," she hissed.

Ignoring her withering scowl, Sean Benton focused his attention on the group, lifted a can of beer and saluted them with a hearty belch. "You were saying?"

"Um." Jeff studied the mellow, watery-blue and visibly bloodshot eyes. "I think we might get some lunch happening."

the announcement

Greg poured a newly-opened bottle into his frosted glass, stopping an inch from the rim to give the bubbling, golden-brown liquid a frothy head at the top. Taking a swig, enjoying the full, velvety coolness flooding his mouth and throat, he licked the foam off his upper lip and smacked them together while inspecting the food cooking on the barbecue. To his left, a mound of sliced onions sizzled on the hotplate, their piquant aroma tickling his nose as he stirred them with the silvery tongs, and with a deft flick of his wrist, he spun a row of steaks arranged neatly across the cast-iron grille to the right, triggering a burst of bright, orange flames that seized the garlic and basil sauce spread upon the crackling meat. White, puffy smoke, thick with the spicy scent, wafted upward and curled past the edge of an enormous retractable canopy Jeff was currently deploying. Satisfied at the coppery tinge on the sausages nearest the edge, he turned to watch while the heavy-duty fabric rolled out along galvanized metal tracks, mounted just within his arm's length on four sturdy, stainless steel poles, two on each level. With a soft clunk, the covering reached its full extent, throwing a pleasant shadow across the table and just over one third of the pool below.

"Huge man. Have shade now. Shade good," Jeff grunted. He clicked the latch shut on a small, black box fastened to the wall six feet from the gas-powered barbecue.

"Mah wife be appreesheeatin' it," Greg drawled. "An' whut in tarnation happen eff'n thar's no eleckricity t'drive thet fine corntrapshun?"

"Got chain on motor. On shiny thing me call pole. Pull chain. Shade move. Shade good."

"If you two don't stop talking like that I'll get Jackie involved." Bustling about the kitchen with Susan, Dee paused to kiss her husband's cheek and smack his buttocks. "Jeffrey, you've already used ten years of your quota."

"Only ten? I thought we were well over," Jeff grinned. "And please don't have Mrs. Cheerful start with me again. I'm sure her eye twitched when I made that innocent and casual remark about the similarity with Suze and this." He tapped the Barbie picture on Greg's torso.

"Innocent and casual?" Susan snorted. "You've had that planned the moment you saw it."

"Spot-on, my dear. But you can't blame me. The fickle finger of fate pointed us to a shop selling barbecue aprons manufactured by Kiwis. A shop in little old Crescent Lake, no less. Amazing." He shook his head. "I was under the impression most things came from China."

"No, mate," Greg laughed. "Not quality like this. That's why everyone found it so funny. Well... everyone except Jackie. Somehow, I don't think a sense of humor is high on her list of priorities."

"Neither is pride in her appearance," Dee said quietly. "I feel sorry for whatever marital issues they've obviously got, because it's certainly taken a toll on her demeanor. She was a very attractive and courteous woman years ago."

"What about Pauly's old man? Changed much?" Greg asked. "He seems to be an okay sort of guy."

Dee glanced at Sean, who was running a chunky hand through his short, sandy-colored hair and leaning to one side, chatting with Jon Fitch, the white singlet he wore stretching over the broad expanse of his tubby belly. "He's, um, well let's just say he's more generously proportioned these days. Aside from that, honey, we don't really know him enough."

"Yep. It's crazy." Jeff turned off the gas cylinder while Greg stacked the cooked and ready to eat food on a large tray. "But hopefully we'll have that enigmatic couple fathomed by the end of the day. And if we're talking similarity again, then holy-moly-crap-a-doodles, put a greasy wig and dirty dress on Pauly, dot his face with red marker, and I'm not sure if I could tell him from his mother. Same height, same build, same facial structure. Seriously, their photo should be under the definition of spitting image in the dictionary."

"You're right with all of that," Greg agreed. "Except the eyes. It's unusual for offspring to have a different color to the parents. Generally they'll inherit that trait from one or the other." He shrugged his massive shoulders. "Okay, I'm organized here, brother. Suze, put the salad down, sweetheart, I'll come back for it. You just go and put your feet up. And, mate, holy-moly-crap-a-doodles?" Greg sniggered on their way to the waiting guests. "I don't know what the heck that means, but I like it. Your company should start making greeting cards. It's definitely the sort of Jeffrey Cooper comedic absurdity I'd buy."

"Hmmm." Jeff nodded. "That's not a bad idea. All right, you wonderfully patient people," he called. "Let the feasting begin."

"Bring it on!" Sean boomed. As the food touched the table he loaded his plate with meat, devoured half a sausage in one bite, and waved the remainder at the level below. "Hey, Jeff," he blared midway through his chewing. "I'm so hungry I was even planning a raid on those guys down there."

Taking a spot between Greg and Tom Harris, Jeff studied the four teenagers seated at the old patio table. Chattering animatedly, they scoffed their lunch and burst into great gales of hilarity that echoed around the backyard when Pauly reached across and tousled Joe's floppy brown hair. "You'd be a brave man, buddy. I think they'd chew your fingers off if you got too close. That's why Stephie put her dog inside, she feared for his life at one stage. Right, honey?" He leaned forward and grinned at his daughter, positioned farther to the left among the women.

"No, Dad. I put him inside because all Austin would do is feed him. He'll end up getting fat," she stated, and joined in on the adult's laughter.

"It's nice to see my funny, good-humored darling back again." Dee patted Stephanie's arm. "Her best friend couldn't make it today and she's feeling a bit lonely being the only girl."

"Awww, sweetheart," Susan smiled. "You're not alone. We'll go for a swim later once those rough boys are finished."

"How long have you known each other?" Rachel Harris asked Dee and Susan.

"Quite a while. I met Susan when she was nearly ten," Dee replied. "I did some secretarial work for her parents, Cameron and

Geena Callahan. They had a law firm in town before relocating to Florida years ago."

"So, what's it like to look at Austin now, Susan, remembering him as a baby and all the diapers you changed?"

"It makes you realize how fast time flies," she said, and grimaced. "But I tend to think of the whole experience as a big positive, because it's certainly prepared me for when I have children."

"Are there any plans?" Sarah Fitch asked.

Sitting next to Greg, Susan shared an inadvertent, momentary look with her husband, completely oblivious to the light-brown, watchful eyes, twinkling above a slowly parting smile on Dee's pink lips. "Susan? I saw that. Something's up. First, there's the non-alcoholic drinks... and you love sharing a wine with me." Her brow rose. "Then, Greg's been fussing over you the moment you arrived. Have you got anything you'd like to tell us?" Suddenly realizing how it must have sounded, Dee quickly made amends. "Oh, I'm... I'm, so, so sorry," she stammered, bringing her hands to her cheeks. "It's just... just... I don't know what came over me. Sweetheart, please, please accept my apologies, I didn't mean for it to come out like an interrogation. It was terrible of me to press you like that. I'm so very, very sorry."

"Dee, it's okay," Susan laughed. "I took no offense, at all. I've thought of you as my sister for a long time, so I guess I shouldn't be surprised when you pick up on things like this. Especially with the help given by Mr. Conspicuous here." She nudged Greg's enormous bicep and turned to face to him. "Shall we?"

"Mr. Conspicuous here says absolutely, categorically yes." Jeff perched himself on the edge of his chair and beamed at them while Dee's hands covered her mouth. "Do it, Suze. Make that announcement, my darling."

Please, honey, please, Dee thought. Say what I hope you're going to say.

"Well... we wanted to tell you something later on tonight, and it was never our intention for this to take away anything from Austin's special day, but... well." Susan looked from Dee to Jeff and back again, over and over, her green eyes shining brightly. "I'm pregnant. We're going to have a baby!"

the raconteur

"Nup. It didn't happen last year and it ain't gonna happen this year, next year, or any year. We go fishing by ourselves. No girls allowed." Taking rapid gulps of his Coke, Pauly exhaled noisily before setting the can down with a heavy thump. "What?" he belched, peering around at the shaking heads.

"Who died and made you king of the world?"

"No one. Wade, that's the dumbest thing I've ever heard. Besides, Austin asked and they don't want to do it. They're not interested. Right?"

Austin regarded the small boy staring at him. "Pauly," he chuckled. "Why are you still going on about this?"

"Because you idiots think they should do stuff with us when they didn't even want to come here for your birthday."

"Jeez, you're a douche sometimes. Coops only invited Tess and her friends to the party, he didn't mention fishing. And since Tess is in California, d'ya think they'd come without her?" Joe's eyes narrowed. "I know what this is, dude. You've got the hots for Shivawn."

"No I haven't. Get lost, asshole." Glowering, Pauly stabbed his finger across the table. "I think it's you…"

A sudden, loud shriek broke the afternoon air. Everyone froze, except Austin, who bolted from his chair, sending it crashing backward as he headed for the second level. With his long, muscular legs pumping, he covered the distance in a time that would make an Olympic sprinter seethe with envy, and came to a halt, frowning, at the top of the stairs. Before him, Stephanie, Greg, Susan, his parents, Henry and Barbara, stood and moved about, all of them hugging, kissing, shaking hands, their faces plastered with the broadest grins he had ever seen while congratulations and excited chatter began.

"Hey! There you are," Jeff exclaimed, and beckoned vigorously.

"What's going on?" Austin strode forward, his hands spread wide. "I thought someone was in trouble."

"Not at all, mate." Draping his arm around Austin's shoulder, Jeff sauntered beside his son, just turned fourteen and already taller by an inch. "Greg. Suze. It's all yours."

"We've got some good news, sweetheart. Or should I say, Uncle Austin."

"Uncle? Me? Huh?" For a second he studied Susan's dazzling smile, his furrowed brow rising when the realization of her words struck him. "Does that mean you're... you're pregnant? OH, WOW!" he yelled at her energetic nod. "That's awesome, I'm so happy for you." Stepping away from Jeff, he stooped to give her a gentle cuddle. "I promise I'll look after your baby forever. And you and Greg, of course." As they separated, Austin saw tears rolling down her cheeks. "What's wrong? Is it something I said? I'm sorry," he added hastily.

Susan gazed into the deep luminosity of his purpley-blue eyes. "Nothing's wrong, darling, it's just been an emotional day so far. I know you'll look after us. It's what you're all about, isn't it? I hope you don't mind me saying this, and I know that you won't, but when I see you now after all these growing years, sometimes I feel sad. Only because I see the little boy I used to dress and feed. Who was so happy and full of excitement when he showed me his new Bert and Ernie pajamas. The child who came running, shouting Sooz-in, and clamping himself to my leg whenever I got here," she giggled. "I loved those times, and I miss them. But now I can go through it all again." Smiling, she reached up to smooth his ruffled hair. "Austin William Cooper, it will be an honor and a privilege to have you and your wonderful family involved in our child's life. I'm the one who should be sorry, honey. I didn't want to spoil your birthday."

"Are you kidding? Susan, you've just made this the best birthday ever. More than you could imagine. It's my honor, my privilege, and I'll always be there for you, like you've been for me."

"Thank you, sweetheart. Have I told you how grown-up you act?"

"Mom and Dad would say it's mainly the opposite. But I've got a slight recollection you've mentioned it before." Austin burst out laughing with Susan.

During the interaction, Dee's hand had once again cupped her mouth as the tears coursed freely down her face, taken aback at the empathy shown by Susan's identical thoughts. She felt relieved, comforted, knowing that another person, a woman, understood the emotional upheaval of watching her babies' growth among the stumbling blocks thrown out by life in general, a contrast to Jeff's reaction on the topic. Within his soothing consolation, he passed it off through seemingly complete indifference, saying things like, 'Time waits for no one, babe. These things happen.' But she knew him better than that, a seventeen year marriage inside a relationship of twenty-four told her otherwise, and if the most loving, devoted man she had ever met wanted to deal with it in that manner, then so be it. In due course, he would reveal the trueness of his feelings, and on that day, she would hold and comfort him, as he had in her time of need.

For the moment, her spirit soared after witnessing the exchange between Austin and Susan, and she knew everything would be okay. Her son just interacted with someone he had known his entire life on a more advanced and intellectual level than she could have hoped for, all the while doing it with total disregard for everyone watching and listening, including his peers, who lingered on the top step, unmistakably hesitant about the unfolding events.

Austin turned to Greg. "Three-Gee," he grinned. "Words aren't enough, bro. I think you know how happy I am for you both."

Pressing his lips together tightly for a split second, Greg's voice cracked when he spoke. "Come here, mate."

"Are you okay, honey?" Jeff murmured. Tenderly, he brushed Dee's tears away as Austin and Greg thumped each other's back in their strong embrace.

"Never better, babe," she nodded. "I'm just absolutely delighted for them, and so very, very proud of our son."

*   *   *

"I don't know how you did it," Dee warbled. "I would've let that cat out of the bag the second I arrived." She squeezed Susan's hand and laughed along with the other women. Gathered together at one end of the table, they chatted about names, diaper brands, and general child-rearing advice while trying to include the quietest person there, who merely sat with a weak smile and simple nod whenever the discussion about all things baby led to fits of giggling.

"So, it hasn't been confirmed yet," she declared, finally joining with some flat and toneless words during a brief lull in the conversation.

"What hasn't?" Dee asked.

"The unborn child. The pregnancy." Like an oil slick on the gently undulating surface of a filthy and congested, third world harbor, Jackie's greasy hair flowed sideways when her head twitched in their direction.

Susan scanned the woman sitting directly opposite. "No, not yet. We only found out this morning, but we'll be making an appointment to see my doctor on Monday," she smiled.

"Mmmm," Jackie hummed, and directed her attention upward.

Shaking her head, Susan turned away from the dreary expression. "That's why we were so late in getting here, Dee. We had to get a testing kit from a drug store in town and ended up using the whole packet. I have never experienced a wait like it, but the result was positive three times. Add the fact that I missed my period, which is like clockwork for me, and it's fairly conclusive. Besides, I can just feel it."

"Honey, you are positively glowing. And Greg looks... well." She glanced to her right at the group of men standing near the table, busily inspecting two sections of an extremely long fishing rod. "He's the happiest I've ever seen."

"He is so excited about fatherhood and thinks it's simply perfect how the baby will be born in America, but conceived in New Zealand," she laughed.

"YO! Three-Gee! Heads up," Austin's resonating hail sounded behind them. He hurled a white, oval-shaped ball toward Greg, who flung his hand out and plucked the object from its curving flight. "Thanks again for the awesome presents," he said, trotting across with his friends.

"You're welcome, brother. Hopefully that rod might do the trick and land us an elusively pesky Legend Fish. This mate of mine back in NZ says it's the best he's ever used, and he's fished off the beach, rocks, lakes, lagoons, boats, whatever. He reckons that carbon-fiber shaft will nearly double over at its tip, and with a good technique you could cast it for hundreds of feet."

"Can't wait," Austin grinned. "We'll be going on Tuesday." He pointed at Greg's hand. "Hey, do you think it'll be okay to throw that around in the pool, or will the water wreck it?"

Greg flicked the ball upward, where it rasped against the massive cover at its spinning apex before thumping back in the towering man's grasp. He handed it to Austin and nodded. "It'll be fine once the chlorine's rinsed off. After a while it might get affected, but that's no problem, mate." He tapped a logo printed on one side. "I know a guy who works for this company and he can get me these anytime, no worries at all."

"Cool! But I'll look after this one, of course."

"I know you will, bro." Returning Austin's thumbs-up, Greg smiled while the teenagers made a jostling run for the stairs, and turned at the pat on his upper arm.

"Nice catch just then," Jon Fitch remarked. "Do you play football over here? With skills like that you'd have to be a wide receiver or maybe tight end."

"No," he replied as the men returned to their seats. "Not here. I used to play a bit of rugby union years back, but had to stop."

"I've heard about that rugby thing," Sean stated. "Never seen it, though. How good a player were you?"

Greg shrugged. "I dunno. I wasn't too bad, I guess. It's been a while now."

"You sure look fit and strong for someone who doesn't play anymore," Tom Harris observed. "How do you keep in shape?"

"If I can find the time, I get to the gym now and then. But it'll probably be impossible once the baby comes along, and our shop keeps us really busy, so in a couple of years I'll be half this size."

A loud shriek, mixed together with raucous laughter, sounded from the level below, and everyone at the table looked down to see Austin jogging to the pool, Pauly slung over his broad shoulder. Pausing at the edge, he jumped long and high, releasing his friend a millisecond before impact. The water surged up and outward, sending a huge, exploding fan of twinkling beads through the bright sunshine.

"Pauly!" Jackie half rose and twisted in her chair as the two boys surfaced with enormous grins. Her bony hand gripped the armrest, green-blue veins protruding against the tight, pasty-white skin of her knuckles. "Pauly, are you okay?" she yelled, her voice trembling. "Austin, be careful. You'll hurt him, doing that."

"Jackie," Sean growled. "Don't be stupid, they're just fooling around. Stop mollycoddling the freakin' kid and leave 'em alone, for Christ's sake."

Ever so slowly, Jackie lowered herself to the cushioned seat. In her sockets, dark-gray eyes, the color of freshly-poured, wet concrete, aimed a smoldering, iceberg-melting stare upon Sean. "He is my son," she snapped, and gritted her teeth, the right side of her upper lip curling back. "And don't you dare use the name of my Lord and Savior in your foul-mouthed rants again. God hates you."

For a few seconds, the adults gawked at Jackie before exchanging uncomfortable, stunned glances. Susan and Dee shared a quick peek, their foreheads creased, while Jeff looked at Greg, who raised his eyebrows and gave a small grimace. Mercifully, Austin's shout broke the embarrassing silence.

"Three-Gee! Are you gonna come for a swim? We should get a game of pool rugby going, bro."

"Uhhh, yeah, that's the best idea yet, mate, and I'll be there real, real soon."

"What about you, Dad? Hey, what about all the guys? We'll draw up teams."

His statement brought a cheer of acceptance from his friends, and a deep, overall murmur of consensus from the males gathered at their end of the table.

"Should I bring Duke outside now?" Austin continued. "He can come for a swim, as well."

"No, buddy, Stephie and Duke are fine by themselves and the pool is not an extra-large bath for canines, thanks very much. You see, Suze," Jeff chuckled. "Now there's a prime example of his opposite moments." He joined in on the sudden hilarity, immense relief at the distraction palpable to everyone.

"Greg, if you don't mind my asking, why do Austin and Stephanie call you Three-Gee?" Rachel asked.

When the huge man dropped his shaking head, Susan answered with an impish smile. "That's my fault. It happened the first time I brought him here to meet my extended family. At the start, the children were terrified. Actually, that's wrong. Stephie was terrified and Austin simply stood there, watching him. Poor Stephie, it was only a couple of weeks after the incident at the kin…" Pausing, she reached across and rubbed Dee's hand. "Anyway, Austin was five and Stephie was three, and I thoughtlessly made a joke that he was a giant named Greg. Well, Austin just said 'Coooool' while Stephie burst out crying and hid behind Jeff's legs."

"No, I'm pretty sure it was the other way round," Jeff quipped.

"You fool," Dee laughed. "Susan, ignore him and carry on with your wonderful story."

"Poor Stephie… and poor Greg." Susan smiled at her husband. "He didn't know what to do at first, but then he did something that was really amazing. He sat down right where he was and said to Stephie that he wasn't a giant, he was just a big person. I can still see the image of her beautiful, wide eyes peering around the side of Jeff's trousers. Greg said that he might be big, but he wasn't mean and rough, and if she wanted to call him a giant, then that was okay with him. All this time, Austin is still standing there, in the sitting room, at

Greg's side, and he blurts out, 'Yeah. You are a giant, and your name is Greg.' He was silent for a moment... you could virtually see the little cogs spinning inside his head." Susan giggled at the memory. "And he said, 'If you're not mean and rough, then you must be gentle. You're Greg the Gentle Giant. GGG. Three-Gee.' Then he jumped on him and started wrestling, and before you know it, Stephie is all over him too. And... well... there you have it. It was the most incredible thing to watch, wasn't it, Dee?"

"It sure was, honey. They've loved him ever since, and it's one of the reasons why I know you'll make an absolutely fantastic father, Greg."

"Thanks, Dee," Greg beamed. "That's a really nice..."

A single, powerful sob disrupted his remaining words, and they all looked at Jackie, who raised a hand to wipe away the tears spilling down her cheeks. Her features had softened visibly, and her moist eyes blinked rapidly as she gazed at Greg. "How did you and Susan meet?" she whispered. "Was it here, in tow... in town?" Her husky voice crackled at the end.

"Not in Crescent Lake, no." Greg leaned forward. "Jackie, are you all right?" He glanced at her husband, who finished a long quaff of his beer and deposited it amidst the many empty cans on the tabletop. Settling farther back into the soft padding, placing his elbows on the armrest, Sean steepled his fingers under his chin and fixed an intense stare upon his wife.

"Please. Carry on," Jackie murmured, a faint smile twitching the corners of her mouth.

"Okay. But I'll keep it short how I ended up here. I don't want to bore you all." Greg swept his eyes over the silent, expectant faces. "Years ago I played rugby in New Zealand, then moved to England to try it over there. In one game, I injured my knee, and after it healed, I thought I'd travel around America before heading back home. While I was in Colorado I met Susan and the rest is history in the making."

"Well, son-of-a-gun." Everyone turned their attention to Jeff as he shook his head and laughed. "Gregory Matthew Kirk," he breathed. "Sheesh! Talk about modesty. Mate, if there's an award for the quickest account ever, you've just won it, hands down. I nearly said something earlier with your 'played a bit of rugby, I guess I wasn't too bad' part, but the opportunity was lost at the time. Now, my friend, these good people should hear from the genuine raconteur." Jeff rolled his hand in Susan's direction. "Suze, your version, please."

"That was a fairly edited description," Susan chuckled. "Babe, I think I should embellish the tale just a tiny bit. You deserve it." Shifting her weight, she noticed Jackie alternating her observation among Greg, Jeff, Dee, and herself every few seconds. "Greg played rugby at a very high level in New Zealand, and was so good that he should've been selected for their national team, the All Blacks. In fact, at the time, his exclusion caused quite a bit of controversy with the general public. Rugby union is absolutely massive over there."

"If I may, I'll interject for just a few seconds, Suze. Other than Henry, have any of you guys watched rugby before?" Jeff cast his sight over the remaining men.

"I have," a voice next to him rumbled.

"You don't count, ya big lump, and to quote my gorgeous wife, 'you fool.'" Jeff and Greg grinned at each other. "We watch the All Blacks on ESPN whenever we can. They're the best rugby players on the planet and the toughest team to beat. Anytime you want to come around and catch a game, you're more than welcome. You ought to see these guys. They don't wear helmets and pads, and before kickoff, they do this challenge called a haka. It looks fantastic and scares the crap out of the opposition. It's great. Anyway, sorry for cutting in there, Suze."

"That's okay, Jeff. I know how much you enjoy your rugby," she smiled. "So, it wasn't long after the non-selection when Greg was offered, and accepted, a contract to play in England, for a team called Harlequins, but he injured his knee during a game only a few months later."

"How bad was the injury?" Jon asked.

"Severe." Susan looked at Greg.

"Well, it ended my career," he nodded. "I ruptured the posterior and anterior cruciate ligaments, snapped tendons, tore my quadricep, and had my kneecap relocated to the back of my leg."

"Ouch!" Tom cringed. "How did that happen, buddy?"

"While this guy was tackling me another bloke fell on my leg and basically pushed the whole thing inside out. Then after I went down, I got trapped on the bottom of a maul and rolled over with it still stuck under everyone. Apparently, it was even heard by some spectators in the stands and they'd said it was like a gunshot going off. I can't remember much about the event, the medics got some morphine into me pretty quick. If I hadn't been stuck and rolled the damage might not have been so bad, but, you know, these things happen." Greg shrugged his massive shoulders, his lips pressed firmly together.

"Shit." Sean shook his head. "You poor bastard."

"I like to think every cloud has a silver lining, mate, and in this case I met mine. On top of that, I can walk fine and still exercise. It's all good."

"True." Sean took a quick look at Jackie. "Hey, what's a maul?"

"I'll explain later. Suze won't be too happy if I stop her now with some rugby chat."

"Excellent decision, babe." Susan blew her husband a kiss. "Anyway, after months of rehabilitation Greg decided to travel the States, and was exploring Colorado on his way to the east coast when his rental car broke down on the outskirts of Castle Rock. I was coming back from Denver, having just completed a computer studies course, and this really nasty storm kicked up. There was thunder and lightning, torrential rain, a howling wind, and I passed this dark, empty car on the side of the road. I wasn't going fast, I couldn't, I could hardly see a thing, and a few miles on I saw this person trudging along, his head down. He stopped, turned toward me and stuck his thumb out, but I drove straight past, doing something that Jeff had always drummed into me. Never pick up hitchhikers, there's too many bad stories about it." Susan giggled when she peered down the table and saw Jeff's wide grin. "I checked him out as I went by and he was absolutely drenched. He looked so lonely and miserable, the poor thing. About a mile down the road, something told me this guy was okay, that obviously he was walking away from a broken-down car, and I figured I could offer him a lift to the nearest rest stop where he could sort it all out, and if I got any bad vibes then I'd just hightail it out of there. So, I went back, pulled up and asked if he was all right. I heard his funny accent, got a good feeling that he was fine and gave him a ride, which ended back at my place. And no." She wagged her finger back and forth. "There was nothing like what you're all probably thinking." Susan laughed along with the others. "I recall Dee conveying wise words to me a very long time ago about knowing when that special someone comes along, and she couldn't have been more correct, because he was, and is, the consummate gentleman, and before you know it, we're dating, setting up our own business, married, and as of today, expecting our first child. Now that, my darling husband, is the short version."

"Wonderful, wonderful!" Rachel exclaimed, clapping her hands. "How romantic."

"Honey." Lifting his enormous frame from the chair, Greg ambled the brief distance to Susan, squatted, and kissed her cheek. "Didn't I already tell that story?" His blue eyes flashed as he gazed adoringly at his wife.

During the sudden blast of merriment nobody heard Jackie's low mumble. "And the rest is history in the making."

the altercation

Simultaneously, Greg and Jeff pushed themselves off the lowest step and glided into the tepid depths of the pool. Bringing their forward momentum to a halt, they paused in the shaded area and looked toward the house. Gentle waves lapped around them, the result of some frolicking play by the other males currently enjoying their swim.

Greg sighed. "This is a nice temperature compared to last year. Not so cold when you first get in." He pointed farther along the right-hand wall, at a large hot tub standing two feet above the coping stones. A molded, chute-like spout projected from its closest side, releasing a cascade of deliciously hot water, flowing and churning into the pool's deep expanse. "The initial chilliness has gone with that clever little setup."

"Nothing much gets past you," Jeff chuckled. "And through heat loss, it'll never get too hot in summer, even with the volume of water being continuously circulated from the tub."

"What a great system."

"Yeah. Crafty old Ben. He's pretty good with the plumbing side of things." Jeff nodded at a sizeable, wooden hut standing near the outer limit of the decking. "Along with pumps, chemicals and cleaning gear and so forth, there's also a gas heater, so we can also heat the pool by itself, just from the tub, like today, or both at the same time."

"Fantastic. I can't wait to try it in winter. In fact." Greg grinned. "I can't wait at all. How about swapping houses?"

"Sure. I'd also donate two uncivilized louts commonly known as the Cooper children, but because of that whole penniless issue I had to sell them. A week today, they'll be working some bazaar in Morocco. Kind of fitting, really, considering it's the style of this pool, and what a great way to recoup the expenses. There's even a slight possibility I'll miss them."

"I heard that, Dad," Austin laughed. He coasted up to them with Sean at his side and splashed his father with one great fling of his arm. "I hope you got a good deal."

Jeff shrugged. "Wasn't too bad."

"You gotta real first-class place, buddy," Sean remarked. "I like this, it's a nice design. Specially that." He gestured to their left, where the pool wall curled in and out across its entire length in an attractively wavy pattern.

"Thanks. It's taken a bit of time, and a lot of reminding from Dee. But... happy wife, happy life," Jeff smiled.

"Mmmm. For some," he muttered. "How big is this thing, anyway?"

"Forty feet long by twenty feet wide. Depth of about six and a half feet there." Jeff aimed his finger at the house. "With a steady gradient leading to a little over four feet at the other end. We deliberated for a few weeks on the size and finally decided on going large. And when I say we, I mean Dee. No rhyme intended."

"I'm with you on that one," Sean sniggered. "Hey, talking about large, that reminds me." Looking at Greg, he ran his eyes quickly over the man's massive slab of a chest and huge, muscular shoulders. "I was going to ask you something before. Now don't get me wrong when I say this, 'cos obviously you're a big enough guy and anyone would have to be crazy to rile your bad side, but Jeff's kids call you a gentle giant. So what were you like when you played your game? You can't be gentle when you've gotta win, right?"

Greg nodded. "That's right. On the field I was different. I wasn't dirty or nasty, but I did give it everything."

Jeff laughed. "Oh boy, here we go again. Sean, we've seen footage of him and let me tell you this... he was one hell of a player."

"Yeah," Austin cut in. Standing just outside the shadow cast by the gigantic covering above them, his eyes shone a light, vibrant blue. "They called him The Wizard, 'cos he could do magic when he had that ball in his hand."

"I dunno." Greg ruffled Austin's wet hair. "Maybe."

"You don't sing your own praises, mate." Jeff nudged his friend. "So let us hum this little ditty. His position was lock forward, and you need to be extra big for that. He was six foot eight and a half inches, two hundred and ninety five pounds of lethal, killing power. A wrecking machine when he played rugby and a book loving gentleman when he wasn't."

"Three-Gee and Susan own this awesome bookstore in town," Austin added. "You should check it out sometime. Hasn't Pauly told you? We've been there loads of times."

"Nah. He doesn't tell me stuff anymore." Sean looked over their shoulders at Pauly, who was throwing Austin's ball around with the other men. Motion on the upper level caught his eye, and he watched as Jackie turned away from the laughter and chatter to gaze down at her son. "We used to talk, but lately things have been..." For a few moments, he fell silent before directing his attention back to Greg. "What sort of books?"

"Usually our specialty is the rare and antique kind, although we have expanded the business to include mainstream material. Pauly thinks we should start selling comics, as well."

"Huhhh," Sean grunted. "I don't read much, unlike him." He focused on Pauly again. "But that'll most likely change in a couple of years."

"Well." Jeff exchanged glances with Greg and Austin. "We should get this game going. The afternoon's slipping away already."

"Dad, there's only nine of us. We need an even number. Maybe you should ask Steph or Henry again, they might want to play now."

"No, mate. Stephie's enjoying herself talking with the girls, and Henry's quite right with what he said. You young hooligans would end up killing him. Besides, Greg's on our team, remember? It's no contest, this game is as good as won."

"Really?" Sean's brow rose. "We'll see." Grinning, he clapped Greg on the shoulder. "Now I know you have a weak spot, you're going down, big guy. I'll show you how we do it in America."

"Game on," Greg nodded. "Lads," he called. "Let's go."

*   *   *

"Three-Gee," Wade screamed. "Three-Gee!" Waving his hands frantically, he jumped from side to side before surging through a gap between his father and Pauly.

Greg let Joe seize his arm, lifted him and the ball effortlessly above the churning water and tossed the oval object to the excited teenager. As Wade caught it, Pauly rushed toward him, straight into a textbook parry when his friend dodged the attack by planting his hand on top of Pauly's head and pushing him under the choppy waves. Charging forward, his arms pumping fiercely, Wade thrust himself full length to the end of the pool, hollering loudly at another point scored while Pauly came up coughing, spluttering and rubbing the water from his eyes.

"Nice one, mate," Greg called. "And great effort, Pauly. Just watch his hand and grab that arm if you see it coming up."

"Dude, I thought you were gonna throw me out of the pool then," Joe laughed.

"Not possible, brother, you're too big and strong for that." Greg clamped Joe's shoulder and gave him a quick, friendly shake. "Wade, Sean's getting bored. He can have first possession now."

"Yeah, yeah," the man grumbled when the ball landed next to him, spraying fat droplets in his face. Snatching it up, Sean looked at his son. "Pauly," he barked. "Tackle him, goddammit. The rule's simple enough. As soon as you've got him, he has to release the freakin' thing, and since he's the only one in front, he's got no choice but to pass it backward, away from the goal line. Shadow the guy. Put your arms out wide like I showed ya. Sweet freakin' Jesus, we're getting thrashed here."

On the level above, Jackie leapt from her chair, hurried to the glass barrier and leaned precariously over the top rail. Wringing her hands, she saw Pauly wipe his long, black fringe across his forehead, glare briefly at Sean, and turn away when Austin swam close to his side.

"You can do it, mate," Austin said. He lowered his voice. "Hey, you've probably noticed that Wade keeps stepping to his left every time. You should fool him by…"

"Pauly." Jackie's shrill tone carried around the backyard. "Are you okay? Are you hurt, darling? I think you should come out of the pool now. Yes. You should come out. You must come out."

Behind him, Jeff heard the forced, heavy sigh a split second before Sean's angry yell. "Jackie, would you shut up already? That's about the hundredth frickin' time you've said it. Have a good look here." Breathing deeply, he rotated a tight circle, his arms gesturing wildly. "He's with five grown men. This guy could lift eight of him. One-handed." He brandished a dripping finger in Greg's direction. "There are also three teenagers, one who's two and a half times his size and can save his scrawny little ass if he had to. Has anything ever happened when he's been fishing? No. He's fine. So for Christ's sake, would you just butt out, leave him and me the hell alone, and just let us enjoy ourselves."

Slowly and surely, Jackie made her way to the stairs, not once taking her wide and staring, smoky-gray eyes off Sean. "You and your filthy language," she rasped. "You and your filthy attitude."

"Oh, I'm the filthy one, huh? When's the last time you looked in a mirror? The last time you had a shower? Washed your hair? Brushed your teeth? Sit the hell down and shut your trap, you've embarrassed us more than enough today."

"How dare you. I'm sick of you talking to me like that." Taking small, shuffling steps she started her descent. "I'm sick of you talking to Pauly like that."

"I've told you to stop treating him like a freakin' baby," he snapped. "Maybe then he won't act like one and I won't have to say anything."

"He is my child," she screeched. The spots on her neck and face vanished, swallowed instantly by a ghastly red glow that swamped her pale skin.

In the pool, Pauly went the exact opposite. He turned a pasty white, all the color draining rapidly with the sight of his parents' freely open altercation. "No. No, please, not now," he muttered, and closed his eyes against the last glimpse of everyone's gaping mouth.

"Yep, you're right there," Sean blared, nodding fiercely. "So go out and buy him another video game, Jackie. Another TV. Another computer. Another smartphone. That'll make it all better. You send the kid off to school looking like a damn pauper and then get him any other crap he wants. I'm just a simple, low-paid carpenter. I haven't got the money for his weekly demands."

Reaching the bottom, Jackie inched her way along the wooden deck. "You know what we've been through. You know I want to keep my baby safe. You know I have to, and I'll do anything for that, YOU FUCKER," she howled.

"Oh my God," Susan whispered while Dee dropped her head and wrapped an arm around Stephanie's shoulder when her daughter virtually climbed onto her chair to snuggle in closer.

"Sean, Jackie. Come on. Let's back it up a bit here, okay?" Jeff implored. "We'll all have a nice, hot cup of coffee, relax, and try to work things out."

"Jeff." Sean's shoulders slumped. "I appreciate it, really. But there's nothing that can be done right now, not unless you or any of these other, good, normal people are shrinks. She's got a problem, and she just flat refuses to fix something that goes back a long, long time."

A strange, high-pitched whine suddenly began. At the start, everybody peered about the property, confusedly trying to trace the sound, until its source became all too apparent when the horrendous and ear-piercing drone escalated to a full blown, unleashed scream. "I... hate... you," Jackie seethed, the moment it died on her lips. "You promised me. All those years ago, you promised. And I married you. I married you when you're nothing compared to him, you... you... you motherfucker. You're nothing, you hear? You're nothing but a... a... a fucking... fucking cun..."

"Whoa, whoa, WHOA, ENOUGH," Jeff roared, his hands high in the air. "No one here should be subjected to your hostility, especially the children. What the hell makes you think you can come to my home and act like this in front of my family, my guests?" His faded-blue eyes, normally so calm and friendly, blazed like wildfire. "It's time you both left. I want you off my property. Now," he growled. "Pauly, you're more than welcome to stay. I'll drop you off late..."

"NO!" Jackie's sight flew from Jeff to her son, pinning the small, trembling boy where he stood. "Pauly, get out of the pool, gather your clothes and go straight to the car. Don't make me say it twice. You," she spat at Sean as her son trudged silently through the tranquil water. "You're not coming. You can walk."

"Is that so? You won't get far in my car without my keys. You see what you've done? You've ruined Austin's birthday, you stupid bitch. You've ruined Greg and Susan's special day. You've ruined everything for everyone, including our sham of a marriage. So why don't you stay a while and explain that? You need help, woman."

Speechless, blinking rapidly, Jackie spun on her heels and stormed off. Coming to a halt at the patio, she looked back and smiled.

"Thank you very much for such a nice day, Deangela," she called sweetly. "Thank you, Jeffrey. Happy birthday, Austin. God loves you all. Pauly! Hurry up."

Pauly flinched at the harsh scold and rushed about, collecting his tee-shirt and shorts. Barely able to make eye contact, his head sagging, he shuffled backward. "Thanks, Jeff. Thanks, Austin," he murmured and scurried to his mother.

The moment they disappeared around the corner Sean climbed out of the pool, slipped his singlet on and stretched it over his stout, glistening belly. "Well. I... um." Rubbing the dark stubble on his chin, he gazed at the wordless, staring faces. "I guess that's that. Jeff, you're right, of course. It was... um... unfair for this to happen at your home, and you people shouldn't have been, ahhh, exposed to our problems. I'm really, truly sorry this happened. Thank you for your hospitality, Jeff. You're a good guy. Thank you, Dee, thank you everyone. Austin, you're a great friend to Pauly and I hope this hasn't destroyed it. Happy birthday, buddy, if you can call it that now. I can make it up to you someday, all this, I'm... I'm just not sure how."

Among his last words, before he turned and trudged across the deck, Sean's body sagged and his eyes seemed to dim, his vitality seeping away visibly with each passing second.

the crossroads

Standing near the top of the driveway, watching the departing guests turn right onto Fairview Terrace, everyone waved a final goodbye when the cars gave a brief, tooting honk and coasted down the road.

"We'll get going, as well," Henry yawned. "The afternoon excitement has taken its toll. Thanks for having two old fogies over for your party, Austin, it's been... hmmm." He pursed his crinkly lips and nodded. "Interesting."

"When it comes to action-packed birthdays, you can always depend on us," Jeff grinned. "It's Cooper guaranteed."

Henry chuckled. "That's what I'm afraid of. If I didn't hold you and the family in such high esteem, I'd have run you out of town years ago."

"Cain't do that no more, Sheriff Evans," Jeff burred. "Once you tamed the Wild West, those days are over. Besides, I think you're out of your jurisdiction."

"An ex-cop is never out of his jurisdiction. But the sort of ruckus that happened today." Henry shrugged. "Now I leave it up to you young whippersnappers. And by the way, you handled it extremely well... Jeffrey." He laughed heartily with his neighbor, the furrows in his face deepening as his mouth opened wide.

Barbara gazed from Dee to Susan. "Men," she puffed, shaking her head. At seventy-eight, the same age as Henry, she looked in remarkable health, and shared her husband's attributes of gray hair, a cheery, kindly manner, and deep love for Austin and Stephanie, whom they thought of as particularly well-mannered. After fifty years of marriage, the raising of three children, now out into the world with families of their own, retirement had brought an enjoyable and special closeness with Jeff, Dee and the happy couple she addressed. "Once again, congratulations to you both," she cooed. "We'd love to hear how the visit goes with your doctor. Just ring Dee and I'll find out from her."

"Don't be silly, honey, I'll call you as soon as we know. And thank you so much for all the wonderful advice."

"You're more than welcome, my dear," she smiled, returning Susan's warm hug. "I'm just so over the moon for you."

"Are you sure you don't want to stay?" Jeff asked. "We're all going in the spa. Not too hot and not too cold, it's perfect for a beautiful evening such as this."

"Another day, maybe." Henry winked grandly at Jeff and Greg. "Methinks one of us here is wrinkled enough."

"We all saw that, so don't try saying you were talking about yourself," Dee giggled. "Barbara, it's time you got him away from the terrible influences called Kirk and Cooper."

"That's the best idea yet," she agreed. "Goodnight, everyone. Say goodnight, Henry."

"Goodnight, Henry," he grinned.

Austin and Stephanie sniggered while Barbara rolled her eyes, grabbed her husband's arm and steered him toward their home next door.

"Goodnight," they all chorused.

"I'll come over and mow your lawn in the morning."

"Thanks," Henry called over his shoulder. "That'd be nice, Austin. But don't make it too early, son. Have a sleep in."

"Okay," Jeff enthused, rubbing his hands together. "Let's go and marinate for a couple of hours."

Chatting among themselves, they followed him to the right, and Austin studied the shadowy trees where he last saw his mysterious mentor. Where are you, he pondered. You told me it'd be a few years and it's been seven. A lot longer. Is that it, then? You're gone and that's it?

"Wow!" The sudden exclamation broke his gloomy musings, and he nearly walked into Susan, who slowed her pace when they entered the backyard. The setting sun spread a vibrant array of pink, orange, and yellow across the western horizon, and Austin wondered what captivated her so much, for she had seen it many times before, even from the very rear of the property while they stared, awestruck, at the magnificent display reflected upon the snow-covered Rocky Mountains. Moving to her side answered his question once he spotted Susan's fixed sight. Jeez, stupid me, he thought, shaking his head. They haven't seen it yet!

"Yeah, this looks a bit different at night."

"Wow," she breathed again. "That's an understatement, Jeff."

Beneath a darkening sky, the mildly rippling pool water glowed luminous-blue, a contrast to the effervescent, churning hot tub, which threw a reddish hue through hazy steam that coiled and sashayed in the peaceful, July air.

"So this is where you disappeared to before. Are there any other surprises?" Greg asked, and laughed when the color changed in the tub, progressing slowly from its rosy tinge to a soft, mossy green.

"Good timing," Jeff chuckled. "The spa's got six colors, each running on a five minute cycle. I think the next one was described as sapphire blue in the booklet. It's a few shades darker than the pool."

Greg smiled. "Looks fantastic, mate. LED or fiber optic?"

"All LED," Jeff nodded. "We had the pool done when it was out of commission for the other building works. There's strip lighting on the steps, around the perimeter near the coping stones, and the whole lot's hidden nicely in the tiling. Do you recall how murky the pool was without them?"

"Greg, honey, he teased the kids that Jaws might be in there and just ended up freaking himself out," Dee giggled.

"Dad," Stephanie groaned. "Can we get in now?"

"Sure. If we're all ready, let's go."

While they climbed into the hot tub, Jeff sniffed deeply at the faint, bitter smell of bleach that entered his nostrils, processing it speedily and judging the chlorine level to be near perfect. Pushing a button on the wide rim, he reduced the amount of bubbles streaming from the many nozzles, and as the water settled, above the soft gurgling and quietly popping froth, a loud, collective sigh of contentment escaped everyone's lips.

"Mmmm... this is heavenly," Susan purred, gliding her arms leisurely below the surface.

"Careful, Suze," Jeff grinned. "If you use those words, there's a certain person who'll accuse you of blasphemy. Hellfire and brimstone upon thee, heathen witch."

"You know," Greg chortled. "Apart from all the profanities, the strange thing is I didn't see Jackie wearing any holy objects, like a cross. And you'd think people that zealous about their faith would display some type of artifact."

"Exactly," Jeff agreed. "We didn't even know she was religious. Did you, son?"

Austin shrugged. "It's news to me. She's never said anything before and there's nothing in the house that gives it away."

"Hmmm. Babe, what was she like when we were in the pool?"

"Well, she didn't cuss, but she didn't chat about God either. I suppose she was a tiny bit more talkative." Dee looked at Susan. "Would that be about right, honey?"

"Yeah. A bit," Susan nodded. "All I know is there wasn't much love between her and Sean, and for a family gathering her language was atrocious, even in the heat of the moment. Pauly must be taking it pretty hard. Austin, does he show any visible signs of distress?"

"No." The teenager frowned. "Nothing that really jumps out at me. There are times when he seems... I dunno, moody, grumpy, but I guess anyone can be like that if you're not happy about something."

"You're spot on, mate. Good or bad, everyone's got their own little mannerisms, and if his mum and dad fight a lot then it would certainly bring you down. Maybe you should keep an eye on him some more, and ask Wade and Joe not to poke fun at him about today."

"Greg's right, darling. But not too gung-ho with Pauly, just be discreet about it. You don't want the poor boy getting nervous or angry with constant questioning about his state of mind."

"No problem. Anyway, Wade and Joe won't do that. Even though we all joke around with each other, they feel sorry for him and said they don't like what Jackie did. And trust me, Mom, I won't jump in straight away, I'll approach the subject very slowly. Which kinda brings me to something else." Austin paused for a few seconds, inspecting the water while it switched to a subtle white. Glancing at Susan and Greg, he saw the muted color shining faintly on their faces. "Something I've been meaning to ask you guys."

"Is it about the dreams, sweetheart?" Susan enquired softly.

"How did you kno..." Wide-eyed at first, he narrowed his sight, and with a small smile, peered at his mother. "Mom, when did you tell them?"

"We've known since you nearly merged with the pool wall," Greg admitted. "That's a scary and exceedingly serious event, mate, and if you want to talk to someone about the how's and why's of these things happening, then we're always here. The decision's all yours whenever, brother."

"No one's ever going to pester you, buddy," Jeff added.

He was at the crossroads again, and the same dilemma brought memories flooding back. Austin exhaled strongly. Should I do it? he thought. Sit here and tell them about this dude who visited me, told me all this weird stuff and then just disappeared. Weird stuff. Huh! Yeah, let me tell you what really happened outside the kindergarten, what really happened with Duke. About the dreams. The dreams that are so real I can't breathe, so real I don't know if I'm awake when I am awake. Susan was dead, you know that, some profoundly deep and unfamiliar part of his essence whispered. What? What does that mean? What is this? She's right here! He planted his sight on the gorgeous woman sitting opposite him, whose dazzling smile and beautiful nature he held close to his heart. I can't do it. They'd think I'm crazy! Of course I can't. Look at them. They trust me. I tell them to do that. They think I'm responsible, mature. And I am. I don't how, I just am. I can't destroy it, and I won't. The truth is too much and even I don't understand it, so how could they? I won't put that doubt in their minds. I can't. "Sounds like you guys have done a Pauly situation on me," he laughed.

"Son, don't be angry or upset, please. We love you, all of us." Dee swept her hand through the hazy air. "We're your family, and we stick together and try to help one another when we can."

"I'm not angry, Mom, and I'm not upset with anyone. You said I could talk to you, Dad, Susan, Three-Gee... and I didn't. So, I blame myself."

"Don't do that, honey." Susan shook her head. "Not wanting to talk is such a normal reaction. Austin, let me enlighten you on a couple of things about this handsome lump here." She patted Greg's shoulder. "He sacrificed a lot to make a life with me. His home, his family and friends, the game he adores and misses... everything to start a new existence in another country. That's a really hard thing to do, and I didn't realize how much until I saw what he left behind in New Zealand. He never told me, but he definitely showed me, and it seems to be a family trait, as well. They don't shirk on their responsibilities, don't broadcast to the world what they've achieved, and if I hadn't seen recordings of Greg playing, and heard him called Wizard, he would never have told me. Darling." Susan smoothed Greg's spiked hair. "Can I tell Austin the real explanation behind your rugby nickname?"

"I don't know," he grinned. "Can you?"

"May I tell Austin, you big smarty-pants," she giggled.

"Can I stop you? If not, you may."

"Jeffrey Cooper, this is all your fault," Susan blurted at Jeff's laughter. "Dee?"

"It's pointless, honey, we've tried. They're like two peas in a pod. We should just concentrate on Austin before it's too late."

"Yeah, you're right. He's our only hope now." With a smile and a quick spray of water at her husband, Susan turned back to Austin. "On our holiday, we met up with a few of his old teammates, and I found out the nickname wasn't just for his sporting ability, it originally came from his fascination with learning new things. When the squad travelled around on buses and planes, he continuously read alternative books, articles, journals, that sort of stuff, so they called him Wizard because of the information he knew. This one time, a player was being interviewed on TV after a game and said Wizard scored the best try he'd ever seen. Apparently five guys were hanging off him while he simply dragged them along." She prodded Greg's massive chest. "And from then on commentators referred to him as 'The Wizard' whenever he played."

"That is so awesome!" Austin stared at Greg. "Five guys! Three-Gee, you're a legend, dude."

"Nah, someone counted wrong, it was probably one or two. Mate, do you see what Suze is getting at in her delightfully rambling way? Now, I'm no authority on the subject, however, I have read a little bit, and as Mum said, we're all here to help one another when we can." Greg leaned forward. "Tell me about these dreams, brother."

Austin swallowed. "Okay." But only the dreams, without Wotlinski or Tess, he thought, and spent the next twenty minutes recounting everything, from the strange beach to a tar-like entity, the burning planet with its spectral apparitions, and the habitual method of his waking, always momentarily confused, disturbed, emotional, and breathless at times, especially with the blazing world's closeness. "It's no big deal, they're just stupid dreams," he concluded. "I have them, and then I get over it."

"Austin, why didn't you tell us about the other ones?" Dee reached across and stroked his cheek.

"I didn't want you and Dad to worry. Like I said, Mom, it's no big deal, and if I hadn't sleepwalked then you wouldn't know about it."

"It is a big deal, you could've been killed. And these dreams keep repeating, don't they?" Her light-brown eyes glistened while they searched his face.

"Yes," he murmured. "Are you disappointed with me?"

"No, sweetheart, I'm sad you've gone through this alone when there's no need to do that."

There is a need, Mom, he thought. You wouldn't be like this. You'd be saying I'm a liar, I'm stupid, childish.

At the prospect of his continuing deception over family and friends, a dull gloominess settled, struggling with the large, thankful part of his mind telling him he was right to say nothing on the surreptitiously forbidden topics.

"Austin." Susan moved through the warm, mildly swirling water, pulled him toward her and wrapped her arms around him in a tender embrace. "For a while there you looked like a man having the weight of a thousand burdens taken off his shoulders." Releasing him, she drew back and frowned. "And now you don't. Greg. What can we do to assist him?"

He couldn't help himself, and Jeff sniggered at Susan's expression, a mixture stating that the matter is of intense importance and we shall advance in a straightforward, no-nonsense approach to find a solution.

"Yes?" Susan retreated to her seat. "Is there something productive you'd like to add, Jeffrey? Oh!" Her brow rose. "Oh dear. I'm sorry, Jeff. I'm not normally like that."

"Maybe it's a classic example of residual Jackieness," Jeff laughed. "Suze, don't worry about it. If you want to know about peas in the pod, what you did then is something I've experienced before with two pregnancies. Mate." He looked at Greg. "You've got another seven, maybe eight months left, and good luck to ya. I'm not sure I'll be around, I might go fishing."

"Really?" Austin perked up. "If it's fishing, count me in. I am so there."

"That's fine," Dee stated, inching closer to her daughter. "While you're living on dirt and grass Stephie and I are going to Disneyland. We'll also take Susan because Greg will probably run off with you."

"Hooray!" Stephanie cried out, and hugged Dee.

"Me?" Greg feigned a look of complete outrage. "I would never do that." Planting his hand alongside his lips, shielding them from Susan, he whispered loudly. "Jeff, Austin, get the bags packed, I'll meet you by the front door. We'll get the bait later." Doing a magnificent double take, he peered at his wife, his eyes darting back and forth. "Oh. Um. Yeah, hi. Ahhh... there you are. So, ummm, how are things... ahhh, what was your name again?"

Among the peals of laughter, Susan poked her tongue out. "Can we get serious, you two? And if either of you say, 'I don't know, can we?' then, then...grrr." She shook her head.

"Okay, my darling, you're right, the night grows late." Greg rubbed her arm and turned his attention on Austin, his temperament transforming the moment their sight locked. "Mate, let's put the banter to one side and chat about a few things. These recurring dreams, how often are they?"

"It varies," Austin shrugged. "Sometimes they're every night for about a week, and then I won't have them for months. Like now, I haven't had one since the beginning of the year. Three-Gee, it's no big deal." I feel good, he thought. Really good. I love the joking between these guys. They've cheered me up so much.

"Okay," Greg nodded. "Well, if you do get curious, we've got some great material on dream interpretation and sleep disorders."

"Do you think it's a result of the comics, cartoons and movies he watches?"

"It's entirely possible, Dee. Look at all the imagery they're exposed to from a very early age. They suck it up like little sponges, incorporate it into their own reality, their playtime, and let the subconscious have complete freedom with it during sleep. There are still many theories on why we really sleep, and other than the obvious rest for our bodies, specialists tend to think this is the stage when the brain collects and reviews your experiences of the day, decides what's to be stored in your long term memory and discards the unwanted information. And that's where the dreaming starts. The generally held belief is that dreams are the result of the mind becoming active during the last stage of a normal sleep cycle, REM sleep, or rapid eye movement, and that's exactly what it means. Beneath your eyelids the eyes flit around as if you're seeing something visually, like TV or a movie."

"But what do the dreams mean?" Stephanie asked.

"That's a great question, sweetheart." Greg flicked his gaze around the silent, expectant faces. "Am I boring anyone yet?"

"Hell no." Jeff shook his head. "This is fascinating. Carry on, mate."

"Terrific," he smiled. "Dream analysis is a hard thing to figure out. From the first apelike humans to our current incarnation, every civilization in the world has a unique and particular method of interpreting what they mean, even attaching their own symbols as well. Babe, if you want to add something, just jump right in."

"No need, honey, you're doing a fine job. I couldn't put it better myself." They grinned at each other.

"This hot tub is awesome. I think I might live in here from now on." Greg paused and stretched his arms skyward. "Okay, mate," he addressed Austin. "Let's try your dreams. This vision of being in space, whether you're hovering above Earth, or at various distances from that huge planet, could be construed as something like a flying, falling, or chasing dream. It also has all the qualities of travelling or escape. The significance of the planet and that weird beach, I don't know. As I said, brother, they're hard to understand, and further research is needed to give an ideal answer. The black creature-human-thing and the ghost people... well, like Mum noted, they could all be miscellaneous leftovers from X-Men or suchlike. The fact they're recurring is, yet again, open to conjecture, with any number of possible solutions, and from what I remember, it boils down to this. Basically, they're drawing attention to some sort of problem in your life, and the subconscious being what it is, it won't let-up until that issue's resolved. They're as common as Jeff's bad jokes, all very normal stuff, and probably worse with your standard, hormone-driven teenager."

Jeff chuckled. "What about the sleepwalking?"

"Ahhh, yes. Somnambulism." Greg blew his cheeks out. "Big word, big subject, and a whole new beast. You know, loads of research is still being done on sleepwalking, and at the risk of sounding repetitive, it's once again full of speculation. There's one theory suggesting it's the result of a delay in maturation, which for me is blown right the hell out the window when you take Austin's maturity into consideration. Another one says it could be hereditary, yet another says a lack of proper development in the central nervous system, and so on and so on. There's a veritable mound of data and theses written about it. We could sit here all night and still not have an answer by morning. By the way, do you know if there's a history of it in your family? Did either of you sleepwalk as children?"

Shaking their heads at the same time, Jeff and Dee gazed at one another. "Not that I know of," Jeff offered. "Funny, isn't it? Even with the incident, we've never asked ourselves that question before."

"Greg did. Once, like Austin," Susan revealed. "On the final night of a rugby tour in Japan, he was found wandering the hotel lobby half naked."

"I don't hold any truth to those preposterous allegations," Greg countered. "Even with the possibility of some alcohol being involved. A microscopic amount. Besides, we won every game, I told Suze all about it, and she understands."

"Susan?"

"You heard right and wrong, Dee," she sniffed, rolling her eyes. "It's something he did tell me, it is all true, and no, I do not understand."

"Anyway." Greg grimaced. "Let's get back to Austin. Mate, I hope that's helped you out, and with a bit of research we might find some articles slightly interesting. At the very least we can eliminate any type of genetic discrepancies, like, umm, I dunno, maybe that thing Dad has... you know, a psychological illness." Rising from the water, laughing raucously, he and Jeff slapped a resounding high-five.

"Yeah, thanks," Jeff droned. "I was trying to keep that from the boy for as long as possible." His dry statement only brought on more roars of hilarity.

"Don't take any notice of them, darling," Susan remarked to Austin. "You're the only normal male here, by a long way."

Somehow, I don't think so, he thought, smiled as warmly as he could, and peered over the top of the hot tub when some movement grabbed his attention. Below them, Duke scratched at a stack of towels lying on the patio pavers. He raked the large articles together and circled his new, fluffy bed several times before plonking himself down in a tightly curled slumber, on the exact spot where, in a little over four years, during a beautifully mild, clear, Saturday evening in mid-September, merriment and festivities would come to an end, giving way to carnage, loss and sorrow.

Chapter Eleven

The Girl

Outside Halfmoon Mall, under a large, shaded entrance, Austin lowered himself onto a wide bench-seat and felt an immediate coolness when the molded metal touched the back of his legs. Beside him, thick paper crunched as Stephanie unwrapped her burger, releasing the mouth-watering aroma of grilled meat and melted cheese through the warm air. His stomach rumbled while she screwed the wrapper into a tight ball before depositing it next to a drink and fries positioned between them.

"Thanks for buying me this," she said, looking up at Austin.

"No worries, Stephie."

"Are you sure you don't want some? How about we go halves?"

"It's okay, I'll be fine. You must be starving, so eat up, enjoy, and I'll just grab something later. Anyway, Three-Gee's probably got food at the shop."

"So, what do we do now?" Taking a slow bite of her lunch, she studied her brother's face.

"Hmmm." Austin watched the people coming and going across the parking lot, and chuckled when a young boy, no more than four or five years old, scurried to his mother after the third frustrated and firm calling of his name. "When you're finished, we'll ask at the service desk again. The place is packed and someone might have handed it in."

"Mom and Dad are gonna be really hacked off."

"Yo, Austin," a voice called, and they swung their heads to see four teenage boys exiting the mall, the glass doors behind them rolling shut with a discernibly rattling thump.

"Hi, guys. How's it going?" Austin grinned.

"Pretty good, dude," the lead one replied on their approach. "Dunno if I'll be saying that next week. Hey, we saw Pauly and he told us you were out here. We've got something for you. Actually, it's for your sister. Xander found it." Half-turning, he gestured to a brown-haired lad, who lingered behind his companions, throwing wary, reluctant glances Austin's way. "Come on, dude, give it back, we've gotta go."

Xander moved to the front. Hesitantly, his sight flitting from Austin to Stephanie, he brought forth a small, black leather handbag and held it out. "I think this is yours," he muttered.

"Thank you," Stephanie exclaimed. "Wow!" She balanced the remaining burger on her thigh and rubbed her fingers vigorously before accepting the proffered item. "Where did you find it?"

"Banana Republic. Near some sh…" he mumbled again, and stopped when the tall youth rose from his seat, his right hand extended.

"Thank you very much for returning it," Austin smiled. "That's really decent of you, bro."

Stepping back, Xander merely stared at the outstretched arm, his gray-blue eyes narrowing, growing harder and darker by the moment. "Whatever," he snorted. "I'm outta here."

"Um. Okay. Well… thanks anyway." Stephanie peered at the figure as he strode to the sliding doors. "Is he okay? He seems to be in a bit of a hurry."

"Yeah, we're catching a movie. Nitro Circus. Hey, do you two wanna come?"

"Another time," Austin replied. "We have to go soon. But cheers for asking, mate."

"No problem. Later, dude, we've gotta run. See you at school on Tuesday. Our first day in hell," he grinned.

"Yeah," Austin laughed, giving a thumbs-up. "Take it easy, guys."

Bustling toward the entrance, the teenagers paused to chat with three girls on their way out, and when one of them spotted the young man taking his seat again, her face brightened.

"That was really stupid of me, Austin," Stephanie moaned. "How could I forget? While I was waiting for you and Pauly, I checked out a pair of shoes in there."

"Doesn't matter now, Steph, it's turned out fine. And speaking of Pauly, I told him we couldn't stay long." He checked his new digital watch, a hefty gadget bestowed with all sorts of nifty features and given by his parents for his fifteenth birthday seven weeks ago. "Where are you?" he grunted.

"Austin! Hi!"

His head shot up at the excited cry, and the irritation melted away, banished instantly by an overwhelming happiness when someone special hurried across to them. Swiftly, he got to his feet, his six-foot four-inch, well-built frame towering above anyone in the vicinity while he gazed at her slim, athletic body and long, crinkly blonde hair that framed a gorgeous face, the cutest he had ever seen. A now familiar reaction infused his soul, his entire being, and for a few seconds, when she came to a halt only a foot away, he found himself adrift within her ecstatic, amber eyes as they clenched onto his. In their gold and coppery-colored depths, he saw thin, yellow streaks spread around her jet-black pupil, like the first rays of light from behind a passing, summer storm. "Tess! Hi, how are you?"

"I'm great, thanks," she beamed. "How are you?"

To him, it seemed as if all the stars in the universe shone from those open lips, and in a flash, his spirit soared. "I was feeling a bit grumpy, but suddenly..." He hesitated, momentarily unsure of letting his emotions take command of his tongue. But logic lost when passion informed him the brain would have no immediate involvement due to a prior engagement elsewhere, and was therefore taking control of any subsequent dialogue. "Suddenly I'm feeling fantastic. Tess, you've just lifted my day and made everything about it so much better."

"That's... that's a beautiful thing to say." Reaching out, the girl ran her fingers down his muscular arm, gently, slowly. "Thank you."

At her touch, Austin's heart fluttered while a hopefully undetectable quiver coursed through his body, making the hairs stand up on the back of his neck. Like nothing he had experienced before, even with the bizarre incidents throughout his life, the powerful surge was the strangest, most wonderful sensation ever. "It's true," he hummed. "Every time I catch sight of you." Straight away, he felt a hot flush on his skin. Closing his eyes, he shook his head. "Am I blushing?"

"I think we both are," she whispered.

His lids lifted to see a rosy tinge spread over her cheeks. "It's a good thing we're not standing near a road or in the parking lot," he chuckled. "We'd be bringing all the cars to a screeching halt with our impersonation of human traffic signals."

Tess laughed, a smooth and silvery melody to his ears. "You sound very grown-up, talking that way. But I like it," she added quickly. "It seems... right for you."

"It's Dad's fault," Austin grinned. "I blame him."

"I know what you mean," she nodded. "Because of mine we only got back two days ago."

"D.C. and New York, wasn't it?"

"You remembered!" Her hand found Austin's arm again. "I'm really sorry I missed your birthday. I promise I'll be here next year."

"You're on. Third time's a charm. Anyway, you should come over for a swim sometime soon. That pool's been yearning for you the last two summers."

"You sweet talker," she giggled.

Swallowing the last mouthful of fries, Stephanie took a sip of her drink and regarded the smiling couple. "Ahem." Her pseudo-cough broke the silence.

"You're right," Austin commented to his sibling. "Where are my manners? Tess, this is my sister, Stephanie. Stephie, this is Tess."

"Hi, Stephanie," she cooed, wiggling her fingers. "It's really nice to meet you. I've seen you at school loads of times before. You're very pretty."

"Hi. Thank you," she smiled. "Just call me Stephie, or Steph, if you want. I'm not used to..."

"Austin! AUSTIN!" Everybody stared at a short boy sprinting out of the mall, his scrawny arms thrusting, swinging a fully laden plastic bag wildly back and forth. It thumped against his hip while he scampered past the teenage girls strolling across to Tess after bidding farewell to their male companions. "W... Wot..." Nearing the seat, he doubled over, his free hand flapping about. "It... it's..." he gasped, and twisted his head to enable a quick, upward peek at his tall friend.

"Jeez, you're popular today," Stephanie remarked.

"Mate, stand up. What's going on?"

The boy gripped his thighs, hoisted himself straight and wiped a layer of sweat from his brow, his gaunt chest heaving with each wheezing breath. "Wotlinski. Been following me. Him and his fucking gang. Tried to get my new games. New clothes." Glancing over his shoulder, he shook the bag. "Even my iPhone. Said he warned me about no bodyguard. Fucking prick." He slumped onto the seat beside Stephanie. "Why does the whole school have to be here today? Why the fuck does he? Austin, you should get him. Punch him. Put him down again, the fucking asshole jerk-off."

"Pauly, I won't be punching anyone, and would you please stop swearing in front of Tess and Stephie."

"They don't care," he grumbled, his twitching elbow dismissing the girls.

"Ahhh... yes, I do care," Stephanie declared. "And there are other people walking in this area. People with children."

"Fine. Sorry," he huffed, flashing a sidelong glance. "Stephie."

"Hi, Austin. Is everything okay?"

"Yeah, it's all good, Alisa. Hey, Shivawn. How's your vacation been?"

"Oh shit," Pauly yelped. "Here they come!" He slid toward Stephanie, nearly knocking the drink out of her hand in a desperate attempt at concealment behind the two females joining them. All together, they turned when three teenagers sauntered through the clattering doors and a raucous, grating laugh echoed around the glass entrance.

"I see's ya, Smally. Hidin' wiv the dykes. Look'a them's ugly bitches," Wotlinski sneered. "Spishly that one's." His cold, menacing eyes settled upon Austin's composed and unmoving face. Keeping his distance while he skirted the quietly observant group, the gang following in his footsteps, Wotlinski pointed directly at Tess. "What'cha fink, Tyrell?" he bayed, pushing back scruffy, blond hair above his plump, ruddy skin, redder and shinier than usual. "The only slut I'd fuck is that's. It got's nice tits. Big 'n' juicy."

"I was so wrong," Austin growled. He marched forward. "I will be punching him."

"Austin, no," Tess cried.

"Austin!" Stephanie yelled.

"HEY! What's going on here?"

"Ain't none nuffin' going on." Wotlinski glowered at the security guard who marched around the corner, his polished shoes clacking on the large paving stones that formed a walkway to the parking lot.

"Yeah?" The guard stopped. Sunlight glinted off the metal nametag pinned to his uniform as he depressed a large button on the microphone clipped above the pocket of his gray shirt. Fastened to a belt at his hip, a two-way radio bleeped loudly. "Lewis to base. I've got three, positive-match O.I.S. outside the North entrance. Over."

"Copy that," a metallic-sounding voice squawked. "Apprehend, Lewis. Base to Wilson, Hernandez. Are you receiving? Over."

"Wilson here, receiving loud and clear. Over," came a reply.

"Please assist Lewis and Turner at North entrance. Three-numbered, positive-match offenders in sight. Over."

"Copy, base. We're close and on our way. Over."

"Copy that. Advise of any further backup. Over."

During the final response, the guard aimed a finger behind Wotlinski. "Move to the wall," he ordered.

"Go fuck ya'self's, nig..."

the student

"He called him a what?" Wide-eyed and open-mouthed, Dee stared at Stephanie as a generous dollop of mashed potato slid off the ladle held suspended in mid-air and plopped onto Austin's hand. "Whoops. Sorry, honey," she said, smiling at her son.

"Well, he didn't exactly say the whole word, only part of it, because right then the other guard appeared and he was also African-American. Those little piggy-eyes nearly popped out of his fat, horrible head." Stephanie shuddered. "Ugh, he's such a creep."

Gathered together for dinner, they sat around the island bench while Dee served their food and Stephanie recounted the early afternoon incident. Scraping potato off his hand, Austin restrained a sigh at the quantity of steaming peas, corn kernels and carrot she dished out, and stirred the vegetables halfheartedly when his mother deposited a small lump of butter on top. Watching it dissolve speedily into a smooth, oily liquid, he prodded the massive steak taking up half the space on his plate before puffing out his cheeks.

"What happened next?"

"That's when they took off. The other idiots ran straight at the guards," Stephanie giggled. "And Wotlinski went for the entrance. He might've escaped if Austin hadn't caught him."

"Stephie's just being nice, Mom." Austin shook his head. "He wouldn't have gotten away. Two more guards came through the door about ten seconds after I tackled him, so he was heading directly toward them. It turned out they'd been shoplifting, harassing the staff and customers, and damaging mall property."

"Really? Wow!" Dee patted her son's broad shoulder. "It's Super Cooper to the rescue. Nice work, sweetheart."

"This, uhhh, Watlinksee," Jeff said. "That name rings a few bells." Looking up from an open, leather-bound ring binder placed beside his meal, he peered over the top of his reading glasses.

"Dad, it's Wot-lin-ski. We've just been talking about him for the last ten minutes. Get with the program."

"Stephie, be gentle on the elderly. At the moment, there are a lot of things happening in his poor, aging, decrepit mind." Dee grinned at her husband.

"You missed a few, babe. Add overworked, exhausted and awesome. Anyway, what's with this elderly stuff? We're the same age."

"No, no, no, you're confusing me with someone else. That promotion has muddled your senile brain."

"Fair enough," Jeff laughed. "I'll change my title from chief executive officer to chiefly discombobulated. So, the Watlinksee person." He deposited his eyeglasses on the thick ream of paper, picked up his utensils and chuckled at Stephanie's shaking head. "My sight may need spectacles to read, but my poor, aging, decrepit mind holds a pretty good recollection of the playground bully." He began cutting into his steak. "Am I right, son?"

"That's him." Austin's fork hovered in mid-air, a single pea impaled on one tine. "He's terrorized just about everyone. I remember when he pushed Stephie to the ground at kindergarten and threw punches at her. I also remember getting in trouble for stopping it."

"Mmmm." Jeff chewed his mouthful and nodded.

"That was ten years ago, honey," Dee noted. "You've got a good memory."

Austin smiled wryly. "There are certain incidents at that kindergarten I'll never forget, even if they're ever so slightly blurred."

"No truer words were spoken, sweetheart. Has he bullied you?"

"Never, Mom. The guy's a coward when he knows what might happen if he does. But I can't and won't stand back when he tries it on with anyone. Especially someone loads smaller than him, like Pauly."

"What happened with Pauly?"

"To be honest, Dad, not much. Wotlinski got angry with him on his first day at school here and didn't back off. Then he swore at a girl who told him to leave Pauly alone and I kind of put him on the ground. That's it in a nutsh..." Austin stopped when he noticed Dee's frown. "Mom, I didn't hit him," he finished hastily. "I just advised him."

"Don't worry about it, buddy. It sounds like this brute is becoming worse, so he gets what he deserves."

"Jeffrey!" Dee protested. She pushed a few stray strands of silky, black hair behind her ears and gaped at her husband. "I thought we dealt with this when he was very young, yet it's still happening. And what's worse is, you're now condoning his actions."

"Oh come on, Dee, lighten up. The only action here is a few cautions to an obnoxious bonehead and that's all it's been." He held his arm out to Austin for confirmation.

"Up to now," Austin murmured. "But today I was gonna punch his lights out."

"Mom, I told you what happened," Stephanie chipped in. "What he said to us, what he said about Tess. He's a disgusting, filthy animal and Austin hasn't done anything wrong. Besides, Mr. Foley must've thought what Austin did to that fat pig was okay. He was such a cool teacher, soooo funny. He joked with Anna this one time about bringing a horse to school, and she thought he really..."

"Hold up, Stephie, hold up." Austin put his fork down and leaned forward. "What do you mean he thought it was okay? Did he see the whole thing?"

She shrugged. "I think so. He said Wotlinski bullied Pauly and you gave him his... ummm... what word did he use? Uhhh... comenupcent or something."

"Comeuppance?" Jeff offered.

"Yeah, that was it! Thanks, Dad," she smiled. "And you never got in trouble. He absolutely raved about you, Austin. He said he was really concerned about Pauly when he first met him and thought something might happen that day, but you took care of him and it turned out okay, 'cos Pauly totally changed after that. Awwww, yeah, I forgot to tell you," she exclaimed, tapping her forehead. "He said he's really looking forward to seeing you around high school this year. How great is that?"

"Fantastic. He's an excellent teacher." Austin's brow furrowed. "You know, I remember him being at the window, but didn't realize he'd seen it. He never mentioned anything. Steph, how do you know all of this?"

"He was saying goodbye on the last day before vacation and how we'd better behave ourselves, 'cos he'd be waiting for us at high school. Then he walked around the room talking to different people and stopped for a chat. That's when he told me about it, and you, saying you were the best student he ever taught. How you always looked out for everyone and acted so responsibly in class. He said no one could beat your manners and maturity, and laughed when I said it wouldn't be a problem," she grinned.

"Ah-hah! You see, babe." Jeff spread his hands, an exaggerated expression of triumph on his face. "Strike one for me. You even vocalized it before with Super Cooper to the rescue. Our son wasn't the one causing trouble, Dee, and in this day and age it's a damn pity more kids aren't as morally inclined as him. If you recall, I wanted to name him Fred Flintstone, which I'm fairly sure doesn't mean resolute guardian and determined protector, or whatever the heck it is."

"You fool," she laughed. "You are an intolerable fool and I love you dearly." Placing her hand upon Austin's, she squeezed it gently. "Both of you. I'm sorry, honey, your father's right. I should be saying how proud I am, not getting irritated because you watch over your friends and family. What you did was honorable."

"Thanks, Mom. Um, can I ask a question?"

"Of course. Anytime."

"Why the sudden change of heart? For a second there, I thought you were really annoyed with me."

"I was, honey, and again, I apologize. We've got the finest son in the world." Dee searched the blue-purpley eyes regarding her. "But in spite of that, I'm still too hard on you at times like this. What I should be doing is asking you the questions, seeing if you're the one that's all right. Like now." She indicated his full plate. "You've hardly touched a thing, which is very strange. What's wrong, my darling? Are you feeling okay? You're not hurt after today, are you?"

"No, not at all." Austin shook his head. "I don't mean to sound arrogant, but the tackle worked perfectly. With the amount of blubber he's got to cushion the blow it was more fun than bouncing on a trampoline." He smiled at his father and sister's bursting laughter. "Three-Gee trained me well and said he's very pleased. By the way, they're coming over tomorrow. I think Susan needs a break. She seemed a bit overwhelmed, so I'll take the twins for a swim while they relax with you guys. We'll take them for a swim," he amended, chuckling at Stephanie's pout.

"Thank you, sweetheart, that's really nice. But if you don't feel well then we better be careful with the babies."

Austin slid the cold meal forward and crossed his arms on the bench top. "Don't worry, I'm not sick, I'm just not that hungry tonight. You know I think your cooking is the best. It's always delicious. It's just... uhhh... I've got something on my mind, and no, Mom, it's not a dream, I haven't had any weird ones for ages. Maybe all the research I did with Three-Gee helped, I dunno. This is different, this involves a... a..." He gazed at the faces of his family, all of them loved and cherished, held deeply, strongly, immeasurably in his heart and soul. "A person," he sighed heavily.

"A sigh person," Jeff remarked. "That is some serious stuff. You've got to watch out for those sigh people, son, they'll sneak up on you. Tell me something, mate, is this sigh person of the female variety? Sometimes called a sigh girl? Honey," he said to Dee's withering scowl. "Put your little eye-daggers away and observe his grin. That mouth of his is nearly stretched inside out."

"Yes," Austin laughed. "The sigh person is a sigh girl. Mom, it's okay, I was fully expecting it, and I'm also ready for Three-Gee's contribution tomorrow. If I can survive their banter when my voice broke, I'll survive this. I'm kinda surprised Stephie didn't tease me about it all afternoon."

"Austin, Austin, Austin. There's plenty of time for that later," she responded, and giggled as he flicked a pea in her direction. "But seriously, Mom and Dad, you should have seen how happy they were together. It was cool."

"How exciting!" Dee clapped her hands rapidly. "Tell us about her, sweetheart."

"Okay. Ummm... well, Stephie's already brought up her name. It's Tess, Tess Anderson, and she's always gone to my schools. Actually, we've been in a few classes, although we never talked much." He shrugged. "You know what it's like with guys and girls when you're younger. But this year we've chatted a few times and, I dunno, today it kind of seemed different, like something happened that changed things. I don't really know how to describe it, it was... special. I felt something else." Austin looked at his mother's radiant smile. "I can't put it any better than that, Mom."

"You don't need to, honey, I completely understand." She shared a delighted glance with Jeff.

"The weird thing is, it was probably the best and worst time I've had. I'm not talking about the matter with Wotlinski, he's a piece of nothing to me and I don't care about that." He stopped, and drummed his fingers on the top of his forearm.

"Don't hold back now, mate. We're all ears."

"I won't, Dad, I'm just figuring out where to start." Pushing himself upright, he alternated his attention from one parent to the other. "Okay, first, let me tell you what was happening. We were on our way to see Three-Gee, Susan and the kids, as you know, and Tess was going ice-skating with her friends. In fact, they left not long after the guards hauled those idiots away. Naturally, the best part was the chance meeting with Tess, but the worst..." He shook his head. "The worst part concerns another person and his behavior before we all went our separate ways."

the enemy

As the bus doors clanked shut and the rumbling engine roared, Austin gave a final wave to his sister while she lifted a hefty bag onto her back before making her way among throngs of noisy, active children crowding the pavement. Twisting on the spongy, foam seat, its vinyl cover squeaking with his movement, he stared aimlessly through a water-mottled and dirt-streaked window for the four minutes it took to arrive at his own destination. With its brakes squealing, the bus shuddered to a halt, and he saw her standing alone on the wide, concrete path, searching the roadside vehicles and multitude of people inundating the vast, front expanse that welcomed students to Crescent Lake West High School. Grabbing his backpack, his head bowed against the low ceiling, Austin followed everyone down the aisle and straightened himself once he reached the bottommost step, just when his name rang out.

"Austin!" Her ecstatic face wore the same radiant and captivating smile.

During their hasty approach to one another, he once again experienced the euphoric rush of three days ago, and as they stopped, two feet apart, he gazed at her while the rich, heady scent of her perfume washed over him, mixing pleasantly with an aroma of freshly cut grass, damp and clean after the pouring rain that fell in the early morning hours. "Hi, Tess. Wow," he breathed. "You look fantastic today."

"Thank you." Peering up at him, the morning sunshine ignited her amber eyes, creating a bright sparkle in their constant golden-coppery hue. "I wasn't sure if I'd already missed you."

"Yeah, I'm sorry about that. Pauly wasn't at his stop and I asked the driver if he could wait a while. But he never arrived, so I don't know what's happened. He's either sick, or can't be bothered coming in 'cos he thought it'd be wet all day." Austin shrugged and looked toward the now cloudless, azure sky. "That's the second most beautiful thing to greet me so far and a wonderful surprise. Thanks for waiting, Tess." His heartbeat quickened at the touch of her silken skin when she nuzzled her fingers into his.

"You're charming, you're welcome, and you're a sweet talker," she beamed.

Across the broad, grassy area, down the right-hand side of the main building, three teenagers entertained themselves by throwing a football around, and as the biggest in the trio tossed it to one of his associates, he spotted the tall, solid frame of Cooper through a sea of heads and bodies. Standing stock-still, he bolted his vision on his enemy and the bitch, both displaying blatant signs of shared happiness. His dark, pig-like eyes glittered, and his lips pulled back in a vicious sneer, right before the football thumped powerfully into his temple.

"It's probably nothing, Tess, and I'm sure everything will be cool," Austin said. "My folks had some great ideas about it."

"You talked about Pauly?"

"Yeah," he nodded. "The other night. Stephie was telling them all about the mall. She really liked how you called her pretty, so don't be surprised if you've got yourself a best friend forever."

Giggling at his giant grin, Tess studied the color of Austin's irides, a luxuriant ocean blue, shining vibrantly in the dazzling light. "She's absolutely gorgeous. Her hair, her skin… so beautiful. She looks way older than someone who's nearly thirteen. You're very lucky to have a sister like her. Actually, we both are. My sister, Melissa, is really special. She's always been there for me."

"I didn't know you had a sister." Austin's brow rose. "What grade is she in?"

"She's not anymore. She just finished high school. We're a bit different in looks and personality, but that's never stopped us being close. Like you and Stephie. I can see she means a lot to you."

"I feel the same way for anyone I care about. Always have."

"Austin Cooper," Tess frowned. "You act very grown-up. Does early maturity run in your family?"

"Not that I know of," he chuckled. "I've always been told women mature quicker than men."

"That's very, very true." She slipped her index finger back and ran the tip of her manicured nail across the soft pad of his thumb, sending a tingling, tickly tremor racing up his arm. "And the reason why we're better. We're more advanced."

"You'd get on well with my mom, she has the same opinion. So does Susan, Aunt Michelle, Stephie, and Dad and Three-Gee. Although I've only seen them agree to things like that when they're outnumbered by females. They reckon it's the best action a man can take, and you won't hear any arguments from me."

"You've been given some very good advice. Umm… what's a Three-Gee?"

Austin laughed. "Three-Gee's not a what, he's a who. Although, I'd imagine when most people meet him, 'what the' are probably the first words they'd think. His real name's Greg, and his wife Susan was my babysitter. They've got two awesome, little…"

"Coops! Good to see you, man."

Turning toward the cheerful greeting, Austin and Tess watched two teenage boys strolling through the crowd. Both were of medium build, almost the same height, and yet inches shorter than their lofty, able-bodied friend.

"Hey, guys. How's things?"

"Dude, we've got some news," Joe called. "Loads of it." Nearing them, he spied the couple holding hands. "And it looks like we're not the only ones. Holy crap, he was right. Did this happen at the mall?"

"Yeah." Austin's grip on Tess tightened briefly. "Hey, wait a minute, who was right? How do you guys know? I haven't seen you since we went fishing on Friday."

"Pauly told us." Wade swung his head left and right. "I don't know where he's gone. He was here about ten minutes ago."

Austin's brow shot straight up. "Pauly's here?"

"Yeah, his dad dropped him off," Joe replied. "You should've seen it. Their old, beat-up car comes screeching to a halt, the door gets flung open, there's loads of yelling happening and then Pauly steps out. Actually, it was more like pushed out. He slams the door shut, and dude, for a second, I really thought he was gonna kick it in."

"How did you see that?"

"Luckily for us we were passing by that tree." Joe gestured to where a tall, American Elm proudly spread its expansive, leafy canopy next to the school border, a low, brick wall with wrought metal barriers positioned between thick and sturdy columns.

"Whoa."

"I know!" Joe mirrored Austin's wide eyes. "Jeez, his old man can be something else. But nothing, absolutely nothing like the old lady." He circled his finger around his ear. "Remember your birthday last year, Coops? That was some heavy shit going down with them."

"Totally," Wade nodded, and fell into a momentary silence with his friends.

"So, guys." Austin broke the blank expressions and memories surfacing in each mind. "Is that the news, or is it something about this new haircut?" With a sly grin, he ran his hand back and forth over

Wade's scalp, the extremely short, spiky buzz-cut prickling his fingers on the upstroke.

"You're doing better than me, Coops, 'cos I couldn't stop laughing when I saw his melon. I mean, what the hell is going on, dude? Is it an impersonation of a toilet brush, or are you joining the army?"

"You wish you had this," Wade announced over Austin and Joe's cackling.

"Nah, man, I think I'll stick with my own style." Joe tousled his shoulder length, mousey brown hair. "I don't want the girls thinking I'm some sort of escaped convict. Hey, talking of criminals, that's one part of the news. We saw Wotlinski checking you before, Coops. But we're so sorry for disturbing you two lovers." He fluttered his eyelashes at the couple.

Tess giggled while Austin sighed heavily. "Yeah, yeah. Come on, Joe, respect for the lady, please. And so what about Wotlinski? He's just a brainless idiot. I couldn't give a damn if he's watching me."

"No. Austin, listen up." Wade's demeanor changed instantly, and his face hardened as he fixed an unwavering stare upon his life-long friend. "We were some distance away and could just see the hatred pouring out of him."

"He's right," Joe agreed. "Austin, you've always riled him up by being the only one who could stop what he enjoys doing. And now." He let out a huge breath. "Now I think it's worse. Now I think he's uber-pissed with you. Dude, I'm totally serious, you've gotta be careful with him. I've never joked about it, Coops, he wants to get you something bad, so imagine what that crazy bastard's like after what you did at the mall."

"Hmmm. Okay, point taken." Austin surveyed the large area, his intense gaze sweeping quickly over the crowd. "I don't see him. Where was he?"

"Over there." Wade pointed to an empty spot near the corner of the building. "He's gone now. He was throwing a ball around with that douche Jones and some other guy, until one of them launched it straight at the side of his fat head. Not once, but twice, and really freakin' hard."

"Hell of a shot, Coops. They took full advantage of him glaring at you and Tess. Maybe not the first time, but definitely the second. Jeez, he got nailed. You should have seen the look on his face." Joe and Wade's loud guffaws brought amused glances from those people closest to the group.

"And when they almost choked on their own laughter he started chasing after them," Wade said, still sniggering.

"Damn, I wish I'd seen that. But maybe it's knocked a bit of sense into his thick skull. Nah, what am I saying?" Austin scowled. "That's impossible for him, and right now he's probably drooling over the chance to bully other kids, especially freshmen. I think it's time we had another lighthearted chat."

"Austin, no, don't. Please." Tess' sweet smile failed to mask the concern clearly evident in her eyes. "There's something seriously wrong with him and I don't want you getting hurt. Everyone knows he's a bully. He's always been that way and nobody can change it, not even you."

"I can't let him persecute anyone, Tess."

"I realize that because I've seen it before." She brought their still-linked hands up and gave his a reassuring pat. "You don't have to do a thing. Leave it to other people. Leave it to the teachers here so they can deal with it. That's what I did when he pushed me over, and he got after-school detention."

"He pushed you? When? Where was I? Why didn't you tell me?"

"It was years ago," she laughed. "In grade two or three. Austin, I think there are times he does it on purpose just to bait you. He wants you to get in trouble. Forget about him, he's not worth the hassle."

"It's not that easy when he won't forget," Joe grunted.

"Yeah, you're right, Joe, but so is Tess. Nothing's ever happened. It's all talk, 'cos he knows that fat ass will be on the ground if he tried anything. And if he did, then I'd seriously consider getting rid of him on Facebook."

"What?" Tess' jaw dropped open. "He's a Facebook friend? Are you kidding? You haven't even sent me a request yet." Her incredulous expression vanished when Austin squeezed her hand amid Wade and Joe's amusement.

"He is kidding," Wade chuckled. "There are four teenagers in America who don't have a Facebook account and Austin's one of them. The other three don't even know what a computer is. Actually, we'll have to include Wotlinski, 'cos he wouldn't. No way in hell. Hey, have you ever thought why that loser's never been expelled?"

"Funnily enough, I asked Dad the same question, bro," Austin replied. "And it's a good thing I do know what a computer is." Grinning, he nudged his friend's arm. "Because we checked it out on the net, and apparently you can only be expelled if…"

"Joe. Wade," a voice behind them hollered. "What the fuck are you guys doing? Let's go inside, it's too fucking wet out here."

In the nick of time, Tess wriggled her fingers free of Austin's, an instantaneous reaction to Pauly's surly and demanding intrusion as he trudged along the path leading from the main building. Joining the group, he peered up at his friends' faces.

"Hey, Austin. What's happening? Have they told you yet?"

"Mate. Here's Joe, here's Wade," Austin stated, pointing at each one. "Here's me. The person you just greeted." He prodded a thumb into his own chest. "Are you forgetting someone else who deserves the courtesy of acknowledgement?"

"Huh?" The skinny young man glared. "Austin, what the fuck are you going on about, you idiot?"

"Jeez, Pauly, your eyesight's like your height, dude. Totally defective." Joe shook his head. "Tess is standing right here, you freakin' hobbit. I know we're all gigantic in your world, but try looking toward the sky now and then."

"It's the hair. All he sees is this long, black veil. Damn hippy. Get a number three clipper cut like mine."

"Shut up, fuckbags," Pauly chuckled and glanced quickly at Tess. "Ummm. Yeah… ahhh… hi."

"Hey," Tess sang cheerfully. "I'm sorry we didn't get to have a proper chat at the mall the other day. Everything was pretty rushed after all that excitement."

"I guess," he mumbled.

"Did you do any cool stuff during vacation?"

"Ummm... no... yeah. Uhhh... went fishing... and... uhhh... swimming. Mmmm."

"Wow! Awesome. I bet that was nice. And you also went fishing? I've never done that, but I'd like to try it sometime. Is it good fun?"

Dropping his head, Pauly scuffed the toe of a grubby, white sneaker across the pale and nearly-dry concrete. "Ummm... I dunno... yeah," he burbled. "We like it. Right, guys?" He raised his vision briefly.

"It's all that and a bag of chips. Tess, you and the girls should definitely come along for the laughs. Like last Friday. It was really windy and we thought Pauly might get blown into the lake and eaten by the Legend Fish. Hey!" Joe tapped his index finger to his temple. "How's this for a great idea. If it's like that next time, we should tie a line to you, just in case. Might be our only opportunity to catch it, dude."

"Fuck you," Pauly snapped. "You're jealous 'cos I always caught more, you shithead butt-munch."

Austin sighed. "Pauly, please stop swearing in front of Tess. We don't mind, but other people might. Can you do that for me?"

"Okay," he replied, and flushed a deep red when the tone of his voice rose, pitching a full octave higher. Turning to one side, he coughed loudly. "Sorry... um, I, um, it's... ahhh... look, just stop with the questions."

"Come on, mate, it's only one thing."

"Not you. Her." Pauly stared at Tess. "Why are you asking me all that stuff?"

A shrill, piercing bell rang, its electronic peal reverberating across the open space, notifying all students that classes would commence in five minutes. When the obtrusive clanging waned, a collection of sounds increased and intermingled, from groans and mutters, to the rustling of bags and clothing as a mass progression started toward the front doors.

"Here we go. Man, I hope he doesn't annoy me so much this year," Pauly remarked. "I had enough of that in grade four." He turned his attention back to his tall companion. "So. Whaddya think? We've got him again. Homeroom teacher and our first lesson."

"Am I missing something?" Austin frowned.

Pauly looked at Wade and Joe. "You haven't told him yet?" he boomed, and rolled his eyes. "Holy shitass crap, you two fucktards are goddamn, fucking useless."

the teacher

The early morning sunlight streamed on an angle through the windows, illuminating the microscopic, twinkling specks of dust that spiraled through the air, a result of the sudden movement as everyone pushed back from their desks. The momentary scuffing of chairs on a wooden floor preceded the odd thump while they stood straight and placed their right hand over their heart.

"I pledge allegiance to the flag of the United States of America, and to the republic for which it stands, one nation under God, indivisible, with liberty and justice for all," Austin recited. Dropping his arm, he took his seat again and waited patiently while the teacher moved a thick stack of papers and perched himself on the table edge.

"What a wonderful start to our day," the teacher said. "The rain has stopped, the sky has cleared, it's warming up nicely, and all of you are in attendance for what promises to be a spectacular year ahead." With a cheery smile, he scanned the expectant faces watching him. "I notice a large number of what can only be described as my ex-pupils, wondering why on earth they had the misfortune of becoming my current pupils once more." He paused when laughter rumbled around the room. "Well, it's always been my desire to teach high school, but certain events led me to where many of us first became acquainted, at your tender age of seven and eight. And now my current pupils have got the jump on me, leaving one person in this class as the freshman. Guess who that is," he grinned. "I also see that I am in the company of adolescents who have matured very rapidly over the six years we've been apart, and many of you who have grown to immense proportions." He looked straight at Austin.

"What about Pauly?" someone at the back called out.

The teacher held his hand up to calm the abrupt surge of boisterous hilarity. "We all develop in our own unique ways, ladies and gentlemen. Let's not forget that, and let's not make fun of anyone. Mr. Benton, it's good to see you. How have you been?"

Seated three rows back, directly behind Austin, the small teenager shrugged. "Fine, I guess," he answered, and received another eruption of laughter when his voice squeaked sharply. Lowering his head, he tried to hide the unanticipated, burning flush that attained an enormous coverage, even travelling to the top of his ears.

"Hang in there, Mr. Benton. It's a natural change, which won't take too long. Mr. Cooper, we meet again. I must say what a tremendous pleasure it is to renew my association with you for a second time. And how have you been?"

"Not bad, Mr. Foley. It's good to see you, too." Austin nodded. "You're looking fit and healthy. How are you?"

"Just wonderful, thank you. However, it is possible I might be losing even more of my lustrous mane." Chuckling, he tapped the top of his head, on a smooth, bare spot that now covered a larger area, leaving a distinct and rounded contour farther back. In the middle, a small, short tuft of brownness stretched a few inches toward his forehead, defying the baldness and continuing recession of his hairline. "That's very nice of you to ask about my welfare, and in all honestly, it's the sort of response I would have expected. Right." He checked his watch. "Before we begin, let's go through a couple of things. During the first thirty minutes each morning our activities will include your subjects for the day, along with any work that requires completion, and as homeroom teacher, I am here to guide and assist you with that. I will treat all of you with the respect and dignity befitting your status as future pillars of our society and as the young men and women you are so rapidly becoming. I would like those ideals to be reciprocated in this room. Any questions?"

"Yeah, can we go fishing?"

"Ahhh, Mr. Harris, how I have missed your fervent sense of humor," the teacher declared over the bursting laughter. "And how I wish I could say yes. Regrettably, there would be punishment tomorrow in the form of detention, myself included," he smiled. "So, in lieu of that, I'll try to keep your mind occupied with thoughts other than more vacation. If you could come to the front, please, and distribute these to your classmates." While Joe walked to the teacher's desk, conversation among the students began. "It's very nice to see you," Mr. Foley murmured, using the gentle burble to cover their exchange. His brow rose as he handed over a sheaf of papers. "I trust you haven't slipped back to any old habits, influenced by certain wayward individuals. One in particular."

Joe grinned. "If you mean what I think you mean, then no, that part of my stupidity is over. It's all good."

"Outstanding. I can see the beneficial effect of another certain individual. Well done, Mr. Harris. Well done." He patted the teenager's shoulder, picked up a clipboard folder by his side, and flicked through several pages secured by a large, spring fastener. "Okay, sophomores, it's time to get started," he called. "Welcome to a full hour of social studies, our first subject of the day. During this semester and into the next, we will be studying ancient civilizations, covering a variety of topics such as their military strength, how far they spanned, language, culture, resources, trade, any connections with other nations, and all at a specific period in their development. Your esteemed colleague is now dispensing information relating to a major assignment, which we will examine now. On page one we have a list of seven ancient civilizations. Rome, the Middle East, Egypt, Greece, India, China, and the Americas, Central and South. It is you, my prominent, young scholars, who are wholly responsible for the selection of two that we will research together. Successful completion of this subject will be based on written material and a unique event, a new venture, never before implemented within the walls of this magnificent establishment and one which requires absolute, mandatory participation. That means all grade ten students in their respective classes are involved." He paused while a soft buzz carried around the room. "Ladies and gentlemen, focus your concentration on the second page, please. This is where the fun part begins."

Getting to his feet, Mr. Foley strolled through empty spaces among the desks while the crunch and rustle of turning paper carried over the whispering rustle of shifting bodies and the occasional, gentle cough. "At some point during semester two we will be presenting our acquired knowledge in the form of a theatrical production to your parents, family, guardians, and the entire school community. In addition to that, this class has been given the honor of deciding not only a theme, but also a date for the hosting of our extravaganza. I would like to think this is due to our imminent position as the number one group of students at Crescent Lake West High."

Heads turned and animated conversation broke the silence. To the right of Austin's wide shoulders, Pauly saw Tess spin in her chair and beam at his tall friend before another girl tugged on her arm, instantly diverting her to one side with a rush of excited chatter. Leaning forward, nearly tipping his desk over, Pauly jabbed Austin solidly in the back. "Dude, we'll pick Greece. It's gotta be Greece. No, wait a minute, what about India? No, no, it's Greece. Austin, we'll go with Greece. And for the other one maybe the Middle East, or ummm... I dunno, I'll come up with something. But for the date we'll go with... ahhh..."

"Okay, okay," Mr. Foley laughed. He stopped at the front and raised his hand. "Wow, what a fantastic response! With such unbridled enthusiasm, I feel extremely assured that we'll do a great job. We will be the best. Let's get down to business, because once our three decisions are made, I will present them to the faculty for approval, and we can commence our real work. Sophomores," he beamed. "The moment is here for us to bring our democratic way of life into practice. It's time to vote, so indicate your choice with a raised hand, ladies and gentlemen. We shall start with the first on our list. Rome."

Austin glanced at Tess, and casually lifted his arm the instant he detected her motion. Looking rearward, a warm smile lit her face when she saw his hand pointing straight toward the ceiling tiles. "Pssssssst," he heard immediately behind him, but didn't turn around. Placation of the hisser would have to wait until lunch.

"Twenty out of twenty-six," Mr. Foley announced. "An overwhelming result for the first selection. Okay, hold your hand up for the Middle East... and... well... only one vote. Apparently that is not a popular choice."

Dropping his arm, Pauly muttered to himself while glaring at Austin's back.

"Right, all those in favor of Egypt."

Through a swiftly taken, backward peek, Tess gauged Austin's preference, and mirrored his action by stretching her fingers high in the air, never noticing the bony jaw that clenched shut below vigilant, hazel eyes, narrowing, scrutinizing her every move.

"Another crushing victory. Twenty-three out of twenty-six. You fantastic young men and women have picked two marvelous civilizations with Rome and Egypt. Congratulations. However, what could be a more demanding task is the era in which our studies are based. Those cultures existed for a long time, and whatever period we decide on will be the theme of our dramatic production. So." Placing his clipboard on the desk, the teacher examined his students. "Are there any suggestions?" He frowned at one individual. "Mr. Benton, you look like you're about to explode. What's with the red face? If you have an objection, submit it now before you yield to some sort of injury."

"I don't have one," Pauly squealed.

"People, remember." Mr. Foley interrupted the sudden amusement. "We do not take enjoyment at another's expense, please. My apologies, Mr. Benton. If I was a betting man, I would have put everything on there being an incredibly significant issue happening right then, but perhaps it's this increasing heat the summer still has upon us, and for that reason, let's speed things up a bit. So, consider the key topics involved with the study of these two civilizations, sophomores, because they all fit the bill perfectly, particularly with their military strength, the extent of their power, and the connections with each other. Therefore, I propose we concentrate on a tumultuous stage between Rome and Egypt. The end of the pharaohs and the beginning of the emperors. A time of growth, politics, war, treachery and mistrust. What would your feedback be if I mentioned the following names? General Marc Antony and Queen Cleopatra the Seventh. Ah-hah," he chuckled at the spirited reaction. "I thought it might grab your attention, particularly from the female faction. Girls, do those audible 'oooo's' hint at your approval of the idea? Keeping in mind that this is also the theme of our play." A rowdy cheer met his question. "Guys, in this case, democracy's out the window and I recommend most heartily that we consent to their feminine wisdom and inclination. That means we'd be foolish to argue or disagree with their choice, and I can sum it up with two words in your terminology these days. Epic fail. Now there's some helpful advice for life."

Laughter exploded around the classroom, and Austin nodded his head when Tess half-swiveled, gave him a wink and quick thumbs-up before turning back. "Mr. Foley, can I offer a date for the play?" she asked.

"Of course, Miss Anderson. And it's very nice to have this opportunity to see and teach you again. What do you have in mind?"

"Um. Well, I didn't know the full story about them until recently, and I thought it was really sad, but really romantic as well," she smiled. "So, perhaps Valentine's Day would be a good time. Is that okay?"

"With that delightfully astute tender, Miss Anderson, I shall now utilize my own advice." Mr. Foley's eyes twinkled as he settled on the edge of his desk once more. "That is not a good time. That is a great time. An undeniably fitting time. I'm also thinking we could base this play on Shakespeare's version, or create something ourselves. Ladies and gentlemen, do you have other proposals?" He gazed around the room. "Anyone? No? Okay, if you're all happy with that decision, then I see no requirement for a vote. I'll present our selections to the powers that be and inform you of their approval. Sophomores, we've got a lot of work to do regarding this assignment. Along with research and written material, there's the staging of our production, including details such as additional character roles, auditions, clothing, set design and construction. But right now, give yourselves a round of applause. You have made this remarkably easy and should be proud of your achievements this morning. I have a strong feeling we'll give the best play this school has ever seen."

Clapping his hands enthusiastically, Austin whirled around and grinned at Pauly, who sat there unmoving, his face an impassive block of stone. "What?" the tall boy protested, alert to the frosty glares swinging between him and the pretty girl diagonally to his right.

the denial

As Pauly ambled down the busy school hallway, a muffled, guttural snickering penetrated his deep musings, and with a hasty glance to the rear, he felt his blood chill at the closeness of his seemingly eternal tormenter. Gripping the shoulder straps on his backpack, he bolted toward the open doors, ran along the path and paused, relieved, when he saw the three youths moving away from him across the lawn. The biggest person threw his middle finger up, just before his menacing stare went straight past him and settled on something near the brick wall boundary. "What the..." Pauly whispered. "Why didn't you follow me?" Frowning, he tracked the line of sight, turned back and lifted his own digit high in the air, and with a huge smirk, reversed among the homeward bound students, heading for the single obstacle to any of Wotlinski's nefarious ambitions.

"I'll see you tomorrow, right here," Austin called. "Same time."

"Same bat channel," Tess responded. Smiling widely, she waved goodbye.

"That chick is so awesome," Joe blurted. "Coops, did you see how she put up with Wade's constant jabbering about superheroes during lunch? I reckon she needs a medal."

"My constant jabbering?" Wade laughed. "You're the one who should've been gagged. It's no wonder she knows everything about Batman now. But let's change the talk to this dude." He shook Austin's arm. "You sly dog. Nice one, bro. After all these years, you've finally hooked up with each other. And since they seem pretty keen on it, we are so taking those girls fishing." He pointed at Tess and two of her friends, strolling toward a parked bus. "Seriously, though, I'm really happy for you."

"Yeah, man, the same goes for me."

"Thanks, guys," Austin grinned. "Maybe we should do it soon, before this warm weather ends."

"Hey," a quiet voice murmured.

"Well, look who's here. The prodigal hobbit comes slinking back."

"Joe, stop calling me that, you stupid fu..." Blinking rapidly, Pauly brought his outburst to a close and softened the scowl on his face when he glimpsed the blond-haired, portly teenager and his cronies farther down the road. "Yeah, okay," he chuckled. "You got me again. Hey, we should ring Peter Jackman and tell him I'm the perfect size for a hobbit. We heard he's making another Lord of the Rings movie, right?" Pauly gazed at each of his silent companions. "C'mon, whaddya think?"

"Jackson," Wade declared.

"What?"

"The dude's name is Peter Jackson. And he's already finishing the next trilogy, which isn't Lord of the Rings, it's The Hobbit. You're always crap with stuff like that."

"Yeah... well..." He shrugged. "You know."

"We know what, Pauly?" Joe's brow rose. "I'll tell you what we do know. We know you're acting like a total douche, but we don't know where you've been during all our breaks today. What's up? Is it that shit with your old man?"

"What shit? What are you going on about?"

"Me and Joe saw it this morning, dude, and it's obviously bothering you."

"Shut the fuck up, Wade. Nothing's bothering me, and even if there was, it's none of your fucking business. What the fuck's up with you guys?"

"Take it easy, mate. We're just seeing if everything's cool."

"Austin," Pauly snarled. "Why? What's it got to do with any of you? Go and get fuc…" For a second time he stopped midsentence when an image of those squinty, pig-like eyes flashed in his mind. In the brief instant of their close proximity he had seen the unmistakable and overpowering desire to do him serious harm, an even darker malevolence, stronger than ever, flickering within their depths. Mentally kicking himself, Pauly sighed heavily. "Look, I'm just kinda pissed with a few things. My old man's an asshole, and I'm not interested in some stupid, shit play. I mean, what's with that? The subject's social fucking studies, not drama."

Austin ran a calm eye over Pauly, appraising the white, tattered sneakers, scruffy jeans, and light-brown, shabby tee-shirt. Apart from maybe two inches of extra height and the long, black hair hanging over his ears and down his neck, his external appearance had remained the same since that first day when he shuffled into their class a timid, nervous boy, and in the ensuing years Austin watched an often baffling personality grow bigger than the short, skinny body accommodating it.

"I think the play's gonna be totally awesome."

"Jeez, Wade, you're such a fuckin' faggot sometimes."

"Pauly, come on, man, don't talk to him like that. Don't talk to any of us like that. Holy shit, you sound like a fat jerk-off we know."

"Get fucked, Joe, I do not."

"Yeah," Joe nodded. "You do." He stared defiantly at Pauly for a moment before focusing on Austin. "Our bus is here, Coops. Catch ya tomorrow."

"No worries." Austin fist-bumped his two pals.

"Later, dude," Wade said. "Hey, Pauly, just remember who your friends are, and the guy who's always supported you." He dipped his head at the tall teenager by Pauly's side, spun around and walked off with Joe.

"What's wrong with them?" Pauly asked, pointing at their backs. "It was a joke."

"It's got everything to do with your behavior today, mate."

"Whaddya mean? I've hardly seen you guys."

"Exactly. You disappeared at every break. One second you're there, the next you're gone. By the way, it's a pretty neat trick. I knew another person who was really good at that. Two people, actually," Austin grinned.

"I was at the library."

"The library? You? When did it get a Playstation and comic book store?"

Pauly burst out laughing. "Austin. Jeez, dude, you kill me sometimes. Comic books. Playstation. I wish," he sniggered. "Nah, man, since you were busy I left you alone."

"I wasn't busy." Austin's brow furrowed. "Where did you get that from?"

"Here's our ride." Grabbing Austin's sleeve, Pauly tugged his arm. "Come on."

"Aw, right, so you are catching the bus," Austin stated as they crossed the road.

"Well, duh, how else am I supposed to get home?"

"Pauly." Austin shook his head. "Yesterday, you called to say you'd see me on it this morning, and when you weren't at your stop I asked the driver to wait. He did that for five freakin' minutes, mate."

"Yeah, the old man's working somewhere close, so he dropped me off. I just thought you'd figure it out. Sorry if that fucked you up, I'll ring your cell next time." While their bus pulled up to the waiting students, he kicked at a large weed sticking out of a crack in the sidewalk, scuffing the plant and grinding it to a mushy, green pulp that stained the coarse concrete surface.

Austin leaned down to Pauly, his low voice carrying over the opening, clanking doors and incessant jostling and thumping of bodies entering the vehicle. "What are the other few things you're pissed with? Is it me? Is it Tess? Is it because I didn't pick the civilizations you wanted?"

Without a word, Pauly joined the queue, made his way to the back of the bus and looked at Austin when he dropped onto the seat beside him. "It's all of them. You picked Rome 'cos she did, and she picked Egypt 'cos you did. I saw it."

"So what?" Austin shrugged. "Mate, it doesn't matter, we can still study them together. Besides, my mom's Italian and Rome is in Italy. She'll love it. Imagine what would happen if I didn't make that choice."

Pauly rolled his eyes. "Your mom's American."

"That's right. But her family origins are in Italy. I reckon I probably own most of Ferrari, Lamborghini and Maserati. Supercars, bro. I might even let you touch one. And because of that, the question now is, do you love the choice?"

"You're an idiot," Pauly laughed. He slammed a window shut when the engine roared and a cloud of oily-smelling, gray-white smoke billowed outside the small pane next to him.

"Why are you pissed at me and Tess?"

"I'm just angry with my dad. And Mom. She's getting worse with her nagging about God and stuff. I wish she'd just fuck off and leave me alone."

"Tell them about things."

"What?" Pauly exclaimed. "You're kidding me, right? Austin, nothing's gotten better since the last time we talked about shit at home, so what the fuck makes you think they'd listen to anything I'd say."

"Okay," he nodded. "Mate, I'm just trying to help. Hey, see if you can stay at my place this weekend. We can start work on our assignment."

"Awesome. But fuck that work shit, we'll go fishing." His eyes widened. "I'll also bring my new games. Dude, I am so gonna kick your ass." Grinning widely, Pauly punched Austin's muscular bicep. "And I'll say sorry to Joe and Wade in the morning. Let's see if they wanna stay, as well. It'll be a fishing and games ass-kicking for you guys. Austin, don't worry about shit, 'cos who knows, things will probably be different tomorrow, man."

Pauly began a vivid description of his Playstation accomplishments, and Austin half-listened while he examined the various notions that churned through his mind. Due to Pauly's undoubtedly arduous family life, he was prepared to understand the erratic and contradictory manner, the escalating use of his bad language, and the odd occasion when pangs of jealousy would rush across his face if Austin had something new and trendy, only recently displayed with the new digital watch that Pauly rotated in his hands during an inspection of the device.

Weird, Austin thought. You always seem to have some pretty cool stuff. But that's not the problem here. The real problem is Tess. I like her, she likes me, and things are not going to be different tomorrow, mate. I know what you mean by that, Pauly, and it hasn't escaped my attention how you never offered an apology and how you didn't even answer my question.

Sighing inwardly, he contemplated a way in which to raise the issue again, how to explain it free of any conflict, because that, clearly, was going to be the easy part, with his release of denial and unavoidable acceptance being the hardest.

Chapter Twelve

The Storm

In the chilly, early-evening air, three people stood outside the school auditorium, a huge building behind and to the right of the main block. White, puffy breath streamed across a metal-clad door as two teenagers leaned in to watch an intriguing contest between their teacher, a shiny, silver key grasped tightly in his gloved hand, and a lock's stiff, unmoving pins.

"I'm not sure if this is frozen or simply a maintenance issue. Ah, there we go," the teacher said when the cylinder rotated with a loud click. Jiggling the key free, he turned around. "Austin. Tess. Please remind me about it in the morning. I don't want to be doing this each time we finish, especially in these conditions." He tilted his head to the dark sky. "I hope the forecast is wrong. After all the hard work and with everything arranged for this week, it would be such a shame if the weather disrupted us. We've only got a couple of months until the show, and that's not long at all when you think about it."

Austin studied the snowfall tumbling through a radiant beam cast from a large halogen lamp mounted on one end of the high, brick wall. "It looks like it's getting heavier, Mr. Foley."

The teacher nodded. "You're right. I think we had best depart now."

"Do you have far to travel?"

"Not far at all, Tess," he replied. "Fortunately, it was still a twenty minute drive today. The town roads were very accessible, and for that reason I'm optimistic our rehearsals will continue. Even though it's nearly Christmas vacation, it'll be business as usual." He waggled his finger at them. "So no moaning."

Austin laughed along with Tess. "Not from us. This is an awesome way to finish the year."

"We've been looking forward to it," Tess exclaimed happily.

"Your enthusiasm is a wonderful sight." Mr. Foley smiled widely at his pupils. "Thank you for staying longer this evening, I really appreciate the assistance. This additional preparation will make tomorrows practice a lot easier, although, in saying that, you both seem extremely comfortable in the roles. I guess I can only describe it as a certain... hmmm." He narrowed his eyes slightly. "Chemistry between you. It's very distinctive and if my understanding of theatre is accurate, then you'll be creating an incredibly authentic performance."

Austin grinned at Tess. "Thanks," he said. "Actually, after we finished the auditions last week I was given another comfortable role because of this. Fishing champion of the year."

"Really?"

"Yeah. When the part of Marc Antony came down to me, Pauly, or Joe, we made a bet that whoever won would be awarded the title."

"High stakes indeed. If I were you, I'd be demanding some sort of engraved trophy."

"I'm not sure that's such a good idea, Mr. Foley. Even though it was just a bit of fun, Pauly's not too happy with the result, and I don't blame him. All through summer, he was the one catching the most fish. And the biggest. But I'm sure he'll get over it, he usually does with that sort of thing."

"He'll have to. While Mr. Benton's rendition was impressive, the fact of the matter is, yours truly surpassed all others. As did your Cleopatra, Tess. It's truly splendid, and I can't wait to see both of you in full make-up and costume." He reached down, picked up a brown briefcase at his feet and deposited the silver key inside before patting the young man's shoulder. "Just remember, Austin, you can't please everyone. I say that even though I know my statement reaches no agreement with your moral fiber," he chuckled. "Let's go. Are you both okay getting home? You told your parents about the extra hour tonight?"

"Dad's picking me up on his way back from work. He should be waiting for me already."

"And everything's sorted with my mom," Tess nodded.

"Excellent. All right, I'll see you tomorrow."

"Okay," the teenagers chorused. They watched their teacher walk toward the faculty parking area, then turned and trudged across the brightly-lit path.

"Wow, it's really coming down now," Austin noted. Brushing some snowflakes from Tess' hair, he pulled his beanie off and placed it over her head. "There, that's better."

"You're so sweet." She smiled at him and linked her arm through his as they rounded the main building. Approaching Shamen Drive, her pace slowed when she saw a lone vehicle parked alongside the pavement, an enormous, black SUV. "Uhhh, my mom's not here yet."

"That's okay, we'll just wait in the car until she arrives," Austin said. He scanned the road's emptiness in both directions, oblivious to the dark tinted window that rolled down silently. "But I've gotta warn you, Tess. Although Dad doesn't usually brag about things, it's guaranteed he'll harp on about his new toy."

"Son, son, son. Dear, oh, dear." Jeff's voice carried over the deep, mighty rumbling of the engine. "This is no toy. This is a machine. A seriously serious machine. A six-speed automatic, five-point-four liter, three-valve single overhead camshaft vee-eight, generating three hundred and ten horsepower within three hundred and sixty-five pounds of pure, raw, terrifying torque." Leaning across the passenger seat, he grinned, gave a funny grunt and tapped the console. "Have I mentioned that this toy. Correction. This seriously serious machine, is all mine? It's entirely possible I forgot to tell y... oh... oh, my goodness... hi, Tess, I didn't realize you were there."

"See what I mean?"

Tess giggled at Austin's shaking head.

"Come on, hop in," Jeff chuckled. "Another five minutes and you'll end up looking like the most realistic snowpeople I've ever encountered." He swiveled around to face them after they shook the snow from their clothing and clambered onto the seats.

"Ahhh," Tess sighed. "It's so warm in here." She took a deep breath, savoring the rich aroma of pristine, pure leather and freshly-installed carpet.

"Toasty warm and the perfect heat setting for this weather, which was probably the outside air temperature the last time I saw you. How have you been, Tess?"

"Really good, thanks, Mr. Cooper," she grinned. "It's nice to see you again."

"Nice to see you, too. How did tonight's rehearsal go? More enjoyable than the first?"

"It sure was." She flashed a radiant smile at her tall companion and prodded his side. "Especially when our teacher said we've got chemistry togeth..." The muted, relentless ringing of an old, 1940s style telephone cut off Tess' next words. Grabbing her bag from between her feet, she unzipped a front pocket, pulled the bright pink material apart and clattered through a variety of possessions before her clanging cell phone emerged. "Hi, Mom," she bubbled cheerily after glancing at the brightly glowing screen.

Gazing at her, Austin thought of a unique bond that had progressed and strengthened throughout the course of the school year. He cherished the relaxed manner of their relationship, the way in which she welcomed his interests, shared his conversation and was, quite simply, good, fun company. And right then, when she had smiled at him, he also thought of his feelings, and felt one in particular deepen all the more with a glimpse of the same emotion shining deeply in her eyes. But the happiness that flooded Austin barely one minute ago dispersed immediately when he observed the distress spreading across her merry face.

"Is she okay?" Tess stared out the side window. "That's good... no... no, Mom, it's not your fault, don't be silly. We all make mistakes, so don't say that. I didn't even check mine. It's been in my bag for hours." She listened briefly, leaned inward and studied the intensifying snowfall beyond the windshield. "It's getting really heavy here, as well," she said, noting the wipers continually sweeping away a thick, white covering on the glass. "What do I do? Apart from Austin and his dad, everyone else has gone. I was waiting for you in their car." She paused. "Austin Cooper." In the momentary silence, a woman's voice, faint and garbled, floated out of the device clutched in Tess' hand. "Yes, Mom, that Austin, and yes his dad's right here. I'll pass you on now."

Jeff pressed Tess' cell to his ear once she handed it over. "Hi, Carol, this is Jeff." His suit trousers made a fleeting screech on the leather seat as he slid around and faced the front. "Yes, it was a quick introduction last time." He listened for a while. "I'm sorry to hear that, but glad it's not serious. Carol, of course it's not a problem. It's no inconvenience at all. Anything else we can do, you just name it. I'll give you my cell and home number, and we'll call the minute we get back."

Tess looked at Austin's furrowed brow. "What's wrong?" he asked.

*   *   *

Jeff stared out the dining room door at the dense, white snow that blanketed the patio. "The storm has eased off a little," he said into the phone. Flicking a switch by the molded wood casing, he plunged the outside area into darkness and turned away from the now brightly-mirrored glass. "But apparently it'll get stronger tonight. And although it might seem hard to believe, given your circumstances, I actually saw our tax dollars working for us. We've had plows coming through here regularly, and the drive to Denver was clear all the way. They're doing a great job. Unfortunately, if you haven't got the machinery in the outlying regions, it's a case of waiting for help, which I'm sure will be soon, Carol." He strolled into the hallway, heading for the living room to his left. "Tess is handling it all remarkably well, and Dee's still clucking away, puffing out her feathers. It's like having a giant chicken in the house. The second you both finished talking she rushed off to scratch up some extra straw for Tess' bed." Smiling at the tinny laughter bursting from the handset, he paused at the doorway before entering the cozy room. "Yes, George informed me he'll ring tomorrow and for you to expect a call from Tess when I drop her off at school."

"Poor thing, going through something like this. It's horrible," Dee was saying. "Don't worry, darling, everything will be just fine." She looked up as Jeff settled on the sofa beside her.

"You're more than welcome," he said. "I'll talk to you in the morning, okay? Take care. Bye."

"How are they?"

"Dealing with the incident admirably, my love," Jeff replied. "Carol's positive the fall didn't break any bones." Placing the phone on the cushioned armrest, he smiled at the occupants of two large, walnut-colored La-Z-Boy recliners, angled adjacent to the brightly glowing fireplace. The faint pop and hiss of blazing wood carried in the momentary silence. "We've got to be thankful it didn't turn out a lot worse, Tess. Your mother was able to make it there before getting completely snowed in, and your grandmother seems to be in high spirits considering she's got one monster of a bruise appearing on her hip."

"Mom will be so annoyed with herself." Tess shook her head from side to side, her long, blonde hair swishing across her shoulders. "She'll feel as if she's let us down, especially Dad. She's proud of the fact that she's usually pretty good with situations, and even told me it wasn't always like that, so leaving her cell phone at home would've bothered her all day."

"Everyone makes mistakes, sweetheart," Dee purred. "She was extremely worried, and yet look at the fantastic job she did in just getting there. The journey must have been horrendous. I'm amazed she actually managed it."

"That's what I said to her, Mrs. Cooper," Tess beamed.

"Honey, seeing as you're staying with us until Friday, I'm gonna kind of insist that you call us by our first names. It really is okay." Dee smiled warmly. "Remember when we saw you last? When you came over for a swim and met Susan and Greg? Was that September?"

Tess nodded eagerly.

"Well," Dee carried on. "Let's start early and we'll make it a permanent thing, because it took months for Susan to stop calling us Mr. and Mrs. Cooper."

"And I got the name Mr. um whoops Jeff for ages after that," Jeff threw in. "So call her Mrs. Dee for a while or even Mrs. C. I'm sure Fonzie won't mind." He patted his wife's leg and gave a tilted, double thumbs-up. "Aaay," he droned.

"Dad," Austin laughed. "That's terrible. You're getting worse." He looked to his side at the beautiful, young woman nestled comfortably in the chair's soft, luxurious padding, held her gaze and felt the happiness cleanse his soul again with the sight of her wide grin and shining, amber eyes, dazzling and vibrant once more. After the anxiety he had seen in them earlier, combined with her forlorn manner, he thought how difficult it must be for her to maintain any semblance of fluency amid the worry of her family and the arrival at an unfamiliar place with barely known people, barely known parents, and he gave silent thanks to his mother and father for the way they eased her troubled mind and heart. Deep down, his affection for her intensified at the strength and courage she displayed.

"Thank you," Tess said. "I'll try my hardest, but I'll probably be a little bit like Susan. I've never been allowed to address an adult by their first name. It's just something my dad's always drilled into me. He's... um..." She shrugged. "Kind of old-fashioned. Set in his ways. It must've taken a lot of convincing from Mom to stop him doing something."

"Your father did come across as a particularly efficient man," Jeff noted. "In our brief chat he seemed very incisive, very competent. Those are good traits to have. What does he do for a job? Is there a military background by any chance?" A faint smile lifted his lips.

"Yes." Tess' brow furrowed. "There is. How did you know that? He certainly wouldn't say anything until you'd met, and neither would Mom. She's been told never to..." Her eyelids closed tightly shut. "He used twenty-four-hour time on you, didn't he?"

"Yep." Jeff chuckled at the exasperation loaded in her voice. "That and a couple of other indicators gave it away. I'm under strict instructions to have you at school by precisely zero-seven-hundred-hours local, and you're to contact your mother within fifteen seconds of our arrival."

"Oh my God." Tess dropped her head into her hands. "Mr. Cooper, I am so…" Taking a deep breath, she blew it out forcefully and looked up. "Jeff. I am so sorry if he was rude to you. He doesn't mean to do it, he really doesn't, and I've tried telling him how to talk to normal people, but he just seems to refuse…"

"Tess." Jeff spoke softly, soothingly. "Sweetheart, he wasn't rude at all. He was very polite and simply expressed the facts as they were meant to be heard. I like that. It shows I haven't got a dumbass on my hands. I could do with that sort of conduct in London right about now."

"And honey." Leaning forward, Dee whispered secretively. "I don't want to alarm you, but Jeff's not normal. He's a damn fool."

"What she said." Jeff gave his wife a playful nudge. "Tess, do you think ringing at seven in the morning is a bit early? They might still be asleep."

"Nana might," the young woman replied, still giggling. "But Mom won't. She's always up at that time, cooking breakfast, doing the washing, that sort of thing. She told me everything changed when she married the army and now it's all kind of ingrained in her to get up when Dad gets up."

"So it's the army," Jeff observed. "He'll be the first G.I. I've met. What does he do?"

"To be honest, I have no idea," Tess laughed. "This may sound silly, but he's never told me his role. He's very guarded about his work. I think he's involved with training at Fort Carson with some type of airborne division or something, and I once heard him talk to Mom about Iraq. But after nine-eleven, he's been doing a load of stuff in New York and D.C. We all went there during summer holidays when he got his promotion, and now the one thing I know for sure is he'll be getting an office in the Pentagon. Did he say he was in Washington with my sister, Melissa?"

"Yes, he did tell me that."

"She absolutely loves everything army. Ever since she finished high school, she's gone with Dad on all of his travels, and sometime next year she'll be the latest Anderson to enlist. I am so surprised Mom hasn't seen them arrive in a helicopter with a full medical team," she declared, and laughed along with Austin and Jeff.

"What about you, honey? Are you interested in joining?"

"Not at all, Dee." She shook her head. "It's not my sort of thing, and that's probably why I'm never told any stuff. I'm really close with Mel, but she wouldn't tell me anything if Dad swears her to secrecy. She'll follow his orders word for word. Actually, Jeff." Tess brightened visibly. "You two have got something in common. Her second love. Cars."

"Awww, no." Austin rubbed his forehead. "That's done it," he grumbled, tousling his brown hair. "I thought we might have escaped more of Dad's waffling tonight."

"Waffling? Me?" Jeff protested. "Mate, I'll have you know that's high-quality drivel and not a syllable less. If it's waffling you want, you should try my so-called manager. Even the English don't understand what the heck he's talking about when he's speaking their own language, in their own country. After I arrive, I'll have to get the Royal Family involved. Maybe the risk of having his head cut off will do the trick."

"What's happening in England?" Tess asked, her voice low. "You're not moving there, are you?"

"Oh honey no, we're not moving," Dee said quickly, noting the tone and slight waver in the girl's words, along with a profound dismay in her downcast expression. "Jeff's going for a few days in January to sort out some problems with his new manufacturing plant."

"Wow!" Smiling widely at Jeff, Dee's assuring statement having an obvious and immediate effect, Tess shifted her weight in the chair, angling herself toward Austin in the process. "Your job sounds really important."

"Naaah," he hummed. "I'm just your standardized, run-of-the-mill, regular pen-pushing desk jockey."

"You are not!" Dee exclaimed. "Tess, don't listen to him. He's a bit like your father. If the question's ever raised he says he's just a worker in a factory, when in actual fact he's the chief executive, who's taken a moderately successful business, restructured it, and turned it into one of the most profitable paper-producing companies in the United States. And in March of this year, based on his design, he instigated an expansion into London where they're now producing greeting cards, which has been seriously jeopardized because the manager is completely useless at making decisions when it comes to..." Dee paused as she glanced at her husband's wide and staring eyes. "What?"

"You're hired," he announced. "You are so hired. You and Greg. The greeting card idea was his, and now both of you should be running the show."

"Babe." Dee grinned. "You couldn't afford us, honey. Especially me. And all I'd do is just show you up something silly. How would you feel if the shareholders and board took away your reward for such hard work and vision, and gave that poor excuse of a jalopy to me?"

Jeff shrugged. "Doesn't matter. There'd still be a brand new, straight off the production line, Lincoln Navigator Ultimate parked in the garage." He knitted his fingers together, crossed his legs and circled his thumbs around each other. "Did you know it's got stability and traction control, a four-wheel, anti-lock braking system, and eighteen-inch, chrome-finished, all-season tires? Tess, we should be the ones mounting a rescue mission. I'm sure that four-wheel-drive bad boy could power over the top of any snowplow, if we tried."

"Mom." Austin dropped his shaking head. "Why did you do that?"

"I seem to remember there weren't any criticisms from you and Stephie when we picked it up. Furthermore, I noticed there being a difference of opinion as to who was riding shotgun, leaving poor old Mom, very, very old Mom, driving on her own." Jeff tilted his head back and peered to the right, at the person slumped beside his wife. "My official finder of all the wonderful information had a fun time. Isn't that right, my darling girl?"

Silent throughout the entire conversation, Stephanie moved her sight away from the orange glow of the fire. "Mom," she groaned. "I don't feel good. My throat's sore, I've got a really bad headache and my body feels all achy." Thirteen by only three months, every year she looked more and more like her mother with the same long, shiny black hair surrounding smooth, bronzed skin. Light-brown eyes, droopy and bloodshot, blinked slowly.

Dee regarded her for a moment before turning to Jeff. "Great," she sighed.

the driver

In the expanse of bright light cast by the car's strong headlamps, Jeff cruised past large mounds of compacted snow pushed to the curbside and spilling onto the dark and deserted sidewalk of Shamen Drive. Near the kindergarten, close to the spot where his daughter almost died, his cell phone chirped noisily from its hands-free cradle mounted beside the climate controls. With a quick glance at the glowing screen, he pressed a button on the steering wheel. "Jeffrey Cooper," he announced cheerily. "Husband, philanthropist, taxi driver."

"Philanthropist?" a voice snorted from the speakers. "Pffft! Replace it with a more appropriate term."

"And what would that be, my love?"

"Fool," Dee stated.

"I knew you'd say that," he chortled. "Probably because you remind me on a daily basis. What can I do for you, babe? Do we need milk? Flour? Eggs? It's Friday and you promised there'd be brownies waiting for me at home."

"I did, and they are. So, no, we don't need any food. I've done all the grocery shopping today, got some more medicine for Stephie, smashed a bottle of merlot in the mall parking lot, then swore because of that in front of a lovely, young family walking by me at the time. Unintentionally, of course."

"Of course," Jeff agreed. "Tell me, is that the wine we would have been taking to Suze and Greg's tomorrow night?"

"The very same. There's about eight glasses worth I could drain out of my jeans and sneakers."

"Hmmm. The connoisseurs will love it. You'll savor the substantial, fruity tang," Jeff crooned, his tone pompous, nasally, and with a slight lisp. "The delightful, elegant taste of Deangela's pants and footwear is a simply marvelous flavor."

"You fool," Dee laughed. "What are the roads like, honey?"

"Well… they're kind of flat with a few potholes, and some are a little bumpy. I think the plows must have taken a chunk out here and there. And before you call me a fool again, babe, because you've already breached the allowed number, they're fine." Jeff peered out the windshield at some delicate, dainty snowflakes, illuminated briefly on their lazy dance through the air. Every thirty seconds the wipers swept away a thin and velvety dusting. "The snow's been cleared from that storm we had this morning and it's just a light fall happening now. If you haven't heard, the weather reports are good, so there shouldn't be any problems with George collecting Tess tomorrow."

"Yeah, I saw that. I was watching the news when Carol rang to tell me their plans have changed a bit. George is picking them up first, dropping Melissa and her nana back home, and then he and Carol are coming at some time around midday to get Tess. But they won't be staying long, 'cos they've got loads of stuff to do."

"Fair enough," Jeff remarked. "It'll give me the chance to go shopping with Austin. He wants to get everybody's Christmas presents, including his special gift for his special someone. And speaking of our leading thespians, I'm just about at the school now."

"Okay, honey. I'll see you all soon. Drive carefully."

"That goes without saying, babe. I've been extra worried this week. If anything happened to Tess I'm sure George would have me tied to a target range in the middle of nowhere and you'd never see me again."

"Then you'd better add extra alert. Our next wedding anniversary is eighteen years of married hell, and you know what that means, right?"

"Go on," he chuckled.

"I'll sum it up in two words. Private jet. One last thing, honey. I'm still the sexiest person in the world who's always cutting off…"

Jeff stabbed the red phone icon on his cell's colorfully shining screen. "Ha!" he exclaimed in the sudden silence, and straightened the cradle after it swiveled aside with his quick jab. "Not this time, my love." Approaching a long line of vehicles idling at the curb, he pulled in behind a beaten and battered Chrysler, the blue paintwork faded, dirty and peeling. No sooner had he stopped than it lurched sluggishly away, spooling huge clouds of dense, white smoke that lingered in the still and frigid air while the decrepit car crept along, spluttering and clanking loudly on its journey along the road. He turned when the rear door opened abruptly and Tess climbed inside. "Well, fancy that," he exclaimed, watching as Austin held it ajar until her legs were safely within the warm interior. "Queen Cleopatra and Marc Antony. What are the odds of two historically famous characters wanting a ride with me?"

"I'd give it a billion to one," Austin replied. Closing the door with a soft thump, he dashed around to the other side and scrambled onto the seat. "Jeez, it's cold out there," he muttered, dumping two bags in the footwell.

"Sure is. You'd think it would be snowing by now. How are you, Tess?"

"I'm really good, thank you for asking. How are you, Mr. um whoops Jeff?" Her eyes twinkled as she pulled her seatbelt down and clipped herself in.

"I don't know what method of communication you're using, but somehow you and Suze are in cahoots." He shared a wide grin with the pretty girl. "I should never have opened my big, fat mouth with that one. Kudos to you, darling, and I'm absolutely fantastic, thanks. Tonight will be payment for all the hard slog we've done this week." Leaning to his right, he peered in the rearview mirror. "Hi, buddy, how's things?" Usually placid in appearance, his son's hardened face pivoted from an intense stare through the window. "No regular, chirpy smile, mate? What's up?"

Austin shrugged. "Just Pauly doing his typical stuff."

"Okay." Jeff nodded at the reflection. Unfastening his belt, he twisted around and propped himself up on the center utility compartment. "What happened? Am I to understand he was at practice this time?"

"Yep." Austin pointed at the windshield. "That was him leaving right in front of us."

"Really? In that old clunker?" Jeff peered backward and saw the red taillights farther up the road. They disappeared as another vehicle pulled out and blocked his view. "I thought they had a brown Cadillac. Who picked him up?"

"Sean. Pauly was late again this morning, 'cos they broke down on the way. He said they were gonna have to borrow another car, so that must be it. Not sure which is the worst of the two, although I suppose that one's still running."

"Austin, that's terrible," Tess blurted, giving him a playfully stern expression.

"Yes, Austin. Terrible. Awful." Jeff winked at Tess. "Awful, awful Austin."

"I saw that, Dad," he laughed. "And the corners of your mouth are twitching." Austin looked at the young woman by his side. "You know what he's been like, Tess. Why hasn't he accepted that we're friends? Like Wade and Joe. They don't mind all of us hanging out together, so why shouldn't he?" His features softened, and a scant smoldering permeated his cheeks when she reached across to massage his forearm. Giving her a quick smile, detecting the same pinkish hue, he directed his attention back to his father. "I apologize if I seemed grumpy before, Dad, and by the way, thanks for cheering me up, but sometimes Pauly can be so pigheaded and bitter." Austin sighed. "Even spiteful. Here's some perfect examples. During rehearsal, we're both doing some dialogue and he yells out asking Mr. Foley if Tess is standing in the correct place. Right in the middle of the scene. And about ten minutes later, he does the same, saying the ending should be changed to have us both die, 'cos that's what really happened. Then after, when we're all standing outside and wishing each other a Merry Christmas and everything, he tells Tess she'll probably have a really good one since she won't be seeing me."

"He's got a tough life at home. Maybe it's affecting him more than we think."

"I know, Dad, and I feel sorry for him, I really do. You know I've tried talking with him about the way he behaves, and even though it's not all the time, it's enough that he's not doing himself any favors treating us like this. Treating Tess like this."

"I agree, mate, and the only thing I can offer is this. Eventually, he will realize that." Jeff flicked his gaze from one to the other. "For now, let's try and forget about it. I need my big, burly shovel-buddy happy and ready for a bit of snow clearing as soon as we get back, or we'll never immerse ourselves in that beautifully hot pool. Mmmmm," he hummed, closing his eyes momentarily. "Hot pool, sizzling tub, and the likelihood there'll be delicious marshmallows mixed with hot chocolate whilst we peruse a hopefully clear sky for satellites. Come on, let's get out of here." He swung back onto his seat and clipped himself in. "Austin, old bean, during our travels homeward be a good fellow and explain the splendiferous optics reward to Tess, who very soon will owe me ten bucks because I ate dinner quicker than her."

The engine's throaty growl blended with the sound of Tess' tinkling giggle while Austin gazed out the window again. And grinned.

the swim

Laughing at another of Jeff's spontaneous comments, Tess laid her cutlery on her plate, the metal clinking faintly upon contact with its glossy, porcelain surface, and leaned back in the La-Z-Boy, contentedly assessing her days spent at the Cooper residence. With the experience daunting at first, it changed rapidly from the moment she set foot in the house. Jeff and Dee were so warm, so welcoming and friendly, that by the time three hours had passed, curiously, she felt like part of their family. She liked all of them enormously, and after observing their banter, combined with the serious parts of their conversation, Tess considered her stay the best extended sleepover ever. The fun, relaxed, and pleasant atmosphere before curling up in a cozy bed for the night was bliss when compared to anything she had endured at her friends' places. There, she was in a sleeping bag, crammed together with everyone on the floor and repeatedly asking Shivawn to be quiet once the chatter ceased and they all tried drifting off to sleep. Her eyes lifted to the tall teenager seated next to his father on the sofa and ravenously consuming his meal. Pauly, she thought, you don't know how wrong you are. I've got a funny feeling Christmas vacation won't be as happy for me as it should be.

"All finished, honey? Would you like some more?"

"No thanks, Dee." Tess smiled at the woman in the adjacent chair. "I'm really full now."

"Was it okay?"

"It was absolutely delicious. You're such a good cook."

Austin's overburdened fork stopped an inch from his readied lips. "Dad," he whispered loudly. "There's something wrong with Tess. What do you think Mom's put in the food?"

"Beats me," Jeff muttered. "But don't make any sudden moves. Pretend we're unaware of her sneaky and wicked plan. Just smile and nod, son. Smile and nod. Hi, babe," he beamed, wiggling his fingers at his wife. "Nothing to see here apart from two guys finishing their scrumptious dinners."

"Pesky men-things." Dee angled herself toward Tess. Taking a momentary hold of the girl's hand, she gave it a gentle squeeze. "Ignore them, my darling, and if we're lucky they might go away."

Beyond the closed door, a muffled thudding and clattering echoed from the hallway, and everyone turned when Stephanie and Duke entered the living room. They all watched as the dog bounded across to Austin and dropped his backside on the soft, fawn-colored carpet before resting his paw on the young man's thigh.

"Hello, Duke," Austin purred. He placed his free hand on top of the paw, smiled at the single lick it received and chuckled when the malamute popped up, heading for a whirlwind tour of the others, the small and shiny silver bell on his blue collar chiming madly. Following his happy circuit, he lowered himself fully at Austin's feet and rolled over, awaiting the desired rub of his fluffy fur while his tail thumped frantically against the floor.

"That is soooo gorgeous," Tess cooed. "My heart melts every time I see it. He must really love you."

"He loves everyone, Tessie. Don't you, Dukey-boy," Austin warbled. Jeff and Dee shared a swift, secretly amused glance as their son reached down to scratch the dog's tummy.

"Not true," Stephanie huffed. "Well, not completely true," she added. Taking the empty seat on the sofa, she sneezed into a large handkerchief clasped outside a tie-dyed, fleecy blanket wrapped tightly around her upper body. "He does love everyone, but he loves Austin the most." She elbowed her brother's arm. "You stole my dog's affection ages ago."

Austin frowned. "And hello to you, too, Steph. How do you come by that?"

"Oh, uh, yeah," she babbled. "Hi. Sorry, I didn't mean to sound grumpy or nasty or anything. I'm just saying." She sneezed again, and wiped the bright, cherry-red skin around her nostrils. "You're always the first person he goes to, and you're the only one who gets that paw on the leg thing. He doesn't do it with me. Or anyone."

"This sounds interesting," Tess remarked. "Why does he do that?"

"It's because... um..." Austin fell silent. Resuming his meal, he gazed at the extensive collection of family photos on the wall to the right of the fireplace, his sight lingering on the one that showed him at eleven years of age, taken only three weeks after his perilous ordeal with Duke. To his great and yet suddenly short-lived relief, assistance came in the form of a response from his mother, who happily narrated the entire event, and how Duke began his ritual the next day when her son sat in the very same chair that had been pierced by the strand of metal he picked off the table to inspect first-hand. Austin's old, inner turmoil stirred, and raised its festering head to gloat delightedly at his situation, daring him to reveal his mixed bag of dishonesty and fabrication.

"And for the past four and a half years, Duke's done it every time he sees Austin," Dee said. "Isn't that right, honey?"

"Mmmm," Austin whirred, feeling sick to the core now that Tess was involved in his deception. It didn't start the next day either, he thought.

"In fact," she continued. "If Austin's standing, then Duke keeps nudging his leg until he's forced to either sit or kneel so their little ceremony can be carried out. It's very sweet."

"Still doesn't explain why Duke loves him more than his owner."

"It sure does, Steph," Jeff grinned. "You're overlooking the fact they're trash buddies. Just go to a garbage dump, roll around there for a while, and if you end up stinking as much as they did, you're a complete shoo-in."

"I'm a complete what? Mom!" Stephanie protested when Dee joined in on the hilarity. "You're meant to stick up for me when they're laughing."

"But I always do, sweetheart," Dee countered, still chuckling away. "I was just thinking about the expression on your face and the way your little nose went all wrinkly when we were giving Duke a bath that night." She looked at Tess. "Stephie was beside herself the whole time they were missing, and I'll never forget how overjoyed she was when she saw them coming up the driveway, knowing they were safely home. We all were."

"It must have been a horrible wait. And Duke is such a beautiful dog. I always wanted my own pet, but now it's probably too late. I gave up asking years ago."

"Why's that, darling?" Dee asked.

"Well." Tess propped her elbow on the armrest and laid her chin upon the tops of her fingers. "Even though it never happened, and I'm so glad it didn't." She smiled at Austin. "For a while there was an ongoing possibility Dad would be serving overseas. But it seems like his promotion to lieutenant general has pretty much guaranteed we'll be staying in America. Plus, there's also Nana's fall. She's getting on in life and I don't think Mom would be too happy leaving her alone now. She'll be really concerned."

"Your dad's a general?" Austin's eyebrows shot straight up while his jaw did the exact opposite and dropped wide open. "An army general? Holy crap, Tessie, I remember you saying he got promoted, but you never mentioned his rank."

"Didn't I?" Tess frowned. "I'm sorry, I thought I had. That's what most of the stuff was about in D.C. We went to this long and totally boring function. Mel kept poking me in the side 'cos I was nearly falling asleep at the table. Sorry," she finished softly.

"You don't have to apologize, honey." Dee rubbed Tess' forearm. "Not only have you had a lot on your mind lately, but you don't have to say anything about your father's title. I'm just really looking forward to meeting your parents tomorrow, and I'm sure there's nothing to cause you any worry. Except him, obviously." She pointed at her husband. "You will be on your best behavior, mister."

"I am always a good boy," he objected. "Tess, don't listen to that crazy Italian woman. I'm the one who should be worried. I promised a lovely time in the pool and spa tonight, and if the general's daughter is disappointed, I'll definitely end up being used as target practice."

"Jeff! How can you say that? He wouldn't even consider such a thing." Tess gaped at him, her stunned expression giving way to a slow and sly smile. "But I guess we'd better make sure. I'll have a foot-rub after the swim, breakfast in bed, the latest cell, preferably a Galaxy or iPhone and then the newest models on release... um... fifty, no, make that a hundred thousand dollars in small, unmarked bills, the ten bucks I'm already owed, and your car, without all the fancy information. I've heard it and I don't need it, 'cos you'll be driving me."

Jeff's roaring laughter bounced off the walls. "I like this girl. I really, really like her," he declared, wiping tears from his eyes. "I think we've got another honorary Cooper sitting right there and a new challenger to the throne. Bravo, that was magnificently said. Game on, young lady, game on.' Clapping his hands together, he peered jubilantly at his smiling family. "Let's get this show on the road. Steph, have you got your swimsuit for Tess?"

"Yeah, I put it in her room. Mom, can I come for a swim? Please, please, please," she pleaded. "I feel loads better. Pretty please with honey and sugar?"

"No, darling, I'm sorry, you're not. You're only starting to get better and I don't want you getting any worse. I'm amazed the rest of us are still fine. Jeff, did I tell you how Stephie got this? Anna went to school on Monday completely choked with flu. Why are there some parents who insist on doing that when they know their sick children will infect everyone else? It's ridiculous and so totally irresponsible."

"Dee, you're like my mom," Tess said. "Now I'm convinced you two will get on really well, 'cos that's just the sort of thing she would say."

"Is it? Then she must be an incredibly resourceful, intelligent, multi-skilled and undeniably top-notch, wonderful person."

Austin rose, watching as his mother and the girl he considered his very special friend lean in closer, giggling, their heads nearly touching, and a huge smile spread his mouth wide, propelling his former despair down to its deep and dark, resident pit.

*　　*　　*

Jeff unlocked the dining room door and turned from his examination of the yard. "Are we all ready? It's mighty cold out there," he said, bouncing his eyebrows up and down. "Now. Much the same as last year, I'll sound like a fussy old fart, but I reckon it's better to be safe than sorry. We should prepare for this. We don't want any sort of falling catastrophe. Tess, take extreme care on the patio and deck. It could be slippery, and we don't want you joining the bruised hip brigade. You and Dee get to the pool as quick as you can. Austin, I can't even remember the last time you were sick, so if you don't mind, you can be our robe manager and put these in the clothes shed." He shook the front of his thick, dark-burgundy, toweling gown, one of a matching set they all wore. "I pretty much know you won't mind."

"Of course not, Dad. It's a good plan. You guys give them to me at the pool," Austin informed them. "And I'll take it from there."

"See? That's ma boy." Jeff patted his son's shoulder. "Steph, what are you going to do?"

"I dunno," she shrugged. "Suppose I'll stare at the TV. Maybe go on Facebook. Can't imagine doing anything else."

"Au contraire, my pretty and contaminated young offspring. You could clean your bedroom. Or pigsty as I refer to it."

"Dad!"

"You're right," he grinned. "First, wash the car, paint the house, and get our delicious brownies ready for when we come in. Then you can have the night off. No, scrub that last item. We don't want our brownies handled by a DAFEC. That's an acronym for diseased and filthy exasperated child, by the way."

"Dad," Stephanie grumbled.

"See? That's ma girl." Jeff hugged his daughter. "I'm only joking, sweetheart. There'll be other occasions. You just watch TV with Duke, rest, and get all nice and healthy again."

"Okay," she mumbled. "I hope you all have a nice time. I'll close the door, if you want."

The frigid air nipped at the exposed skin on their faces and lower legs the moment they stepped onto a diagonal path cleared through a two-foot-deep accumulation of snow. Tess squealed delightedly, and her gown flapped as she scurried hand in hand with Dee across the pavers. Pausing at the coping stones, they disrobed hastily and handed their garments to Austin before leaping into the balmy water. With bulging, cloudy breath gusting from his mouth, Austin dashed around to the other side and stopped at a small, wooden shed located next to the hut containing the gas heater and other equipment. A new addition to the area, Jeff had the shed built during summer, successfully deterring Duke's continuous and often amusing infatuation for making beds out of anything left lying about. Placing all of their toweling robes on a bench-seat inside, Austin spun and traversed the decking with great, bounding jumps, luxuriating in the liquid warmth that enveloped his freezing body the instant he dived in.

"What happened to the extreme care part?" Jeff asked when his son surfaced in front of him.

Austin grimaced. "Yeah, sorry about that, Dad. I had it all under control, I was just starting to lose feeling in my feet."

"Fair enough," he nodded. "It's time we invested in some suitable footwear, and nothing like those toe-tangling flip-flops we tried last winter. Stability wise, they were no better than running a marathon in scuba fins. We'll check it out at Halfmoon tomorrow, mate."

"We need decent lighting too, honey. It's well overdue." Dee pointed to a halo of muted illumination cast from the single, external fixture. "That's never been enough out here. A couple of spotlights on the wall should do the trick."

"Terrific idea, babe. Maybe something for the deck, as well. What do you think about recessed LED along the border? We could also have it going up the stairs and put pole lighting around the kitchen and table, all on different circuits and dimmer switches. I reckon it'd complete the whole scene superbly. Needless to say, that means there'll be no jet for you in the foreseeable future."

"Not likely," she chuckled, curling her arm around Jeff. "Come on, my fantastic husband, let's give these two a bit of breathing space and chat about the finishing-off details to this place."

While his mom and dad drifted away, Austin gazed at Tess as she glided lazily to him. At her wet and slicked-back hair, shining brightly in the vibrant, blue glow. At the glossy sheen on the smooth and silky skin of her face and neck, and at the wide smile that formed her mouth when she fixed her glistening eyes upon his.

"Hi," she murmured, draping her arms atop his shoulders. "Do you mind if I hold on? It's too deep for me to stand."

"I am yours to command, my queen," he grinned.

"Sweet talker," she giggled.

"Are you having a nice time?"

"The best," she gushed. "I've never done this before. Everything about your home is gorgeous and I absolutely love it."

"You seem very happy," he noted.

"I am. But I'll really miss all of this. You've got a wonderful family, Austin. Your parents are just so cool. Your mom is adorable and your dad is the funniest guy I've ever known. He cracks me up every time. I have never had conversations like that with my dad. Ever."

"Do you both... get along? I hope you don't mind my asking," he added rapidly, his brow raised high.

"I don't mind at all," Tess frowned. Her forehead flattened out instantly at the realization of his swift words. "I'm sorry," she sighed.

"Sorry for what?"

Squeezing her lips together tightly, she stared across the gently swaying water and its translucent, misty curtain that twirled out of the radiance and into the still, pitch-black night. "For not telling you about my father. I feel bad. A big part of me wanted to, but a bigger part was afraid, I guess. I even had the opportunity months ago when Wade cut his hair really short and you and Joe kept saluting him all day."

"Aw, yeah," he snickered. "Jeez, that was hilarious. Good times!"

"They were," Tess nodded. "And they still are." She touched her fingertips to his cheek and ran them down a bristly, subtle covering of darker hair sprouting on his jawline and chin. "Austin, Dad is a lot sterner than Jeff, and I'm a bit worried about tomorrow. I've been worried the whole time. I don't want his... umm... differences to affect..." She paused. "Us. Don't get me wrong, we get on really well and I love him loads, but change doesn't come easy to him, and he's very set in his ways. I can't even remember the last time I heard him laugh. Actually, no, I'm wrong. It was at his promotion when he was talking to Mel about some saying they had at Fort Carson. They altered 'you can't teach an old dog new tricks' to 'you can't teach an old dog new tricks, but sure as hell can you teach a soldier a thing or two.' And when Mel said it would now be a daughter, he gave this simple, little grunt, which is about all you'd get out of him in the humor department. It's in his blood, he can't help..."

"Hey," Austin beamed. "I get to meet a real general. How can that not be the awesomest thing ever?" He took hold of her arms and slid her along his shoulders, bringing her closer until mere inches separated them. "And don't be sucked in by Mom and Dad. They're pretty strict as well. You just haven't seen it yet, Tessie."

"I love how you've started calling me that," she purred, scrutinizing his features. "This is probably a really stupid question, but has anyone ever said you have the most amazing eyes?"

"Mom has been known to mention it from time to time. She says they change color depending on the light."

"They do!" Tess crooned. "Right now, they look light-purple. It's absolutely beautiful. At other times, they're a lot darker, stronger, and then they can be different shades of blue, or a mixture of both. They're stunning. I adore them. Every time I see you, I wonder what color they'll be. Every time I see you, I think how handsome you are, and then... every time I... I... I want..."

Austin's absolutely beautiful, light-purple, stunning eyes widened immensely when she leaned in and kissed him, pressing her soft, tender lips fully against his. Twice in a matter of hours, and for only the third time since their impromptu meeting at the mall, they blushed simultaneously as Tess launched herself backward off his broad, muscular chest, kicking her legs wildly and dousing him in a deluge of white, frothy foam.

"Ahhh... honey," Dee whirred, goosebumps plastering her arms in spite of the beautifully warm water swirling about her neck. After observing the expressive and romantic contact on display, she peered at the current splashing war they waged and smiled. A wistful smile filled with nostalgia and emotions, both joyous and sorrowful. Joyous because she witnessed what was obviously a momentous event in their developing bond, confirming an intimacy she and Jeff had already identified, and sorrowful because it reminded her of an age where all the great experiences of a young adult life were still in front of them, a fairly selfish and yet predictable sentiment, she thought, given that it was always gone for her now.

"Mmmm?" Jeff lifted his sight briefly before bending forward again to resume his intense examination of the countless shiny, silver flecks glinting in the floor's sapphire-blue depths. "Babe, you know, I think we should've picked the bigger tiles. The ones we liked at the very beginning."

"I don't, honey, they're fine. What I think is, we need to talk with those two over there and probably soon. Probably now."

"You're right," he said, glancing toward the blasts of laughter and high, gleeful shrieks. "That sure is a lot of delightfully hot water being thrown out. Wasteful, hormone-saturated teenagers."

"No, silly," Dee sniggered. "But you couldn't pick a better way of explaining what happened. Judging by the astonished look on our son's face, I'd say they just shared their first kiss."

"Nawww." Jeff watched as Tess climbed on Austin's back, keeping a tight hold while he towed her toward the hot tub and its tumbling overflow, burbling and bubbling into the pool below. Passing under the constant stream, the disrupted surge spread forcefully like a watery umbrella over their heads, splaying their hair flat. "Well," he said, turning to Dee. "To be honest, I'm not surprised. They've spent a great deal of time together this semester, and the indicators have all been there. The coy smiles, the touchy-feely stuff, and now he's got a pet name for her. Those little love-chemicals must be running around like a bull in a china shop."

"Exactly! Oh, God," she sighed. "It's time for that conversation."

"Which is?"

"The one involving s-e-x."

"Supremely exotic Xanadu? What the heck has that got to do with things? Or is it the other one?" Jeff frowned. "Ummm... actually, I can't think of anything else that starts with an x. Hang on, X-ray. Is that even a proper word? Xenon. Yeah, there's one. It's a gas, and I'm pretty sure it starts with an x and not a z. What about Xmas? How could I forget that, it's just around the corner? X-rated. Now I'm cooking. And quite appropriate considering that's the topic we're just about to discu..."

"Jeff," Dee cut in, scowling. "You're not funny. We've got to think of a way on how to deal with this. I definitely do not want to make either of them uncomfortable, especially Tess. She's such a sweet girl."

"Haven't we already covered this subject with Austin? And they also get sex education in high school."

"Yes. But it's different when you're outside that classroom environment. We don't know how much Tess has discussed the issue with her parents, and you're forgetting we were near their age when we became boyfriend and girlfriend."

"We were sixteen."

"Babe, it's only a matter of months until they're sixteen. I'm just trying to make sure we're all on the same page here."

"Okay," Jeff nodded. "I agree. You've got some extremely valid points, honey, and you're emphatically correct. We don't want Tess feeling uncomfortable. Or Austin. He may be relaxed exchanging views without her around, but he could get mightily embarrassed when she's part of the conversation. Personally, I don't think that'll happen, he's a level-headed guy, and Tess is very comparable to him in many ways. She'll be able to talk with us about this. But if I'm wrong, shoot me. Or get George to. No, wait, that's the worst idea ever."

"It's not, it's brilliant!" Dee grinned. "Thanks for the brainwave, darling."

"About what?" Jeff's sparkling blue eyes narrowed. "If you do that shooting thing, you'll never get the jet."

"I must admit, the prospect is rather tempting," she laughed. "But believe it or not, there's something more useful. How's this? We've already got Susan, Greg and the kids coming over for New Year's Eve, so why don't we invite George, Carol and Melissa? As well as being a great way to become better acquainted with them, it also serves as an approach to Tess. We can tell her how much we like her, what she means to us, and lead on to the other subject with no trouble at all. What do you think?"

"Babe." Jeff smiled at his wife's excitement. "You are a genius."

"I know," she beamed. "Honey, let's make a night of it and host a New Year's Eve, fun-in-the-pool party. Austin's going across to clear Henry and Barbara's driveway tomorrow, so he can ask what they're doing. We'll send invitations to Jon, Sarah, and Tom and Rachel... ahhh... that means I'll have to get..." Dee trailed off and started counting on her fingers, bringing each one down to her palm while staring at faraway spot beyond her husband.

"Don't kick me when I suggest this, but what about the Benton family?"

"Uh-uh. No way." Dee shook her head vigorously, flicking strands of wet, black hair from side to side. "Jeff, are you kidding? After the mess that woman caused last year, do you really want to risk her destroying a perfect socializing opportunity with Tess' parents? Besides, we've not seen or spoken to her since, and Austin's said she hasn't changed one bit, so as far as I'm concerned, Jackie Benton is banned from this house until she does. Pauly's welcome, but only if you're happy to pick him up. I suppose you'd be dropping him off again if Sean's having trouble with his car."

"Yeeaaah," Jeff hummed. "That's no problem. And it's a pity their marital woes have made the situation awkward for Sean. He's an all right sort of guy. A bit gruff, maybe, but he's okay. Every time he brings or collects Pauly, he dead-set refuses to come inside, and now he just stays on the road beeping the horn. But I've got to admit, for about five months I've been doing the same thing. There's only so much I can take of a completely motionless Jackie staring from an upstairs window. Alfred Hitchcock would've been proud of her performance."

"I don't want to talk about her, honey," Dee stated. "That woman's not an important topic. They are." She nodded toward the far end of the pool, where Austin and Tess held on to the coping stones, talking quietly, their heads nearly touching.

"I couldn't agree more, and there lies the ultimate in chatting environments, my love." Jeff aimed a dripping finger to the teenagers' left, at a dense and orange, fuzzy steam that rolled and sauntered from the hot tub above them. "We'll all be relaxed, at ease," he whirred, studying the color as it shifted to a dusky, shimmering yellow. "And able to seize the opportunity for an undisturbed, carefree powwow. However, these circumstances require the subtle touch of sensitivity and diplomacy, so watch and learn, for you about to behold a master at work, charming wife of mine. Hey," he called. "Thingy and the other thingy. That's right, you two lovebirds. Flap those little wings and get yourselves over here."

"Jeffrey Peter Cooper!" Dee chopped the water in front of him. "Sensitivity? Diplomacy? You're about as subtle as an earthquake."

Observing her disgruntled expression, he stroked his wife's cheek. "Babe, they know I'm only teasing. I'll apologize to Tess, because this is an important issue. And she's very aware of my ability to be a damn idiot. All they did was cackle on the way home tonight. Not with me, but at me, the cheeky buggers."

"You and Greg with your Kiwi-speak. You're both the same."

"We are? Then he must be an incredibly multi-skilled, intelligent, resourceful and undeniably top-notch, wonderful person."

"You fool," she giggled, and peered at the laughing, smiling teenagers, aware that the closeness perceived between Austin and Tess were exact echoes of their own relationship.

Chapter Thirteen

The Lake

Standing close to the window, his arms folded, Austin studied the bitterly cold, yet magnificent day outside, and squinted as his eyes passed briefly over a feeble sun inclined toward the horizon, the bright star sliding across a cloudless, pale-blue sky, a stark contrast to the storms plaguing the last week of school. Only four days of sporadic snow had interrupted his well-deserved vacation since then and he deemed it a perfect manner in which to see out the previous twelve months.

Sighing deeply, he glanced at his watch, subconsciously tapping his foot while various contemplations jostled for attention. Tess and her parents would be here soon. He still hadn't met Melissa, with just a brief talk on the phone being their initial introduction, and because she was partying with friends for New Year's Eve, saying her final farewells before enlisting, he didn't know when they would meet.

In the sixteen days after Tess' departure, he found himself mentally marking off the calendar, startled by how much he missed her. Excluding the weekends, this was the longest time they had been apart, and realization came that he never felt like this with other friends. Male friends. Their companionship and familiarity paled drastically compared to the incessant yearning he experienced for her. What made it worse was the lack of steady contact. Except for the odd text message, their last conversation was on Christmas Day when he rang her home and politely asked Mrs. Anderson if he could pass on festive greetings to Tess. As it turned out, he spoke to everyone, wishing them all a Merry Christmas, even her beloved grandmother, who had made a swift recovery after her fall due to continuous care from her daughter and grandchildren at the family home.

"You okay?"

Austin swiveled to the person in the open doorway. "Yeah," he nodded. "I'm fine, Dad. Thanks for asking."

Entering the front sitting room, Jeff joined the tall, strapping teenager at the window, and together they watched a skein of Snow Geese loudly honking their way over the rooftops dotting the hillside, lured back by the unexpected, favorable conditions. "I know that expression. I've been to that place and seen it before. You're feeling a bit empty, aren't you?"

"And more." Austin's lips tightened. "It's strange. I've never felt like this. I've missed her so, so much." Dropping his head, he stared at the carpet. "Sorry, that must sound really stupid, really ridiculous, and really weird."

"Not at all, mate. Sometimes what you consider stupid, ridiculous, or weird is all too often the truth."

Don't I know, Austin thought. With a wry grin, he turned and fixed a steady gaze on his father. "Unfortunately, I imagine that's a statement most people wouldn't believe."

Frowning, Jeff searched the somber eyes three inches above his. "I wish I had a dollar for every time I've mentioned your incredibly mature outlook, and two dollars for saying how fortunate we are to have a son like you. I'd be a very rich man." He thumped the solid, meaty part of Austin's upper arm. "You've heard this already, but I'll tell you again. Your mother and I are extremely happy with that little meeting we all had in the hot tub the other week. Both of you acted very responsibly about the whole topic, and we're really proud. I know you'll take on board what was said, and I also know you'll do the right thing, Austin, no matter what the circumstances."

"I appreciate that, Dad. It means a lot. And I'm lucky I've got you and Mom always ready to listen. I promised I'll respect and care for Tess, and I'll show the trust you've placed in me."

"I've gotta admit there are instances when I might even like you," Jeff said. "Come here, ya big lump." Laughing heartily, the two men embraced. "Have a great time when you're ice skating, okay? Sure you don't mind the biggest lump taking you guys to the lake?"

"I don't think there's anyone who could stop him," Austin beamed. "When we spoke yesterday, Three-Gee raved about finally driving the Lincoln. He said he's gonna be extra generous seeing as how it's New Year's Eve and do a direct swap with his car. But he's keeping the baby seats."

Jeff chuckled and shook his head.

"And, Dad. I'll make sure Tess is well looked after when we go. I have to. If I don't, I think her father would somehow have me killed. Probably by his own hands."

"You sound worried on that one."

"A tad." Austin heaved a sigh. "He's pretty nerve-wracking."

"You got that right. When they collected Tess, I actually felt quite intimidated by him, just in those fifteen or so minutes they were here. Me! The CEO of a large company, who's used to meeting and greeting and hiring and firing. He's a lot different in person than simply a voice over the phone, that's for sure."

"I know." Austin's eyes widened. "I told Tess not to worry about it, but jeez!"

Jeff nodded. "Your mom thinks it was the uniform. She says he'll seem a lot different today when he's not wearing one. So, we'll see, because when he's dressed up there's definitely some sort of an aura. With all of those medals, ribbons, and bits and pieces, I'm surprised he could move. The weight of that stuff would be incredible."

Austin laughed. "Thanks, Dad. You've made me feel a whole lot better."

"No problem, mate. Job done. I'll bill you later. You know, I think once you get past that rough, gruff, hardened soldier-shell, I'm sure he's a nice enough, normal man. Just act naturally and you'll be all right." He poked Austin playfully in the stomach. "Anyway, quit your whining. At least you get to take off for a couple of hours. I have to stay and convince him the government doesn't need this land for an assault course."

Motion in the corner of Austin's eye caught his attention. "Battle stations," he declared as a luxuriously sporty sedan came into view, cruising unhurriedly along Fairview Terrace.

"Thaaaat," Jeff hummed. "Is a spectacular vehicle and one worthy of a proper inspection this time. Look at those contours, son. Right, I'll tell Mom the party's starting, and you wait for me at the front door. Come on, buddy, let's leave before we're spotted. They might think it's a household of staring freaks. Before I forget, Suze rang to say they're coming over earlier, probably in another half hour or so."

"Cool! We'll get some decent skating in." Austin clasped his arm around his father's shoulder while they crossed the room. "Dad, can I ask you not to go on about your car? Please?"

"Fair enough," he said, and nudged his son's ribs. "I'll just mention his." They parted company at the door, with Jeff sniffing deeply at the delicious aroma of a slowly roasting turkey that flooded his nostrils as he neared the kitchen. "Chef and assistants," he announced on entering. "Your attention, per favore. In about three minutes our esteemed guests shall cross the threshold of this sacred abode."

Dee glanced at him during her industrious task of chopping vegetables at the island bench, the shiny, flashing blade in her swiftly moving hands thudding upon a chunky, wooden cutting board. "Sacred?" she snickered, tipping a mound of diced carrots into a large, stainless-steel pot. "There's only one reason this isn't holy ground and he's walking toward me right now."

"Great comeback, honey. It seems my throne is under attack from all sides lately." Jeff looked around. "Where are Stephie and Anna?"

"Upstairs. I'll have them start on some potatoes after we've welcomed our esteemed guests, as you so eloquently phrased it."

Jeff moved behind her, wrapped his arms around her waist and nudged her long ponytail to one side. "I love you," he whispered in her ear. "How are you feeling? Are you okay?"

"I'm good, darling. Being busy always keeps my mind off this time of year." She squirmed around in his grasp, giggling when he tickled her. "I don't know how I could manage without you. Thank you for being my rock," she breathed.

"Forever," he smiled. "Later, when everyone is settled and chatting, we'll quietly slip away and light the candle." He gave her forehead and the tip of her nose a quick peck as the front doorbell chimed loudly. "Here they are and here I go. Rumor has it that if you keep a high-ranking army officer waiting for more than two rings they make you wash their car while doing a hundred press-ups. Which may not be so bad because apparently Greg's keeping mine after today. I'll just conceal George's in the garage and feign ignorance to its uncanny disappearance." Grinning, he spun on his heels and marched into the hallway.

*   *   *

Susan rolled the dining room door open a fraction and popped her head out through the narrow space. "Austin," she called. "Pauly's on the phone. He says it's urgent."

"Okay, I'm on my way," he answered, and turned to the group of people inspecting the outdoor kitchen. "Excuse me, I'll be back soon." With a quick grin at Tess, he raced down the stairs and across the deck. "Thanks, Suze," he beamed when he reached the patio pavers.

"No problem, sweetheart. Greg's talking to him at the moment." Shivering, she closed the door hurriedly after he jumped inside. "Brrrrr. It's cold out there."

"Is it?" His smiled widened. "I didn't notice."

"Of course not," Susan chuckled. "Weather conditions are completely irrelevant when you've got the warm fuzzies for someone keeping you snug and cozy."

"Are my emotions that obvious?"

"Let me put it this way. Be careful of any wind changes or that terribly pleased expression could become a permanent feature." She giggled as Austin hugged her to him, and linked her arm through his while they strolled to the living room.

"These things happen," Greg was saying when they entered. He scooched across the sofa cushions, making room for Susan to flop beside her husband. "Hey, here he is now, so take it easy and I'll catch you later." He paused. "Okay, mate, same to you. Cheers. See ya."

"Thanks, Three-Gee." Austin took the receiver. "Yo, Pauly! Are you ready to go, dude? We should be on our way shortly."

"Don't bother," he snorted, his disgruntled tone came over a line sizzling with interference. "I can't make it."

"What? Why? Are you kidding me?" Austin looked at Greg, who shook his head, obviously having heard the tale already.

"Nup. I'm fuckin' grounded. The old man didn't like something I said and my punishment is looking after Mom, 'cos she hasn't been too good for a couple of days. The fucking bastard," he spat. "So that's me out. Sorry, dude, I really wanted to go."

"Jeez." Austin ran his free hand through his short, brown hair. "Well, I'm glad you called before we left. Thanks, mate."

"Oh." There was a brief, crackling silence. "Are you two still going?"

Austin's eyebrows shot up. "Uhhhh... yeah. This was organized a week ago, Pauly, and you know Dad hired the skates for us yesterday. Plus, everyone's arrived earlier so we could have a good amount of time doing this. Just because you've been a dickhead doesn't mean me and Tess have to miss out." Nothing but a hissing noisiness issued from the other end. "Pauly? You there, mate?"

"Fine," his dull and neutral voice responded. "Then go with her... mate." The contempt seeping from his last word teamed up with a harsh click and the sudden drone of a dead line, and Austin stared, unseeing, as he dropped the phone slowly from his ear.

Reaching for the television remote on the armrest, Greg paused at the sight of Austin's thickly creased brow. "Everything all right, brother?"

"I don't believe it. Get this." Austin plonked heavily on the edge of the nearest La-Z-Boy, tipping the recliner forward on a wildly slanting incline. "Pauly just hung up on me. He got himself grounded and then acted like it was a big shock that we were still going, a 'how-dare-you-go-without-me' sort of thing. The way he spoke before he ended the call, it sounded like..." Exhaling strongly, Austin dropped his gaze. "Like he hated me. It's probably a good thing Joe and Wade have gone away, 'cos I know Joe would ring and give him an earful. They've said heaps of times how he's been nothing but trouble ever since we started back at school this year."

"And it's a situation that can only be dealt with in the next, my darling, so don't let it bother you now. Just go and have fun with Tess, and then we'll have even more fun welcoming the New Year in together." Susan patted her husband's solid thigh. "Greg's ready to leave whenever you are."

"Thanks." He smiled warmly. "Are Willow and Adam asleep?"

"Finally," she laughed. "It's all very amusing and time for games when they get to stay in Uncle Austin's room. Do you need to get in there, honey?"

Shaking his head, he pushed himself upright, halting the chair's turbulent, swinging action with a well-timed placement of his foot. "No, it's all good, Suze. The car's packed and ready. Are you sure you're fine with Three-Gee taking us? We'll probably be gone a couple of hours."

"As you say, sweetheart, it's all good. I've got your mom, Steph, Anna… even Carol. That should be more than enough to handle the little monkey twins. You two head out and enjoy yourselves. But just be careful, Austin. Remember that research we did on spotting unsafe ice, okay?" Her expression was both loving and all business.

"Gotcha, Suze. I won't forget. By the way, what's wrong with that?" Scowling, he pointed at the family's large television, positioned on an angle in the corner of the room. Pixilated squares and rectangles distorted the usually crystal-clear, high-definition image, which disappeared every few seconds when the screen flashed to a brightly flickering lime-green.

"I dunno, mate. It's been that way for about fifteen minutes and every channel's the same. Even the phone was playing up."

"Yeah, it was doing that with me, too." Austin shrugged. "Must be this weird and awesome weather, Three-Gee. Well, I'll see you soon, bro. I'm just gonna check how they're doing outside." He stepped to the sofa and gave Greg a fist-bump before striding toward the hall and bolting from sight.

Turning her gaze from the empty doorway, Susan prodded her husband's beefy chest. "Guess what I'm thinking."

"I get two," he said, rubbing a spot on his left pectoral muscle. "That little nail of yours is awfully strong, and no, I'm not climbing on the roof to muck about with the TV antenna."

"You're right with the first one," Susan laughed, and rasped the pad of her index finger over the short stubble on his chin. "No, I'm thinking you should invite Austin to Philadelphia next summer. That book auction will have loads of stuff he'll find really interesting, and it's a great way to spend a weekend with the person he absolutely idolizes." She curled up sideways to Greg and rested her weight upon him. "I've always been fascinated with how little time it took for Austin to integrate himself within your cultural speech pattern. It's the most classic example of a deep male bonding I've ever seen."

"He's an awesome guy, babe." Greg stroked her arm as she wrapped it around his midriff. "The best. I may throw around a certain slang word like it's going out of fashion, but with Austin I mean what I say when I call him brother. It's not just a colloquial term. I really love him as if he was one. Jeff included. They're like the male siblings I never had."

"My point precisely, sweetheart," she murmured. "The connection transcends mere friendliness. It truly is a relationship that's more kin than anything."

"And the same goes for you." Greg touched his head to hers. "Austin's a lucky fella to have two beautiful sisters in his life."

After sliding the dining room door shut, Austin crouched on the pavers and casually laced his shoes, glancing up now and again to monitor the group touring the backyard, specifically Tess' parents. In the short duration when they met outside the garage two weeks earlier, George, resplendent in his uniform, shook everyone's hands while Carol thanked them profusely for the kindness shown throughout the emergency. Consequently, they had accepted the party invitation, commenting on it being a perfect and suitable way to socialize and express the gratitude they felt for their assistance. And as Tess raved about the entertainment area and the wonderful time she had during her stay, George was not stupid enough to neglect the momentary interest she displayed in Jeff and Dee's son. At every opportunity, he studied Austin, relishing the chance to establish the teenager's character and integrity by way of an inborn and finely-honed talent. Initially forming a positive opinion, the next stage would be evaluating any noteworthy influences, and when Susan and Greg arrived at the party fifteen minutes later, even his eyes widened slightly at the sight of the powerfully built man who stooped to enter the living room, carrying his children effortlessly in each arm while his extraordinarily stunning wife brought two bags brimming with baby supplies. But watching their interaction buoyed his approval once Austin demonstrated a continuing courteousness, good sense, and maturity well beyond his tender years, and George nodded at the young lad as he rejoined the group, moving into a sizeable gap between himself and his wife when they all stopped by the edge of the pool, directly opposite the hot tub.

"You'd never guess it wasn't real," Dee hummed. She ran her hand down the sleeve of a plush, full-length coat Carol wore, its brown fur soft and silky-smooth to the touch. "It's very chic."

"Thank you, Dee," Carol replied. "I don't like the idea of killing animals for the sole purpose of clothing, and I'm always being asked if it's genuine. There have been a few times I've thought of selling the damn thing, but it's just so comfy and warm." Four inches shorter than Dee, she was a slim, attractive woman, with auburn hair elegantly layered to the shoulder and high cheekbones beneath faultless skin, like her daughter standing by her side. A broad smile and friendly, blue eyes settled on Austin before skipping nimbly around the scenery once more. "This is a wonderful design, especially the way you've put the decking around that beautiful tree. What do you think, George?"

"Yes, it is extremely nice indeed." Dressed in a buttoned, dark-gray suit and knee-length, black trench coat, George had his hands tucked firmly in his pants pockets, his wrists holding back the edges of the finely-tailored garment. With his rock-hard, cold face, tidy moustache and a jawline seemingly set in granite, he bore a striking resemblance to the clean-cut version of a lawman out of an old Clint Eastwood spaghetti western, the only things missing being a horse standing faithfully by his shoulder, a cowboy hat, a pair of Smith and Wesson six-shooters strapped to his hip, and a thin cigarette dangling from the corner of his mouth. Turning to the right, his strong, commanding voice addressed Jeff. "For recreational activities, and needless to say, we are taking these climate conditions into account, at what parameters do you set the water temperature to achieve an optimal and satisfying use?"

"Dad!" Tess leaned forward, flashing a noteworthy glare in his direction. "Can't you just ask how warm it is?"

George swiveled her way, his brow creased. "My apologies. I was under the assumption I did."

Struggling to keep his composure, Jeff faked an instant curiosity with the fiercely shuddering cleaning device creeping along the pool floor. It was like the skits between him and Stephanie, only George was completely serious, and he came exceedingly close to great gales of laughter. Coughing once, he collected himself magnificently. "Well, currently we've got ninety degrees Fahrenheit, and the hot tub at one hundred and five. But because of the overflow feature." He indicated the small, gurgling waterfall. "I've been finding the deep end is exactly one-point-two degrees hotter." What the hell, thought Jeff. This high-flying army guy must encounter an unbelievable number of people every year, and can't expect them all to be like him. "Hey, I'll let you in on a secret," he said, grinning widely. "After many exhaustive attempts, I am now proficient in an art I'm referring to as utterly wrinkled digits. By the time one hour has passed, you'll have what appear to be scraggy, little sausages hanging off the end of your hand."

Austin slapped a palm to his forehead, and dragged it slowly over his face from top to bottom while Tess giggled and Carol laughed gently, her merry eyes twinkling at the sight of her husband's smile.

"Hmmm, yes," George rumbled softly. "Sausages."

"You are coming in later, I hope." Dee made a drastic attempt to alter the subject. "Austin, did you remind Tess about the swimsuits?"

His neck cracked at the speed of looking at her, alarmed by the sudden involvement. He had a brief, scary vision of a squeaky-voiced answer while trying his hardest not to snicker at his father, who promised during breakfast that he would keep the wisecracks to a minimum, and most probably none at all. Obviously near impossible for him to achieve, it had started as soon as Greg entered the house.

Tess came to the rescue. "Yes, Dee," she announced. "He told me."

"But we're not sure if we'll go in," Carol stated. "In fact, George didn't bring his."

"I wish I had now, it looks rather appealing," he commented, surveying the twisting, gauzy mist floating up from the glittering blueness.

"You'll be glad to know they're wrapped up with my extra pair of jeans, Dad, just in case you changed your mind. Except for a towel. Sorry, I only brought mine. But you can use it, if you want. Or maybe we can borrow one. Would that be okay, Dee?"

"Tess, sweetheart, of course."

"Although there is a leasing fee," Jeff teased. "Along with locker costs, payment for responsible use, et cetera. I'm afraid the charges are exorbitantly high, and blame Dee on that one. Ever since we survived the Mayan apocalypse she's been a bit…" He rolled his eyeballs ahead of a sweet smile at his wife. "But we'll gladly accept American Express, cash, checks, or the last and only viable option, which is a two thousand and twelve, silver, E-Class Mercedes-Benz. Is it possible you have any of those?" He beamed at Tess, who sniggered quietly before performing a brisk double-take when her father did something that thoroughly contradicted everything she knew about him, in particular the statement she had made about his humor. And in the space of one minute, his actions caused her jaw to drop twice, the first being a deep laugh that rolled from his throat, sending large, steaming clouds of breath gusting skyward as his mirth resonated in the freezing, motionless air.

"Well then, it seems I may be going in after all. Tess." George looked at his daughter. "Forward planning at its best. Well done, darling. Exceptional work." And he grinned.

"No problem, Dad," she beamed, her eyes shining brightly.

"We can start a game of pool rugby," Austin suggested. "Dad, how about me and Three-Gee against you and Mr. Anderson? We'll have a sick time."

"I don't know, buddy. Other than it sounding incredibly one-sided, George, Mr. Anderson, has to go back to work in a couple of days, and it wouldn't be too good if he turned up with an unintended black eye."

George swung his gaze to Jeff, his right eyebrow hoisted high on his forehead. "Pool rugby? Intriguing," he chuckled. "I have no idea what that is. As long as the endeavor does not induce this aforementioned sickness, then it's been a very long time since anyone's given me a shiner. Count me in." With a prompt wink at his host, a signal no one else saw, he did something that took the others by surprise, dropping Tess' jaw for the second occasion when he spun unexpectedly toward Austin. "And if you want to make use of my name, Cooper, it will be General Anderson, not mister," he growled. "Is that clear? I will not have a young upstart like you disrespect me in such a way." Through his short-cropped, dark hair, the few noticeable streaks of gray that gave him a smart, debonair flair glinted in the mid-afternoon sunshine, and his trim moustache bristled while he held the teenager's astonished stare.

Swallowing hard, Austin considered the solemn, intelligent eyes, remembering their active, continuous roaming during the tour, assessing both the details of the territory and every object it contained. Even though they were the exact same color as his youngest daughter, so far he had not detected any of the care and tenderness always present in hers. Yet now they didn't match his tone, and Austin thought he saw a touch of merriment within their depths. For a fleeting moment he was sure he caught Tess' humor there. "Yes, sir." He straightened, pushing his wide shoulders back.

"Excuse me, General Anderson, but isn't that strictly for army personnel? Sir?"

"As a rule," George nodded. "However, next time exercise caution over valor, and always address an officer by rank and surname, whether talking about, or to them. Most especially to them. And in this case, you are excused. What's your height, son?" The question came from out of nowhere.

"Ahhh… about six-foot-four, sir, although I'm not entirely sure." Austin kept a firm gaze on the man. "That was the last measurement, which Mom took during our summer vacation."

"You've grown some more," he announced. "I would put you at around six-five. Precisely four and half inches above me. Remarkably tall for your age. What do you desire? Do you have a calling?"

"Sir?" Austin frowned. "I don't understand."

"A career. What are your ambitions? At nearly sixteen years of age, I knew my mission in life. What is yours?"

"I don't know, sir. With the way I am, I guess law enforcement is a possibility."

"The protection of the people. A commendable vocation. Have you ever considered taking that protection to another level? The defense of your country?"

"Sir, no I have not."

"Mmmm. Do you have a favorite color?"

"None that I'm aware of, sir."

"Do you know the number of tanks the United States Army has on home soil?"

"I have no idea, sir. I've never…"

"Estimate."

Tess' eyes jolted from one to the other, unsure of what was going on. She glanced at Dee and her mother, who didn't see her. They were gawking just as much as she was. Looking at Jeff, relief flowed when he smiled broadly, gave a quick thumbs-up and mouthed a silent, 'It's okay, Tess, it's okay.'

"Um." Austin drew in a deep breath. "I would imagine there are thousands."

"And how many do we need?"

"Sir, enough to protect our country and keep it safe from invasion."

"What if it's an aerial strike? Are they effective?"

"No, General Anderson. Their use is for land-based assault only. Fighter aircraft apply for that scenario. Personally, I would utilize a favorite of mine, the F-22 Raptor, because of its maneuverability, stealth, and the advantage of further ground attack."

"Mmmm." George flicked his sight over the young man's brawny, soaring frame. "Good. At what time were you contemplating a departure?"

"I was hoping we could go soon." Austin pulled back the sleeve of his jacket. "It's nearly three o'clock and the sun will be setting at a quarter to five. Exactly sixteen forty-five hours, sir. I went online to confirm that information."

George appraised him a moment longer, withdrew a hand from his pants pocket and held it out to the teenager. "Very good," he murmured, shaking the reciprocating grasp. "Your maturity matches your stature, Austin Cooper. I have the utmost confidence in your ability to watch over my daughter."

The reversal was astounding, and even though the eyes looked set in stone again, his voice had taken on a new resonance. If anything, it sounded warm, much like his steely grip... and extremely complimentary.

the beasts

"This machine rocks," Greg hooted over the rumbling purr of the engine. "Like a big, gray, rocky thing that's found in the Rockies and often called a rock. Jeff's lost it now and it's mine, mine, mine. He can keep the baby seats." Drumming one-handed on the dashboard, he looked in the rearview mirror and nodded at the rowdy laughter behind him.

Only minutes from their destination, they passed the area where Austin and Duke had reappeared all those years ago, and the teenager automatically swung his head to the window, peering out at the spot. It was something he found himself always doing on the way to his favorite hobby, whether by bike or the current form of travel, and a momentary flash of movement, a blurred glimpse of pastiness opposing the pristine snow had him twisting around, straining upon the seatbelt's restraint in the hope of catching another sight. Their velocity, coupled with the rising and falling of the straight road restricted it, and Greg's next statement took over, pushing the foolish thought that he had seen anything out of his cheerfully whirling, unconvinced mind.

"Okay, guy and gal, I'm happy with your knowledge of ice safety and Suze will be really pleased when we tell her you've passed the exam with flying colors. Mainly you, Tess, because you didn't read the info we had. You must have been skating loads to know all that."

"A few times with my friends. But only at the rink next to Halfmoon, with no danger of going through thin ice."

"A few times?" Austin blurted. "Three-Gee, she lives there. They've even got a stand named after her. And she cheated. The proof is right here. She kept looking at the answers." Holding up a piece of paper, he waved it about, the document's crumpling rustle drowned out by Tess' giggling and his cackles when she reached across to poke him in the side.

Greg glanced over his shoulder, chuckling at the playfulness between them.

*   *   *

In early summer of 1831, the first, weary settlers of Crescent Lake mopped the sweat from their brows while they stood on a rocky outcrop and gazed at the sight of a huge, unspoiled body of water twinkling in the hot, midday sun. This was their prize after a long and arduous journey from the east, particularly with the slow, winding trek through such a densely forested territory, and after reaching the pinnacle of the toughest hill yet, they unanimously decided a place to call home lay below. Naming their new colony came easily on the way down the steep rise because the lake resembled the semi-circular profile of a partial moon, and following their rest and refreshment on its shore, another motion passed to build farther away in the hope of preserving the stunningly natural beauty. Nearly 60,000 people now populated the district, and even though the last half a century had seen rapid growth, to that day the official decree by the original inhabitants protected a considerable area of land surrounding the water's edge, still preventing the construction of any suburbs. Complying with that law was the lakes accessibility from just two directions, both of them roads on the smallest and tightest parabolas of the curved shape. And on the initial entrance created by those pioneers, a black Lincoln SUV slowed as it came off the blacktop and crawled across a graveled trail, the stones, shingles and pebbles crunching beneath its wide, rubber tires.

Greg pulled in close to one of the many picnic tables scattered about the flat, snow-covered leisure area, and inspected a lone vehicle parked ten feet away to his right. "There's another car, but I can't see anyone." He squeaked around on the seat. "At the moment it looks like you're on your own. You've got about an hour and a half until sunset, so have fun you wild and carefree young adults. And if there's any problem, give me a call. It's my life on the line here, too."

"How's that, Three-Gee?" Frowning, Austin bent and picked up two pairs of skates near his feet.

"Before we left I also reassured Tess' dad we knew what hazards to keep an eye out for, and he looked me up and down and said, 'Good. But if they require your assistance I expect a commendable report. I do not want to hear you were warming your ass instead.'"

"I am so sorry, Greg." Tess shook her head. "He had no right to speak to you that way. He's been acting strangely all afternoon."

"No worries," he beamed. "I like him, he's quite a character. He reminds me of my coach when I played in London. He was also a no-nonsense, hard-as-nails bastard. Whoops. Sorry, Tess, I don't mean your old man's a bastard. In his case I mean a no-nonsense, hard-as-nails, really, really lovely human being."

The three of them laughed.

"Anyway, you got your cell, bro?"

"Sure have." Austin patted a jacket compartment high on his left chest. "And Tess has got hers. Are you gonna be all right, Three-Gee?"

"Mate." Greg lifted a newspaper from the front passenger seat. "I'll be fine. I've got my New Zealand Herald to read, sent over by my dear old mum, and in case you never noticed, the sound system in my new car is awesome. The thing is, I will be keeping my ass warm and dry. Unlike you two," he grinned.

*   *   *

Austin pulled his socks up a bit more and wriggled his toes before tugging his jeans over the skates bound tightly around his ankles. Tapping the black leather twice, he swayed as he straightened, and adjusted his beanie while gazing out across the enormous, frozen expanse they faced. Vapor rose like ghostly limbs from a thin veil of mist obscuring the distance, and in the vast forest surrounding the lake, towering trees struggled to show their evergreen needles through a thick coating of snow lying heavy on their sturdy structures.

"Oh, wow!" Tess gushed, her breath blowing puffy, bulging balloons. "Austin, have you ever seen anything so gorgeous?"

"I have, actually," he nodded. "She's standing by my side and I'll be holding her hand once it's free from securing that very bright, pink scarf around her neck."

"Sweet talker," she crooned. Placing the trailing ends down her back, she flicked her long, blonde hair over the top and squeezed his hand the instant their gloved fingers entwined.

"Just don't tell your dad we're doing this. I bet there's an interrogation planned for me when we get back and I'm already making a big mistake. In fact, it's almost certain I'll have to pay Three-Gee to keep quiet."

Her head sagged as she turned to the tall, young man. "Apologizing for my father seems to be a frequent thing at the moment. He's treating everyone like they're in the army. First Jeff, then you, then Greg. I was mortified with what he did by the pool. I don't know what's gotten…"

"Tess." Austin tilted her chin up until she peered straight into his eyes, which right then, in the weak light of a late afternoon sun, funnily enough shone a cool and frosty blue like the water beneath its layer of thick whiteness and the pale sky above. "Hey, I'm the one who should say sorry. I was only joking. Obviously, I'm not near to Dad's level. Listen, I think anyone who loves his daughter as much as he does would have done it, 'cos I know I would. When we were just about to leave Dad told me what he did was a test. Apparently it's a technique that some employers use for staff promotions and hiring and stuff. All the wacky, rapid-fire questions assess a person's moral fiber and potential. He reckons I handled it really well. Trust me when I say I'm the same as Three-Gee. I also like your dad. He's awesome. And your mom. They're both good people. I get the feeling they like my family, as well, so that means they're good people, but maybe a tad on the crazy side."

"Thanks," she giggled. "I think. Am I included in your crazy theory?"

"Tessie, you're the wackiest of the lot. Come on," he announced above her laughter. "It's time these two wild and carefree young adults had some fun." As one, they stepped from the shoreline onto the solid, unyielding ice.

"Austin, where did you find all the information about tanks and raptors and aerial ground whatever the heck they are?"

"Too easy. And you should know. The clue's in that new and totally wicked figurine you got me. Watching X-Men finally paid off," he grinned.

In the car, Greg looked up from the broadsheet spread upon the steering wheel, smiled at the scene of two teenagers rolling gently across the lake, and chortled when the tallest one landed heavily on his backside, nearly dragging his girlfriend with him.

*   *   *

"Awww, man!" Austin picked himself off the cold and wet surface. Again. In the last fifty minutes he had tumbled more times than he cared to remember, and his backside was taking an awful, soaked beating.

Tess whizzed up to him. "Let's move, babe, this is too patchy, as well. It looks like the whole of Colorado has been here, so we'll try someplace else."

"Yeah, yeah," he chuckled. "This part looks okay to me, just like all the others we've tried. It's okay to say I suck, 'cos I know I do."

"If you're not used to skating, it does take a while to get the hang of it," she said, brushing his dark-gray jacket. "Besides, you're getting loads better. There've even been times when you've got good balance. Another ten or fifteen minutes and you'll end up with only a few thousand bruises on your butt. I think you should take a photo of it after we get home, 'cos when you do decide to join Facebook you can use it as your profile picture." With a musical giggle, she took off, gliding effortlessly away from his snickering.

Austin glanced over his shoulder when he caught up with her, noting they had rounded the first of many heavily-wooded hillocks jutting out into the lake like tiny peninsulas. On that one mile stretch of land the contour was fairly irregular, with about twenty projections thrusting their way into the water and creating small coves as it began making the gradual, curved, left hand turn forming the smallest arc of Lake Crescent.

"Wait up, Tessie. I'm gonna ring Three-Gee, he won't be able to see us now." Lightly, he dug the heel of his skates into the ice, managing to slow his progress without a floundering fall this time while she came drifting back. Turning a tight, polished circle, she stopped a couple of feet away, her eyes twinkling above rosy-red cheeks and pearly, streaming breath.

"This is awesome," he declared, stripping off his gloves and nodding toward the thick forest. "We've fished off most of these points and it's really deep around this area. I can't believe how quickly you can get here this way, 'cos usually it's a hell of a trek through the woods." He dug around in his pocket, pulled out his phone and flipped its clam shell open with a nimble flick. Scrolling through the contacts list, he tapped a button. "Yo, Three-Gee."

"Everything cool?" came the immediate reply.

"Yeah, mate. So cool, it's frozen."

Tess heard Greg's strong laughter emanating from the speaker.

"I'm ringing just in case you're wondering where we are," Austin explained. "It was too chopped up, so we've gone left around that first big headland we went fishing off last summer. The one where you caught that whopper. We'll head around a bit more and then come back. Is that okay?"

"That's fine, mate. What's the ice like out there?"

"Clear, blue, and getting a lot smoother, dude. I can see what might be a pressure ridge not far from us. There's a long line of white, which is probably the ice poking up. But we won't be going anywhere near it, 'cos we're sticking close to the shoreline. Hey, just think, Three-Gee." He bent, and peered intently at the thick crust. "Below us the Legend Fish is swimming around somewhere. He could be staring at me right now."

"Anything's possible," Greg's voice floated from the cell. "And we'll get that big boy soon. Bro, this car's still sitting in the parking lot. Are there any other people near you?"

Straightening, Austin twisted about, searching the huge location. "No, mate, it's just me and Tessie."

"Hmmm. Okay. Well, they must be around someplace. Then again, it could be broken. It looks a bit old."

"I guess." Austin clasped the phone to his ear with one, broad shoulder and pulled back the sleeve of his jacket. "We've got about a half hour left, Three-Gee, so we'll see you in a bit."

"Okay, take it easy."

"You too, mate. Later." He closed the phone with a crisp snap, slipped it back into his pocket and yanked his gloves back on.

"Let's go then, slowcoach. You're it." Tess tagged him on the arm and rocketed away, laughing as she snatched a quick, rearward peek.

Austin smiled, and tried to match her pace, his arms flapping and his body swinging like a drunken trapeze artist. Mercifully, she slowed and waited, the two of them knowing there was no way he could catch up. Performing a graceful pirouette, she skated backward when he neared, and they coasted leisurely that way for a while, their vision locked, a soft swishing the only sound other than the thumping beat of his heart at her captivating beauty.

"So what's the full story with Pauly? You never got the chance to tell me."

"Yeah, check this out. It sounds like he's fighting with his dad again, and when I told him we were still..." Austin's mouth slammed shut, his lips fusing firmly together while his face hardened, the jaw muscles clenching and unclenching furiously as he swung his head back and forth, scanning both forest and icebound water.

"What's wrong?" Tess followed his search. "Are you okay?"

Austin glanced at her frown. "Did you feel tha... ah, no, I mean did you hear. Tess, stop." All at once, he dug his skates in forcefully, bringing their meandering coast to an abrupt end at the sight of a huge and familiar beast slinking among the dense and dappled trees on a projecting section of woodland about forty feet away to their diagonal left. It was a popular spot he and his friends often visited, as the land dipped sharply into the deep water at its tip. Studying that hard-sought place brought on the instant recollection of a muggy Tuesday during summer vacation the previous year when, much to everyone's great amusement, Wade had managed to throw himself into the shimmering blueness while casting Austin's massive, sixteen-foot fishing rod. And in final daylight on the last day of the year, the sun's fading rays glistened off the creature's slimy skin, highlighting its darker splotches against the horrid pale. Sidling into clear view, it vaulted from the shadows in the exact place where his friend had fallen and landed with a savage crack on the frozen lake, its enormous paws spread, the thick, arched claws piercing the ice easily and holding it fast. A sustained and powerful growl issued from the barrel-shaped chest and brawny throat.

"Duke?" Austin whispered, his brow furrowing heavily. "It can't be. You're not... we're not. I'm... here." Something inside him stirred. Something entrenched, and waiting for a moment such as this. An ability that had lain dormant for nigh on sixteen years, almost released far too early twice before while still nothing more than a toddler and a young child. Now, he was not. Now, it wasn't premature. And now, there was no one to stop him, no hooded man, no disrupted fall to a dusty, valley floor. Nothing. At that precise point of awareness, he remembered everything from his infancy. All the blurred and buried memories from a child's level of perception transformed into clear-cut, well-defined recollections, and at the forefront was the image of a broken, destroyed body, someone he loved dearly, lying at the end of a lit hallway. This time, he needed no unfathomable, unknown part of his psyche. Susan was dead. It was a certainty. As certain as the death stalking its way toward them.

Tess spun at the unexpected disruption of a wonderfully enjoyable and peaceful end to the afternoon, and on seeing the monster, her life flashed in reverse, beginning with the cheerful, friendly teasing she had laughingly endured from her friends about the activity today and party later that night.

In the cavernous depths of Austin's suddenly fierce eyes, a bright, white light flickered. "Tess," he rumbled. "Come here. Slowly."

His resolute voice broke her detachment. Taking a half-step backward, she turned to face him, and with one question forming on her already open mouth, verbal communication fled at the sight of more beasts spreading out to the rear.

"How many are behind me?" Austin watched while two gigantic swarms came crashing through the underbrush on the next outcrops of land. They made a direct line for their lone comrade tracking to his right, rapidly and effectively cutting off the couple's prospects of freedom. "Tess, how many?" He looked at the girl staring past his shoulder. At her shiny, blonde hair, prominent under her dark, knitted beanie. At the bleached appearance to her usually lustrous and radiant skin, and at her noiseless lips, fluttering beneath wide eyes that filled with an all-encompassing and saturating fear. Moving carefully, attentive to the approaching mob, he twisted sideways, gauging there to be at least seventy or eighty encircling them, blocking any hope of retreat. Some skulked, creeping aggressively with their sight locked resolutely on the pair, while others trotted nimbly onward, their curved claws scratching the ice and hurling sparkly, glittering particles into the waning light. A raucous clicking and pounding heralded the extra arrivals, and Austin turned back, estimating the number at around three hundred that joined a steadily rotating ring.

They were everywhere, and identical copies of the alternate family dog, excluding the eyes. Whereas his had remained soft and playful, these oozed a fervent malevolence and hate. As they prowled, the same defined, bulging muscles rippled under a thick coat of the revolting substance, the frigid temperature inhibiting the gooey, lingering strands that ran and dripped off Duke's strong legs and belly at the other place. Not one sound issued from them, they merely opened their giant mouths, a teeming amount splattered in darkly-drying red, and drooped their fat, luminescent tongues over the black and dagger-like teeth.

Austin recalled their length and sharpness during his close inspection, and most definitely recalled the extreme comfort and thanks he gave for the loving pet being on his side. These were not. These did exist for one purpose. Running, attacking, overpowering. Shredding. The killing machine that sent a vicious shiver racing up his spine so long ago. A tremor, resolve, not fear, and a hundred times more powerful, travelled through his body, and the twinkling white light in his irides glowed when Tess stepped around to gape at the creatures. With her back to him, she trembled violently, and blinked through the tears that spilled down her ashen cheeks as she found her voice at last.

"Aus... Aus... Austin," she sobbed. "Wh... wha... what are th... th... they? I don't... I don't wa... I don't want to d... d... die."

The second her croaky words ended, and like a silent, psychic message, the pack stopped their circling and parted, revealing a much larger version striding through the clearing, snapping and snarling at the heels of those too slow to withdraw before its advance. The obvious leader, it was twice their bulk and another four foot taller. It clacked to a stop at the edge of the group, and with glittering saliva dribbling from the teeth and gums, actually leered at them before shaking its mammoth head.

Preoccupied by his constant and vigilant check on the surrounding beasts, Austin had only taken scant, cursory glimpses of its threatening approach, but his vision nipped back when he heard the tinkle, to see objects dangling from the leader's tiny ears, one on each, held by a six-inch-long, coarse twine fused to its skin. On the right swung an incredibly aged and yellow tooth, Duke's missing canine, the string punched through a rough hole in the root, while on the left, tied to the battered plastic buckle, his dark-brown leather collar swayed, all of it dull, twisted and withered. At every movement, the small, tarnished bell chimed mockingly.

Tess whimpered, the lost, hopeless cry thudding into Austin's very essence, like a sledge hammer slamming into his soul and lodging itself there, spiraling its reverberations outwards. He could only imagine what her face looked like, for if it matched the shuddering body of someone so cherished, he knew a glimpse would shatter his heart.

"We're not dying today, my darling," he murmured. "Not here. Not now. Not ever. You're someone more than special to me, Tess. You always have been. And I couldn't bear losing that now." Total composure came over him when a thin wire of heat ignited within his entire frame, spreading its warmth throughout his body as fresh, hot, rejuvenated blood coursed through superheated organs, pumping itself speedily to the surface of his skin.

It was partly the tone... so confident, so tender... but mainly his words that gave Tess the strength to rip her gaze from the fearsome scene and spin away from the nightmarish chiming of the monstrous animal still throwing its head about, flaunting its prize. What she saw caused no more shock or distress than the events already witnessed, and in a bizarre moment of clarity, she understood the vision was normal. For Austin. She couldn't analyze it better than that, a logical and cognitive thought process needed for such an accomplishment didn't exist right then. Later, however, as she sat in a chair peering miserably at the other people in a dimly lit room, she had already established what her instincts, her innerness, knew from the very beginning. That Austin William Cooper was no ordinary person, no ordinary man, for surely that's what he was, she could not think of any boy that would ever measure up to him... physically, mentally, powerfully... and mesmerized, she studied his eyes while they continuously changed color.

It was like some sort of frenziedly-viewed chart, the way they couldn't decide on which to accept. From an emerald green to a scarlet red, then sky blue, dark gray, hot pink, royal purple, bright yellow, vivid black... shades Tess couldn't even name flared for a microsecond before splintering into a myriad of dissolving shreds. She always adored the way ambient light conditions naturally changed them, but this effect had nothing to do with that, it came from within, for they simply burst into life, vibrant and dazzling... and her jaw sagged when a distinctive pattern flared unexpectedly, twinkling at first before blazing with the intensity of a star gone supernova.

In the three months leading up to Christmas, Austin had worked hard doing added chores to boost his allowance and implement a plan for buying Tess a gift. Remembering this one lunchtime at school when she talked passionately about a particular animal with its amazing colors, her absolute favorite since a very young age, he knew precisely what to get after seeing something perfect at the mall no more than two weeks later. Immediately upon entering the store, he asked if they could put one aside, and collected it during his festive shopping spree with Jeff. Later that night, sitting cross-legged on his bed, all prepared to wrap it in a snowman-themed paper, he held it close to his face and examined its features, the vividly reflected colors moving in his eyes while he slowly revolved the cuddly toy, hoping she would like it.

Following friendly, holiday greetings at the Andersons' arrival, the two teenagers rushed to the kitchen and exchanged parcels across the island bench. Elated, she ripped the paper off and clasped a large, fluffy tiger to her bosom, grinning widely before placing her gift in his hand. Once he removed a detailed, metallic statuette of Wolverine, they moved around the counter and hugged, pressing against one another eagerly. With the feel of her warm, supple body touching his, and the aroma of her clean, silken hair drenching his nostrils, Austin closed his joyful eyes, the ferociously burning eyes that ceased their baleful glare at Duke's doppelgangers when he lowered his head to Tess' gorgeous, tear-streaked face. "Tessie. Sweetheart," he purred. "Come to me." Tearing the gloves from his hands with two quick thrusts, he dropped them by his feet and held his arms out wide.

Around his inky, depthless pupils, she saw the vibrantly shining orange and black stripes in motion... flowing, rippling like the skin of the majestic animal in a full, predatory stalk, and without hesitation, entered his strong embrace. Instantly, she felt his heat and a wave of serenity radiating through her, caressing and soothing her spirit, creating a feeling of love and security that she so desperately needed.

And then they attacked.

the escape

They took great delight in watching the smaller one, the female, quivering at their approach, and the irresistible stench of her fear fueled the anticipation of a plan running to perfection. After dealing with their target, they would increase that terror, flinging her from one to the other before ripping her body to pieces and feasting on its remains, their hunger, their bloodlust, still unfulfilled, even with the fate of those earlier. Then something went wrong. At the last second, she moved to him, she held the human, the intended possessor of The All, The First, and he stripped their reward away. His alarm was minimal, his power radiating, just as expected, for their master prepared them of that sureness, and still did, with the ongoing, telepathic link they received. But this absolute loss of pleasure caught them unawares, and as the delicious scent of her dread disappeared completely at his touch, they surged forward, howling furiously, ready to take advantage of a specifically instilled ability that would overcome his renowned trick.

One fine, hot morning during the summer trip to New York City, Tess accompanied her mother and sister to the Empire State Building while her father attended to his duties at Fort Dix. Other than the fantastic view from the breezy platform, which literally took her breath away, the one thing she never forgot was an amazing journey in the elevators. They raced upward so fast it felt like her whole body remained several floors below, catching up only on the nearly-as-swift deceleration. And that strange sensation she felt right now, with her arms wrapped tightly around Austin's waist, tentatively freeing her life-saving clutch the moment he spoke.

"Let's go, babe. But be really careful and don't touch them, or we'll be in trouble again." Austin bent to retrieve his gloves, and stuffed them into his jacket pocket, all the while searching the stationary mob, confirming a tapered, yet clear path behind the leader being their solitary exit. "This way," he stated. "We'll be going in the opposite direction to safety, but I guess it doesn't matter. We should be long gone by the time my influence comes to an end." Austin grasped Tess' hand and pulled her gently along behind him while she stared at the creatures, wide-eyed and open-mouthed. Moving warily past the gigantic beast-boss, she tugged on his arm, bringing them to a stop, and he aimed his glowing tiger-eyes on her.

"What are they?" she whispered. Releasing his hold, she studied the horde, motionless in their leap to the now-vacated spot, and shivered at the razor-sharp, black fangs glistening within their gaping jaws. "I can see through them. I can see through everything. Look at the greenness on some of the trees. The color's nearly gone." Turning to Austin, she placed her fingers tenderly on his cheek. "What's happened to your eyes? Austin, what the hell is going on?"

"I don't know, Tess. Believe me when I say I don't really know. This kind of weird stuff has happened to me a couple of times before, and I don't know what it is, or how I'm doing it. There's only one person who does, but he's not here. And what do you mean? What's wrong with my eyes?" He leaned over to peer at the lake's icy casing. At first, on the way down, he thought it a result of the dull, deserting light, but on raising his head he verified what the creature's reflection to his left had briefly shown. They were starting to move, the legs ever so slowly shifting, along with the pale, purple-splotched bodies that began solidifying, looking more and more dense with every passing second.

"They're like my Christmas present from you," Tess replied. "No, sorry, what I meant to say is..."

From his pocket, Austin's cell dinged its annoying manufacturer's jingle. With the device never properly customized, it was something they planned to do later after Tess had failed to convince him that his phone needed upgrading, and instead suggested a website she used for downloading ringtones. Right then, he had no choice but to ignore it, absolutely certain the call was Greg doing his obligatory check. "Tessie, we've got to leave." The struggle to keep alarm from his voice created a far too-cheery tone. "Let's talk about it at home. Maybe when we go for a swim." He grabbed her hand and pushed off, the resistance lessening when she equaled his speed.

In front of them, the pathway had narrowed when the beasts commenced sealing the gap, still enough to get through safely, but only in single file. Austin switched grips, took a firm hold of her jacketed arm and back and shoved powerfully, propelling her ahead of him. She flew across the ice, hunched over like a speed skater, and cleared the open ring seconds before a slow, high-pitched droning began. Catching up quickly, he seized her hand again and glanced over his shoulder at the mob. Barely translucent, they were undeniably mobile, their slow-motion pace increasing along with the god-awful whine.

"What's happening?" Tess bawled, keeping a close watch on the flashing surface in front of her. "I think I saw them moving."

"They are," he shouted back. "This is a lot faster than outside the kindergarten. I don't know why, 'cos we didn't touch them." And at the moment, we're going away from safety, he thought. *We should prepare for this, Jeff's sage advice cautioned. We don't want any sort of falling catastrophe.* Dad, mate, you're not a fussy old fart. You're the most switched-on, awesome and best father a son could ever have, and without you, I'm nothing. "Tess," Austin boomed. "Listen to me."

In the corner of her sight, she saw the orange glow of his eyes, and glanced across at him.

"We're heading the wrong way, honey. They'll get us out here, so you need to do exactly what I say, when I say. Understand?"

"Come on, bro," Greg mumbled, turning the radio volume down. "What's going on?" He wasn't sure if he had heard something over the song, and flung the door open, hauling himself onto the crusty ground when Austin's automated voicemail cut in. Scanning the area by the outcrop of land, his last sighting before they disappeared, he checked the sun's position to his right, its hazy yellowness dazzling his vision as it peeked just above the trees, then ran at an angle toward the lake's edge, veering left across the large clearing and heading for the first, jutting section that still blocked any view. The second he neared it, a distant babble of loud howls and clobbering chilled him to the core, and he began a trunk-dodging flight into the main forest.

The brisk and gelid air prickled the delicate skin on her lips, and tore over her face with an exhilarating, bitter sting, moistening her already damp eyes. Under any other circumstances, it would have been a refreshingly blissful ride.

"We've got to turn around," Austin called above the deafening buzz. They were zooming along, gathering more and more pace, and any undisclosed, major route changes would risk that untimely fall. "The car's behind us, so just a nice, steady curve to the right when I say now. Are you ready, Tessie?" He studied her nod of accord. "Now!" As one, they swept into an arc worthy of the finest professional skaters and smoothed out to a gliding, straight line with the danger now farther away on Tess' side. Austin peered over her, checking the progress of the horde. "I think we might make it, babe. But if something happens, I'll hold them off while you go. You're much better on these things, so skate hard, skate fast, and don't look back. Just get to the car, okay?"

"No!" she yelled, squeezing his hand through her woolen glove. "Where you go, I go. I'm not leaving without you, we're in this together."

Right at that moment, the droning amplified, detonating into a full-blooded, brutal wail when the beasts resumed their attack in normal time and collided in on the empty place, the crunching and cracking of heads and bodies echoing across the lake. Tess whipped her head to the sound... and screamed, something she analyzed later on, in the same chair, hating herself for doing such a stupid, reckless act. Because Austin was correct. Even with the others, they had a chance at getting away safe and sound, but when her shriek reverberated above the loud commotion she watched in horror as they wheeled toward them, racing away on an angle of interception. An added burst of speed that pulled on her arm brought her attention around to Austin, who was slightly in front now, nearly dragging her as his long legs powered them along. They were pumping furiously, spraying out a torrent of shaved ice behind his flashing blades. He's got to be kidding, she thought. How the hell does he figure I'm better? He's out-skating me!

"I've got bad news, babe." He looked over his shoulder at her. A thin sheen of sweat lined his forehead, and his tiger-eyes shone brightly. Slowing, he came level, and pointed with his free hand.

"Oh shit!" she screeched, fighting the fear that bloomed again.

To their left, an entirely new group came thundering out of the mist and fading light, about half the number already zeroing in. Austin checked right once more, and grimaced when he saw the pack split. Twenty or thirty moved forward and farther out while the rest made a direct line for them, with the monstrous leader bringing up the rear. Bellowing triumphantly, it trampled over the top of any stragglers that got in its way.

"Tess!" Austin yelled. They were drawing nearer, their ice-piercing claws and brawny legs propelling them into a gallop, their long, green tongues flapping from the side of every open mouth. "I've got a plan. I don't know if this'll work, but if it does, we'll have one shot at it. We're going to the pressure ridge, so when I say now, we're doing a sharp left. Ready? NOW!" Swerving violently to the side, Austin felt Tess starting to slip, and took most of her weight on his arm, only pulling her upright as they stabilized. For a split second during the turn, he caught sight of a distant movement, a yellowish shimmer, out past the snow-covered danger on the ice, and recalled seeing the same phenomenon in his early childhood. But the feeling of something very close to his back wiped the event from his occupied mind.

Other than the ceaseless clattering and rare, excited yelp, they were mainly stealthy killers, so he risked a quick glimpse behind, his orange and black striped eyes widening when he saw the beasts no more than twenty feet away, prepared to strike. Another two or three bounds would bring certain demise.

"TESS! DON'T WORRY, TESSIE," he hollered. "I'VE GOT YOU, BABE."

Letting go of her hand, he grabbed the sleeves of her milky-white jacket, and in one swift motion lifted the stunned girl into the air and swung her in a half-circle to face him, catching her collar and yanking her quaking body hard against his.

Panting heavily, her pink scarf threshing madly around her head, she tucked her arms in and gawped dazedly over his shoulder, finding enough breath for the already too-late warning. "AUSTIN," she screamed as a beast struck him, right when she saw a flash of orange and experienced the strange, fast-elevator sensation. The impact rammed them forward, with Austin twisting while they fell. He landed on his back with a bone-juddering crash, still holding firmly on to Tess even when she dug her elbows forcibly into his solar plexus.

"Ooooffffff." The exhalation puffed from his lips as he slid ahead with the girl stretched on top, finally slowing to a stop thirty feet from their destination. Gasping, he slithered from under her and struggled to his feet, keeping a guarded watch on their attackers, transparent and static for a second time. But not for long. Studying them, he made out the legs and jaws moving progressively, the solidness recurring and the descent of those suspended in flight beginning.

"Come on," he wheezed, half lifting, half dragging Tess, his skates scrabbling for purchase while he hauled the exhausted teenager onward.

His cell rang when they approached the darker, thinner ice. Ignoring the phone yet again, he hurried about, bent over double and nodding his head at a long line of snow. "Okay, this should be fine." Straightening, he examined the converging beasts. Of the three groups, two were coming directly at them, the new mob from the left, the leader and its lot from the right, and the third performing their flanking maneuver, away from the action. It looked like they favored the faster option this time, with the backup surrounding stratagem again. But if his idea worked, it could give them the moments they required to pull off one final escape.

"Tess, catch." Digging the cell from his pocket, he tossed it to her. "It's Three-Gee. Tell him we'll be there in ten minutes. Make it quick, babe, they're coming at us loads faster and I don't know how many more times I can do this... this whatever the hell it is I'm doing."

With his last word scarcely out, he started jumping expansively around the area, high, bounding leaps with his legs drawn up tightly and plunging down the instant before contact. Shockwaves exploded through his ankles and the blades rang shrilly at each strike, but judging by the emphatic cracking as the fissure splintered in all directions, his punishing task was paying off, and he doubled his efforts.

Greg slowed his plundering dash to a trot when Tess answered the call, but his relief vanished as he heard her panicky, rushed voice and a harsh thudding, clanging, and crunching in the background.

"Greg." She gulped for breath. "Hi, sorry, we'll be there in ten minutes."

"Tess, what the hell's going on? Why have you got Austin's phone? What's all that noise? How far down are you? How far away?" He came to a complete stop, realizing the queries had sounded quite severe with his concern, and forced a calm tone while staring into the shadowy woods. "Where are you? Are you okay?" His soul rocked, gripped by a horrifying despair, when the guy he considered his brother suddenly hollered a command. "TESS, THEY'RE COMING. OVER HERE, NOW!" A piercing shriek seared his eardrum, followed soon after by a distinct, rattling smash, both instantly before the sinister nothingness of a disconnected line.

"Austin? Tess? AUSTIN!" In the three seconds it took to shout their names, he made two decisions. Ring Jeff and George, and get to the lake. Immediately. And in that same time he also analyzed the sound, the one sound prior to losing communication, the one sound he dejectedly and most categorically confirmed... the definite crash of a phone, so recently in the hand of a young woman he was growing very fond of, and now undeniably shattered when it fell from her grasp.

"Shit, shit, shit," he hissed. Whirling to the right, he broke into a suicidal sprint over the undulating terrain, trying desperately to keep sight on his frenziedly-moving fingers and the face-whipping branches he bulldozed through, all the while disregarding a knee screaming for mercy, having not been through such an exertion for many years.

the savior

I hope that's enough, Austin thought. I can't do any more. He finished with a bludgeoning slam that jolted his frame, and a huge section of ice to his left unlocked from the scattering of wide cracks he had created, scraping against the crust like fingers on a chalkboard as it rocked wildly back and forth. After a quick glimpse to both sides, his mind yelled a chastising, furious order, alarmed at the progress of each pack. I've left it too late, he snapped. It's gonna happen. Get Tess!

"TESS." He darted toward her. "THEY'RE COMING. OVER HERE, NOW!"

Covering the distance quickly, he performed a tight and flawless semicircle in front of the girl, sweeping her into his arms in one smooth, fluid motion. Tess screamed, startled at the unexpectedness of it all, and the cell slipped out of her flailing, gloved hand, momentum carrying it far behind them when he hurtled onward across the disintegrating lake. While they raced back, she watched the beasts fully reenter their phase, and a massive paw trample the still-open clamshell, snapping it from the phone, the device already useless when its cover and battery flew apart on contact with the dense surface.

Compelled by the sustained link, bequeathed with superior intelligence to the rest, the leader stopped, obeying its master's instruction, and rumbled angrily when the two packs disregarded its authority to continue on their incensed and unrelenting pursuit.

Clasping Tess harder, Austin launched over the crumbling ice and landed upon the loosened slab. Briefly surfing its swaying mass, he slid to a stop at its outermost edge, just as a gargantuan ripping, cracking explosion proclaimed the mobs' arrival. In front of him, he glimpsed the animals shattering the weakened covering while they surged forward, unwilling and unable to end their charging stampede, and heard the same happening directly behind, a second before they were flung skyward when the entire pack hurdled onto the large shelf and pitched it vertically, the seesaw action catapulting them back over the heads of their attackers.

Tess stopped her hysterical screeching the moment Austin drew her closer, his striped eyes flaring for the penultimate time, and she buried her head in his chest when the pleasant tranquility poured through her again. As the terrifying freefall slowed, she was sure they seemed to glide above the mayhem and danger, right before the last, unseen strike.

The leader hunkered down against the cold, icy shell, its mighty leg muscles bunched and tensed. Watching them sail overhead, it cast a message and ominous glance to the remaining mob, which heeded its command and came to an immediate halt, lurking farther away from the current pandemonium.

Austin smiled when he turned his head to the left and looked below. The beasts' fury-obsessed leaps had shattered the ice into thousands of segments, and they fell, yowling, into the deep, freezing water, now exposed and readily welcoming its victims. When they went under, none came back up, their stocky legs effectively suited for the persistent chase, but inadequate in these circumstances. He saw some thrashing and struggling by the rim, wide-eyed as they threw their claws out at the crust, only for the sections to snap off with their grasp, the leverage driving them and the ice far beneath the roiling surface. Wrenching his vision from the multitude of flung droplets glinting in the reddish-pink sunset, Austin sensed the threat a nanosecond before the barely glimpsed, peripheral movement, his continually modifying plan splintering like the icy covering when a set of keen, black teeth sunk deeply into the firmness of his right thigh. Knowing he had failed, it was more anger than pain that showed in his tortured cry at the realization of being clamped in the leader's jaws. Plunging suddenly, they landed with a heavy thud, all of them separating, spinning and tumbling as they slid away from the treacherous region, the clattering and clobbering of their flung bodies merging with the final, drowning splashes of the creatures.

A prompt and concentrated coldness drilled its way through Austin's body, making his heart skip a beat, the usually rhythmic, steady thump now lethargic, nearly seizing, and he rolled onto his hands and knees, struggling to raise his head in his search for Tess. Blinking sluggishly, trying to overcome a potent and rapid sleepiness with short, rough shakes of his head, he located her at least twenty-five feet directly to his right, flat on her back, and his spirit sank when he saw the huge leader advancing slowly toward the softly moaning girl. Lightheaded, queasy, exhausted, he watched the brute rear over her while the remaining snarling and sauntering swarm loitered in the background.

Straddling Tess, it gazed down at its victim, syrupy, glutinous saliva dribbling and dropping from its jowls. She sobbed, and her head wilted to one side, her amber eyes blank when they locked onto Austin, her tears only now beginning to flow across the bridge of her nose and cheeks as the creature followed her stare. Pulling its lips back, accomplishing another perfect smirk, its oversized head swung leisurely to her throat, the jaws parting during its unhurried motion.

"NOOOOOOO," Austin screamed. Inside, the smoldering wire, now so very nearly extinguished, suddenly blazed, erupting with explosive power, and the orange and black stripes ignited in his sockets, virtually illuminating the entire area with their brilliance. What he achieved next didn't feel at all like the episodes with the beasts before, and he didn't know how he crossed the distance. It was just a thought... an assertion... that he didn't want to be where he was right then, he wanted to be over there, with Tess. And over there he was, completely and utterly at the creature's shoulder. Stepping back, mustering everything he had, he sprang, and smashed an elbow solidly into its temple, the lunging drive carrying the monster and himself on a plummeting roll over the recumbent young woman, where they skidded to a stop ten feet away.

The other mob paused when they saw Austin leap to his feet, looming above their stunned leader, and positively backtracked while the tall teenager slammed a closed fist to the side of its skull again and again, making the small bell on Duke's collar jingle with each strike. After a dozen, pounding blows he slapped his hand to the bulky neck and held it there as a pulsing, bluish-white ball of energy surged down his arm, hammering into the beast with a force strong enough to make its whole body bounce savagely.

Convinced a half minute earlier that she had lived her last day on Earth, Tess watched, open-mouthed, while the man she loved annihilated his adversary. Having monitored Austin's feats from the moment he appeared beside her, she now fully understood what he meant to her and what he would do for her protection. Fresh tears welled, and her lips curled into a grin when the beaten creature glowed brightly, the escalating radiance causing her to squint the instant it simply vaporized, leaving an immense cluster of flaming embers that swirled about its conqueror and floated off across the lake, evaporating swiftly in the frigid, twilight air.

Spiraling around, smiling affectionately, Austin took two staggering, sliding steps. Tess stared at the tiger-eyes that fizzled out, their usual bluey-purpleness restored, but now hidden by his slowly closing lids. Dropping her sight to the dark blood pervading his denim jeans, she gasped when he sunk to his knees and toppled forward, his body juddering with its sickening thump upon the ice. Scrambling to him, she grunted at the effort of rolling his heavy frame over, and kissed his forehead before pulling his torso onto her lap. "Thank you, my darling," she whispered, gently stroking his damp hair and cheek. "My love. My brave, brave hero."

After the demise of their leader, and their objective met with the human, the link vanished, and the remaining beasts silently approached, their faltering strides a testament to the wariness of any other unanticipated events. But nothing else happened, and they quickened their pace, eager for the imminent gorging of the female. Soon, they would head off to hunt some more. An entire planet was out there, with enough to satisfy the smaller throng forever.

Tess wept, and glared defiantly at their forthcoming death, thankful, at least, that she was holding the one person she adored like no other. Shivering uncontrollably, and through hazy, tear-muddled sight, she blinked when a strangely dressed man materialized from nowhere, the air twirling momentarily with his abrupt arrival. He was, quite plainly, there, like Austin when he appeared beside her, right at their feet and facing the enemy.

As he turned to them his long hair swung, and above a shaggy, dark beard, a pair of whitely glowing eyes regarded the couple, the inspection lingering longest on the taller of the two. A rich, scarlet-red replaced the departing paleness while he delved into a large, tan satchel hanging near his hip, his peculiar garments drifting with the quick action of spinning around again, seeming to alter and mold with his body, the indigo and russet colors elongating and broadening each time. Tess couldn't see what the object was that he withdrew, she only noticed his arm rise, prior to his deep, booming voice.

"Don't run, little doggies!" He gave a hearty laugh when the entire mob reversed, their long, spiky claws scrabbling on the ice, distributing a finely grated spray as they struggled for grip. Rotating, they galloped speedily away from the trio with a high-pitched whimper. "Get back here," he called. "Where are you going? I've got a nice treat. Something different to chew on, you bastards."

Advancing several feet, he swept his upright arm from side to side in a fast, semi-circular motion. Ribbons of green and yellow light jetted out, bright, fat, and expanding into a heaving, bubbling wall of fire that chased after the retreating throng, overtaking and consuming them with the intensity of burning magnesium. Their remains detonated into a myriad of crackling ashes that flickered and danced when cool, light breezes carried them into a thickening mist rolling across from the opposite shore.

The man pivoted, and hurriedly stuffed the object in his bag while staring at the nearby treeline. "Crap on a stick," he muttered. "The guy's built like a silver-back, with a dodgy knee, and he's still damn fast." Crouching at Austin's side, he laid a honey-brown hand above the teenager's heart and lowered his head close to the comatose face. "What have you been doing, boy? And how?"

Tess wiped the moisture from her eyes, her mutely wobbling lips struggling for a correct manner in which to address this oddly clothed savior. With a bundle of questions and statements on her euphorically drained mind, the choice among thank you, who the hell are you, what the hell was that, and what the hell is going on wrestled to be the first one heard. The terminology varied greatly, with a few noteworthy words sprinkled somewhere in the sentences, and a fit of frenetic giggling nearly erupted when Greg came crashing his way through the forest, suddenly vocalizing her thoughts after leaping high and long onto the lake's rigid surface, slipping and regaining his balance quickly before commencing a difficult, slithering sprint toward them.

"HEY! WHO THE HELL ARE YOU?" His roar echoed across the frozenness. "GET THE FUCK AWAY FROM THEM. NOW!"

The man sighed, turned his gaze from the huge, stumbling figure and leveled it at Tess. "Girl!" he barked quietly. Unsurprisingly, she saw the scarlet had gone, replaced by a beautiful, chestnut color that darkened in the descending gloom, friendly and caring, even with his harsh, hastily whispered speech. "Pay attention. I know Austin. Right now, he's in trouble and I need to get to him before it's too late. Tell no one of the creatures. They wouldn't believe. You say it was wolves. A large pack of wolves. Any questions about the fire or lights, they were flares. You say I had them. Do you understand me, girl?"

She nodded wearily, ahead of two loud, resonating noises. The first sounded like a pistol firing, followed immediately by a deafening, thunderous bellow.

"RRRAAWWWWRRRRGGHHHH!"

Their heads whipped around, in time to see Greg clutch at his knee, the leg buckling as the giant man collapsed heavily to the ice. With a loud groan, he heaved himself upright and hobbled to them, dragging his damaged limb.

"I… said… get away… from them," he snarled between clenched teeth.

"Okay, okay." The garments tightened on the man's body when he pushed himself back from Austin and plonked onto his haunches, raising his hands in the air, palms out. "I haven't harmed him, my friend. I was simply passing through and thought these two young ones could use some assistance."

Red-faced, puffing, sweating, Greg glanced at the man's appearance, taking in the scruffiness of his features along with the weird, almost earthy clothes, and figured him for some sort of hippy or wandering hobo. Grunting at the action of propping himself on his good leg, he leaned over, pressed two fingers alongside Austin's windpipe and examined his brother. "Awww shit, mate. What's happened? Tess." He looked at the silently crying girl, and in the closing spell of pinkish light, she watched the tears trickle down his scratched and bruised skin. "Are you okay? Are you hurt? What's with all this blood? Did he do this?" Greg inclined his head at the silently observant man.

"No." Her head quivered. "He… he saved us. I'm not hurt, it's Aus… it's Austin. Gre… Greg, we've got to…"

"Shhhhh." He reached out and stroked her face. "Come on, let's go. Your dad and Jeff should be here any minute. Tell me what happened on the way." Tensing the muscles in his arms and torso, he hoisted Austin and draped him gently across his wide back, grimacing with the weight on his injury.

"Heyyyy... uhhh." Rubbing his bushy beard, the man squinted up at Greg. "You want me to lend a hand there? That knee don't look too good."

"The knee will be just fine. Thanks for the offer. And thanks for your help. Tess, let's go." Greg turned, drew in a colossal lungful of freezing air, and prepared himself for the most agonizing run of his life.

About the Author

Liam Taylor was born in Auckland, New Zealand and currently lives in Queensland, Australia with his partner, children, two cats, and an acre of forever-growing grass.

Buoyed by his love of sci-fi and the exceedingly strong belief that we are not alone in The Universe (probably not a good idea to get him started on the subject, either... he'll bore you to tears!), he began writing his debut series several years ago, culminating in the publication of this, Book One: The Naissance.

www.ingramcontent.com/pod-product-compliance
Lightning Source LLC
Chambersburg PA
CBHW060602030726

47498CB00005B/1497